EAST WIND RETURNS

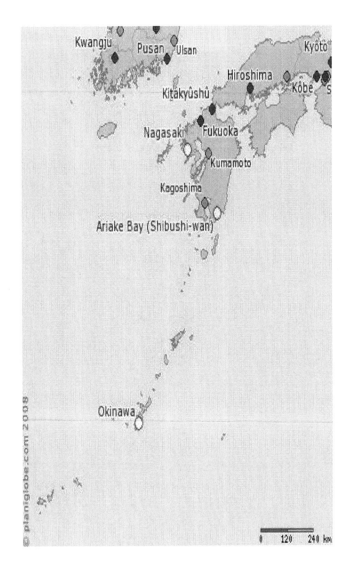

Okinawa and Kyushu

EAST WIND
RETURNS

A Novel By
William Peter Grasso

Cover design by Alyson Aversa
Map created at planiglobe.com

East Wind Returns is a work of historical fiction.
Apart from the well-known actual people, events, and
locales that figure in the narrative, all names,
characters, places, and incidents are the products of the
author's imagination or are used fictitiously. Any
resemblance to current events or locales or to living
persons is entirely coincidental.

DEDICATION

To Peggy, my tiny dancer, who makes everything
possible

Chapter One

July 1945
New Mexico Desert

The lone steel tower rises above the desert emptiness in the early morning sunlight. At its apex is cradled America's first nuclear weapon. This weapon, the product of the top secret Manhattan Project, promises destructive power on a scale that few have dared to envision. Several years in development under heavy security and in the isolation offered by this desert, it provides the possibility for unparalleled dominance of the United States over its World War II opponents--as well as its allies. Now, with Germany finished and American troops poised on Japan's doorstep, it offers the United States another avenue to force Japan's unconditional surrender, ending the war once and for all.

If it works.

It is estimated that the force of this anticipated explosion will equal that of 20,000 tons of TNT--equivalent to 2000 of America's biggest bombers carrying conventional, high-explosive bomb loads. All from just 13 pounds of plutonium.

Miles from the tower, General Leslie Groves, Manhattan Project director, and his chief scientist, Dr. Robert Oppenheimer, stand in the control bunker and squint downrange through the thick glass of the slit-like windows as they oversee the final preparations.

Developing this weapon had proved difficult both technically and psychologically. The strain of the many conflicts that had raged between these two men over those years is manifest in every brusque utterance. Oppenheimer is sure he knows what Groves is thinking:

We shouldn't even be in this position, with the whole damn project riding on this plutonium bomb...We should have had that uranium bomb already. Didn't even need to test the son of a bitch. Foolproof, they said. But the fire...and that radioactive hotspot it left that we can't get within a mile of...all the enriched uranium we had, ruined. It had to be one of those commie scientists sabotaging the project...

Oppenheimer wished that fire had not happened, too. But he sharply disagreed with the General about its likely cause:

It must have been some idiot military policeman who caused it, failing to properly extinguish the cigarette he knew was against all regulations. When given a choice between conspiracy and negligence, I'll choose negligence every time...especially when dealing with the military.

Two facts were inescapable: they no longer had enough enriched uranium to make a simple, if inefficient, atom bomb, and it would take quite some time to enrich more uranium. They had plenty of plutonium, though, but this type of bomb, while superior in destructive efficiency, was not so simple to build. They would have to test it to be sure the 5000 pounds of high explosive could successfully squeeze the 13 pounds of plutonium to critical mass. There was another problem with this bomb: it already weighed 10,000 pounds, the maximum load that could be carried in a B-29's bomb bay.

In the control bunker, the safety checks are complete and range clearance confirmed. It is time to push that button.

With a nod from General Groves, Oppenheimer lifts the safety guard on the panel before him. As they drop shaded goggles over their eyes, Groves says, "This better be one hell of a bang, Robert."

With his finger resting on the button, Robert Oppenheimer is not sure if he is reaching out to destiny or damnation. There is only one way to find out. He presses it.

Not a breath is drawn for several seconds. Then several more seconds. But there is no bang--just a wisp of smoke from the top of the tower and a dull *thud,* like a distant firecracker, several seconds later. There is no blinding flash. No shock wave crushing structures to splinters. No intense heat to incinerate flesh in an instant. No desert floor turned to glass...

And no mushroom cloud. Just the sound of the wind across the parched sands.

Hungnan Island, Occupied Korea

Professor Isoroku Inaba stands on the coastal bluff and stares, awestruck, out to sea. The blinding flash has extinguished; the professor and his party--scientists and military men--remove their shaded goggles and watch as a towering mushroom cloud billows to the heavens 30 kilometers out to sea. The delayed rumble of the explosion, painfully loud despite the distance it has traveled, assaults their ears. Seconds later, a sudden, warm wind--the weakened remnants of the explosion's shock wave--sways them and sends caps flying.

3

The military men excitedly proclaim it *a divine wind from the east.*

What Professor Inaba has just witnessed is an unbelievable success, a success he had grave doubts would ever be achieved and a secret wish that it would not be. He is a physicist who has explored peaceful uses for nuclear energy. Like most of his fellow scientists, however, he had been forced to develop weapons for Imperial Japan. When summoned by the Emperor, you went.

The nuclear device he developed had just detonated with a force equal to 15,000 tons of TNT. A fleet of derelict vessels had surrounded the device to a distance of 5 kilometers to measure the blast's effect. Those vessels had been torched by the blast, swamped by the shock wave and sent to the bottom.

A saki toast is prepared. Raising his cup to his assembled staff, Inaba's voice trembles. "Gentlemen, pray the Emperor protects us, for we are damned."

A colonel of the Japanese Army stands apart from the others and quietly downs his saki in one quick swallow. While the other military men remain gleeful-- despite the Professor's dampening words--this colonel is somber. As his cold eyes stare at the far-off mushroom cloud, he mutters to himself, in perfect English: "You are wrong, Professor. It is the American cowards who are damned."

The White House, Washington, D.C.

Harry Truman slumps in his chair, trying to accept what his Army Chief of Staff has just told him. "So, General Marshall," Truman says, "you're telling me the test was a complete failure?"

"Yes, Mister President," George Marshall replies. "The weapon did not detonate."

Truman sighs, stands and walks to the Oval Office window, seeing his own look of distress reflected in the glass. "First that goddamn fire ruins all the uranium...and now this plutonium bomb doesn't work. Isn't that just peachy, General?"

"We all hoped for a better result, Mister President."

Secretary of War Henry Stimson sits across the room. Seventy years old and in failing health, Stimson had been a major proponent of nuclear weaponry in Franklin D. Roosevelt's administration--and now in Truman's. But Stimson had let George Marshall do all the talking this time. Henry "Hap" Arnold, Commanding General, US Army Air Forces, also sits in uneasy silence. Arnold's boys will be the ones delivering the atomic bomb--if there ever *is* an atomic bomb.

There are two navy men in the room: Admiral Ernest King, Chief of Naval Operations, and Admiral William Leahy, Chief of Staff to the President. They listen in guarded silence; both know better than to speak at a time like this.

The newly appointed Secretary of State, James Byrnes, is seated by Truman's desk. A confidant of the new president, it is his style to pepper bearers of bad news with accusations thinly disguised as questions. But as he turns to begin a verbal assault on Marshall, Truman cuts him off. "Hold on a second, Jimmy."

Then the President turns back to Marshall. "Where does that leave us, George?"

Immediately, Truman wished he could reel his use of the familiar name back in. He knows full well Marshall can only function in an atmosphere of

5

professional formality. He vividly recalled the time FDR had casually called Marshall "George" in conversation and Marshall's firm but polite demand that such informality cease. Marshall had taken Truman's slight stoically, but it was a slight nonetheless. Even a brand-new president has to cater to the temperaments of subordinates.

"Excuse me," Truman says. "I mean *General* Marshall."

Marshall looks relieved. Protocol has been restored. "Thank you, Mister President. General Groves informs me his people have isolated the problem. The casing for the high-explosive triggering device is rupturing before the atomic reaction can be achieved. He still believes that with a modification to this casing we'll have a serviceable weapon."

Truman scowls. He is not interested in technical details. "And how long do they expect this to take?"

"He believes they can be ready to test again in two months."

"Shit," the President says. "But if the next test is successful, we would still have a weapon ready for use in the western Pacific by October?" He pauses, then adds: "Of *this* year?"

"Yes, Mister President."

Truman is silent for a few moments. Admiral Leahy seizes the opportunity to speak. "Mister President, if the wide-scale firebombing of Japan hasn't brought them to the point of surrender, why do we continue to hope this one atom bomb will? General LeMay's tactics have already wiped out entire cities, have they not?"

Truman, pretending to be deep in thought, tries to ignore Leahy's question--and the painful truth at its core.

Now Admiral King speaks up. "The only thing that will bring them to their knees is to continue the naval blockade. They'll starve. They'll have to surrender."

"Bullshit. That could take years, Admiral. We don't have that kind of time," Secretary of State Byrnes says.

"Amen to that, Jimmy," the President adds.

King is not finished. "So we are to blunder ahead with this invasion, Mister President... and get another million or so American boys killed?"

Truman's face reddens. King is a master at rubbing him the wrong way. Marshall reads the meaning in the malignant glance the President sends his way: *Put this arrogant asshole in his place.*

"That's a wild assumption, Admiral," George Marshall says. "You've seen the studies. We all have. The scale of casualties for the invasion is expected to be no different than at Normandy, Iwo Jima or Okinawa."

King smirks. "You're willing to bet on that, General?"

"Yes sir, I am."

"I am, too," Truman says, but his tone convinces no one. Not even himself. Then, shifting to a confident voice that belies the uncertainties of his first three months as president, he says, "OK. You have my full approval to continue the testing on the atom bomb. Let's get this damn war over with by 1946...one way or the other."

George Marshall saluted and left the Oval Office, very glad the ordeal was over. In a way, he was also glad the atom bomb test had failed. Like most of the scientists and generals, he feared the rush to use the nuclear weapon and the massive power shift it could bring to warfare and world politics. *Once that cat is out of the bag, where will we all end up? Even some pipsqueak nation with an atom bomb can turn the balance of power inside out.* At least now, they could put off dealing with it for a few more months. Maybe, by some miracle, the war would be over by then--and cooler heads might prevail.

Neither George Marshall nor anyone else in the US command knew that the Japanese had successfully developed a similar weapon--but it did not share the Americans' problems. Japan's bomb was not designed to be delivered by an aircraft. Size and weight were not obstacles.

Chapter Two

It is a traffic jam in the sky. The air above Kadena Field on the island of Okinawa is thick with US aircraft being brought into a ragged landing pattern by overworked air traffic controllers. A building thunderstorm approaches from the west. Lightning illuminates its darkened, towering clouds from within, like flickering Chinese lanterns. The controllers are running out of time to get everyone on the ground before the storm hits.

In the holding pattern, Captain John Worth smoothly pilots his F-5--a twin-engined photo reconnaissance airplane based on the P-38 "Lightning" fighter--into line for landing behind a string of bombers and transports. The three-hour ferry flight from the Philippines has been routine and dull--until now, with that storm rolling in quickly. He will be glad to be on the ground and out of this cramped cockpit, which is becoming a steam room in the warm, tropical air of low altitude.

The bloody, three-month-long conquest by US forces of the Japanese on Okinawa is finally over. The island is now being turned into a major staging area for Operation Olympic: the invasion of the southernmost Japanese home island of Kyushu, only 350 miles to the north.

Kadena and the other airfields on Okinawa had been major Japanese airbases. Now they will be home to over 2000 US aircraft. These planes, along with those still based in the Philippines, the long-range B-29 bombers in the Marianas, and naval aircraft from the carriers of Admiral Nimitz, represent the collective might of US airpower in the Pacific.

John Worth's plane has no guns but an array of five sophisticated cameras in its nose. Although looking almost identical to a fighter aircraft, it is not a fighter at all--and John Worth is not a fighter pilot. He flies a machine that takes pictures. Swaggering fighter pilots--who gladly supported the notion that they were the elite of aviators, strutting around with all the confidence and assertiveness of brothers in the most prestigious fraternity--call recon pilots "kodak" or "camera boy" with derisive delight. The fighter jocks have unflattering names for everyone else, too: bomber pilots are called "dump truck drivers"; transport pilots are "garbage men."

The cameras of a photo recon plane are a strategic weapon more valuable than any fighter pilot, though. Photo recon aircraft provide the generals with pictures of enemy troop dispositions, topography, shipping, bomb damage assessments, even weather patterns--the intelligence needed to make sound military decisions. Getting the pictures while surviving enemy fire requires the unarmed recon pilot to possess high degrees of skill and courage. Sure, they would love to have guns. But their planes just cannot fit all the equipment necessary to perform multiple missions and have enough performance left to not be sitting ducks. As John Worth's first commanding officer had told him, "Fighter pilots are expendable. Photo recon is indispensable." Despite those wise words, John still feels like the second string football player he had been in college not so long ago.

John turns his airplane, named *f-stop,* to a short

final approach. He watches as, a mile ahead, a transport touches down hard on her left gear, then bounces to her right gear and slews sharply off the right side of the runway. She comes to rest abruptly in the high weeds with her nose spun around to face the just-departed runway. A knowing smile crosses John's face. "Well, ol' girl, we've got a bit of a crosswind right to left," he says aloud as he pats her throttles. *It would be nice if they mentioned that,* he thinks. But he imagines the air traffic controllers are having as much trouble as the pilots seeing the primitive wind sock in the center of the field. *Oh, well! No different from New Guinea or the Philippines, I guess...Maybe I really am nuts for still being here.*

The controller's voice barks in John's earphones: "Focus 4-7 from Kadena tower... You want to go around? That guy's sitting right on the edge, ain't he?"

"No thanks, tower," John replies. "I don't have the gas for that. There's plenty of room."

Crosswind landings are always tricky. A one-wheeled landing with the F-5 could blow a tire and cause her landing gear to collapse. John coaxes *f-stop* to the ground, working hard to keep her wings level. Despite the effort, he is calm; he is no amateur at this high-stakes game. The touchdown is close to flawless, something the embarrassed transport pilot, from his unfortunate ringside seat, cannot help but notice as *f-stop* rolls past his mired aircraft.

John speaks softly to his airplane as she decelerates: "Whoa, girl, whoa...Nice job, baby...Smoother than a G.I. haircut."

John Worth is only 23 years old. He has been at war for three years, with 3000 hours of flying and hundreds of combat recon missions to his credit.

He has never lost an airplane.

He could have gone home a long time ago.

Chapter Three

August 1945
Imperial Palace, Tokyo

"This is insanity!" Those were the words Prime Minister Suzuki spoke when told of the Japanese Navy's plan to utilize the nuclear weapon. Suzuki had mighty hopes that this meeting of the War Council would consider ways to negotiate an end to the war. But negotiation seemed to be the furthest thing from the Navy's mind.

Admiral Toyoda, the Navy Chief of Staff, ignores the Prime Minister's obvious distress and gets down to details. "We will mount the weapon on an I-15 Class submarine and detonate it in the harbor of San Francisco."

General Umezu, the Army Chief of Staff, sits quietly, observing the proceedings. Foreign Minister Togo, also silent, anxiously paces the floor.

Highly agitated, Suzuki says: "You cannot be serious, Admiral. The Navy's poorly executed attack on Pearl Harbor had ultimately served only to rouse a sleeping giant. Now this giant and his insidious Russian ally are poised to destroy us as a people and you wish to antagonize him once again?"

"Nonsense," Toyoda replies. "The American people and their new, guileless president are tired of war. An attack of this magnitude on their homeland would finish off their will to fight."

There is silence as Prime Minister Suzuki considers those words, but after a moment, he shakes his head in rejection. "Admiral, I fear the only thing that would be finished off is the Americans' reluctance to totally incinerate us." Gesturing toward the window, Suzuki continues: "Look upon the burned-out heart of Tokyo. Imagine 1000 fire-bombers doing the same to every Japanese city."

It is the admiral's turn to shake his head. But before he can say another word, General Umezu asks, "Admiral, perhaps you would share with us the details of your plan?"

Toyoda looks offended by the request. "The details of the Navy's plan are of no concern to the Army."

"I beg to differ, Admiral," War Minister Anami says. "I believe all present have a right to hear those details."

A large map of the Pacific hangs on the wall. Less than pleased, the Admiral approaches it with pointer in hand. "Very well. The weapon is to be mounted to the deck of our one remaining I-15 Class submarine at the Hungnan Weapons Development Facility in Korea, under the direction of Professor Inaba and his staff. This submarine will, of course, be manned by a *special* crew, who will bring honor to the Emperor and themselves with their deaths. The submarine will cross the Sea of Japan, enter the Sea of Okhotsk, and cross the northern Pacific." Pausing for a moment to shoot a defiant glance at the Prime Minister, he continues: "...following the route of our fleet's *great victory* in December 1941."

Toyoda pauses again to savor his reclamation of the Navy's honor, but the delay is met with nothing but impatient faces and a chilling silence. Defiantly, he

14

launches back into his monologue.

"It will pass north of the Hawaiian Islands and continue to the western coast of America. Once near the Golden Gate, it will submerge and enter the bay when the submarine nets are open for other maritime traffic. Our spies have been very successful obtaining shipping information of this sort. Once inside the harbor, it will surface adjacent to the San Francisco docks and the crew will detonate the weapon."

"How far is the voyage?" Umezu asks.

"9000 kilometers."

"And what is the range of an I-15 submarine?"

Toyoda is getting testy. "More than sufficient for a one-way journey."

"And how do you propose to do this on an ocean you no longer control, Admiral? Your *victorious* navy now litters the seabed."

"General, may I remind you that nautical matters are best left to the Navy. Besides, all US naval victories have been the product of luck. We will yet turn the tide."

"Will this submarine's performance be degraded by its external cargo?" the general asks, ignoring the admiral's bravado.

"No, General, the I-15 was designed to carry an attack float plane on its foredeck. Transporting the weapon will pose no impediment... even when submerged."

General Umezu has saved his most critical question for last. "Admiral, how long will it take to detonate the weapon after surfacing? And why must it surface at all? Wouldn't a detonation while submerged at a shallow depth be just as devastating?"

Toyoda smirks confidently. *The general is speaking from ignorance--a position of weakness. It is*

time for me to put him in his place once and for all.
Like a headmaster disciplining a student, he says, "We must surface, *General,* to connect the electrical power for the detonator. The weapon would not be watertight otherwise--"

Umezu interrupts. "I ask you again, sir... how long?"

How dare this Army toad interrupt me? If this pointer was a sword...

"Kindly allow me to finish, General... We estimate five minutes to complete the preparations for detonation."

Waves of astonishment and disapproval wash through the chamber.

General Umezu shouts above the discord. "They will not survive five *seconds,* let alone five minutes, on the surface of an American harbor, even with the bold assumption that they arrive undetected!"

War Minister Anami raises his hands for quiet. "Admiral, I am sure the Emperor applauds your determination, but I fear your plans will not alleviate our most immediate problem. The Americans are sitting on our doorstep and we are almost powerless to stop them. The Russians may join them at any moment. We possess only one nuclear weapon. If we are to employ this terrible device at all, logic dictates that it must be used against the American invasion force directly. I suggest that the Army and Navy consider this and be prepared to present other proposals in one week's time."

Somberly, Prime Minister Suzuki nods in agreement and closes the meeting.

As the War Council departs the chamber, each member knows that despite the War Minister's polite and diplomatic language, the San Francisco plan would never be adopted. What they do not know is that it would have failed for a totally unanticipated reason.

The secrecy and isolation in which Professor Inaba and his scientists had been forced to work allowed a conspiracy to blossom undetected. When told of the San Francisco plan, they had agreed among themselves to sabotage the weapon.

Inaba's device was not originally designed to be submerged. All such weapons require an electrical source to set off the high explosives that initiate the nuclear reaction. Inaba's successful test weapon had used a simple battery and timer. The submarine crew, however, would have to connect the electrical source after surfacing by first removing a bolted-on, watertight hatch, then connecting the requisite wiring. They would then play out their final act in this world by triggering the explosion with a hand-operated generator.

Inaba and his staff installed defective seals on the hatch. When the submarine submerged, the interior chamber of the device would flood, ruining the high-explosive charge. Their atomic bomb would become nothing but a soggy piece of radioactive junk.

Chapter Four

They say flying is hours of boredom punctuated by moments of sheer terror. This is true of civil aviation. For combat flying, it is hours of intense apprehension punctuated by moments of sheer terror.

John Worth is in the apprehension phase of his first mission from Kadena, north-northeast of Toko-no-Shima approaching 10,000 feet. This puts *f-stop* just above a deck of patchy cumulus clouds, making her easily visible only from above. At least the threat of ground fire from the islands below, still held by the Japanese, is minimized. But ground fire is the least of John's concerns. Enemy fighters are still the biggest threat. Mechanical problems with his aircraft follow a close second. At least the weather is cooperating. No storms today, so far.

Today's mission is to get pictures of the northern seaport areas of Kyushu, the southernmost of Japan's four home islands and, by consensus of US and Japanese strategic analysis, the next logical place for the US forces to invade. MacArthur's Intelligence Staff (G-2) would use these photos and the many that would follow from future missions to assess the defensive build up they felt sure was well underway. John is the leader of "B" Flight, one of three flights with four aircraft each in his squadron. *Flight Leader* is something of an administrative title, as recon pilots usually work alone.

Other pilots from John's unit are flying elsewhere

over Kyushu, as well as over Shikoku and Southern Honshu. A few of the squadron's pilots are not flying due to medical reasons, real or concocted.

Flight surgeons had learned to accept the occasional faked maladies--migraines, earaches, stomach problems and the like--just as commanders had learned to overlook the occasional maintenance problems that caused mission aborts yet could not be verified. The doctors were more concerned with the far less frequent occurrences of medically unfit airmen who insisted they were ready to fly. John Worth had never faked a medical problem to avoid flying. In his words, *that just wasn't right.*

Leveling off, John trims the aircraft and sets power for fuel-efficient cruise. Kyushu is 350 miles from Okinawa, straight up the Ryukyu Island chain, about an hour and a half flying time in the F-5. His left hand lightly plays the levers that control the engines: throttle, mixture, RPM. The sound from the two 1400 horsepower Allisons settles into a synchronized drone. He doesn't need to check the engine gauges: his senses, sharpened by much experience, tell him that they are running just as he wants. But he takes a peek, anyway.

His head moves constantly, scanning the instrument panel, then swiveling to the sides and rear, checking the sky for other aircraft, especially those that might want to kill him. Even without the deck of clouds below him, he lacks downward visibility in level flight. The wings and engines block most of that. Sliding his backside around on the parachute that served as his seat cushion, he settles his body in for the mission, which will take almost five hours, and all that time he'll be staring at the remains of insects on the windshield, splattered there during takeoff. He wonders how many more are lodged in his radiators and air intakes or plastered on the props and leading edges of the wings and stabilizers.

His right hand gently grips the control yoke, the left hand free for reaching levers, knobs and switches as necessary. John is at one with *f-stop*. He knows all too well that airplanes are machines that happen to fly, a complicated collection of mechanical devices moving through the sky in close formation, needing the pilot only to suggest it move fast enough and point it in a safe direction.

More islands slip past as John follows the Ryukyu chain north to Japan. Now less than 15 minutes from the southern tip of Kyushu, he has yet to see another aircraft, friend or foe. *f-stop* is behaving herself. The clouds below are beginning to thin, and in a moment he should see the mountains looming out of the distant mist. His drop tanks would be empty very soon. He would not release them unless forced to by the need for a speedy escape. Even though they are streamlined and weigh practically nothing empty, the aerodynamic drag of the tanks slows the plane down a bit. Besides, the fighter boys have plenty of spare drop tanks; recon squadrons do not.

Right on schedule, the drop tanks empty and the mountain peaks appear. He begins climbing to 20,000 feet and skirts the east coast of Kyushu, heading north, staying a few miles offshore. There are few clouds now; he can see some of Admiral Nimitz's warships below, further offshore. Eastern Kyushu, to his left, seems to be all narrow, coastal plains with waves of rippling mountains inland, their grayish-brown peaks topping out at 5000 feet, shrouded in mist. The bases of the mountains are also shrouded in mist; just hints of green glimmer through.

Passing 15,000 feet, he suddenly has company: distant specks growing larger off his left wingtip, slightly higher, moving south. Despite the growing coldness in the cockpit, he feels sweat in his helmet and oxygen mask. His gloved hands grip the controls tighter.

Directly abeam, their silhouettes are unmistakable: Japanese fighters.

An experienced voice deep within John begins to bark commands as if coaching some rookie:

"Gotta see what they're gonna do..."

"Keep scanning! Don't get jumped from behind!"

"Fly the airplane, idiot! Don't let it get ahead of you."

But the Jap planes never change course. They have not seen John's airplane because it is between them and the morning sun.

They become bright pinpoints, quickly fading and vanishing in the clear blue sky at altitude... and then they are gone.

The whole encounter has taken just 5 seconds. That's how the moments of sheer terror happen.

f-stop reaches the Bungo Channel, the wide strait separating Kyushu and Shikoku. "Let's get to work, ol' girl," John says aloud, and deploys the dive brakes. Rolling the aircraft left past 90 degrees with a smooth turn of the control wheel, he pulls back a bit on the yoke, retards the throttles and sends his aircraft plummeting downward and turning to the northwest.

Once on the northwesterly heading, he continues the steep descent to 5000 feet, then stows the dive brakes. As he approaches Beppu Bay, his first objective, he drops smoothly to 500 feet and opens the throttles.

He passes over several Japanese airfields crowded with aircraft along this northern coast, but no enemy rises to meet him; the Japs just don't have enough fuel left to be chasing lone intruders across the sky. They don't even have enough fuel to conduct proper training flights; best to save it for Kamikaze attacks against high value targets, like troop ships and aircraft carriers.

There is always the chance, though, that somebody would suddenly be on your tail.

Of course, it hadn't always been like this. Not so long ago--although it already seemed like another lifetime--swarms of Japanese fighter aircraft roamed the sky above New Guinea, piloted by very experienced and very deadly warriors. Speed and surprise had been the only weapons John possessed. Even more recently over the Philippines, although fewer in number and with pilots of lesser experience and abilities, Jap fighters had still been a terrifying menace.

There hadn't been any anti-aircraft fire, either. At low altitude, traveling at over 350 mph, people on the ground don't hear the aircraft until it's right on top of them. Then, it's too late: you've already missed your shot.

The pictures from Beppu Bay would not be very informative; there was little going on there, just a few barges at the docks. The pictures from his next objectives, Kokura and Shimonoseki, would also be uninteresting. B-29's of Major General Curtis LeMay's 20th Air Force had mined the Shimonoseki Straits, the narrow, twisting passage between Kyushu and Honshu that linked the Sea of Japan with the Inland Sea as well as the adjacent ports. Some estimates put the resultant maritime traffic reductions at 90%. It certainly looked that way, from John's vantage point.

Now he turns his aircraft to the southwest and heads directly to Fukuoka, about 30 miles distant, descending even lower and following the contours of the land between the low hills on either side.

OK, girl... we've got one more job to take care of.

That job was to photograph bomb damage from a B-24 strike that should have occurred about an hour before. The four-engined B-24's had come, dropped their bombs on Fukuoka's port facilities and were heading back to Okinawa, but they were behind schedule on target. The smoke rising from their targets is still fresh; the anti-aircraft gunners are still on alert. Four Japanese fighter aircraft, of a type code named "Tony" by the Allies, hurtled past *f-stop*, slightly above and in the opposite direction. They had risen to challenge the B-24's and might have had some luck: one of the B-24's was trailing smoke as she flew away to the south. Seeing *f-stop* clearly below, the Tonys roll on their backs and dive in pursuit.

John gets a little help from an unexpected source. The anti-aircraft gunners, trying to get a bead on the low-flying bullet that is *f-stop* at this moment, actually are shooting behind the F-5. The tracers weave their bright arcs well aft of her tail, directly into the path of the pursuing Tonys. The Jap fighters have to break off the attack to escape the "friendly" fire. They would not have caught up to *f-stop*, anyway; she had too much speed and too great a lead.

Nevertheless, John is soaked with sweat and tense as a banjo string. If he had to make a radio transmission right now, his voice would be a tell-tale sign of fear, an octave higher than normal.

He has gotten the pictures, though, and after anxious seconds that seem like hours, is climbing over the Sea of Japan, heading south, back to Okinawa. A moment of relief engulfs him like a fresh breeze.

"Welcome to Japan, ol' girl," he says, patting her throttles before resuming his scan for adversaries.

But he sees no one. They are alone in the sky again.

Chapter Five

John's fuel and oxygen supplies are in good shape, so he climbs back to 20,000 feet for the trip to Okinawa. Far below, the wispy smoke trail from the wounded B-24 grows more dense. After about 15 minutes, he catches up with the crippled bomber – she has two engines shut down and a third trailing smoke-- and the two P-51's that had lagged behind to protect her. The fighters orbit above the stricken, slow-flying aircraft as their pilots worry about fuel.

John chats with the P-51 leader on the standard hailing frequency.

"We figure it's gonna take them another two hours to make Okinawa," the fighter pilot says with a heavy drawl. "We've got about enough gas for another 30 minutes of this ring-around-the-rosy shit. Hey, Kodak, you ain't doing anything much... you'll be in radio range of home way before us... How about giving bomber command a heads-up about this busted dump truck?"

"No problem, little buddy," John says. "Wilco... You take care now."

The P-51 leader is in a chatty mood.

"You can bet on that, Kodak... Sure would be nice if the Marines mopped up some more of those islands down there. We could use the extra landing strips."

John could not agree with him more. Those rugged green islands--the Ryukyu chain – were just jagged mountain tops sticking out of the sea. And they were teeming with airstrips. It looked like they carved one out of the trees and foliage everywhere there was a piece of flat ground. They would make wonderful emergency landing fields for American planes in trouble.

John checked his navigation charts. Even with the slight headwind, *f-stop* is making good time. No sooner does that comforting thought pass than she lurches, yawing hard right, then drops her right wing. The smooth, muffled drone suddenly sounds labored – the right engine is losing power. "Shit! Damned supercharger's acting up!" John mutters as he scans the engine instruments. They tell the same tale as the seat of John's pants: manifold pressure on the right engine is dropping erratically. He pulls both engines back and descends.

The trip home just became longer and more dangerous. They will be lower, slower, and more vulnerable to fighters. And now they just might run out of gas.

John levels off at 10,000 feet, finally able to match the power of the two engines without superchargers. The drop tanks--long empty--will have to go: their extra drag could be the difference between making it home or not. With a flick of two switches, they detach from the wings and tumble to the deserted sea below.

The sea is not deserted for long. Now it is full of US Navy warships, battering the islands north of Okinawa at will. *At least if I have to ditch, I have a pretty good chance of getting picked up quick around here*, John thought, *provided some trigger-happy swabbies don't shoot me.*

As promised, John informs Bomber Command of the B-24's problem when he gets within radio range. A few minutes after that, Okinawa looms ahead, the mountains of the north clearly visible. It is time to start down: he gets busy with the *Before Landing* checklist. The fuel gauges begin to flirt with the low end of their scales.

Keep them running, girl... This is gonna be real close!

Time seems to drag. This mission should have been over a long time ago. Preparations for landing make the cramped cockpit a busy place. As the descent takes them through thin, patchy clouds, John doesn't even notice that the brilliant blue sky of altitude is fading to the less-vibrant hue of sea level.

Air traffic control tells him to plan a landing to the west-southwest, so he hugs the east coast until clear of the mountains. There are plenty of other aircraft approaching the island. A controller's voice barks in John's headphones: "Focus 4-7, how about orbiting for a few minutes while I get this flight of transports down? They're running on fumes."

A quick glance at the fuel gauges tells John what he already knows all too well.

"Unable, Kadena. Unable." John replies. "I'm pretty low on gas myself."

"All right, Focus... we'll sandwich you in. Do you have visual on traffic to your south?"

"Roger, Kadena. I've got them."

At least a dozen C-46 and C-47 transports are approaching from the opposite direction, clustered in V-shaped groups known as the "finger four" formation. As they begin to peel off for landing, forming a ragged, downward sloping line to the runway, one of the transports turns wide to accommodate *f-stop*. John snuggles his plane into the landing queue.

He taps the fuel gauges one more time, just to

make sure they're not lying. They don't budge--not even a needle's width. He begins to consider one more option to ensure making the field.

Maybe I should shut that right one down... It'll be no sweat making the fuel last on one engine...

But he knows better. Flying on one engine always feels a lot dicier than two. And if you have to *go around*--abort the approach, climb away and circle for another try--an F-5 can get *real squirrelly* when you pour the coals to just one engine. Many pilots have died after losing one of the engines during takeoff. Their planes just rolled over and augured into the ground.

I'm going to leave them both running, thank you.

The ground is now close but not close enough. Flaps down...gear down...and in a few more moments, *f-stop* is on the ground and taxiing to its spot on the squadron ramp.

She is guided to a stop by her crew chief, Staff Sergeant Chuck Jaworski. He holds up the closed-fist signal that means *set brakes*. Technicians immediately begin removing the film cartridges from the 5 cameras, load them into a jeep and speed off for immediate development. John would join the Intelligence staff people shortly, who would debrief him on the mission and evaluate the photos.

As the props spin to a stop, John rolls down the side windows of the canopy and releases the upper section. Jaworski, a bull of a man, towers above him on the wing, folds the upper canopy back out of the way, straddles the cockpit and effortlessly lifts the tall, sturdy but very stiff Captain Worth out of the cockpit by the armpits. The weather has turned. The storm has finally arrived and is unleashing its rain. John can tell right away Chuck is not pleased.

"You're a little late, ain't you, skipper? And where the hell are my drop tanks?" Jaworski asks.

"Right supercharger dropped out at 20,000 feet, Sarge…lost power… fluctuated…"

"You weren't trying to get away from anybody at the time, I hope?"

"No… not then."

Two of Jaworski's mechanics stand by the aircraft's nose, awaiting instructions, getting wet.

"Petrillo, Lucas…" Jaworski says, "get a look at the right intercooler and waste gate ducting… we've got ourselves a sick supercharger here."

Glancing at the supercharger, which protrudes slightly from the upper side of the right tail boom behind the engine, Jaworski says, "Well, she didn't blow apart, anyway…" and steps over the cockpit to the right wing. John follows him. Petrillo and Lucas get to work removing the access panels at the rear of the engine nacelle.

Chuck Jaworski is 27 years old; something of an old man in this Army. He is married with two kids, who he hasn't seen since late 1942; a tough survivor of the hardscrabble steel mills of Pittsburgh. A highly skilled mechanic and intuitive troubleshooter, he has been John Worth's crew chief for the last three years. The bond of respect, admiration, and trust between the sergeant and the captain is immeasurable. When not around other people, they call each other by their first names, indifferent to the breach of military etiquette.

Petrillo and Lucas remove the nacelle panel covering the suspected ducting. Jaworski kneels on the wing and begins to feel around the still hot ducting with a gloved hand, ignoring the steady rain that turns to steam on contact with the ducting.

"Here it is… this duct clamp is blown… leaking at

the waste gate… that's why you lost power," Chuck says, correct as usual. "Lucky you didn't melt the tail boom off."

John kneels and leans forward to look down into the nacelle, but his body, still stiff from over five hours of sitting in the cockpit, just doesn't bend the way he wants. Instead, he topples forward, his right forearm plunging onto a sharp edge of the now-exposed ducting. The cut is deep…there is lots of blood.

John grimaces as he pulls the arm back, yelling: "Ah, shit!"

"That's gonna need stitches, Captain," Chuck says.

"Yeah, yeah, I know… Corporal Petrillo, hand me one of those clean rags, please. I'll just wrap it up and walk over to the hospital. I could use the exercise."

John turns to Chuck. "Just tell them I'll be a little late for debriefing, Sarge."

Chapter Six

John Worth made his way to the hospital dispensary adjacent to the airfield, his bleeding forearm still wrapped with the rag. The rain had let up a bit.

As he entered the dispensary tent, crowded with scores of sick and injured soldiers and airmen, busy nurses, and medics, the first thing--and the last--he saw was the nurse at the triage station, Second Lieutenant Marjorie Braden. The harsh electric lighting in the tent illuminated only her, with a surprisingly soft glow. Everybody and everything else was in olive drab shadow and made no sound.

She was pretty enough, even in fatigues and without make-up; a little taller than average, with lithe body and chestnut hair--probably shoulder-length, now tied back--and green eyes that flashed like beacons of awareness and purpose. She seemed to know exactly what she was doing and spoke in a direct, no-nonsense manner that was authoritative but not intimidating. John stood in the tent's entryway, a man transfixed.

Impatiently, she calls out to him: "I can help you over here, sir... but how about knocking the mud off those boots first?"

Wordlessly, he complies.

"OK, Captain, what've we got here?" she asks, peeling off the bloody rag.

"Hmm... looks like you'll live... just needs some stitches."

She cocks an eyebrow and with just a touch of sarcasm, asks: "Should I start processing your Purple Heart right away?"

John snaps out of his trance. *And a sassy one, too, this nurse…*

"Nah… don't bother, Lieutenant. I've already got one." He replies with a shy smile, his voice matter-of-fact, almost humble, trying like crazy to mask this spontaneous attraction to her--and failing.

But he has gotten her attention, too. Marjorie Braden reconsidered her opening lines:

OK, Marge… start over! This guy standing in front of you may be some kind of war hero and you're mouthing off like some little smartass!

She starts over by putting her finger on the leather name tag of his flight jacket and reading aloud: "Captain J.P. Worth. What does the J.P. stand for?"

"John Peter"

She writes that down on the form in front of her. Centered on his name tag are the embossed pilot's wings.

"What do you fly, Captain Worth?"

"I fly an F-5," John says. Seeing that she has no idea what an F-5 is, he adds, "That's a P-38 modified for photo reconnaissance."

"A P-38! So you're a fighter pilot."

"No, I'm not." John's voice is still matter-of-fact, almost apologetic. "I fly photo recon."

Lieutenant Braden thinks: *Am I hearing this right? This guy in front of me flies a fighter but talks like a down-to-earth kind of guy. He doesn't swagger and he's not waving his willy in my face…What's his game?*

Marge decides not to assign a medic to do the stitching. She will handle this one herself.

"How'd you get cut, anyway?"

"I was looking at a supercharger with my crew chief... it gave me problems on my last flight. I slipped and sorta fell into the nacelle..."

"Wow! A pilot getting his hands dirty! Didn't you read the Officer's Manual?"

John laughs. "No, I guess not."

While she stitches, they engage in the ritual performed by all those in the service meeting for the first time, asking *where are you from?* His answer is Des Moines, Iowa. Hers is Chicago.

The small talk turns serious. He answers her questions about photo recon: what its purpose is, what flying the missions is like. Marge is incredulous his plane has no guns, only cameras, but he still flies into harm's way regularly, all the while insisting he is not a fighter pilot. *He's telling me this like it's no big deal... it's just his job. And I don't think all this modesty stuff is some kind of put-on! He's sincere!*

Marge Braden is surprised to learn he is only 23, just a year older than her. He seems so much older. And there is something else...

He's got the saddest eyes I've ever seen.

In her mind, all the elaborately designed filters military nurses employ to select suitable mates from the vast pool of available men begin to signal in unison: *this one definitely passes the test, Marjorie...* which is a good thing, because she really likes this guy.

Then her stomach begins to grumble. Loudly.

"Did you miss lunch?" John asks. He's not trying to mock her; he's genuinely concerned.

"Yeah," she says, a bit embarrassed. "I try not to eat the hospital food... it's *soooo* lousy."

It was time to throw caution to the wind. In the

bustling circus Okinawa was becoming, he might never see her again. Besides, this is war. We could all be dead tomorrow

The debrief he is supposed to be attending is all but forgotten.

Gingerly, he makes his move. "Could I get you something to eat? From the Officers' Mess, maybe?"

"Well, we're kind of busy right now… but I'll tell you what. I'm off at 0400. Want to meet there for breakfast?"

Chapter Seven

In accordance with Foreign Minister Togo's directive, the Japanese Army and Navy leaders hurried to develop new proposals on how to best use the nuclear weapon against the American invasion. Their air forces--both Army and Navy--had never been part of the equation: they had no aircraft capable of lifting a 20,000 pound load, the weight of Professor Inaba's device. In fact, no air force in the world had such a capability. Even the mighty American B-29 bomber, while having the ability to carry a 20,000 pound payload, could not carry a single object weighing that much: the load had to be distributed between its two bomb bays. Not that the Japanese hadn't tried. They had once attempted to increase the payload capacity of their highest performance bomber, the twin-engined Ki-67 "Hiryu," code named "Peggy" by the Allies, by using a rocket-assisted takeoff system.

The normal weapons payload for a Peggy was 2400 pounds.

Stripped of all non-essential equipment and carrying minimum fuel, she was given a 15,000 pound test payload. As the severely laden aircraft struggled to accelerate on takeoff role, the pilot fired the rocket motor. The Peggy staggered into the air, but the thrust of the underslung rocket caused excessive nose-up angle of attack. The pilot fought to maintain control, but the instant the rocket expended its fuel the plane stalled and, dropping its left wing, plummeted the 800 feet to the ground, killing the pilot and destroying the aircraft.

The Imperial War Council decreed there would be no more test flights of this sort. Suicide must be put to more expedient uses.

The Navy's new plan sought to destroy the invasion fleet before it reached the beaches of Kyushu. Unfortunately, they had no practical way to do it. The problem was the same one that plagued their San Francisco plan: how to place the weapon on the surface of a sea teeming with opposing vessels, beneath a sky full of opposing aircraft.

They probably had a better chance of sneaking into San Francisco Bay than the middle of the invasion fleet.

The "middle" was a somewhat relative term, too. Where would that be on a fleet that stretched across the horizon and occupied more than a hundred square miles of ocean? Choice landing beaches stretched around southern Kyushu from Miyazaki in the east to Kushikino in the west, some 100 linear miles of coastline. One nuclear weapon could devastate, at best, five square miles and destroy some of the invasion fleet, perhaps as much as 25%, but not all.

No, the Navy's role against the US invasion of Kyushu would be the same as at Okinawa: Kamikaze, but on a grander scale. The Japanese Navy had left about 3000 such aircraft, hundreds of suicide motor boats laden with explosives, plus the handful of destroyers and submarines still operational. The rest of the Imperial Fleet's might lay at the bottom of the sea, lost to the "luck" of the US Navy. They never realized it was not "luck" at all, but their signal codes had long ago been broken and their plans revealed in the intercepted radio transmissions.

The Army had a more practical plan for the defense of the homeland, code-named Ketsu-Go; a part of this plan--called Ketsu-Go 6--covered the defense of Kyushu. It took no great strategist to determine southern Kyushu was the next logical landing place for US forces. It was in easy proximity to Okinawa, the Philippines and the Marianas. The meager road and rail network coupled with the central and northern mountains would make Japanese reinforcement of the southern defenders physically difficult and easily interdicted by US air power. Once US airfields were established on southern Kyushu, almost all of Japan, including Tokyo, was within the range of any US combat airplane, not just the long-range B-29's.

Even with a massive Kamikaze onslaught against the invasion fleet, the Japanese Army General Staff was certain American troops would succeed in landing on southern Kyushu. They could not stop them with the conventional forces at hand--but Professor Inaba's device was anything but conventional.

Ariake Bay, also known as Shibushi-wan, lies in the southeast corner of Kyushu, central to the likely invasion beaches. The General Staff had determined this area to be most critical to their defensive plan. Destroying the invaders at this location would divide the attacking forces and greatly hinder the landing of reinforcements and logistical support. Once cut off from each other, the divided attackers to the north and west could be defeated in detail.

Here was the perfect place to employ the nuclear weapon: hidden in plain sight 1 or 2 kilometers inland, with high ground to the rear, shielding the island's interior from the blast; a deadly trap of unbelievable killing power, planned to be detonated about 48 hours after the first wave, when most of the invading

American devils would already be on shore.

Chapter Eight

0400 is a busy time at Kadena's Joint Officers' Mess, where Lieutenant Braden and Captain Worth had arranged to meet. Pilots and staff officers start their day long before first light; and of course, nurses have to eat, too, but they found it usually more convenient to eat at the hospital mess, as it was closer to their guarded, barbed wire-encircled living quarters. Also, it was far away from the constant, often unwanted flirting and frat house shenanigans of the numerically superior male officers.

John Worth, stitched up arm and all, had just finished collecting a tray of food and was pouring himself a cup of coffee when Marge Braden and a few of the other nurses from her night shift cautiously entered. Seeing John, Marge bid her fellow nurses goodbye and headed toward him, breezily tossing off fervent offers of a seat and lustful attention from every group of men she passed. Not so long ago in combat theaters, nurses were forbidden from leaving their hospital without armed MP escort for protection against friendly as well as enemy troops. Okinawa, however, was thought to be as secure and orderly now as any stateside base. While fraternization was still officially forbidden, the regulations were "unofficially" relaxed and the natural urges of men and women quickly surged to the forefront. It blew across the officer ranks--both male and female--like a blast of fresh air, relieving some of the boredom and uncertainty of a stalemated war with no end in sight.

"Good Morning, Captain Worth!" Marge says, gushing a bit. "Sleep well?"

"I was OK except for the agonizing pain in my arm... some butcher sewed me up and..."

Marge interrupts with mock indignation. "Hey! With all due respect, sir, I'll have you know you were sewn up by one of 5th Air Force's finest!" Grabbing his arm, she gives it a cursory inspection. "And I must say the work still looks damn good, too!"

"No, really... it's great... I'm just kidding, Marjorie. Where should we sit?"

"How about right here, Captain?' I'll be right back... gotta get some food in me before I faint... No coffee, though! This is almost my bedtime!"

When she returns, they sit facing each other on what you'd call a picnic table back home. They talk in the way two strangers of opposite sex do, drawn together by chemical attraction and circumstance, desperately trying to get to know everything about each other as quickly as possible. Children only yesterday, their entry to adulthood is shaped only by war.

"So you've got a Purple Heart?' Marge asked.

"Yeah... two, actually. Nothing serious." There was that matter-of-fact, almost apologetic tone again.

"Do you want to tell me what happened?"

"Well... the first one was from ground fire... flak... over New Guinea. My plane got a little messed up... shattered the canopy... I think I had more plexiglass in me than metal."

"You're lucky you didn't bleed to death up there," Marge says, her green eyes wide and serious.

"I think I would have run out of gas before bleeding to death. It really wasn't that bad, just very noisy."

"And the second time?"

"Actually, the second one was on the ground in the Philippines. Our airfield near Lingayan got attacked... some Jap fighters managed to get through and shot the place up pretty good... got the fuel farm... big explosion, big fire... a lot of guys got burned real bad. I just got hit with some flying debris."

"Thank god you're OK," Marge says. Then she adds: "I was in the Philippines, too. Our hospital unit was at Leyte. That was our first post overseas. We got there December, last year... Too bad we didn't meet there... although that wouldn't have been very likely. We were sequestered like prisoners."

"Big place, bigger war...I guess I just wasn't that lucky back then," John says, managing to sound ironic and smitten at the same time.

Marge smiles back. "I'm feeling pretty lucky myself lately. Got any other medals?"

"Just a bunch of Air Medals."

"What did you get them for?"

"Flying a lot."

After a quiet, contented moment, they finish eating and go back to discussing the history of each other. They already knew each other's home towns; they had performed that ritual yesterday at the dispensary.

"Des Moines, huh? Did you live in the city itself?"

"Nah... On a farm, about 20 miles out."

"A Farm Boy! I'll bet you're from a real big family, too."

"I'm the oldest of five boys and two girls," John says.

"Yeah...I figured you for the big brother type." Then Marge starts to giggle, enjoying a private joke.

"Oh, gosh! Farm Boy… Farmer John!" she says.

"Oh, please… not Farmer John! That was the name of my first airplane. I didn't choose it, though… the other guys in the squadron did, the old timers. I was the new green kid… the minute they heard my life story one of the ground crew painted it on my plane… I never liked that name."

"OK, Farm Boy, I promise I'll never call you Farmer John again!"

"You've got a deal. So tell me about growing up in Chicago."

"It was great! We actually live in Highland Park… that's just north of Chicago…"

"I know where it is," he says. "I've been to Chicago a bunch of times."

"Oh, good! Anyway, my dad is a lawyer, my mom's an English teacher… and my older brother is a naval officer. His destroyer was in the Atlantic but we don't know where he's going now… and I've got a kid sister still in high school."

"Highland Park, huh? Daddy a lawyer? All right… your new name is "Rich Girl!""

Her smile vanishes. "Oh, no, John. We really aren't rich. Please don't call me that."

"Well, richer than my family, that's for sure...but OK, fair's fair. I'll ditch the nickname. But tell me, how did your folks feel about you joining up?"

"They weren't very happy, but then again, they weren't happy when I chose nursing school over college, either. They knew they couldn't stop me, though.

OK, Farm Boy, now tell me about your family. Hmm… from Iowa, I'll bet you're Methodist… or Lutheran."

"Actually, Marge, no. I'm Catholic."

"Really! I didn't think there were any Catholics in Iowa! Are you devout?"

"Hardly. Consider me lapsed. What about you?"

"We were brought up Episcopalian like my daddy, but I'm hardly devout. More like disinterested. I've got a streak of my Tennessee Baptist mother in me... she's from Knoxville."

"Disinterested?"

"Yeah... I guess it started when I was 15. I was always kind of a skeptic, but during a summer trip to Tennessee, some Baptist pastor tried to proposition my mom. That did it. Religion seemed like such a joke after that. Imagine, a *man of god* trying to pick up women..."

"Well, can't say I blame you."

"Wait, John, there's more. After Mom told him to get lost, he started sniffing after me."

"Oh, no! He didn't try to..."

Of course he tried! But I slapped him one real good. Kind of knocked him on his ass, actually."

John laughs with relief. "So let me get this straight. You're smart, you're beautiful...and you're a real tough cookie."

"I'm not so sure about the *beautiful* part... but you better believe the other two, Farm Boy!"

"Trust me on the beautiful, OK?" he says with a big smile.

"If that's your opinion," she says, smiling back.

Chapter Nine

Professor Inaba had been caught by surprise. Until this moment, he had no idea the San Francisco plan was dead. Now he was told the Army would deploy his device and he was being commanded to have it ready for transport within 24 hours. Military personnel were swarming all over his facility in preparation for the move.

The Professor was disheartened the military no longer planned to submerge his device; his plan to sabotage the weapon had been rendered irrelevant and there was no time or opportunity to implement another. He and his staff watched, dejectedly, as the 10 ton weapon--resembling a very large beer barrel--was hoisted onto a flatbed rail car. Once dockside, it would be loaded onto the deck of an Imperial Japanese Navy destroyer, one of the few left afloat. Inaba's only hope was that the Americans would send this destroyer to the bottom of the Sea of Japan, taking his device with it.

The crossing of the Sea of Japan to Fukuoka, Kyushu, some 300 miles distant, would be made over the course of 3 nights, preferably in poor weather. While no US Navy surface ships had yet to enter the Sea of Japan, US submarines and aircraft roamed there with little opposition. Poor visibility and rough seas would improve the odds against the American threat. The 24 hour deadline was timed to coincide with just such a forecast.

The first two nights of this journey, following the western Korean coast, passed without incident. On the third night, as the destroyer with its deadly cargo departed the southern Korean coast for the final, 100 mile leg of its journey, the American submarine USS Sturgeon had just surfaced and was making its way north through the Tsushima Strait near Shimonoseki. On the conning tower's small deck, in the veiled moonlight, the captain, Lieutenant Commander Bradley Stark, was discussing the deteriorating weather with his executive officer (XO), Lieutenant Ward Grayson. Sheets of rain were falling all around them on the roiling sea. This weather had just foiled their chance to attack some merchant ships.

"How's the battery charge coming?" Captain Stark asks his XO.

"Full charge should be in another 2 hours, sir," Grayson responds.

"That's a long time on the surface in this crappy weather. We'll be rolling all over the place. We can't afford another torpedo falling off its rails… and I don't want to be burying anyone else at sea if I can help it."

After a solemn pause, Captain Stark says, "Let's reverse course… maybe stay out of the really rough stuff for the next couple of hours… go back towards Nagasaki… sun will be up in about 4 hours, and I want to be able to dive without worrying about the batteries. I can't believe we chased those tubs for so long and never got a shot! Turn left to course 210."

"Aye aye, sir"

The Japanese destroyer captain, Commander Ito Fuchida, estimated the final leg of this voyage would take six hours. That would put them into Fukuoka about 0500, long before sunrise. The storm had whipped up the sea quite a bit, but they were still making satisfactory headway. He was concerned that if the sea got too rough, the deck would be awash and he might lose this mysterious object lashed to it, that thing that looked like a gigantic beer barrel. The Army Colonel in charge of it steadfastly refused to tell him what it was; he only referred to it as a "secret Army project."

Just before 0300, Captain Fuchida sensed the problem even before he was summoned by the intercom from the engine room. One of the two diesel engines was pulled back; they were losing speed rapidly.

"Captain," a voice from the intercom barks, "the port engine is overheating. The cooling inlet line has ruptured. There is some flooding in the engine room, but it has been brought under control."

Furious with this sudden bad luck, Fuchida asks, "Can you repair the cooling line?"

"We can make temporary repairs but there will still be sea water leaking into the engine room. The port engine must remain at 'idle/stop' until cooling flow is restored. Otherwise, it will seize."

"How long until the engine can develop power?" the Captain asks, his voice demanding.

"The repair should take about one hour. After that, the engine should cool in about 10 minutes and be ready for full power."

Captain Fuchida leans over the chart table and calculates that at this agonizingly slow speed for one hour, they would still be in the Genkai Sea off northwest Kyushu at sunrise: easy pickings for American submarines and aircraft.

On the USS Sturgeon, Captain Stark is also receiving bad news.

"Chief says we've got a problem with the batteries, Captain...one bank isn't taking a charge...doesn't know why yet," the XO says.

Stark delivers his concise reply through clenched teeth. "Shit!"

With their battery power cut in half, the two electric motors that propel the sub when submerged will have less than an hour of power; hardly enough time to stalk and sink your prey and make an undetected escape. They would be forced to remain on the surface using the two air-breathing diesel engines.

From the lookout post above the conning tower comes the cry: "Contact off starboard beam!"

Captain Stark scans the sea to the west, but he has to wait until his boat rises on a swell again to see anything other than walls of gray ocean on both sides. When it does rise, the Captain, his binoculars pinned to his eyes, says, "Looks like a Jap destroyer, probably... starboard bow, about 1500 yards."

Then his sub slides back down into a trough. This cycle of rising and falling repeats itself two or three times a minute.

"Is that son of a bitch even moving?" Grayson asks.

"He must be," Stark replies. "He's gonna pass behind us. Ready the aft torpedo tubes. Get me a range as soon as we pop back up!"

"Do you think he's alone, Captain?"

Stark's impatient reply cuts the cold, wet air like a knife. "I don't see anybody else, do you?"

The range is proving difficult to estimate, however. After a few abortive attempts, Grayson says, "I swear, Captain, this guy is hardly moving... but he's going down in a ditch, too. Most times, I can only get the top of his mast. We're gonna have to change course left to even get a shot with the stern tubes... and I think he's further away than we first thought. I just can't get a decent plot in this fucking rain!"

After a few more minutes with no success, Captain Stark calls out: "We're getting too far away... Helm! Hard left, all ahead one half...come to course 030... let's get a better angle for a shot with the forward tubes. He's got to be moving!"

Halfway through the sub's turn, the men on the conning tower lose sight of the destroyer. When they arrive at the specified course, rather than their prey being dead ahead as they hoped, it is gone.

"What the hell?" Stark says. He pauses in exasperation, then adds, "You know, you're probably right... this guy must be almost dead in the water... he's gotta be to the west... he couldn't have slipped by us, could he?"

"I doubt it, Captain."

"Forget it," Captain Stark says with a sigh, giving up the chase for the second time that night. "Come left, back to course 210, all ahead full...Sun will be up soon. Have we figured out the fucking batteries yet?"

As the American sub completes its slow, full circle, still rising and falling with the heavy swells, the Japanese destroyer, its engine repaired and now making normal speed, passes unseen to the south. Almost two hours later, it completes its voyage with the sun rising over its bow. Captain Fuchida proudly enters in the ship's log: ENGINE REPAIRS COMPLETED UNDERWAY. CROSSING SUCCESSFUL. NO ENEMY VESSELS SIGHTED.

In the early morning light of the clearing skies, as the sub's lookouts see the smoke from the destroyer's stacks far to their port stern, Captain Stark is never more painfully aware of the old cliché "...like two ships that pass in the night."

Chapter Ten

General Takarabe was deeply distressed. He commanded the 57th Army, a force of 150,000 men that would defend southeastern Kyushu against the American invasion. Ariake Bay, the lynchpin of defensive plan Ketsu-Go 6, fell within his zone of responsibility. Takarabe had just received secret orders from the War Council's emissary. What he was told had left him dumbfounded.

The general was ordered to allow the emplacement of a new, secret weapon inland at Ariake Bay by a "special" unit. He was further instructed, in no uncertain terms, not to interfere with this unit and he was to ensure none of his subordinate commanders did so, either. He felt insulted by this intrusion to his command but he was a soldier and would follow orders.

The general was not told the nature of this weapon. Initially, he feared it was some kind of chemical weapon--a poison gas--but he, like all of Japan's military leaders, was disinclined to use such weapons. The Americans were similarly disinclined; they had vowed to use chemical and biological weapons only in retaliation for their use by the Axis powers. That was a Pandora's Box the Japanese did not wish to open: they knew America's chemical arsenal far outstripped theirs. In the strange code of ethics now governing human conflict, it was acceptable to blow a man to bits but not acceptable to burn his lungs out or decimate his nervous system with gas.

But was the War Council now desperate enough to employ chemical weapons? Takarabe doubted it. He knew the Council was counting on the fanatical, suicidal actions of his inexperienced troops to destroy the invaders. He also knew that no matter how fanatical, you can only die for the Emperor once.

At the Fukuoka docks, it is midmorning of a beautifully clear day. The storms of last night have moved to the northeast, to Honshu and beyond. The nuclear device is being off-loaded from the destroyer that has brought it from Korea. Colonel Minoru Ozawa, the Army officer in charge of the device, is now recovered from the seasickness of the previous night. He watches as the crane lifts the barrel-shaped object, in its steel cradle, off the deck and sets it down on a railroad flatcar. His second in command, Major Hideki Watanabe, bellowing instructions to the loading crew, makes sure the high-explosive triggering device, removed from the weapon for safe transport and weighing slightly less than 100 pounds in its shipping crate, is loaded onto a truck.

Suddenly, to the south, comes the sound of anti-aircraft fire. All eyes turn upward to see a dozen or more B-24 bombers approaching from the southwest at about 10,000 feet, puffs of flak surrounding them. The B-24 has four engines: the noise of 50 or more of these engines seems like the drone of angry hornets as they draw closer.

The bombers are flying straight for the docks. As they enter the airspace above, the lead bombardier has no trouble at all finding the aiming point on this clear morning. At his command, all aircraft begin releasing their four ton bomb loads on the docks some two miles below.

Colonel Ozawa's "special" troops scurry to any shelter they can find. None hide under the railroad flatcar now carrying the nuclear weapon.

The American bombs begin to impact, creating a rapidly moving curtain of crushing shock waves and razor sharp fragments of steel, wood, and concrete. For those far enough away, the noise is like the rapid beating of a thousand bass drums. For those too close, they hear nothing but the screaming of their own auditory nerves, for the blast percussion has shattered their eardrums. Blood drips from their ear canals as proof.

A few of the Colonel's men are torn to shreds, some are bleeding from jagged lacerations but will survive, but all the survivors are, at least temporarily, deaf.

The destroyer has received a direct hit to its superstructure and is now a blazing inferno. Captain Fuchida and most of his crew are killed onboard. Moments before he is killed, the Captain had completed his final entry in the ship's log: MISSION ACCOMPLISHED.

The truck onto which the high-explosive triggering device was loaded is torn apart, as are the three soldiers who had taken shelter beneath it. The triggering device, in its mangled shipping crate, lays amongst the rubble, undamaged.

The anti-aircraft gunners have failed to bring down any of the B-24's.

As Colonel Ozawa and his men stumble about, numb and disoriented, unable to hear anything except the ringing in their ears, no one notices the lone F-5 that streaks overhead several minutes after the bombers have delivered their deadly payloads.

The only thought Ozawa can formulate is *Fucking American Pirates!* Those words resonate in his disordered mind in perfect English, just like the words of his unspoken rebuttal to Professor Inaba's lament on that seaside bluff in Korea.

6TH US Army Intelligence Section (G-2), Okinawa

"What do you make of this thing, gentlemen?" Colonel Tom Watkins, Assistant G-2, asks, pointing to the strange, beer-barrel shaped object clearly visible in the photograph on the dock adjacent to the burning Japanese warship. "Pretty big ration of beer, wouldn't you say?"

No one in the room laughs. Nobody has any idea what it is.

Colonel Watkins has a question for John Worth. "Captain Worth, you took these pictures. Any other observations you'd like to share with us?"

"Well… yes, sir," John Worth says. "There didn't appear to be much activity around the docks, other than what's in the picture, but it struck me as odd that the object in the photo was either just off-loaded or was about to be loaded on a destroyer. Why are they using a warship to transport whatever this thing is?"

Watkins is skeptical. "You're suggesting it has some high military value?"

"Quite possible, sir," John says, "and whatever it is, it looks to be intact… Undamaged."

Colonel Watkins thinks it over for a minute, then offers his conclusion. "It's probably industrial in nature. Just make note of it in the intelligence summary. Now get this package off to Manila. General

Willoughby is waiting."

Then the colonel adds: "You know, Willoughby told me that MacArthur is convinced he's going to just walk onto Kyushu and be the next Emperor!"

Chapter Eleven

Professor Inaba sits in the anteroom of the Imperial Counsel Chamber, exhausted and scared out of his mind. He is sure he has been summoned here, flown in the night from Korea, to be forced to commit ritual suicide for his aborted plot to sabotage the nuclear device.

He wonders: *How had they found out?*

The entire trip had been a nightmare. Rousted from his sleep by soldiers and hustled off into the night, he felt sure they were going to execute him then and there. Instead, he was taken to an airfield and loaded onto a transport plane, its engines already running, and flown in darkness across the Sea of Japan.

Perhaps they plan to throw me from this airplane into the sea below!

But his military escort had done no such thing. After the long and bumpy flight, one that left Inaba weak from airsickness, he was bundled into an automobile and driven into a city he eventually recognized as Tokyo; so much had been destroyed by the fire bombing that it was difficult to identify. Now, at sunrise, he sat outside the Chamber, trembling with fear.

The Professor is a pathetic sight, disheveled and disoriented, as he is ushered into the chamber. There are eight other men already in the room, some from the Army and Navy; some, perhaps, statesmen. Inaba recognizes only General Umezu, who he had met several times during the course of his work on the device.

General Umezu speaks first. "Professor, we apologize for any inconvenience we have caused you, but we require your expertise. Would you care for some tea?"

This could be a trap! It's poisoned! Inaba thinks, his mind reeling out of control. But he manages a shaky reply: "No, thank you, sir,"

Secretary of War Anami speaks next. "Professor, allow me to introduce myself. I am Anami. Let me get right to the point. Do you believe the Americans possess nuclear technology similar to ours?"

Inaba is taken aback by the question; the answer should be obvious. He replies, "Why yes, Minister, of course! Physicists throughout the world have a working knowledge of the technology. Only a few countries, though, have the resources to develop nuclear weapons. They would be ourselves, Great Britain, Germany, the Soviet Union and, of course, the United States."

None of the Counsel takes comfort in what the Professor has just stated. Japan is at war with three of the countries he has just listed and the other is an already defeated ally.

"So then, Professor, you feel the Americans could and would use a nuclear device against the Japanese Home Islands?" Anami asks.

"I can only speak for the *could*, and have already done so, Minister. As to *would*, that is a question for soldiers and statesmen. I am only a scientist."

"I see," Anami says, then yields the floor to Admiral Toyoda.

"How would the Americans deliver such a device, Professor?" Toyoda asks.

"It would depend on its size and weight, sir. Our weapon, as you know, is much too heavy for Japanese aircraft to lift. If the Americans can master the metallurgy to make a lighter casing, it is quite possible for them to deliver it by a bomber aircraft. Our attempts at this failed: we had no choice but to make the casing of iron. Of course, it could still be delivered by a sea vessel, even a submarine, if they could make the device watertight."

Inaba wished with all his heart he could reel back the words he had just spoken.

I have given myself away! Fallen right into their trap! They must already know I planned to sabotage the device by compromising the watertight seals. How could I be so stupid?

I am doomed.

Feeling he now has nothing left to lose, Inaba offers one further opinion. "Gentlemen, if I may… if the Americans used a nuclear weapon, how could you tell? I have seen what my device can do and I have seen the results of the American fire bombing. I can only assume an American nuclear device would have similar characteristics to my own. Quite frankly, the fire bombing is more catastrophic, only less economical to deliver. What would be the difference to a devastated Japanese city?"

The silence in the Chamber is crushing. Inaba feels sure he will faint at any moment.

Finally, General Umezu speaks: "Very interesting point, Professor. Now, if you would be so kind, our staff has some technical questions for you. Please follow the escort. He will take you to them."

This is it. I am a dead man.

Much to the Professor's bewilderment, he is actually led to another conference room, where junior staff officers from the Army and Navy pepper him with questions about his device and the methods to employ it for over an hour. They are especially interested in the map of southern Kyushu: where could the device best be employed against the invasion beaches? Inaba draws circles on the map designating the blast radius. He then corrects their misapprehension that the device could be effectively detonated in a cave on the bluffs; much of the energy would be absorbed by the surrounding earth. He continues to answer their questions despite the fact he is so physically and emotionally drained, he can hardly stand or speak. His throat is so dry that no amount of water provides relief.

When the staff officers are finished, the Professor is driven to his family home in the countryside west of Tokyo. An army officer escorts him to the door. The officer thanks the Professor for his efforts, bids cordial best wishes to him and his bewildered wife, who has joined them at the door, and then drives away.

The Professor's wife cannot understand why her husband, who she has not seen in months, is curled on the floor, weeping, until finally, in that very spot, he falls into a long but fitful sleep.

Chapter Twelve

John Worth and Marge Braden had made the 0400 breakfasts together an everyday occurrence. John was flying almost daily photo missions to Japan and the Ryukyus or weather missions, sometimes to the China coast, unless grounded by the frequent storms or the maintenance requirements of his airplane. Many missions, however, were resulting in no pictures because of bad weather or cloud cover over the objective; such was the lot of the photo recon pilot.

The breakfasts were the perfect start to his day, before the pre-dawn briefings and takeoffs at first light, a few moments away from anxiety of what he might soon face alone in the sky. For Marge, they were the perfect end to her 12-hour night shift, a chance to clear her mind, just for a few minutes, of the injured, the dead and those who might soon be so.

Everyone knew they were falling in love.

Major Kathleen McNeilly, Marge's head nurse, knew it and issued this warning: "Be careful with your heart out here, Marjorie. Pilots may die... recon pilots just vanish."

One morning in their first week together, Marge says to John, "You know, you could take a day off now and then."

"And exactly how would I do that?"

"Be sick," she replies. "We get loads of flyers at the hospital every day with migraines, earaches, upset stomachs, but everyone knows there's nothing really wrong with them. You can tell right away... they just want to sit out a mission. We just give them some sugar pills and pull them off flight status for a day or two. You mean to tell me you've never done that?"

"Nope." He seems annoyed she has even suggested it.

"Nobody thinks any less of them, John."

"Doesn't matter. I couldn't do that."

"Well, give it some thought, will you? And speaking of flying, couldn't you have gone back to the States by now? You've been overseas a long time. Haven't you done enough missions?"

"Well, yeah, I could have gone back to the States. But I'm in the middle of my third tour and I can't leave before it's done."

John can tell from the expression on Marge's face that his answer is far from satisfactory.

"Besides," he says, "I can't see myself behind a desk or as some instructor... not while all this is still going on. From what I hear, pilots in this theatre won't be released until the replacements from Europe are available, and that won't be for a few months, at least."

Marge's facial expression changes. Now, it can mean only one thing: *there's something wrong with you!*

"For cryin' out loud, John... your *third* tour? You could have gone home *twice?* And you *didn't?*"

She places the palm of her hand against his forehead, like a mother taking a child's temperature. "Are you sure you're feeling all right? Maybe you shouldn't be flying today."

Smiling, John pulls her hand off his head but continues to hold it tenderly.

"This ain't like the 8th Air Force was in England, Marge. Those guys only had to fly 25 combat missions. Of course, their chances of surviving 25 missions was about one in three. Our odds are a little better. Here, a tour is longer, maybe 50 missions... supposed to be something like two or three hundred hours of combat flying. Of course, they can always order you to go home, like they did with Dick Bong."

"Who's Dick Bong?" Marge asks.

"Leading American fighter ace of all time... 40 kills against the Japs. I think the brass got afraid he was going to get himself killed. He flew a P-38."

"Just like you!" Marge says.

"No, he had guns. I've got cameras, remember?"

"Hey! You get shot at just the same, don't you?" His continual self-denigration was beginning to wear itself thin.

Not wanting to dwell on the hard truth she had just spoken, Marge quickly moves on. "That reminds me of a joke Nancy Bergstrom told me. She got it from some fighter pilot she knows."

"Nancy? One of the nurses in your group?"

"Yep, that's her. Good old Nancy... the icy Nordic nymphomaniac who has devoted her brief military career to the physical pleasure of Army doctors."

"No pilots?" John asks.

"Nope, just doctors, as far as I know. McNeilly hates that, too. Doesn't think you should copulate with co-workers."

"And that would be Major McNeilly, your boss?"

"Right again. Anyway, she said the real reason the 8th Air Force guys went home after 25 missions was to lessen their chances of knocking up more English girls. Apparently, the Brits felt one Churchill was enough."

"Wait a minute," John says, his face without a hint of a laugh. "Churchill's *mother* was American!"

Marge sighs in exasperation. "OK, Farm Boy, you get an *A* in current affairs, but let's work on the humor a little!"

"Hmm... and how many fighter pilots do *you* know, Marjorie?" He was still very serious.

"Only you, honey."

John knew that could not be true. Women in combat zones are not starved for male attention. In fact, it was necessary to post MPs around the clock at the nurses' quarters to ensure men heeded the signs that read FEMALE OFFICERS ONLY--ALL OTHERS KEEP OUT. And fighter pilots are not shy.

He begins to correct her, but she silences him with a finger to his lips and says, "Don't forget... you're supposed to show me your plane when I wake up later, right?"

Chapter Thirteen

The sky had cleared of American bombers. Colonel Ozawa took stock of his situation. The nuclear device was intact and serviceable, having survived the bombing raid on the Fukuoka docks. That raid, however, had cost Ozawa five men killed and three severely wounded. The seven remaining soldiers were ready to carry on with the mission, despite the wounds three of this number had received. The Colonel and his second in command, Watanabe, had both received minor wounds.

At least now they are able to communicate verbally. Everyone's hearing is slowly returning, although the ringing in their ears would persist, probably to their planned death. It is a shame, Ozawa thinks, that "special" suicide troops had died without extracting a price in blood and steel from the Americans.

After getting his badly wounded to an aid station and leaving his dead with a local commander, Ozawa returns to the mission at hand. It is too soon to position the device at the suspected Ariake invasion site; suitable concealment there had not yet been arranged. Major Watanabe would be sent ahead to find an acceptable location and determine the best of the three available rail routes to move it the 70 miles to the chosen site. For now, it is to be hidden, away from the prying eyes of American airpower, regular Japanese troops, and the public.

The original plan was to store the device until deployment at Ariake Bay at the Kokura Arsenal some 30 miles to the north of Fukuoka. The arsenal, however, had begun to receive a good deal of attention from the bombers of the 5th and 20th Air Forces in recent days, as it was an aircraft production facility. Ozawa was instructed to improvise. He commandeered a large warehouse on the southeastern outskirts of Fukuoka that was miles from the docks as an alternative. The railroad tracks ran right inside this warehouse. This area had not been bombed yet.

The movement from the docks to the warehouse began smoothly enough, in stark contrast to the carnage several hours before. The small locomotive sent to tow the flatcar carrying the weapon is balky at first; to get it moving, the engineer has to repeatedly strike several steam valves with a mallet. These valves had been giving him trouble for a while, but there were no spare parts available. This is a nuisance but it does not impede progress.

Slowly, the locomotive begins to pull the flatcar away from the docks. It is risky doing this in broad daylight; the chance of air attack is high. Leaving the device exposed on the docks, however, is a greater risk. Ozawa now has barely enough soldiers to provide security here and at the Ariake Bay location Watanabe would select. It only takes one man, however, to activate and detonate the weapon, and each member of the Colonel's team has been trained in these tasks and is ready to carry out the orders.

After several minutes underway, the train is stopped by a track switch that will not move. The engineer's assistant pulls on the lever with all his might, but it will not budge. On closer examination, one of Ozawa's men finds debris, probably from the bombing raid, lodged in the moveable section of the track. After producing a crowbar from the locomotive cab, the debris is dislodged and the track switch repositioned.

The engineer begins his mallet blows to the steam valves once again, but as the locomotive starts to move, a flight of four US Navy fighters, gull-winged F4U Corsairs, streaks low out of the north, following the train tracks. Strafing trains is great sport for fighter pilots: the thick geyser of steam that shoots suddenly skyward when the boiler is punctured is dramatic and unimpeachable evidence the train has been rendered useless. Provided, of course, the boiler does not blow apart like a bomb and knock its attacker from the sky.

Closing on the train from behind, the Corsairs slew from their echelon into a line formation, one behind the other, opening up in turn with their .50 caliber machine guns as each plane reaches close range. In fact, they are too close: the machine guns, mounted three in each wing, are bore-sighted so their rounds converge 300 yards in front of the aircraft. They would be much closer than that to the train when they fire. With the target centered in their gunsights; the projectiles would straddle the target.

The flight leader, US Navy Lieutenant Bob Kelly, anticipates this and kicks his rudder from side to side during his brief gun run, yawing the aircraft to shift the impact of the rounds, but he sees no geyser of steam result from his shooting. As he pulls up and turns west for a better look, he sees that none of the aircraft in his flight has achieved a kill, either. His frustration boils over.

Son of a bitch! We can't shoot for shit!

Kelly's problems are suddenly amplified as six Japanese "Tony" fighters appear out of nowhere behind his flight, spread adjacent in a "finger" formation. He calls for his four aircraft to regroup into two sections, each with a leader and a wingman. The leader would attack; the wingman would protect the leader's tail. Kelly and his wingman turn north in an attempt to gain altitude and get behind the Jap fighters. The other section continues their full-throttle climb to the southwest, acting as *the bait.*

The Tonys respond: two Japs peel off to pursue Kelly and his wingman, the other four continue in pursuit of the bait. Seeing this, Kelly and his wingman roll on their backs into a *split-s* maneuver, a half loop that rapidly heads them in the opposite direction. They pass below their pursuers and begin the chase of the four Tonys pursuing Kelly's other section.

Kelly thinks to himself: *Where the hell are all these fighters coming from? They keep telling us the Japs have no trained pilots, they have no fuel...It's all bullshit! More times than not we end up having to tangle with somebody! Or am I just unlucky?*

Fortunately for Kelly and his group, these Japs are not very experienced. A few maneuvers in their direction and they disperse in panic. With the Tonys fleeing, Kelly brings his group higher, to a tactically more advantageous altitude. Once there, no Jap fighters are to be seen. Checking the fuel and ammunition remaining, Kelly decides they have played long enough on the doorstep of the enemy. It is time to return to the carrier, which is some 100 miles east-southeast of Kyushu. The encounter had lasted three minutes but felt like three hours. Tomorrow is another day.

It is closer to sunset than Kelly planned as his flight enters their carrier's landing pattern. Landing a Corsair on the boat is hard enough in daylight;

darkness makes it a harrowing experience. During its developmental period, the Navy had initially rejected the Corsair for carrier use. Aerodynamic modifications to the prototype had moved the cockpit aft, so the forward fuselage and big round engine in front blocked the pilot's forward view of the floating "postage stamp" that was the carrier deck during landing. Only after a curved approach was perfected, with the aircraft constantly turning from the downwind leg to the threshold, with the deck and the landing signal officer always visible out the side of the cockpit canopy, was the plane approved for carrier deployment.

Kelly is last in line to come on board the carrier. As he waits in the holding pattern in the fading sunlight, he cannot stop his mind from wandering. He flashes back to his days at Yale, which he had left in early 1942--his junior year--to volunteer for Naval flight duty. A Bostonian from a wealthy family, he joined up for no other reason than patriotism and had flown combat missions in the Pacific since early 1944. His industrialist father had arranged to pull some strings and keep his idealistic son out of the military, but Kelly refused his father's help. Their relationship, never close, was strained and, perhaps, irreparable.

He tries to clear his head as he begins his approach but fatigue is taking over; his focus is not perfect. The landing signal officer, somewhat fatigued himself, is on the verge of waving him off but does not; this last plane has a stable sink rate after all, and he isn't enthusiastic about another approach in even less light. Kelly lands long, his tailhook barely snagging the last of the four arresting wires. Like an exhausted bird, the Corsair slams to the deck and lurches to a halt, its whirling propeller just feet from the flock of parked aircraft crowding the deck ahead.

Any landing you can walk away from is a good landing... but I definitely stunk the place up with this one.

At the post-flight debrief, none of the pilots in Kelly's flight remembers anything significant about the train they had strafed. The gun camera film is equally vague. The conclusion is quickly reached that the obscure, cylindrical figure briefly visible behind the locomotive and tender is a tank car, probably carrying fuel or oil. Kelly and his flight get credit for a "probable" neutralized target, despite the lack of firm evidence. No intelligence significance is attached to the mission debrief report, other than the presence of ineffective Japanese fighter coverage. It is further noted that effective immediately a directive is in force to cease attacking trains until further notice. The intelligence staff suspects they are being used to transport American POWs to forced labor in the invasion area. The pilots think the directive strange, but hell...war is strange.

Colonel Ozawa is relieved to find no damage to the nuclear device and no new injuries to his battered unit. He clearly remembers the sharp "clank" sound--loud and rapid--as bullets bounced off the iron device, leaving it unharmed and shielding his men and the locomotive. A disquieting thought crosses his mind: *What if an American bomb scored a direct hit?*

Would that cause the nuclear reaction to occur? Ozawa does not know. He only knows how to hook up the wires, depress the firing handle, and sacrifice his life for the Emperor.

When the nuclear device is finally parked in the warehouse, hidden from sight, the Colonel gives a sigh of relief and lets his battered troops get some rest.

His mind ponders the irony that, save for a decision made by his father almost 20 years ago, he might now be fighting for the other side.

Ozawa had been born in Hawaii, the son of Japanese parents. His father had moved the family back to Japan in the mid-1920's, after the death of his younger brother. Ozawa was grateful his father had made that decision. He despised Americans; it had been an American Army officer, a major, who had killed his brother. An *accident*, the police report said. That fateful evening, the two boys were walking home on the darkened road when the younger boy was struck by the Army man's car. The American officer claimed he had not seen the boy.

He might have been able to see, Ozawa believed, had he not been dead drunk. Returning from a social function, the inebriated major lost control of his vehicle in a turn. As it veered crazily toward the Ozawa boys, they tried frantically to jump out of the way. His brother wasn't quick enough.

Ozawa could never forget the words the American major had uttered--without emotion--as he stood over his dead brother: "Too bad...I killed the little chink." His equally inebriated female companion urged the major to just drive away, but the police had been summoned and were already approaching. Once on the scene, the policemen did not detain the American officer. He was never prosecuted or disciplined in any way.

Ozawa vowed he would forever hold all white people in the same disregard they exhibited to Asians. Americans and their allies could not be bothered to tell the different Asian peoples apart: chinks, nips, slants, dinks, wogs... they were all the same. During the early war years in Malaya and Burma, he encountered many

British POWs. He had found them comical: haughty fools who didn't realize their day had passed; a dishonorable rabble, not unlike the natives of the lands they had shamefully failed to protect for their king. If Japan was "The Empire of The Rising Sun," Britain was surely "The Empire of The Setting Sun."

But he would forever reserve his deepest hatred for the Americans. It was on them that he would take his apocalyptic revenge.

Chapter Fourteen

Marge sits in the *f-stop's* cockpit, overwhelmed by the array of gauges, switches, and levers that John, sitting on the wing outside, is trying to explain to her. Everything seems so much smaller than she had imagined. The only dimension that doesn't conform to this impression is the height of the wings while the plane sits on its tall landing gear. It took her several awkward leaps, with a lot of help from John, to climb the boarding ladder onto the trailing edge of the left wing root. Once on the wing root, the cockpit is at your feet. You practically fall into its cramped confines.

What a strange creation this aircraft is... so different from the other aircraft she has seen. There is no fuselage to speak of, just a pod jutting forward from the junction of the wings, with the cockpit at the rear of this pod, in line with the wings' leading edges. Extending from the lower forward section of the pod is the nose landing gear, which is as tall as she is and retracts rearward in flight so the tire nestles inside the pod just below John's feet. On either side is the big number "47," painted in red, and the name "*f-stop,*" in black, on the shiny aluminum skin.

Its two engines protrude forward from the wings, one on either side of the fuselage pod, each turning a three-bladed propeller. The plane's height off the ground, provided by its spindly landing gear, is necessary for these blades to clear the ground. Rather than an aft fuselage, two slender booms extend aft from the engine nacelles to the tailplane.

John has been describing the aircraft and its equipment to Marge nonstop, like a military instructor teaching a class of basic trainees. "In the fighter version," he says, "the nose of the pod has four .50 caliber machine guns and one 20 millimeter cannon. Recon planes like this old girl have five cameras instead, looking through small windows that are oriented vertically down and obliquely to either side. We'll get a better look at them from the ramp in a minute. Now, by synchronizing the airspeed, altitude, and shutter speed, I can get miles of continuous, high resolution strip photos of the earth below. Several strips shot on parallel courses give us a mosaic map."

"OK. I think I follow you there," she says, forcing a smile. "And I thought you said you didn't want to be an instructor. You sure sound like one right now."

"No, Lieutenant, you're just getting the special five dollar tour. Relax and enjoy."

"Yes, sir!" she replies, with all the sarcastic tone she can muster.

Marge's head begins to swim again as John continues. "The props are constant speed, electrically controlled and counter-rotating. That cancels out the torque, making her much easier to handle during take off and rapid applications of power."

Yeah, sure, Farm Boy, whatever the hell that all means.

"Each of those big Allison engines has 12 cylinders and develops nearly 1500 horsepower, enough to give *f-stop* a top speed of over 400 miles per hour. Nothing the Japs have can overtake her in level flight."

Marge likes the sound of that. Yet it brings no comfort.

He turns her attention to those two booms extending to the tail. While explaining the engine coolant radiators that protrude from their sides, she becomes fixated with the wheel-like mechanisms atop each boom, flush with the skin and in line with the wings' trailing edges. Turning slowly in the stiff breeze, they remind her of the spinning ventilators on Chicago rooftops. She points to them, interrupting his presentation.

"What are those?" she asks.

"I was just getting to them," he says. "They're superchargers...*turbochargers,* actually. The hot exhaust gases from each engine spin a turbine which turns a compressor that squeezes the thin intake air at altitude so the engines will make full power up there."

"A supercharger... Isn't that what blew out on you the day we met?"

"Hey...good memory! It was that one over there," he says, pointing to the one in the right boom.

Marge had hoped that learning about his airplane would help lessen her growing dread that something might happen to him. It did not seem to be working that way, though.

"But what does all that stuff mean when you're up there risking your life, John?"

He tries his very best to sound reassuring. "It means I can outrun and outclimb anybody else."

It does not matter what he says. All she keeps thinking is: *This is a coffin with wings! He's going to die in this thing!*

But she would not let him see how frightened she is. She summons all her resolve and tries to impress him with some *pilot lingo.*

"Where's George?" Marge says.

"*George?* You mean the autopilot? She doesn't

have one. You've been hanging around too many bomber pilots!" John replies, somewhat crestfallen.

"Never you mind!" She was enjoying this first hint of jealousy.

Marge points to a lever on the cockpit sidewall labeled DIVE BRAKES. "OK... Does that mean you can dive faster than anybody, too?"

"Not exactly. The dive brakes are little fences that pop out of the wing and increase drag. Without them, it's possible to go so fast in a dive that you cannot pull out... it's a phenomenon known as compressibility. If you get caught in it, it's crash and burn."

There it was; that reminder of imminent death again. She struggled to overcome her tumbling spirits one more time.

Dammit! He seems to love giving this little tour so much... Don't ruin it for him!

"John, your first airplane...What happened to it?"

"She got worn out...'war-weary' or 'uneconomical to repair,' as they say in official jargon. She was an F-4, an earlier P-38 recon model. I turned her in to the scrap yard at Nadzab, New Guinea. Then we were assigned a brand new bunch of F-5's, but before we ever flew them, they were taken back for conversion to fighters. Recon got the short end of the stick again. Finally, I was assigned this airplane from another batch of new ones."

"And you've never been shot down?"

"No."

"How long before *f-stop* wears out?

"A long time... she's still going strong."

"You know, that name--*f-stop*--it's kind of cute for a photo plane...like a lens setting, right?

He nods. She probes a little deeper. "Are you *sure* you don't you have a girl back home to name it after?"

"Nope. Don't have one."

"Hmm...I'll bet," she says, highly skeptical. "So what made you pick *f-stop,* anyway?"

"Well, all the good names were taken, like *Shutterbug, Celluloid Clipper, Photo Express, Eye in the Sky.* It just sort of came to me."

"Well, I really like the name," Marge says.

"Yeah, me, too. You know, Marge, I really do love this plane."

"I know, honey, I can tell. Forgive me, but I find it a little hard to love."

"I guess I can understand that." Then he adds: "And by the way... the number "47" on the sides... that, coincidentally, was my football number in high school and college."

"How convenient! There's something I've got to ask you, John. It's silly, but..."

"Go ahead, ask."

"You're up there so long some times. What do you do when you have to go to the bathroom?"

"You think about something else."

"Does that really work, John?"

"Well, there is a *relief tube*...I hate to use it... but if you're asking me if I've ever peed myself in the cockpit, the answer is yes, but not for the reason you're thinking."

Marge just stares at him with those bright green eyes, as if to say: *OK, so tell me!*

"Back when I was a rookie in New Guinea, I was lost and got caught in a valley by two Japs flying Zekes...you probably call them Zeroes. Those guys were obviously not rookies. I was too low, too slow, and had nowhere to go. I was sure I was about to buy it, but I was real lucky. Even though the plane got riddled, it was all light machine gun stuff...they must have been out of cannon ammo when they ran into me. Every time I looked in the rearview mirror, all I could see was a big round engine right on my tail. I guess they shot at me until they ran out of all their ammo, then they vanished. I never got a scratch, though, but I did get a big case of the damp drawers. And speaking of being pissed, Jaworski gave me holy hell for all the holes they had to repair!"

As he tells his tale, Marge's resolve collapses. Her face slowly transforms into a portrait of apprehension. She winces when she realizes that John's story is not finished.

"And ever since then," he says, "as a kind of reward for not actually getting my stupid self killed, I've been the squadron maintenance test pilot."

"What, exactly, is that, John?" She is almost too afraid to ask.

"All the planes that get really badly damaged... after they're repaired, I give them a test flight to make sure they still fly OK."

"OH, NO!" Marge cries, grabbing her shaking head with both hands.

John leans down into the cockpit, takes her head in his hands and kisses her forehead. She looks up at him, her green eyes suddenly expressing all the terrible pain and loneliness of the past year in a world at war, and pleads in a whisper:

"Take me away from here. Right now. Please!"

Chapter Fifteen

One week has passed since the War Council's last discussion of the nuclear device.

Foreign Minister Togo assembles the Council once again, still with the vain hope the military leaders would, at last, accept the concept of negotiated surrender. Prime Minister Suzuki silently shares that hope. They both believe that Japan is already defeated militarily. The US Navy's highly effective blockade is literally starving their nation. The war must end.

If not for the Allies' insistence on "unconditional surrender," that would be the Emperor's wish as well; but it certainly isn't the military's wish. Both Suzuki and Togo fear assassination by fanatically extreme junior officers if they dare to differ too strongly with the generals and admirals. They would not be the first statesmen to meet death at the hands of wild-eyed, immature young men in uniform.

The Prime Minister rises first to speak. "Gentlemen, I understand you are ready to propose a plan for deployment of the nuclear weapon. General Umezu, the Army commissioned Professor Inaba's research. I call on you to enlighten us."

"It would be an honor, sir," the General says, placing his prepared statement on the table before him. "As you all know, the defensive plan for the Home Islands is named Ketsu-Go. The section of this plan covering the defense of Kyushu is Ketsu-Go 6. We in the military understand some members of the government consider us deluded fools, but let us assure you we understand our situation clearly. We know we face a powerful foe who rules the sea and the sky. But this foe cannot be allowed to rule our people, control our way of life, or dictate terms to the Emperor. This foe fears setting foot on the soil of the Japanese homeland, as well he should. Our heroic defense of Okinawa was just a prelude to the battle he knows he will face if he invades. He does not understand our values, loyalty, and honor. He possesses no honor and is our inferior. The Kamikaze is a terrifying mystery to him. Unfortunately, the Kamikaze is all that is left of our once mighty Navy and Army Air Forces, but our ground troops are still almost five million strong... although half, of course, are on the Asian continent and, in light of the latest Russian betrayal, probably trapped there, unavailable for homeland defense. We believe our army on Kyushu, numbering over 500,000, can repel the American invaders, who will undoubtedly land on the southern beaches at the conclusion of this typhoon season, less than two months away. Our plan calls for fixing the attackers on the beaches and destroying them in place, before they can establish a foothold and employ the numerous airfields in the area. Close-in fighting on the beaches will negate the advantage the attackers will have in air and naval firepower. Reduced to this level of combat, the attackers will surely succumb to the determination of the soldier defending his own soil."

Foreign Minister Togo rises to speak. "General, we all have the deepest respect for your efforts in these matters, but we are all familiar with Ketsu-Go. How will the nuclear weapon help us?"

"I was just coming to that, sir," Umezu says. "As you know, sufficient enriched uranium was provided by the Germans to create the test weapon plus one additional device. How do we employ this solitary weapon, you ask?" His finger stabs at the map of Kyushu unfurled on the conference table. "Ariake Bay," Umezu continues, "is the most strategically critical point. We estimate three divisions will land there, approximately 60,000 men, one third of the initial invasion force. If the attackers succeed in gaining a foothold there, all the invasion forces can easily link together. Reinforcements and supply would be rapidly available to any and all. By employing the nuclear weapon there, at Ariake, we believe we can destroy half of the forces in the area, about 30,000, and render the remainder ineffective. This will divide and isolate the rest of the attacking forces, facilitating their defeat in detail. Once the Americans are routed on the beaches and plains of southern Kyushu, they will not have the courage or resources to invade again any time soon. Our Kwangtung Army, weakened though it is, will slow the Russian advance in Manchuria; they will not be able to threaten our shores for some time. At this point, and this point only, can we discuss a negotiated peace."

Suzuki, though surprised to hear the words *negotiated peace* in this context, is still more deeply troubled. "What of civilians in the area?" he asks.

Umezu replies: "All civilians will be evacuated to the interior before the invaders land. The propaganda films of civilians preparing to defend their homeland with bamboo sticks may be good for morale, but civilians are of no use to our Army on the field of conflict. They will only be in our way."

In a half-hearted attempt at a joke, the General adds: "Perhaps the Americans would sicken of slaughtering them and lose their will to fight."

Several of the officers present snicker in appreciation of the General's joke, to the horror of Suzuki and Togo.

The Prime Minister then asks: "And what of our troops in the area? Will they be evacuated before the detonation, too?"

"No, sir. That would not be possible. The troops must remain to fix the invaders in place. They will die honorably."

Suzuki's temper flares. "Are these to be *special* suicide troops?"

"No, Minister. These will be regular troops. Only the small special team that actually fires the weapon will know of its existence."

The Prime Minister is now shrieking. "As if this weapon is not horrific enough, is this deceit... this incineration of your own troops... not too awful to contemplate?"

General Umezu calmly looks out the window at the fire-bombed ruins of Tokyo and replies, "No, it is not. All Japanese troops are expected to fight to the death."

"General, do you not see the difference between a soldier who dies doing his duty and one whose duty is to die?"

"There is no difference, Mister Prime Minister."

Suzuki, overcome with hopelessness, turns away.

Then the General adds, "If this plan fails to achieve the advantage we seek, I will, of course, offer my life to the Emperor in atonement."

Chapter Sixteen

Marge and John had spoken not a word during the long walk from *f-stop* to John's tent. He wanted to wrap his arm around her shoulders and feel her body tight against his, her arm wrapped around his waist. He felt sure she wanted that, too. They settled for holding hands--lightly, tentatively--a link easily dissolved if they ran into any of the brass. Their anticipation was powerful but bittersweet: for all they knew, this could be their one and only time together.

The recon squadron pilots had set up their tents as far from the aircraft parking areas as was practical. This was an old habit from the two years spent on New Guinea; if the airfield got bombed or strafed while you were sleeping, the distance lessened your chances of catching some lead. The tents aren't exactly secluded, but they are, at least, away from the continual beehive of activity the airfield has become. Tall and circular, big enough for half a dozen men to walk around in, the tents look like big tops in a miniature circus.

John and his two tent-mates, fellow pilots, had long ago arranged a signal in case one had the rare good fortune of female company. A sign stating, "STAY OUT – AUTHORIZED PERSONNEL ONLY – THIS MEANS YOU!" had been appropriated from the ordnance section. If this sign was displayed at the tent's entrance, one of their number was entertaining a guest and their privacy was to be respected. The options for such company were very limited: nurses, few in number; the infrequent Red Cross and USO girls; or local prostitutes. The sign had rarely been used and never by John.

During their walk, Marge and John pass several of the squadron's mechanics, "wrenches," as he refers to them, in a way that seems to imply nothing but respect.

They bid a courteous greeting, complete with crisp salutes, to the Captain and his lieutenant. Marge is surprised: she had expected voyeuristic leers. Ordinarily, the mechanics would have obliged her. She is with John Worth, though, and to the enlisted mechanics the Captain is more than just an OK guy: *he's an old hand; he's been around, he knows his stuff and never talks down to us. If the Captain is getting lucky with a nurse--who, as an officer, is off limits to us enlisted types – well, it couldn't happen to a nicer fellow. After all, this is war. Anyone from the highest general to the lowest private fornicates if and when he can; to hell with the regulations--you could be dead tomorrow. Besides, everybody has seen them around together; it's obvious they're much more than friends.*

Approaching the tent, Marge balks at first. "Uh-uh, John... Not here. This isn't exactly *hidden*, you know."

John's explanation of the sign seems to ease her fears just a little, and once inside the tent, they find complete privacy in its dim light, walking through the unkempt maze of cots, boxes and cabinets decorated with pin-ups and profane comments on the war, Japs, and superior officers. Marge feels herself relaxing, giving in without reservation to the inevitability of what is about to happen. Eyes wide with mock astonishment, she puts her finger on one particularly vulgar offering and stage-whispers, "Can Colonel Harris really do that to himself?" John puts his arms around her waist from behind and she spins to face him, standing on tip-toes and reaching up to wrap her arms around his neck. "Sure he can," John says. This is photo recon… we've got the pictures to prove it!"

They silence the ensuing laughter with a brief kiss, then a longer one. John guides her to a hammock that hangs in a corner. After removing their muddy boots, he climbs in, then pulls her in on top of him. They continue the delicious kissing.

After awhile, they exchange positions. John raises up on his knees carefully so as not to dump them both out of the hammock. He peels off his shirt, exposing his lean, smoothly muscled torso. Marge smiles approvingly, her fingers tracing the taut contours of his abdominal muscles.

"You farm boys sure take good care of yourselves," she says.

John unbuttons her fatigue blouse and gently runs his hands up under her tee shirt, baring her breasts, kissing each one softly. He undoes her belt, unbuttons her fatigue pants and pulls them off, leaving her lower half in nothing but drab, government-issue cotton panties and socks.

"Fetching, aren't they?" she says, giving them both a case of the giggles as the panties add to the growing pile of clothes on the ground beneath them. They nearly add themselves to that pile as John reaches to his footlocker for a condom, nearly upsetting the hammock's delicate balance.

In a small, dark chamber of his mind not yet overcome by the fine madness, there is dismay that the penetration is achieved without difficulty. But as the motion begins, slowly at first, then building in tempo as they master the hammock's sway, the door to that chamber slams shut and the judgmental voice in his head that whispers *you are not her first* can no longer be heard.

After a time without seconds, without minutes, as she senses that he is about to climax, she tumbles into her own bliss as the sweet electricity begins to course through her body.

Not so far way, another couple has also finished their lovemaking. Major Kathleen McNeilly, US Army Nurse Corps, lies naked in the arms of the equally naked Lieutenant Commander Martha Simpson, a head nurse for the adjacent US Naval base.

Chapter Seventeen

Lieutenant Commander Marcus "Mark" Colton, US Navy, intently studies an aerial photograph he has just, quite randomly, come across. Surrounding him in the Intelligence Section (G-2) of General MacArthur's headquarters in Manila are hundreds of similar photographs and tactical maps. What he has come to see--accidentally--in this particular photo makes him very uneasy.

Mark Colton is a physicist by profession and a Navy officer by circumstance. Recruited from the University of Southern California, where he had been a graduate student under Dr. Oppenheimer at the onset of World War II, he spent two years as a young staff officer on the Manhattan Project. As this project was hopefully nearing its goal, General Groves sent some of his staff officers to combat commands as liaisons for the possible use of the atomic bombs. As the Pacific and Asian theaters against the Japanese were the only ones still active since the surrender of Germany, these officers soon found themselves in Guam with Nimitz, Manila with MacArthur, or India with Lord Mountbatten.

Colton was assigned to Nimitz's staff at Guam, a very pleasing assignment, as staffs tended to reflect the personality of the commander. Admiral Nimitz was personable and easy going. Not so with MacArthur's staff, most of whom adopted the imperiousness of their boss. MacArthur's chief of staff, Lieutenant General

Sutherland, was notably arrogant and abrasive. Coordinating the plans for the invasion of Japan between the two headquarters had, as a result, been extremely trying. The Joint Chiefs of Staff in Washington had the foresight to retain overall command of Operation Olympic, delegating Admiral Nimitz to lead the amphibious invasion phase and General MacArthur to lead the land campaign on Kyushu.

Despite all the interservice friction, the intelligence staffs of the two headquarters had, at least, managed to strike up a cooperative relationship. It was in this spirit of cooperation that Mark Colton found himself in Manila; MacArthur's original representative from the Manhattan Project, an Army chemist of frail constitution, had fallen ill in the malarial Philippines almost immediately. Colton was dispatched as a replacement indefinitely. His first task was to give the "top secret" briefing to all of MacArthur's skeptical staff on the details of atomic weaponry. The briefing would have gone better had there actually been a successful test of the bomb.

Checking the identification information on the photo, Colton determines it had been taken over a week before and depicted bomb damage assessment of the docks at Fukuoka, Kyushu. He summons the half-dozen staff officers in the room to have a look; none of them venture any suggestion as to what the large, beer-barrel shaped object in this photo might be.

Not confident about being the stranger from a different service, Colton begins hesitantly. "You all know I spent the last two years on the Manhattan Project. We used to joke there that 'if the damn thing didn't have to fly, it would look just like a beer barrel.' We have believed for some time the Japanese have access to enriched uranium from Germany. They also have a number of physicists knowledgeable in the field of nuclear reactions."

The brief silence that follows is broken by a booming voice from the back of the room: "So, Commander, you think that's a Jap atom bomb?"

Mark turns to face the speaker, Major General Charles Willoughby, MacArthur's G-2. Feeling even less confident, Colton says, "I believe it's entirely possible, sir."

"And they're going to deliver it by railroad?" Willoughby asks with a sneer. "An airplane could never lift that monstrosity!"

"Why not a railroad, sir? That would be a viable means of delivery on land," Colton replies, feeling more sure of himself now. "You wouldn't have to be right on top of the target to be effective...just close."

Willoughby laughs. "I think you Navy boys develop these vivid imaginations from being at sea too long!"

There is some snickering in the room. Mark Colton feels like he has been hit with a ton of bricks... and he has never been to sea in his life. He has only crossed an ocean once; that journey had been made on an airplane.

Willoughby is not finished with his sarcasm. "And I suppose, Commander, you'll be running to Nimitz with your wild-ass guess as quick as you can."

Colton stands silently, fighting off the scientist's need in him to argue his thesis. Willoughby's ridicule does not matter, though. Informing Nimitz is Mark Colton's duty. He will carry that duty out immediately.

As he turns back to his office, Willoughby says to his aide: "Tell Watkins at 6th Army to run a few more missions up that way. We'll cover our asses and keep an eye on this thing… And advise the Operations boys that Army and Navy tactical air will continue to lay off trains until further notice. Keep using *protecting American POWs* as the cover story. And one more thing… make sure young Colton understands I was just having some fun with him."

Colonel Watkins does as he is ordered and sends recon planes to photograph the Fukuoka docks again. The first two attempts are unsuccessful. On each occasion, poor weather prevents the pilot from getting the pictures. On the third attempt, photos are finally taken from 8000 feet. They reveal that the strange, beer-barrel shaped object is nowhere to be seen. John Worth did not fly any of these missions.

Chapter Eighteen

September 1945

General Walter Krueger, commander of the Sixth Army, felt physically exhausted. He sat among his subordinate commanders in the briefing room of his Manila headquarters, listening as his operations officer, or G-3, outlined the plan for Operation Olympic, the invasion of Kyushu. The G-3's droning presentation was threatening to put the general to sleep.

At 64 years of age, Walter Krueger was truly an "old soldier." Enlisting in the Army in 1898, he had quickly risen through the ranks. He had fought in the Philippines once before--during the Spanish-American War--and also in Europe during World War I. George Marshall had been a close friend for over 40 years. The Philippines campaign, however, was the first combat action he had seen in World War II. His army, one of two under MacArthur, had just fought and won the tough Leyte and Luzon campaigns. The intense, close combat and high casualty rates--over 10%--had taken their grueling toll. It was an infantryman's nightmare. The Japanese had fought a war of attrition, yielding the beaches, then fighting fanatically from every cave, bunker, and foxhole of the heights beyond. MacArthur had, for a time, considered relieving Krueger because of the agonizingly slow progress his command was making, yet had given Walter Krueger the nod to command Operation Olympic's ground troops; he was already in theater, he was blooded, and he was senior.

The information the G-3 was dispensing was old news to Krueger; other issues dominated the general's thoughts as the briefing dragged on. He mentally reviewed his forces, which numbered over 300,000 assault troops with 200,000 support personnel.

The six army divisions slated for the initial assault were already with him in the Philippines, having participated in that now completed campaign. Three Marine divisions would also be in the initial assault and under his command once landed: two were veteran units in the Marianas, the third was in Hawaii and had not yet seen action. The combined force of nine divisions was organized into three corps of three divisions each. There would be three primary landing sites on Kyushu, one for each corps: Miazaki and Ariake Bay on the eastern coast for the Army Corps, Kushikino on the western coast for the Marines.

A fourth corps, comprised of two Army divisions, was in reserve. One of these divisions, the 98th Infantry, was in Hawaii and had never tasted combat. Three additional divisions would provide the follow-up force and secure the adjacent small islands of Tane-ga-shima and Yaku-shima to the south and Koshiki Retto to the west.

"Unfortunately, gentlemen," the G-3 says, his monotone voice booming, "our forces will be composed, to a large degree, of green replacements. In addition to recent combat losses, the demands of the *points* rotation system will send as many as half of our combat-experienced ground troops home before the invasion."

The *points* system: a plan to qualify a soldier for discharge based on time overseas and the amount of combat action seen. It was instituted at the end of the war against Germany in an attempt to alleviate the insidiously creeping war weariness of those soldiers about to be redeployed from Europe to the Pacific. In fairness, it had to apply to soldiers with equal combat time in the Pacific theater, as that campaign still had no end in sight.

It was Washington's hope that the system might alleviate some of the growing war weariness at home, as well.

One of the factors that had kept Krueger's large Philippine casualty lists from growing even larger had been the effective teamwork the veteran combat units exhibited, especially in the face of close infantry fighting against a determined foe. The key to beating the Japanese in their chosen defensive stance was to ensure that each soldier determined to die for the Emperor took as few Americans to the afterlife with him as possible. If a single Japanese soldier could consistently wipe out entire squads of panicky, bunched-up GIs by blowing himself up, the calculus of victory might favor the Japanese.

Experienced US soldiers had learned those lessons. They kept their intervals, used maneuver effectively, and actually fired their weapons. Green troops would tend to cluster, cower, and never shoot. Now, through attrition, Krueger's units would lose that edge. He hoped what was left of his experienced cadre had the time and opportunity to train at least some of that edge back into his inexperienced troops. His only consolation was the Japanese forces opposing him were expected to be equally as inexperienced and fewer in number due to their staggering combat losses and isolation of the large Japanese forces on mainland Asia.

"Now, gentlemen," the G-3 continued, "current intelligence suggests a three to one advantage for the Americans on southern Kyushu. Casualty estimates are on a par with Luzon, Okinawa, and Normandy."

The G-3 turned to the large, wall-mounted map of Kyushu. "Our objective is simple... capture and hold the airfields and harbors of southern Kyushu. The airfields will put almost all of Japan within reach of the entire 5th Air Force, whose current activities barely extend beyond Kyushu. The anchorages will allow the Navy to finally enter and dominate the Sea of Japan with surface ships, not just submarines. By the second day of the operation, our air units will begin relocation from Okinawa to Kyushu."

His pointer swept across the map of Kyushu. "The mountains of central Kyushu," he continued, "delineate a natural line of defense, allowing our forces to easily isolate southern Kyushu from the additional Japanese troops in the north. Were these troops able to move south, the total number of Japanese in the fight could approach our own. Therefore, we will prevent this from happening. There are few roads and even fewer rail lines through the mountains. Sealing them off will be a simple task."

General Krueger's thoughts drifted to the Kamikaze, the effectiveness of which had grown to terrible fruition during the invasion of Okinawa. They would pose the only danger to the Kyushu invasion fleet. It was expected that thousands of suicide aircraft and boats would attack the US fleet, the carriers and troop transports being the prime targets. Krueger resigned himself to the knowledge that there was little he could do protect his embarked troops from this menace. That responsibility would lie with Admiral Nimitz.

One more thing troubled the weary general: the prospect of facing civilians determined to fight to the death. While he considered civilians in pitched battle as militarily ineffective and nothing more than a nuisance, he wondered how his troops would react to slaughtering them wholesale, especially if they were armed only with crude weapons, such as bamboo spears. MacArthur's staff was already preparing tales of "atrocities" by Japanese civilians against US soldiers, to be used as necessary to keep the bloodlust fueled. By all reports, though, the Japanese civilians on Okinawa had not participated in combat; while a very small number engaged in sabotage and assassinations, most were terrified of the Americans and did not fight. Thousands committed suicide, often whole families together, rather than face life under the invaders.

The G-3 had ceased speaking, his briefing complete. General Krueger rises for questions, shedding the demeanor of the tired old man and once more re-acquiring the aura of the determined old soldier, prepared to practice his art.

Turning to his G-3, Krueger says, "Fine job, Colonel. Thank you."

The first question, from a corps commander, is a request for clarification of 6th Army's headquarters location once landed.

Krueger answers: "At the Ariake Bay beachhead."

Chapter Nineteen

MacArthur and his senior staff were fashionably late for their own planning session. His junior staff members, along with Mark Colton, were already waiting in the situation room of his Manila headquarters and deeply embroiled in a debate about nuclear weapons, both American and Japanese. Colton found himself besieged at the center of this spirited discussion, defending both the existence and usefulness of nuclear technology to his highly skeptical peers.

An Army major summed up the prevailing wisdom at the headquarters concisely: "If the Old Man doesn't buy this Buck Rogers crap, then neither do I."

The junior staff did not realize that MacArthur himself had quietly entered the room--most atypically--and was listening to their intense discourse. General Sutherland, MacArthur's Chief of Staff, began to call the junior officers to attention, but MacArthur silently raised a hand to stop him. He wanted to enjoy this exchange firsthand and unfiltered.

Several moments later, the young officers realize the great man himself is standing among them and spring to attention, mortified at their breach of military etiquette. It had always seemed that the General's every movement was accompanied by a brass band and a bevy of photographers. *How in hell had he slipped into the room unnoticed?* MacArthur seems unconcerned, though, commands them to be seated, and strides to the middle of the group, which closes around him, waiting to hear the wisdom of a sage.

In fact, MacArthur really hadn't planned to be at this meeting at all. He changed his mind in a snit, however, when he was informed that Chester Nimitz had chosen not to attend after initially indicating he would. Nimitz had little choice, though. Admiral King--the Chief of Naval Operations and his boss--had summoned him to Pearl Harbor for a meeting. In the petty world of giant egos, MacArthur considered this quite a snub, one he suspected King had intentionally arranged. Now, by his own, low-key presence, MacArthur was looking to appear more "in command," less beholden to superiors. Above all, he would use this opportunity to influence the naval staff to his way of thinking without the countervailing presence of the Pacific Fleet Commander, thereby tilting the planning for the invasion--supposedly balanced between the wishes of the Army and Navy--to the Army's viewpoint.

Such complicated arrangements for joint staff meetings would not be necessary if MacArthur's and Nimitz's headquarters were co-located, but both refused to leave their respective headquarters at Manila and Guam. The Joint Chiefs in Washington had tried repeatedly to get the isolated commanders to reconsider but always stopped short of ordering one of them to relocate, avoiding the blow that would result to that man's status. The Solomon-like solution of relocating both headquarters to a neutral location would be an administrative and logistical waste of time, commodities that Washington was running out of quickly. The headquarters would remain separate but equal.

Looking directly at Mark Colton, MacArthur says,

voice booming, "You're telling me the Japs *might* have an atomic bomb... and they could employ it against our invasion forces on land or sea? Ridiculous! <u>We</u> don't even have one that works!"

Intimidated and terribly nervous, Colton replies, "Sir, we are very close to the final test. Dr. Oppenheimer's team is doing amazing work perfecting a device light enough to be carried and dropped by an airplane. What we believe may be a Japanese device appears much too large and heavy for aircraft. Developing it would have been a much simpler task."

MacArthur laughs. "Commander, I'll believe it when I see it. Gentleman, if we ever <u>do</u> have a working atom bomb, give it to me. It will soften the Japs up for the invasion."

There is only cowed silence from the assembled staff.

A naval captain, one of Nimitz's liaison officers, finally musters the courage to speak. "General, there's much scuttlebutt that the Japs will surrender before we invade. They're being strangled by our naval blockade and bombed mercilessly by the Air Force. Quite frankly, sir, it's growing hard to motivate the training exercises. Nobody wants to be the last man to die in a war that's going to end very soon."

With a dismissive wave of his hand, MacArthur says, "That would all be very fine. Their surrender would make my arrival in Tokyo much easier. But you better not believe this war is going to end quite that quickly! They will not surrender until we can reach out and grab that little rodent Hirohito by the throat! Only our troops on their home soil will achieve that... and if your sailors and marines don't believe that, Captain, I suggest you kick yourself and them in the ass!"

The Navy men were taking a beating today.

An Army colonel rises with a question. "But what about suicide attacks, sir? Won't they fight more fanatically on their home soil...even civilians?"

The fire in MacArthur's eyes was about to burn holes in the questioner. "Fanaticism...I despise that word, Colonel. To me, it represents accelerated suicide... a quicker guaranteed death. How much more fanatical or dead do the vanquished defenders of Leyte or Okinawa become?"

Calm but still forceful, the General continues: "Determination...now there's a word I like. For the American warrior, it is what comes from competence, sound tactics, and steel. That's what wins wars. Dying is not a strategy, it is folly... and no competent general would allow civilians as combatants on his field of battle. If they were foolish enough to do so, we would sweep them aside like any other nuisance."

Yet another naval officer rises and asks, "General, you mentioned use of atomic bombs. Against what would you employ them? Rumor has it that Admiral King and Admiral Leahy have expressed their opposition to using them against cities. They fear it's immoral to use a weapon like this, a weapon that changes the very nature of warfare, against non-military targets."

Now infuriated, MacArthur bellows, "Gentlemen, may I remind you there is no city in Japan that is not a military target. General Willoughby, your people continue to amaze us with aerial recon reports that indicate little defensive preparation in progress on the beaches and plains of Kyushu. Where are all the troops?"

"In the cities, sir, just like on the other home islands...the munitions factories as well," Willoughby says.

MacArthur's body language is making it clear that this impromptu question and answer session is over.

"Let me make it clear one more time, gentlemen. We must invade, regardless of rumors of atomic bombs, Japanese _or_ American. Nothing else will bring that little boy soldier, the Emperor, to his knees. And make no mistake: only the Emperor can make Japanese troops throughout Asia lay down their arms. _I_ will be the man who accomplishes this. Unfortunately, the Joint Chiefs in Washington still make the call whether we actually go or not, but I know General Marshall also believes in this invasion and I trust he has convinced the President of its necessity. Now, let's get down to business. We have invasion plans to refine. One more thing, gentlemen: there will be no discussion of atomic bombs outside this room. Is that understood?"

When Admiral Nimitz, after returning to Guam, was told of MacArthur's remarks, he just smiled, shook his head and said, "Douglas just can't wait to be the king of something."

He also knew that MacArthur would never rest until he exacted his revenge for being driven out of the Philippines over 3 years ago.

Nimitz immediately called for a review of the invasion fleet's defensive plan against submarines. Kamikazes were one thing, atom bombs trying to infiltrate and destroy his fleet entirely another. He was as skeptical as the next man about the possibility of atom bombs, but he prided himself on comprehensive planning for any contingency. Better to be safe than dreadfully sorry.

Nimitz knew something of submarines; he had been Chief of Staff to the Atlantic Submarine Force during World War I and helped develop US submarine doctrine after that war. He realized that it would take a fairly large submarine to successfully carry what was purported to be Japan's weapon. He knew that large submarines numbered very few in the Imperial Japanese Navy.

Were he commanding the Japanese fleet right now, such a submarine would be awaiting its mission in an anchorage on the Sea of Japan in northern Honshu, perhaps near Sakata, just out of reach of American bombers from Okinawa, the Mariana's, or the Aleutian's. It would have to travel over 600 miles to meet an invasion fleet off southern Kyushu, over a two-day voyage on the surface. It would not be able to stay submerged for more than a few hours at a time.

The defenders of Kyushu would have, at best, two to three days' warning of the invasion fleet's approach, assuming it was spotted by long-range maritime reconnaissance aircraft, surface ships, or submarines who could radio a warning before being destroyed. Any vessel carrying the atomic bomb would have to be ready to sail from a port on Kyushu, southern Honshu, or Shikoku.

Nimitz realized that it did not matter if such a sub was currently out of his reach. It would have to be repositioned to more vulnerable waters to attack his fleet. Since current aerial reconnaissance indicated little, if any, Japanese naval buildup around Kyushu, the presence of such a vessel would be very conspicuous and a most tempting target. To effectively employ the weapon, the sub would have to be on or near the surface, easily seen by aircraft in daylight. His most serious problem was if the sub managed to escape detection while in the waters around Kyushu and approached his fleet at night: radar and sonar would be the only practical means of detection.

To ensure maximum safety from a nuclear device, his anti-submarine forces must be able to destroy or sink the intruder at 5 or more miles from the fleet in case the stricken vessel manages to detonate its atomic payload during its death throes. Nimitz's fleet would cover over a vast area--100 square miles of ocean. To lower the margin of error for detection, it would be necessary to predict the intruder's most likely avenues of approach to so broad a target and intercept it as close to the home islands as possible.

Taking all this into account, Nimitz directed his staff to revise the fleet defensive accordingly. Nowhere in the plan were the words *nuclear* or *atomic* to be used, nor were those words to be uttered in any pre-invasion briefing to the fleet's sailors and airmen.

Chapter Twenty

Marge Braden jerks away from her obnoxious patient in Bed Three and flees the ward tent. Outside, she finds her friend and fellow nurse, Nancy Bergstrom, striking a Marlene Dietrich pose as she leans against a stout tent post, playing the seductress even on a cigarette break. She throws back her head against the post, the bun in her white blonde hair acting as a cushion as she exhales smoke rings with world-be-damned defiance. She turns, bemused, as the flustered Marge approaches.

"Nancy, just who the hell is that arrogant prick in Bed Three? If he touches me one more time, I'm gonna have to poison him!"

"Well, Margie, I see you've met Captain Harmon Mann."

"You know him?"

"Yeah... I met him right after we got here. A brief liaison."

The offhandedness of Nancy's admission takes Marge by surprise. "You never mentioned him."

"He's really not worth discussing... just another stupid rich boy... A Yalie. Crappy pilot too, I hear. A real fuck-up. Nobody wants to fly with him. His daddy's a US Senator. You know, Frederick Mann?"

"OK, I've heard of Senator Mann... from Connecticut, right? Very rich...been a senator forever?"

"Yep, that's him," Nancy says, watching more

smoke rings drift away.

"Hmm. But if this Harmon character is so well-connected...and a fuck-up to boot, what's he doing out here at all? All the rich assholes I knew back home ducked the service completely."

"Because, sweetie, the family has big political plans for the boy. *Honorable* war service is a must. Apparently, he tried to duck overseas service but his parents put the kibosh on that. So he'll put a little time in over here and then get shipped back to the States a regular goddamn hero."

With a triumphant grin on her usually deadpan face, Nancy delivers the final blow. "And here's the best part. His fighter plane is named after his MOTHER!"

"His Mother! Oh my God...that's pathetic!" Marge says, giggling so hard she grabs a tent pole for support.

"Actually," Nancy says, "I was kind of attracted to him at first. He seemed charming, in a dumb sort of way. Then I realized he's just your typical, over-privileged rich kid. Nicest thing I can say about him now is that he disgusts me. He's arrogant, shallow, self-obsessed, abusive, and not too bright. Anyway, you know my heart belongs to doctors. He seems to be taking quite a liking to you, though, honeybunch."

"Forget it, Nancy. I know that rich boy type too well."

Nancy frowns. "Oh, yeah, I forgot. You were born with a *silver spoon in your mouth* and all that crap."

"Cut it out, Nancy. That's not true."

A knowing smile crosses Nancy's face. "Yeah, it is, honey."

Nancy takes another deep drag on her cigarette as she thinks *there you go again, Little Margie, dishing up another load of that "I'm gonna marry for love" bullshit.*

"You know, Margie, I do get pissed off sometimes how guys fall all over you"

"Nancy! Look who's talking! Besides, guys here will chase anything in a skirt."

"That's not what I mean and you know it," Nancy says. "I saw how he looked at you. It wasn't just that *I've gotta tap out this one* shit. It's always that swooning *I want to bring this one home to meet Mother*...And when's the last time you wore a skirt, anyway?"

"Same as you, *Nurse Bergstrom*, on the boat going to the Philippines, with guys trying to look up our thighs every time we sat down."

Nancy throws her head back and blows yet another set of smoke rings. "Yeah, those were good times," she says, as the rings dissolve and float away.

Nancy produces a prophylactic from her pocket and waves it in front of Marge. "So what do you think? You gonna give the arrogant little prick a tumble?"

"Nancy! You know I'm with John. For once I meet a guy who's not all full of himself, treats me nice and can stand on his own two feet."

"And he's a good looking stud, too, right?"

Marge frowns, waves off Nancy's assertion and finishes her sentence, "What would I want with some pampered brat like Harmon Mann now?"

"Well, he is loaded, honey."

"That's the problem," Marge says.

"Unfortunately, my dear little romantic, you are going to have to provide medical care to him."

"For advanced athlete's foot, of all things! Don't these idiots pay attention to the hygiene films?"

Nancy laughs. "He probably gave it to himself on purpose, sweetie... walked around in damp socks for weeks, I'll bet... Anything to get out of flying,"

Marge shakes her head sadly. "Anything to get out of flying, huh? Sometimes, I wish John would think of doing something like that. He's obsessed. Nobody should fly as much as he does. I just worry so much."

"You know, Margie, I'm sure I could get the Flight Surgeon to ground him. He owes me a favor or two."

Marge considers the offer seriously for a brief moment, then recoils in shame and comes back to her senses. She could not betray John, no matter how badly she wanted him out of danger. There was another catch: with as much time in-theater as he had, if he could not fly, he would be sent home. She did not want to lose him that way, either.

"Nancy, don't you dare!"

Though very busy with seriously injured airmen and soldiers, Marge Braden eventually returns to check on Harmon Mann in Bed Three. After cleaning and dressing his inflamed foot, Marge says, "Captain, the doctor says you can go, but you've got to check back in every day. If you take care of it like he told you, it should clear up in a week or two. Of course, you're off flying status until a doctor clears you."

"So the Army Air Force is going to have to get by without one of the great fighter pilots of all time?"

"I'm afraid so, Captain."

"Call me Harm," he says, slipping a hand around her waist. "Nancy tells me your name is Margie..."

Sliding from his grasp, she replies, "Actually, I prefer Lieutenant Braden, sir."

"You know, Margie, looks like I'm going to have

a bit of time on my hands. How about you and me getting together? I bet we've got plenty in common. You look like a girl with a lot of class. Your Daddy must be a wealthy man. "

"Oh, I doubt that, Captain, and no, he's not. And I'm seeing someone, so… no, thank you."

"Yeah, I've seen you around with that photo boy," Mann says. "Why don't you do yourself a favor and give a real man a try?"

"Let me know when you find one, Captain," Marge says as she walks away.

Chapter Twenty-One

The mission briefing begins promptly at 0300. Colonel Watkins strides to the front of the assembled recon pilots and begins to speak.

"Airfields, gentlemen, airfields. It's all about the airfields in this first round of the invasion. Nimitz and MacArthur agree on at least one thing completely: eradicate the airborne and seaborne kamikaze before they can get to the invasion fleet and this operation will be a walk-over, because, gentlemen, that's all they've got. Our missions today will be the first in a series to identify the kamikaze airfields so tactical air and naval guns can take them out. Each of you will be assigned a sector for a low-level mission. Some of the fields will be quite innocent-looking when the planes are camouflaged. We believe there are 30 such airfields on the two peninsulas of southern Kyushu alone. So far, we've identified exactly four. Step up to the map table and get your sector assignments. Northern sectors, plan to be airborne by 0430... southern sectors, by 0500. Let's be over Kyushu at first light."

The pilots let out a collective groan at the prospect of night flying over the blackness of the sea. Their F-5's have only the most basic equipment for instrument flying.

John's assigned sector is the southeast corner of Kyushu, from the southernmost tip north to Miyazaki and as far inland as Miyakonojo. As he prepares his maps and briefing notes, he is unhappy that he will miss breakfast with Marge. At least he had had the chance to pop in on her at the hospital a few minutes before the briefing started. She and Nancy Bergstrom had spent a harrowing night keeping a badly burned fueler alive. He had failed to properly ground his tanker and the aircraft about to be fueled. The small spark from the nozzle as it touched the P-47's filler neck instantly set off an explosion and fire that consumed the aircraft and the tanker; 100 octane aviation gasoline is most unforgiving. The fueler was blown from the wing to a patch of ground not yet covered by the growing pool of burning gasoline. Two mechanics working nearby dragged him to safety, but he was severely burned over most of his body. Marge and Nancy were close to exhaustion. Major McNeilly had given John her customary disapproving glare as he quickly departed, able to do nothing more than wave goodbye to his new love.

John walks from the operations tent to the ramp where *f-stop* is parked, her aluminum skin shimmering in the moonlight. He finds Chuck Jaworski finishing the preflight checks. Petrillo and Lucas have just finished rolling away all the servicing equipment except the battery cart, used for engine start. They stand ready on either side of the aircraft, armed with fire extinguishers. If an exhaust belched raw gasoline during start, it could turn into a deadly blaze in seconds unless quickly smothered by the ground crewmen.

"How's she look, Sarge?" John asks in greeting.

"Tip-top, Captain. The camera techs have you set up with colored film like you asked...gonna see through that camouflage real good. Oh, yeah, we changed the number 2 prop governor. The points looked a little pitted. Better to be safe then sorry."

"I appreciate the sentiment, Chuck. I could live without another runaway prop!" John smiled at the irony. Although he hadn't meant the remark to sound quite so fatal, a runaway prop--spinning at some uncontrollable rpm beyond its design limit--could destroy itself, its aircraft, and its pilot.

"I sure hope the weather up north stays good," John says. "Let's get this show on the road, boys."

As John stows his map case in the cockpit, he looks up to see Marge hurrying his way across the ramp. He jumps down from the wing to meet her. She smells of burned flesh.

"I know I stink," she says, breathless from running, "but I just had to catch you before you took off. I'm sorry I didn't have time for you before... that poor boy is in such bad shape."

"I'm glad you did, honey," John says, kissing her forehead. "By the way, Lieutenant Marge Braden, meet my crew chief, Sergeant Chuck Jaworski. We go way back."

Awkwardly, Chuck shakes her eagerly offered hand.

"Nice to meet you, Sergeant."

"Same here, ma'am." Then Chuck turns to John. "You about ready to crank 'em, sir?"

"Yeah... one second, Sarge." Giving Marge one more quick kiss, John says: "Now go get some sleep. I'll be back before you wake up."

"Promise?" Marge asks, her eyes pleading.

"Promise."

Marge stands to the side as *f-stop's* engines come to life, Petrillo and Lucas ogling her from a discreet distance. With a salute from Jaworski, the plane taxies away to join the line for takeoff... and as it lifts into the air, just a few points of colored light and the bright blue-orange glow of engine exhausts, Marge feels the dread that has become all too familiar begin to grow in the pit of her stomach.

Chuck Jaworski catches up to Marge as she walks away. "You've got yourself some kind of hero there, ma'am," he says.

"Why doesn't *he* know that, Sergeant?"

"Wish I knew, ma'am."

Taking off in the dark is always unnerving. Any malfunction is amplified by the lack of clear visual references to the world outside. Fortunately, John's squadron is the only one departing right now. The fewer planes groping around in the dark, the less chance of the fiery, mid-air collisions that are all too common.

The F-5's take off 90 seconds apart, each on a slightly different heading and climbing to a different altitude. *f-stop* is third to go. As John rolls her onto the runway and advances the throttles, everything looks perfectly normal. She leaps forward, accelerates through 100 knots about halfway down, and lifts off gracefully.

Retract the gear, pick up some more speed, 150 knots now... OK, retract the flaps... heading 015... this bird is humming! Keep up this rate of climb... gotta clear those hills to the north.

The hills, of course, are invisible in the early morning darkness, as is the surface of the sea and horizon beyond. The only things visible on the earth below are the dim points of light from the many encamped military units and ships in port, looking no different than the stars above. They give a pilot nothing with which to gauge his aircraft's attitude. He could be upside down and not know it. He must rely solely on a gyroscopic instrument--the artificial horizon in the center of his instrument panel--to keep him right side up.

The recon planes slowly climb to their assigned altitudes for the flight north; a steady, reduced rate of climb at lower power settings that will conserve fuel. There is little chance here of Japanese fighters being up in the dark, much less intercepting you.

As the sun rises, *f-stop* is at 10,000 feet, having just passed the island of Yaku-shima. John would begin his photo run in less than 20 minutes. He begins a slow descent of about 500 feet per minute; that will put him "in the ballpark" to begin his low-level run as soon as he makes landfall. The sky above the southern end of Kyushu contains only light, patchy clouds around 5000 feet. Further north, the conditions look less hospitable for aerial recon and photography. *f-stop* is still behaving well, but John notices the right engine's coolant temperature is higher than usual but still in the normal range.

Hmm...that's odd. Better keep an eye on it.

John can see no other aircraft, friend or foe. Staying to the western side of the small peak at the southern tip of Kyushu, John levels off at 300 feet, opens the throttles wide. Racing above the coastal plain, he switches on the left oblique camera at every area that seems flat enough for an airfield, noting on his mission map where and when the camera is activated; this would be the key to organizing the photos for evaluation later. There is no point turning on the right oblique camera now: there is nothing but empty sea in that direction, and he is too low to make practical use of the vertical cameras. He will save that film for a different pass. If there are any hidden airfields, he cannot tell with his own eyes as the earth flashes by beneath him.

A few minutes later, he is skirting the shoreline of Ariake Bay as he continues toward Miyazaki, the northern boundary of his assigned area. He flips on the right oblique camera, too, as there might be some suicide boats hidden around the bay. The cameras click away, the intervalometer operating the shutters every 9 seconds.

Something whizzes past him on the left side: large sea birds flying in the opposite direction. Fortunately, there are no collisions. He knows all too well what bird strikes can do to an airplane: two squadron-mates crashed after their planes were severely damaged by striking large birds in flight.

Moments later, little red balls stream vertically up, past his airplane: light anti-aircraft fire. In a second it is gone, scoring no hits.

This is getting exciting, he thinks, feeling the tension in his body rising several notches. He is desperately thirsty but does not dare take a hand off the controls to drink. At this lower, warmer altitude, the right engine's coolant temperature is entering the caution range.

What the hell's going on? The radiator flaps are showing wide open...If that's true, the Prestone should be stone cold, fast as we're going. Something ain't right...

Reaching Miyazaki, he turns out to sea and begins climbing. To complete the entire mission, John must make another low-level pass further inland, this time to the south, and if he has enough film left, a medium-altitude run using the vertical cameras. The potential coolant overheat, however, is forcing him to consider aborting the mission and starting back to Okinawa immediately:

If I can't control it...if the temp climbs any higher, I'll have to shut the engine down...if I don't, it'll seize up or maybe catch on fire...

If I gotta go back on one engine, maybe I can get fighter cover...there's supposed to be a couple of Tac Air units in the area...

But if I get jumped on one engine, I'm probably dead.

The crackle of the radio interrupts his thoughts. Two of the squadron's aircraft, working farther north near Usuki and Nobeoka, are aborting due to poor visibility. One has minor damage from anti-aircraft fire, an apparent lucky hit by gunners firing blindly into the overcast at the engine noises overhead. John requests they do the medium-altitude work in his sector on their way back, as he may have to abort himself.

The cooler air of higher altitude has brought the coolant temperature back to the high end of the normal range. He decides to continue the low-level run to the south; at least he will be pointed toward home if he has to abort, and if he was slowed to single engine speed, his squadron mates from the north would overtake him and might look like escorting fighters to any Jap pursuers.

John rolls *f-stop* onto her back and points the nose down, reversing direction in a relaxed "split-s" maneuver. A few minutes later, he crosses the coastline again. Descending to 300 feet, he flips on both oblique cameras and heads south, about 1 kilometer further inland this time. The coolant temperature for the right engine climbs back into the "caution" zone, a little higher than before.

He actually begins to notice partially concealed Japanese aircraft in a few locations; the cameras would pick them up, too. He marks those locations on his map. As soon as the low-level run is finished, he will call for any available Tac Air unit to strike those locations; he is too busy with low-level flying to do it at the moment.

There is much chatter on the radio now. US Army B-25's are attacking the Japanese naval base at Kagoshima. US Navy planes are prowling over the interior, looking to lure Jap fighters into combat, giving away their airfield positions. John begins to feel more confident of getting fighter escort should he lose the engine.

I can't believe nobody wants to shoot at me today.

He allows his mind to drift off the mission and think of Marge for a split second. *She's probably asleep right now... Wish I could be with her.*

That blissful distraction is shattered by the realization that he is rapidly overtaking two Jap fighters, landing gear and flaps extended, as they prepare to land at one of those yet-to-be-discovered airstrips. He pulls up abruptly to avoid a collision but at his far greater speed roars past them, much too close for comfort. The right camera records it all. The startled Japanese pilots almost collide with each other in John's wake--and then *f-stop* becomes just a quickly disappearing speck in the distance. John marks the airfield location on his mission map.

The right engine coolant temperature rises to the top of the "caution" zone.

Reaching the western banks of Kagoshima Bay, John decides this mission is now over. Throttling the hot right engine back a bit, he compensates with rudder trim for the now-asymmetrical force of the engines trying to yaw the aircraft and begins to climb slowly away over the sea, headed back to Okinawa.

An odd thought crosses his mind: *I've never bailed out of an airplane. Gee... I wish I'd told Marge that. Maybe she wouldn't worry so much.*

He finally takes that drink of water.

Over the island of Yaku-shima, at about 6000 feet, the needle in the right engine coolant temperature gauge begins rapidly making its way to the top of the scale.

"AHH, CRAP!" escapes from John's mouth as he begins shutting the engine down, feathering the prop and dialing in a great deal more rudder trim, repeating the emergency procedure he knows by heart and has had to do several times in the past. The sudden absence of the right engine's drone creates a disquieting void, negating any comfort the steady hum of the good left engine might offer.

"Looks like this is about as high as I go," John says aloud as he releases the two long-empty drop tanks to minimize drag. Looking behind, he notices the trail of glycol vapor his right tail boom is now painting across the sky.

No wonder we've got an overheat, old girl... you're blowing coolant.

6000 feet of altitude puts *f-stop* just above a deck of scattered, patchy clouds that extend south, east, and west as far as John can see. Higher still is a deck of broken clouds, which would afford even more protection but is now out of reach. Airspeed slows to an agonizing 180 knots... and still dropping.

Dammit, I'm gonna be late... Marge is gonna be really worried!

John considers announcing his predicament over the radio and requesting escort but thinks the better of it. If the Japs are monitoring, he would be easy pickings for any roving fighters until his own escort was on hand, if it ever arrived at all. He settles in for what will now be a much longer flight home, his head nervously swiveling in search of adversaries with even greater urgency: he is now a sitting duck.

After a few tense but uneventful minutes, a flight of aircraft breaks through the upper cloud layer to John's right, descending rapidly. Their path will take them across *f-stop's* nose. As they grow closer, he realizes they are six "Oscars," a type of Japanese fighter. They might as well number a hundred.

Look at all of them! To hear the intel boys talk, the Japs don't have that many combat aircraft left in the whole country!

John is sure they have seen him, but oddly enough they begin to turn away. In an instant, he realizes why: two flights of US Army P-47s, eight aircraft total, break through the clouds in pursuit of the Oscars, fanning out for the kill. The Japs must think that *f-stop* is a part of their "funeral procession," probably never realizing he has a dead engine.

Hearing the P-47's chatter on the radio, John waits for a quiet moment and announces his presence to the flight leader, who acknowledges with the assurance that John is in good hands, then tells his number 43 ship to *go cover the Kodak downstairs*. That ship rolls out of formation and dives down, looking for *f-stop*. When the P-47 pilot finds her, he pulls up close on her right side, gives John a lackadaisical salute, then accelerates away from both *f-stop* and his squadron mates in the dogfights developing ahead. John can clearly see the squadron markings and the number "43" emblazoned on the tubby but powerful fighter as it flees to safer skies.

John mumbles to himself: "Gee... thanks for all the fucking help, numbnuts!"

The two recon pilots who had aborted their northern missions are well above this action. After hailing John on the radio, they descend to his level to keep him company for the remainder of the flight home.

Five of the photo ships have already returned by the time Marge awakens at noon. *f-stop* is not among them. She tries to control her mounting anxiety by doing some laundry, taking every opportunity to look across the airfield and see what type of plane is on final approach. No sooner has she thrown her dirty clothes in the tub than three silvery F-5's pass overhead and turn to land, the trailing one with an engine shut down. As it taxies off the runway, she sees it is Number 47, John's plane. She nearly sinks to her knees from the tremendous wave of relief that passes through her body. Then she runs all the way to the Photo Squadron's parking area.

John is standing next to Chuck Jaworski by the right tail boom, looking at the streaked stain of leaking coolant running down the boom from the outboard radiator to the tail. Petrillo and Lucas are already opening the radiator fairings to get a better look at the problem.

Looking up the exhaust chute of the radiator fairing, Chuck says, "Ain't no holes in the skin... you weren't hit by any ground fire... one of these vanes probably cracked all by itself and started leaking, then finally let go on you."

The squadron commander, Lieutenant Colonel Bob Harris, drives up, listens to John's story, pats him on the back, and offers him a ride to debriefing in the jeep. Harris is an ex-fighter pilot of no repute. He had not flown today. In fact, he had not flown in weeks.

They all turn to see a female lieutenant running toward them. John tactfully excuses himself and runs to meet her.

A love-struck nurse, no doubt, Harris surmises.

John and Marge collide and dissolve into an embrace in the middle of the ramp.

Harris turns to Jaworski and says: "Uh, oh! Your boy's in love... I'll bet he turns 'ramp happy' before you know it."

Like you, you useless bastard? Jaworski thinks but does not dare speak aloud. "Ramp happy" signified a pilot or aircraft that seemed never to leave the ground.

Instead, Chuck replies, "With all due respect, sir, I disagree. It don't change a thing. It'll probably make him even better."

Since *f-stop* was being repaired, John does not fly the next day. He is waiting for Marge as she finishes her shift at 0400 and they go straight to John's tent, munching on bread and chocolate as they walk the half mile. Once in the hammock, she falls asleep in his arms quickly. John finds himself softly humming "Sleepy Time Gal" to the exhausted nurse lying beside him. He will not be able to get that song out of his head for days.

Chapter Twenty-Two

Nakagusuku Bay, on Okinawa's southeast coast, was renamed Buckner Bay by the US military in honor of Lieutenant General Simon Bolivar Buckner, Jr., US Army, who was killed in action June 1945 during the conquest of that island. It was a fine harbor, and the US Navy promptly made good use of it, filling it with ships of all descriptions. In addition to the vessels bringing personnel, supplies, and equipment, wounded warships sought refuge there to repair and refit.

Tankers were frequent visitors to Buckner Bay, delivering aviation gasoline to quench the 5th Air Force's insatiable thirst. While immobile in port, they are easy targets, each a potential incendiary bomb of incredible destructive power.

On one unusually clear night, a twin-engined Japanese bomber, code named "Betty" by the Allies, gropes its way down the Ryuku chain in search of Okinawa. The plane is laden with bombs; its pilot is determined to crash into the first target of opportunity he can find. It is his appointed time to die with honor. The harbor is the most desirable choice, as the odds of inflicting significant damage will be higher. An airfield would rank second.

Once the kamikaze actually finds the island in the identical blackness of sea and sky at night, he can select and attack a target with little opposition, but finding the island proves to be challenging. Barely trained, the suicide pilot has his hands full just keeping the lumbering craft in the air. The fingers of his right hand play with the fabric of the "belt of 1000 stitches," praying for the good luck this traditional charm, sewn by his mother and sisters and worn around his waist, is supposed to bring. Controlling the plane's two engines is proving especially difficult, as neither are in good running condition. If the night was not so clear, he would have missed Okinawa completely, as he had strayed to the east, drifting with the winds aloft. It is, perhaps, a blessing that a proper landing would not be required, for it is unlikely the pilot is capable of such a feat. The warmth of the ceremonial saki toast before takeoff and the courage it inspired in this sacrificial aviator has long passed.

The buildup of US airpower on Okinawa is now a 24-hour-a-day operation; bright lighting is required at the harbor and airfields so crucial work can continue in the hours of darkness. The glow of these lights ultimately gives the island away and the pilot turns west, back to his final destination, to fulfill his mortal duty. American radar picks up the plane, but the operators assume it is friendly since it is approaching from the east, probably a Navy plane that cannot find its carrier. Picking out a cluster of lights at the edge of the blackness that he thinks might be the harbor, the pilot banks left and dives. Seeing the shadowy outlines of ships at their moorings, he aims for the closest one.

The pilot has misjudged his height badly and is overshooting the target vessel, an empty freighter, at a dangerously high speed, exceeding his plane's maximum maneuvering velocity. Realizing that this could not possibly be a friendly aircraft, the fire of American anti-aircraft gunners begins to erupt all around the low-flying Jap plane, striking it several times in rapid succession but not bringing it down.

Sure that he cannot survive another pass, the terrified, disoriented pilot pushes the nose over, determined to destroy something--*anything*--American. Soon low enough to see reflections on the water he is plunging toward, the pilot instinctively jerks back on the control column. The nose began to rise for an instant, until the elevators on the tail, severely overloaded by the excessive speed, begin to disintegrate, turning the plane into an uncontrollable projectile. The Betty's nose tucks under for the last time and it plunges dead center into a tanker, just arrived, filled to the brim with 100 octane aviation gasoline. The pilot had never even realized the tanker was there. Unwittingly, he has fulfilled his duty.

The explosion and blaze that follow are cataclysmic and rock the harbor. The flames are visible for 100 miles.

John Worth, asleep in his tent, is awakened by the explosion and sees the towering flames clearly, as does Marge Braden, who is on duty at the hospital. On the photo recon ramp, mechanics Petrillo and Lucas are trying to catch a nap as Jaworski hunts down some parts for *f-stop*.

Jarred awake, Petrillo says in his thick Brooklyn accent, "I thought we seen the last of this bullshit in the fucking Philippines!

Lucas looks around, yawns, and drawls, "They ain't aiming at you, Yankee... shut your piehole and go back to sleep!"

The toll is some 50 dead, over 200 injured--most badly burned--and includes sailors, marines, and soldiers who were onboard ships or working the harbor. In addition to the destroyed tanker, two other ships sunk at their moorings and 10 more are damaged... all from one suicide aircraft, one barely trained and expendable pilot.

John and Marge would not see each other for several days; the demands of the injured on the hospital staff are too great. Swiftly and painfully reminded of how close the war still is to them, even on this island overrun with Americans, John begins to fear a kamikaze attack on the hospital, on Marge.

Nurse Nancy Bergstrom, ever the pragmatist, comments as she fills out triage tags, "Well, Margie, at least that slimeball Harmon Mann can't bother you for a while."

The fires at Buckner Bay rage into the next morning, when the familiar downpours of rain return and assist in their extinguishing.

Chapter Twenty-Three

John Worth made some inquiries and found out who was flying the P-47, number "43," that had abandoned him during the engine-out return to Okinawa. The other P-47 pilots just smiled and shook their heads when John related the incident; they were not in the least surprised. The pilot in question was Captain Harmon Mann. John had been worried the cocky fighter jocks might not tell tales on one of their number, especially to a "camera boy," but in this case they opened up gladly.

"Useless son of a bitch!" was perhaps the kindest opinion offered by one of Mann's squadron mates. "I'm surprised they even take him along anymore... nobody wants him as a wingman, and the C.O. would never let him be section leader. He's usually assigned as *lifeguard*. Even then, he usually flees at the sight of another aircraft, even friendlies."

Lifeguards were planes that patrolled the sea routes to and from an objective, spotting and marking the location of downed fliers to facilitate their rescue by naval vessels or flying boats. Lifeguard planes were usually worn out and ready for the scrap heap. Their pilots were either rookies or tired old hands as worn out as their planes. Mann should have had no reason to be classified as either.

The fighter pilot continued to lay it on the line to John. "He has friends in high places, you know. Daddy's a rich senator, so they gotta make the boy look like he shines… but you can't shine shit. Rumor has it he only qualified for cooks and bakers' school, but that got overridden from above and he ended up in flight training on a *must-pass* ticket. The C.O. tried to get rid of him a couple of times, but the orders were squashed by 5th Air Force. We just try to keep him out of our way. Probably the best advice we can give you is to do the same."

Chuck Jaworski had done some checking of his own with buddies in the P-47 squadron's maintenance section. Like the pilots John had talked with, they had no qualms talking about Captain Mann's less-than-stellar exploits in great detail.

Returning to the photo recon squadron ramp, Jaworski finds John Worth sitting in his aircraft, constructing an improved chart table for the cockpit.

Admiring John's handiwork, Chuck says: "That looks really neat, John… I like how it folds out of the way. Much better than the original… but I've just found out some shit that you've gotta hear right now."

"Go ahead… Shoot!" John says as he gives Chuck his complete attention.

"I know you heard that nobody wants to fly with Mann, and you know from personal experience you can't trust him, but this guy is one for the books… pretty much a walking SNAFU. Let's just say he doesn't have much in the way of piloting skills… or balls. He's trashed a couple of P-47's that basically had nothing wrong with them or malfunctions any novice pilot could have handled… even tore one up on takeoff when he forgot to lock the tail wheel… ground looped right off the runway, ripped a main gear off, bent up the wing… They had to send it straight to the scrap heap."

In their years together, John had never heard the

usually taciturn Chuck utter so many words all at once.

Chuck had even more to say. "But the big story is that he shot down and killed his own section leader back in the Philippines. Nobody really saw the whole thing... it all got hushed up like it never happened... the poor bastard got scored as KIA by the enemy... but it looks like he crossed in front of Mann during a tangle with some Oscars and in a blind panic, Mann opened up on him."

Incredulous, John asks: "What about his gun camera film? Wouldn't that show what happened?"

"That's the really fucked up part, John. There is no film... it was *defective*. They think Mann threatened his maintenance crew and made them ruin the film. He had some shit on them that he had saved up until he needed it, caught them stealing booze from the Officer's Club or something like that... so keeping them quiet was real easy. Now the arrogant bastard struts around like nothing ever happened."

"Do you believe all that, Chuck?"

"You bet I do, John...and there's something else I gotta tell you...he's been going around boasting that he's nailing Lieutenant Braden."

"That miserable son of a bitch..." was all John could manage to say. The voice in his head, though, was clear and focused:

Maybe I should just take the advice of those fighter pilots and keep my distance from Mann before I do something really stupid, something that wouldn't do me or Marge any good. I've sure wished a bunch of Japs dead in my life...but never a guy who wore the same uniform as me.

Marge wakes up as usual, around noon, and walks down to the flight line looking for John. She sees him sitting in his cockpit, obviously preoccupied, fiddling with something; looking for all the world like his mind is a thousand miles away...and strangely silent. He would always talk softly to *f-stop*--to *her*--as he worked on her, but not this time. He doesn't notice Marge until she hops up the boarding step onto the left wing root; she is getting pretty good at doing that all by herself.

He seems deeply troubled, pulled into himself like a wounded animal. She has never seen him quite like this before.

"What's the matter, baby?" Marge asks.

"Do you know a pilot named Harmon Mann?"

"Yeah...a real asshole! We treated him in the hospital a couple of weeks ago...for athlete's foot!" she says, laughing.

"Well, he seems to know you, too... been telling people he's sleeping with you... Are you dating him?"

"DATING!!! Oh, Farm Boy! Dating! Here? In the middle of all this shit? That's so adorable! John, you are such a romantic!" Then she hardens her tone in a heartbeat: "Now listen to me, you idiot... I'm a woman in a combat zone. I've accepted the fact that just about every guy I see fantasizes about fucking me. Surely you must know this! So no, I'm not *dating* him, *screwing* him, or anything else. I don't even want to know him."

She leans into the cockpit, wraps her arms around him and kisses him, a warm and deep kiss that did much to clear his foolish doubts.

"I'm in love with *you,* Captain Worth."

With an uneasy smile, John struggles to quell his fit of jealousy. "OK...maybe I'm being a little silly... and I love you, too, Lieutenant Braden." Then he adds, his voice quavering, "But I swear...if that useless bastard ever comes near you, I'll kill him."

Not wanting to prolong this nonsense another second, Marge expels an exasperated sigh. "Swell," she says. "That's my brave warrior talking. Now, can we go get something to eat? I'm starving."

Chapter Twenty-Four

Some food, some coffee, and lots of happy talk had purged the specter of Harmon Mann from their conscious thoughts. They still had a few hours to kill before Marge was due back on duty.

"Let's steal a jeep and go down to the beach," John says. "We'd be all alone, I'm sure."

Marge discards that idea in a hurry. "Hey, *aviator*...look up there! Does that look like a storm brewing to you?"

John checks the darkening sky to the west and, a bit chagrinned, nods in agreement. Marge knows what he really wants, though--to mark his territory--to reclaim her for his own. *Silly boy...I'm something you never lost...*

"Let's just go back to your tent... And hurry up about it, Farm Boy, before we get ourselves drenched."

Once in the hammock, their lovemaking is urgent, frantic, sweaty... and wonderful. They pay no attention to the heavy rain pelting the tent, turning the roadways and footpaths of the base into the usually slippery muck, bringing the business of waging aerial warfare to a halt.

An hour passes. The rain has stopped. The rivers of mud outside the tent have ceased their flow and begin to dry. Both wearing one of John's old football jerseys, they drowse in contented silence, spooned against each other, still damp from their exertions in the subtropical heat. Marge stirs and glances at her wristwatch.

"Is it late, baby?" John asks, entwining his legs in hers, not wanting this to end.

"Nah… We've got plenty of time."

"Good," he says, squeezing her tighter and slamming his eyes shut again.

"John, can I ask you something?"

"Of course."

"Why'd you ever want to be a pilot?"

"Well…when I was about nine, a barnstormer with engine trouble landed on our farm. That pilot was a crazy old guy, flying this patched-up old biplane. Some of the stories he told! I sort of became his apprentice…helped him get that engine running again…"

Marge interrupted. "You could do stuff like that at age nine?"

"Honey, I was born a farmer… and for a farmer, being a good mechanic is a matter of survival. You depend on your machines and you start learning at a very early age how to take care of them. Hell, I rebuilt a truck's engine when I was 12."

"At 12? You couldn't even drive it!"

"Sure I could… around the farm, anyway."

Marge sighs and snuggles even closer against John. "We really are from different worlds… When I was 12, I wasn't even allowed to ride the *el* by myself."

"But I bet you did anyway, Marge."

"Oh, maybe a couple of times…"

"Thought so. Anyway, once we got that plane fixed, he took me up for a ride. We did a couple of loops, rolls, buzzed some cows…It was a riot! That's all I could think about from then on. I tried for years to save up some money for flying lessons, but by the time

I got to Iowa State I was working my tail off just to pay for school."

"But yet you managed to study engineering, work a job, play football... When did you ever sleep, John? Are you sure you didn't join up just to get some rest?"

"Nah. I joined up to meet girls."

He laughs as her elbow flies backwards and jabs him in the ribs.

"Not funny, Farm Boy." But she's laughing, too.

Marge has another question. "John, why does this fighter pilot thing bother you so much? They're no better than you... or anyone else, for that matter."

"That ain't what they think, Marge. When you're in primary flight school, it's pretty obvious that only the cream of the crop gets chosen to fly fighters."

"OK... so they should have picked you, no?"

"Well, I was doing real good in primary. Pretty much top of the class. But toward the end they want you to engage each other in mock dogfights. Guys were getting really carried away, trying to show off, flying way past their abilities. Crashes and mid-airs were happening like crazy. I didn't see any point dying in training... so let's just say I didn't participate fully."

"Makes sense to me," Marge says.

"Not to them, though. They rated me as *lacking aggressiveness,* so I ended up in multi-engine training."

"Lacking aggressiveness? What bullshit! Trust me, Farm Boy, you are *not*! Boy, the Army can be so stupid sometimes."

They lay quietly for a few minutes more , bodies wedged tightly together, dreading the moment they must break apart. Finally, John breaks the silence.

"Everything OK at the hospital?" he asks.

"Yeah, things have really quieted down. If it

wasn't for you flyboys and your never-ending accidents, we wouldn't have any critical care to do at all. We're just getting ready to move with the Japan invasion... if that ever comes. We're one of the first hospital units scheduled to go, you know... as soon as the air units start relocating."

"Oh, good," John says. "I'm glad you're not that busy. That means you might actually get a day off soon?"

"Hey, I've gotten days off before... and I believe you've been the sole beneficiary of them, Captain," Marge replies, elbowing him again, softly this time, aiming for the groin.

"No complaints here, Lieutenant... Well, maybe one..."

Marge props up on one elbow and glares down at him, her green eyes flashing. "You've got a complaint? This I've *got* to hear."

"I've never seen you in anything but fatigues, Marge."

"Wait a damn minute! You've seen me naked! Doesn't that count?"

"Of course it counts, baby, but I'm talking about civvies."

"John, we're in the middle of a war. Who the hell wears civvies?"

He tugs on the football jersey she's wearing. "You know how pilots are. We wear our sports jerseys and Hawaiian shirts when we're off duty."

"Well," Marge says, "I do actually have some civvies...and speaking of Hawaiian, I have this dress I bought in Honolulu. It's blue with big red flowers... It's beautiful! I love it! Sure wish I had some place to wear it, though."

John's enthusiasm sets the hammock rocking

wildly. "Oh, honey, please wear it for *me! Anything* that's not pants. Be waiting for me when I come back from a mission wearing it!"

"Oh, no, John. Wouldn't I look a little stupid standing on the ramp all dressed up like some lovesick tourist, just waiting and waiting and waiting for her man to return? And McNeilly would have me on report in a second for being out of uniform."

"Ahh, who cares about report, Marge? Wear if for me!"

"No, John... It would be just my luck that that's the mission you don't..."

She stops her words cold, ashamed that this deepest, darkest, yet most obvious fear--*the mission you don't come back from*--the fear that must always remain unspoken, had slipped so easily past the guardians of propriety and exposed itself to the light of day.

"Oh, don't be silly, Marge... Please, just do it?"

Her face ashen, she swings out of the hammock and retrieves her pants from the pile of clothes on the wooden slat floor.

"No, John. Some day. Not now."

Chapter Twenty-Five

"STALEMATE!"

Harry Truman looked at that headline and grimaced, angrily throwing the newspaper down on the conference table. It expressed the growing uneasiness of the American public with this long and costly war that had seemingly ground to a halt short of Japan's unconditional surrender.

Turning to Secretary of State Byrnes, Truman says, "What do they expect us to do, Jimmy? Just walk into Tokyo and hand the Emperor the surrender document?"

Robert Patterson was a new face in the Oval Office. He had just replaced the aged Henry Stimson as Secretary of War.

Patterson rises to speak. "Mister President, the American public is ready for this war to end. The prospect of continued operations against Japan, like the bombings and the blockade, going on indefinitely, without Japan capitulating, is unacceptable."

"Tell us something we don't already know, Robert," Byrnes says, with all the arrogance of an old hand upbraiding a newcomer.

Admiral Leahy, the President's Chief of Staff, says, "Perhaps your American public finds the prospect of an invasion of Japan, with many thousands of American casualties, a more appealing outcome? Surely we can make them understand it is in our interests to continue to starve Japan into submission."

Truman shakes his head dismissively.

"It's no good, Admiral," Truman says. "It'll take too goddamn long. This war needs to be a distant memory by the 1948 elections. We need a Japanese surrender in our hands and damn soon!"

Leahy is startled by the President's statement. "1948!" he says. "Why worry about the elections? Give LeMay another six months and he'll burn all of Japan to the ground!"

General Marshall winces at Leahy's last remark. He had never been fully convinced the fire bombing of Japanese civilians that General LeMay was pursuing was a wise policy. *Hypothetically,* he supposes, *were we to lose the war, LeMay and all the rest of us could be tried as war criminals. Worse, the campaign isn't even working...Japan still gives no hint of surrendering.*

Marshall offers this sobering thought. "Invasion is inevitable, but we're not ready to go yet. Training and logistics are not at the required level and, of course, there's the typhoon threat through October."

Secretary Patterson finally gets to speak again. "This Japanese intransigence is difficult to understand. Do they doubt our ability to crush them? What didn't they understand about the terms of the Potsdam Declaration?"

The Allied leaders had met in July on freshly conquered territory at Potsdam, Germany, to reach agreement on the means to consummate the defeat of Japan. A final ultimatum was issued which called for *the unconditional surrender of all Japanese Armed Forces* or face annihilation. In its vague wording, it did not call for the elimination of the Emperor or the subjugation of the Japanese people. It never specifically mentioned the Emperor at all. The US

Joint Chiefs had argued that maintaining the Emperor was essential, as he was the only entity who could ensure the surrender of Japanese troops all across Asia. Those troops would otherwise never give up and would have to be destroyed to the last man.

The Japanese War Council could not agree on the actual meaning of the ultimatum, but on the chance it meant elimination of the Emperor, they chose to ignore it, or *remain silent.*

Responding to his Secretary of War's question, the President says, "They understand it, all right. The Emperor is just stalling, trying to save his own political hide."

Trying to save his political hide was certainly something with which Truman could sympathize.

"We've made our terms clear enough," Byrnes says. "Any further explanation or clarification will be seen as a sign of weakness and unwillingness to complete the task at hand. We've got our post-war position to consider vis-à-vis the Russians. We cannot back down now from our demand for unconditional surrender."

Admiral Leahy throws open his arms in a pleading gesture and says, "Why? It's just a term! Do we really care if the Mikado survives as a symbol so long as we've disarmed Japan? Let's just make it clear to them the Emperor can stay!"

"NO!" Byrnes replies. "We have the future to consider. Any backing down, any weakness we show now will haunt us for decades!"

Patterson, astonished by Byrnes' statement, speaks again. "What weakness? If just a few meaningless words will bring this war to a close, what's the harm? Does it make us any less powerful?"

Flush with agreement, Leahy says: "Exactly! Your

dreaded Russians understand the difference between words and deeds. So do our other allies. Do thousands more American boys have to die for your precious words?"

As Byrnes, feeling cornered, simmers, Patterson adds, "Not to mention untold numbers of Japanese."

Handed this ill-considered attempt at persuasion, Byrnes explodes. "Does anybody here really give a shit about Japanese casualties? The savages deserve everything they've gotten."

Patterson responds calmly. "Mister Secretary, we are talking about *our* boys. Does anybody care about our potential casualties?"

"I do, Robert," the President says.

"As I do, Mister President," Marshall says. "But we mustn't lose sight of the ultimate goal. Leaders from all quarters... political, scientific, military... have proposed we clarify our *unconditional* stance to allow continuation of the Mikado and expedite the surrender..."

Interrupting, Byrnes says, "A naive mistake!"

Marshall finishes his sentence: "...with the exception, of course, of the Secretary of State."

Byrnes lashes out. "And what of your new *atomic bomb*, General Marshall? Will it ever be ready?"

"We are hopeful it will be soon, Mister Secretary..."

"Hopefully not," Leahy says, shaking his head. His comment draws looks of annoyance from Marshall and General Arnold, the Air Force Chief of Staff.

Marshall, growing tired of being interrupted, finishes his sentence once again: "...for whatever use it might be." He was growing especially irritated with Leahy; he expected soft-headedness from politicians but not military men.

Byrnes, eager to maintain the upper hand, attacks once again. "Explain to the American people, Admiral, why we failed to use every means in our possession to save American lives and end this war."

Leahy does not back down an inch. "In your own words, Secretary Byrnes, *we have the future to consider.* Is clarifying our stance not *a means in our possession?* Do we put the onus of this horrific weapon, if it even works, on ourselves and the American people by using it on an already beaten foe?"

Truman decides it is time to take back control of this discourse. "Gentlemen... I don't believe the American people will care how we get Japan to surrender, and I'm open to all *military* possibilities."

The President pauses as Admiral King, Chief of Naval Operations, storms into the room. Angrily, he hurls his uniform cap onto the conference table.

"Ahh, Admiral King," the President says. "Back from Guam, I see."

King says, "Mister President, while you're speaking of military possibilities, Admiral Nimitz has just informed me of a most disturbing one that MacArthur has apparently failed to mention..."

Chapter Twenty-Six

Halfway around the world from Washington, it was mid-afternoon. John had flown a weather recon flight to the China coast that morning. It was not scheduled to be his mission, but he had volunteered. A few Jap fighters had tried to intercept him, but he was too high for them and got away easily. Now he was back at Kadena, pensive and restless as he walks Marge to the hospital; her shift would start soon.

"What are you thinking about, honey?" Marge asks.

"Oh, I was thinking about something Uncle Leo said."

"Who's Uncle Leo?"

"My dad's older brother. He's an engineer for the A.T.S.F.," John says.

"What's the A.T.S.F.?"

"The Atchison, Topeka and Santa Fe Railroad."

Marge laughs. "You mean just like the song? You're not going to start singing, are you?"

"No," he says, laughing, too. "There's no musical score to this story. Uncle Leo's been driving trains ever since he got back from World War I. He was a doughboy... actually saw combat in France. One of his regular runs used to pass a couple of miles from the farm. Sometimes, I'd bicycle to the depot and he'd let me ride with him...Used to let me drive, too, once I understood how everything worked."

"And how old were you when this was going on,

honey?" she asks.

"Ten. Maybe 11."

"Oh, geez! A 10 year old driving a locomotive! My daddy the lawyer would have a field day with that one!"

"I might have scared a few cows, but that's about it," John says. "Once, I drove all the way to Cincinnati and back. I thought my parents would be frantic... probably kill me when I got back the next day... but what I didn't know was Uncle Leo had cleared it with them in advance."

"You didn't tell your parents you'd be gone overnight?"

"I didn't know, Marge! When Uncle Leo told me the itinerary, it was...you know...the chance of a lifetime to a kid."

Her face turns serious, her eyes pleading. "Promise you'll never do that to me. I've got to know when you're coming back."

"I promise, Marge... Really, I do."

She perks back up a bit and says, "But it's pretty great that you got to do that as a kid. You must have been really thrilled."

"You bet I was! To be driving that much machine...learning how the boiler and all the valves worked...making all that smoke and steam...high-balling through miles and miles of farms, towns, cities... You know, I just love the way machines work!"

"Oh, I know that, baby. Watching you around that airplane of yours...the way you talk to it sometimes... It's so adorable..." Then she sighs and says, "But I don't like where the damn thing takes you!"

"Yeah...but she always brings me back."

"She'd better," Marge says. "But get back to your

story. What did Uncle Leo say?"

"Well, he told me about war, what fighting in the trenches was like. He gave me a piece of advice when I enlisted. He said the only thing important is keeping yourself alive. Don't believe all the slogans about duty, honor, country... it's all bullshit... just a way to get you to do their bidding...to do things you wouldn't do in your right mind."

Marge can't believe her ears. He has hit her most sensitive nerve.

"John, I agree with your Uncle Leo completely... but I don't think *you* do! What are you trying to prove, honey? Nobody is forcing you to fly this much...Shit, you didn't even have to fly today! Haven't you done enough?"

John tries to interrupt but she will not be silenced.

"Do you really think that because there are no guns on your airplane, your actions are somehow less important? I love you, baby...I can't bear the thought of something happening to you, yet I live with it every fucking day since I met you... I know this is a war, but please, baby, can you take it a little easy... for me?"

"That's what I've been doing! That thing today was a milk run." John says.

"Milk run, my ass, John! Japs don't chase you on milk runs."

Taking her in his arms, he smiles and says, "I love how you swear when you're mad."

Her fists beat softly against his chest in frustration. "You haven't heard swearing yet, Farm Boy."

"You're not exactly at some picnic, either, Marge. Don't build me up like I'm some daredevil hero. I'm not fighting... I'm just the guy taking the pictures."

Quiet but not comforted, she stops the ineffectual pummeling, resting her head against his chest instead.

"Marge, why'd you join up, anyway?"

"To take care of dumb bastards like you!"

He doesn't have an answer for that one.

"But why do you fly so much, John?"

"Baby, if I sat it out, I'd feel worthless."

"You just don't realize how special you are," she whispers.

He doesn't have an answer for that one, either.

After a kiss, he spins her around, points her toward the hospital and says, "Now get to work, Lieutenant!"

Chapter Twenty-Seven

George Marshall did not like being blindsided. He turned to confront Ernest King.

"That's a very strong accusation, Admiral King," Marshall says. "What are you getting at?"

King, no less agitated than when he stormed into the White House conference room moments before, amplifies his claim. "You know exactly what I'm getting at... MacArthur is holding back intelligence information so as not to disturb his precious invasion plans. I only just found this out from Nimitz..."

President Truman slams his hands on his desk in anger. "Wait a damn minute," the President says. "What are we talking about here?"

King goes for dramatic effect; he takes a big pause before continuing. The only real effect, however, is to further irritate everyone else in the room.

"Mister President," King finally says, "there is an excellent possibility that the Japanese have a nuclear weapon they plan to use against the invasion forces. Navy nuclear experts believe they have photographic evidence of such a weapon on Kyushu."

"You say *Navy* experts... what does the Army think?" Truman asks, turning to Marshall.

Calmly, Marshall begins. "Mister President, we have been advised of this information and General MacArthur does not believe it credible at this time. The object in question has been only sighted once, in an aerial photo. Its actual nature is pure speculation."

"Self-serving bullshit!" King says. "The Army is so hell bent on this unnecessary invasion they'll twist and distort anything that gets in their way... Damn the consequences!"

Admiral Leahy, glaring at Marshall, wades into the fray. "Mister President, if General MacArthur has attempted to withhold this information, I believe his judgment is compromised and I suggest you should consider relieving him of command. Obviously, the invasion must be placed on hold in light of this new contingency."

A livid Secretary of State Byrnes jumps in. "Admiral, just who the hell are you to suggest such a thing to the President of the United States?"

Leahy fires back: "I am Chief of Staff, in case you have forgotten, and it is my duty to advise the President. Mister Secretary, you cannot ignore intelligence that does not fit your agenda! That's just criminally negligent."

"And you cannot fabricate intelligence to suit yours!" Byrnes replies.

Truman has had enough of this. "Gentlemen," he says, "we will put this destructive rivalry behind us for a moment and analyze this issue with all the wisdom, judgment, and leadership we possess. I need the good counsel of all of you. We're going to work through this. Do our nuclear experts believe it possible the Jap scientists could have this capability?"

"Yes, Mister President," Marshall says, "provided they received sufficient nuclear material from Germany."

A pensive Truman weighed the positions of his Army and Navy. The Navy leaders felt that even the possibility of a Japanese atom bomb was a show-stopper for the invasion. Their preferred course of action remained blockade, which they hoped to intensify with operations against the occupied Chinese mainland, securing access to the Sea of Japan. This would completely encircle the island nation with US naval might.

The Army, in the absence of more concrete proof and skeptical of atomic weaponry in the first place, saw no need to delay the invasion.

Leahy offers one further opinion: "The Japanese might not even want to use their bomb on their own soil."

Byrnes rebuts loudly. "Of course they would! Who wouldn't?"

General Arnold, ever the air power advocate, proposes a unique alternative. "Suppose we drop our bomb on their bomb?" he asks.

"You mean the bomb that doesn't work?" Byrnes says, his mocking tone unmistakable.

No one else in the room had a response to Arnold's suggestion. Nobody understood the science well enough to speculate on the possible outcomes. Besides, Byrnes was right: the American bomb did not work. At least not yet.

Truman thought his head might actually explode at any moment. The thought of Japan having such a weapon, regardless of how credible the information or how unlikely the science, brought him to the brink of physical illness. He mustered all his politician's skills to control the waves of impending nausea.

"Interesting idea, General Arnold," the President says. "See what General Groves has to say about that. But it seems to me we'd have to know where the Jap bomb was to attack it with *any* kind of weapon. Do our experts say we could destroy it with conventional weapons without causing a nuclear explosion?"

Marshall, King, and Arnold nod in affirmation, unified at last.

"And do we know where the supposed Jap bomb is?" the President asks.

The three Chiefs of Staff shake their heads, still unified but now in the negative.

"What are we doing about that?" Truman asks.

"A crack aerial recon unit has been dedicated to the search, Mister President," Arnold replies.

Truman speaks softly but resolutely as he turns away, deep in thought. "Better be the best damn bunch of flyboys we've got."

The room has gotten deathly quiet. After a moment, Truman asks: "If they used it against our invasion forces, could the invasion still prevail?"

Marshall replies, "Despite potentially enormous casualties to part of our force, if we were able to employ our reserves immediately, then yes, Mister President, we believe we could still prevail... provided the Japanese possess only one such weapon."

Leahy lets out a long, pained sigh. King whistles softly, a sound like a bomb falling.

Byrnes is coiled, ready to strike as necessary.

Truman looks perturbed, perhaps betrayed, as he says, "So you've given this some thought, I see..."

The President's decision came down to a question of personalities. He had always considered Marshall the textbook definition of the rational man. King had always struck him as a partisan hot-head, and Leahy, while a gifted organizer and mediator, had become too moralistic and academic to be an effective war leader. Arnold was a brilliant advocate for the development of air power but little more. Most of all, Truman distrusted alarmists.

"Continue the invasion preparations, gentlemen.

We go as planned," the President says.

Chapter Twenty-Eight

A late afternoon thunderstorm had caught just about everybody at Kadena by surprise. John, strolling back to his tent after walking Marge to her shift at the hospital, got drenched. So did Nancy Bergstrom, who had been sitting outside the hospital, taking a break while she smoked a cigarette. Marge was busy changing dressings on several injured patients, working with Second Lieutenant Maria Carbone, a new nurse from the Bronx, New York. Maria, barely 20 years old, a friendly girl with a chubby face, was a replacement. She had only been on Okinawa a week, fresh out of nursing school. This was her first duty assignment. Marge and Nancy were showing her the ropes.

"Does it always rain like this?" Maria asks, surprised how quickly the sudden rain turned everything outside the hospital tents into a quagmire.

"I'm afraid so," Marge says without breaking the rhythm of her work. "You got to keep your feet dry. Get used to cleaning your boots daily, and keep plenty of dry socks handy."

"Yeah, I can see that. Hey, Marge, Nancy tells me you're dating a pilot?"

"Dating...that word seems so out of place over here," Marge says, stopping to reflect for a second. "But, yeah, I'm seeing a pilot."

"Wow! I'm really surprised at all the boy-girl stuff going on here," Maria says, wide-eyed. "They told us in training that a field hospital would be like a convent, with your head nurse the Mother Superior and armed guards escorting you everywhere."

Marge looks around, then pulls Maria to a corner of the tent so as not to be overheard. "Well, it used to be like that when we were close to the fighting, but it's different now on this island, on a big base like this... and let's just say *Mother Superior* has got a little something of her own going on... and it ain't with a guy. So it's live and let live."

It takes a moment for Marge's last remark to sink into Maria's innocent mind. When it finally strikes home, Maria's face becomes a portrait in dismay. She whispers: "Oh, my! With another nurse? Here?"

"No, not at this hospital. But close..."

"Oh, thank God! That would be so awkward!"

"Gee, no kidding, Maria!"

Marge chuckles to herself, trying to remember if she had ever been this naïve.

The two nurses go back to tending their patients. After a few minutes, Maria's shock passes and she resumes pumping Marge about her boyfriend. "A pilot! That must be so exciting!"

Marge puts down everything and turns to Maria, giving her the knowing, weary look that comes from hard-won experience. "No, Maria," Marge says, "it's awful...terrifying. I guess if I was his girl back at home I'd only know what he told me in letters, but being here, I see it all, every damn day, with my own eyes. But I love him... he's everything I want in a guy, so I live with it."

Maria decides: *I should maybe shut up for a while.*

Outside the hospital, US military personnel and Okinawan civilians went about their business. It had proved impossible to keep civilians out of sprawling complexes like Kadena, and many were employed for laundry, kitchen police, and general labor. MPs kept a close eye on them; there had been reports of saboteurs and assassins infiltrating US installations.

Yoshio Iwazumi was such an assassin. He had smuggled a disassembled rifle onto Kadena, well hidden in the large basket of laundry he carried. He roamed the area looking for a high-ranking officer to kill. The MPs who were supposed to inspect objects like the laundry basket had given it only a cursory look and let Iwazumi pass.

Yoshio Iwazumi was 42 years old and had not been pressed into military service. He had lived on Okinawa his entire life, never leaving the island once, but he was a loyal subject of the Emperor. He was not a Kamikaze but would die if necessary to defend the Mikado; his wife was already dead, killed by an American bomb two months ago. His two sons served in the Imperial Japanese Navy. He feared, but did not know, that they were both dead, as well, killed as the Americans recaptured the Philippines.

The rain had stopped. Iwazumi struggled through the mud and muck, balancing the heavy basket on his shoulder. It was getting dark; he selected his target by the dim electric lighting that surrounded the hospital tents. He was not completely sure, as US insignia of rank were strange to him, but he believed he had found two army colonels leaning on a jeep, talking, probably hoping to consort with some nurses. How magnificent it would be if he could shoot them both!

He got close enough to have a good chance of success yet give himself an opportunity to escape into the faceless throng. Dropping the basket to the ground, it tipped over and dumped some of its content of hospital bedding into the mud, but that gave him the opportunity to prepare his weapon, all the while looking like he was cleaning up the mess he had just made.

In a few moments, he had the weapon assembled. He stood and turned toward the colonels and quickly pulled the trigger. Nothing happened. He pulled it again. Still nothing. He cycled the rifle's bolt and pulled the trigger again. This time, a shot rang out. It struck the front tire of the jeep and nothing else. All this had taken less than five seconds.

In the instant that followed, no fewer than six bullets from the weapons of several MPs slammed into Iwazumi's body, killing him outright. Three had come from the submachine gun of an MP about 20 feet away, but this MP had fired an eight-round burst. Of the remaining five rounds, two sailed harmlessly through the roof of a hospital tent and two buried themselves into the mud of the roadway.

The last bullet struck Maria Carbone, who was standing a foot away from Marjorie Braden, squarely in the forehead, exiting the back of her skull along with a large part of her brain.

Marjorie Braden was an experienced combat nurse. She dropped to the floor and cradled Maria's mortally wounded head; she knew immediately there was nothing that could be done for her. Marge began to wipe the blood and brain tissue off her own face. When she was done, she moved quickly about the tent to check on everyone else; no other person had been hit.

Nancy had rushed in from outside when she heard the shots. She stood over Maria's dead body, saying nothing. She, too, knew there was no point. In a moment, Marge and Major McNeilly were at her side. McNeilly directed the dumbstruck medics as they placed Maria in a shroud and processed her body to Graves Registration. Then the three nurses joined the others in their section in a group embrace and sobbed uncontrollably for several minutes, after which they regained their composure and quietly returned to their duties.

Word traveled quickly across Kadena Airfield. John was awakened by the duty officer, who told him a nurse had been killed, but he didn't know who. John then sprinted the half mile to the hospital and upon finding Marge he was so overwrought he could not speak. He tried, but nothing came out.

Marge held his face in her hands and whispered, "I'm OK, baby. Go back to sleep."

Still no words would come from John's mouth, no matter how he tried.

Marge's soft voice spoke again. "I love you, John. Go back to sleep!"

John returned to his tent but slumber eluded him. His voice had returned on the walk back. When he joined Marge for breakfast at 0400, all she said was, "She was standing right next to me." Marge ate nothing.

They never again spoke of the night Maria Carbone died.

Each MP involved in the incident convinced himself someone else fired the shot that killed her.

Chapter Twenty-Nine

Robert Oppenheimer looked up from his desk and rubbed his tired eyes, hoping they would focus better on the diagrams his team of scientists was trying to show him.

"We think we've got it, Dr. Oppenheimer. Do you agree?"

A metallurgist from the University of Chicago was doing the talking. They knew the steel casing of their bomb had been failing at the titanium reinforcement bands, allowing the pressure of the high-explosive charge to vent before critical mass of the nuclear material could be reached. The bands had been an attempt to allow light, yet strong, construction of the casing. However, since they were more rigid than the case itself, the bands had actually concentrated the stresses on the case at their edges, resulting in cracks and failure.

After weeks of calculations, experimentation with models, and precision machine work, Oppenheimer's scientists found the bands could be made slightly wider but gradually tapered from their edges to the center of their width, allowing the bands to "give" slightly. This would attenuate the buildup of stress at their edges as it dissipated across the entire band. Their new design added negligible weight to the bomb.

All the recent tests on models had been successful. Machining of a new case, with the tapered reinforcing bands, was in progress. A redesigned bomb would be ready to test in two weeks.

Oppenheimer nods in approval to his assembled team; he likes the look of this fix. Dialing his desk phone, he says, "Good. I'll notify General Groves."

Chapter Thirty

October 1945

Not much happening here; it's become a waiting game where little seems to change anymore...

These were the opening words of a letter Marge was writing to her parents. She did not think the censors would blot out anything she had written so far. Putting down the pen, she looked over at John as he rummaged around in his tent, dressing for today's mission.

"Baby, please don't fly today. Stay here with me."

"Marge, I have to..."

"You don't *have to*. Even your C.O. says you can take some time off. You've gone up every day this week except that day with the big storm... even the day after that, with the high winds and planes cracking up all over the place, you *still* went up."

"Haven't we had this discussion before? Besides, my squadron did OK."

"John! You were the only one in your squadron who flew that day!"

John was secretly satisfied with that fact. His C.O., Colonel Harris, had tried to fly that day, too--for the first time in weeks--but aborted takeoff with *propeller problems*. Jaworski later told John there wasn't a damn thing wrong with Harris' airplane, but the mechanics had cleaned and reseated the connectors on the prop governors so the colonel could save face.

John puts his arms around Marge and says, "Honey, you're tired. Go to bed. I'll be back when you wake up."

Marge sighs in frustration. "Farm Boy, how many times have I heard that? Then I wake up, you're not back, and I end up wondering if you're swimming or dead somewhere...or maybe a guest of the Japanese."

He didn't answer, like he did not hear what she just said. She was resigning herself to the inevitable once again: John would fly.

"Do you know where you're going today?" she asks.

As he pulls on his heavy flying boots, John says, "Yeah....It looks like I've got the railroads on the western side of Kyushu. Other guys will be doing the eastern railroads and the ports."

"You're not looking for airfields anymore?"

"Well, we did find a bunch of them in the last few weeks. Tactical Air has hit them all. We'll go back to them real soon, no doubt. I know I've said this before, but I'm amazed how little seems to be happening on Kyushu. You'd think we'd see heavy equipment for building fortifications, obvious troop movements, gun emplacements, especially in caves behind the beaches, but no... almost nothing! We just keep finding and destroying Kamikaze planes on the ground. At this rate, this invasion looks easier than Okinawa."

"John...they're gonna surrender...they're finished...there'll never be an invasion. Then we can all go home."

"Ah, my beautiful optimist! I wish I could agree, baby, but I think we'll invade, they'll fight like crazy like they always do, and we'll outgun and overpower them just like every campaign before, but they won't surrender until we walk into Tokyo and make them.

Lots of casualties on both sides, though."

He is eager to change the topic. "Hey! Are we going home to Iowa or Chicago?" he asks. "I can finish my degree either place."

"It doesn't matter to me, honey," Marge replies. "After this, any place will be just fine, just so we're together. And I can work in a hospital anywhere. But really, John, everybody's saying they're going to surrender. They can't even control the sky over their own country. You're living proof of that... and may I emphasize *living,* please? You're not going to do low-level today, are you?"

"No. High altitude... That surrender talk is just wishful thinking, Marge." He turns back to his flight preparations, too preoccupied to debate her further.

"We'll see, Farm Boy. You know, I hate that low-level stuff... scares me more than just about anything you do... I see how warm you're dressing, so I figured you'd be up high," Marge says, quite knowledgeable now of the pilot's realm.

"If there's one thing I wish I could change about an F-5, I would make the cockpit warmer at altitude. No wonder the guys in Europe disliked them," he offered.

"You're going to stay here, I guess?"

"Uh-huh," Marge says, yawning. "It really was swell of those tentmates of yours to move out. I'm getting to like this little home away from home, especially since McNeilly gave up on doing bed-checks."

John picks up his weary lover and places her in the hammock. "Do you want your writing paper?" he asks.

"No, I'll finish it later."

He leans over the hammock and kisses her.

Drawing the curtain, John says, "I'll be back

soon."

"You'd better, Farm Boy."

"Count on it, baby."

f-stop leaves the ground at sunrise. Turning north, the weather looks good, at least for the first part of the flight. Clouds are building far in the distance, but for now it is just several patchy decks, thousands of feet apart. John can see a few of his squadron mates several miles ahead and higher, a few more behind him and below. The squadron isn't much for formation flying; they are too used to working alone. At least they can keep an eye on each other if there is any trouble from mechanical glitches or the Japanese. It gives some small level of comfort to at least know where somebody went down. All too often, the whereabouts of recon pilots--flying alone--remain a mystery once they are knocked from the sky.

f-stop is climbing gently to 20,000 feet. John can feel the cold creeping in. The cockpit heater system is a poor design, woefully inadequate for the temperatures encountered at high altitude. Pilots of single-engine craft had it a little better, as the big engine right in front of them helped to warm the cockpit a bit, but the F-5's twin engines, mounted on the wings, afford no such benefit. Pilots who had flown this type aircraft in the European theater suffered badly from the cold while escorting the high-flying heavy bombers. During the harsh European winters, they could never stay warm, no matter how low they flew. Here, in the Pacific theater, with its temperate climate, you could stay warm at lower altitudes without any bulky clothing; pilots often fly low-to-medium-level missions in their shirtsleeves.

From 20,000 feet, John figures he can photograph

the railroads of western Kyushu in two passes, the first to the north and second to the south, then continue directly back to Kadena. There are two rail routes running basically north-south in this area, with several connectors between the two running east-west. The photos from the two passes should make a mosaic covering the entire area, provided no clouds obscure the ground and the cameras do not malfunction. He has enough oxygen and fuel to stay at 20,000 feet for the entire four-hour mission, if he so chooses.

This should be a milk run, provided no Japs feel like coming up to play.

Although he is concerned about the growing clouds sweeping into his path far ahead from the west, the camera run begins routinely. It is almost like a sightseeing tour. John has a magnificent view of southern Kyushu and all that is happening in the air above it. The US Navy is particularly active today; Avenger and Helldiver bombers are combing the coastline, searching for Japanese naval vessels foolish enough to be there and the small suicide boats that might be concealed practically anywhere. Above the bombers, flights of protecting fighters orbit; if they don't expend their ordnance on intercepting Japanese, the escorts will drop down to the deck to strafe targets of opportunity after the bombers are safely on their way back to the carriers. The radio chatter indicates a few Jap fighters have tried to prey on the bombers but are driven off, with one probably shot down.

John wonders where the ones that had been *driven off* are now and at what airfield they are based. In his flights over this big island, he has seen large numbers of enemy aircraft on the ground; he knows those airfields have been attacked repeatedly, but they never seem to get them all. How many planes have actually

157

been destroyed?

He hopes the answer to that question is *enough*.

Halfway through the first camera run, the clouds between *f-stop* and the ground become sufficient to obscure the photography; John descends to 12,000 feet, just below the broken, obscuring deck. He doubts he'll have enough film in the vertical cameras at this altitude to cover the entire mission, so he does a quick recalculation of his planned route to include using the oblique cameras. The photo ships working the eastern and southern areas are reporting satisfactory visibility; they are able to remain at high altitude and maintain a higher speed. In fact, two of the planes are already on their homeward legs. The planes working northern Kyushu and Shimonoseki, however, are now reporting unsatisfactory conditions and are returning home, too, one of them reporting engine problems and calling for fighter escort. They also report some moderate turbulence. John thinks it strange they even mention it, as if they need another excuse to go home. Pilots and crew are usually unfazed by turbulence until the rare times it becomes severe and throws the airplane out of control, usually in close proximity to thunderstorms. Those who realize too late they have blundered into a thunderstorm might find their planes disintegrating around them, the wildly gyrating machines unable to withstand the extreme aerodynamic forces imposed on their structures. All too often, those airman pay for this misfortune with their lives.

John hopes he can fly no lower than this altitude all the way to Fukuoka, his turnaround point. Higher altitudes now would be nothing but cloud layers, some of which look like they could be foreshadowing storms that must be avoided. The cockpit, still cold-soaked from the high-altitude run, refuses to warm up.

Over Fukuoka, John begins the gradual left turn that will bring him to his southerly return leg. With the better downward view the turn affords, he sees the Jap fighters struggling to his altitude: five, he counts.

Damned Japs never seem to attack unless they have a big numerical advantage. It shouldn't be too hard to get away, though...they're climbing and slow...I've got a big speed advantage... should be able to outrun them, no sweat...nobody behind me...yet... may not even foul up my camera run.

A moment later, John becomes aware of the Jap fighters' real target: the flight of 16 B-24's high above, heading north, which had left Okinawa from another airfield before the recon squadron. The F-5's had passed above the lumbering bombers long before either flight had reached Kyushu. He can only catch glimpses of them through the clouds above, but he hears their excited radio chatter: the bombers are already under attack. The fighters John sees are heading to join in that attack. Several bombers are spreading out and dropping into the clouds to try and hide, a very risky tactic during formation flying. The pilots of the other bombers are shouting--no, *screaming*--into their radios, urging those seeking shelter in the clouds to come back while trying to maintain what is left of their defensive formation. Their escorts, six P-51 fighters, are dodging back and forth above the bombers, trying to find the attacking Japanese who are using the same clouds to conceal their approach from below.

The five climbing Japanese fighters are passing below *f-stop's* nose right to left. John is certain they see him; sure enough, one rolls left, seemingly to come around on *f-stop's* tail. The others continue their climb to the east, to the American bombers. John has little reason to be concerned over his would-be pursuer: the

Jap could never catch up. John continues his photo run, flying straight and level.

The radio chatter, filled with tense, sometimes panicked voices, suddenly becomes a loud shriek--the sound of a man who knows he is about to die. Then, silence.

The next voice is that of a B-24 pilot: "Oh my God! He flew right into them... These bastards are Kamikaze!"

The airwaves are again filled with the high-pitched voices of men in peril. They call out locations of the suicide fighters by the hour hand of the clock and warnings of their intent to perform sudden, violent evasive maneuvers. They will try anything to avoid the intentional, mid-air collision that spells death for all on board.

The first B-24 to be knocked down by a Kamikaze was attacked from directly ahead; two enemy planes had suddenly popped up from the clouds below and turned hard into the bomber. The first missed wide to the left, just clearing the bomber's wing as it hurtled past. The second flew directly into the bomber's nose section. There had been no time for the pilots to react and evade. The bombardier, navigator, both pilots, and the flight engineer manning the top turret behind the cockpit were all killed on impact. The remaining five crewmen, unable to bail out of the bomber in its spiraling death plunge, now ride it to the ground. John sees the doomed plane in the distance to his left, tumbling out of the clouds.

A second B-24 is struck, this time by a Kamikaze that had slashes through its left wing between the two engines, causing the spar to fail and the wing to buckle, the tip flying upward as the wing hinges at the impact point, then separates from the aircraft. The doomed bomber begins its death spin to the ground, the fuselage pivoting about on its remaining wing, like some broken pinwheel. No parachutes from this plane, either.

A final calamity befalls this flight of bombers as two of the B-24's seeking shelter in the clouds collide, their propellers chewing up each other's wings, which are now meshed. Structural failure and separation of both wings follows quickly and those planes, too, spin to the ground, taking all their crew with them.

Forty American and two Japanese airmen dead… Four B-24's and two Japanese suicide planes destroyed…all in a matter of moments.

The gunners on the remaining 12 bombers shoot down three Kamikaze; the escorting P-51's claim four more. These unskilled Japanese in deficient aircraft are easy fodder for the more experienced American fighter pilots, who have finally succeeded in locating their foes. The remaining three suicide planes make good their escape, perhaps to seek honor someplace else, perhaps to return to their airfield in disgrace.

As the radio chatter dies away, John checks his own tail once again. He is astonished by what he finds.

Damn! He's still there! At my altitude and gaining on me…What the hell?

John scans his instruments: the engines are running perfectly and his airspeed is right where he wants it to be. How is this piece of junk, an aged "Zero"--probably a Kamikaze--gaining on him? Pretty soon, he'd be in gun range--if this Jap even has guns-- and evasive action will be necessary.

If he could look into the cockpit of his adversary, John would see the reason for this seemingly impossible occurrence: this Kamikaze, a novice pilot, barely trained in this or any other aircraft, had simple pushed the throttle of his stripped-down aircraft to the limit, oblivious to the maximum operating limits for manifold pressure and rpm. The importance of these limits had never been stressed in his perfunctory flight training. What would be the point? You planned to destroy the aircraft anyway.

You could get away with a momentary operating parameter exceedance; everybody did it in combat due to either distraction or self-preservation. The excessive parameters the suicide pilot is forcing on his engine have persisted far past any momentary event, however, and are starting to take their toll on the poorly maintained machine. The Zero has begun to vibrate as the engine approaches self-destruction. When John looks behind again, the Zero is closing in, apparently trying to sever *f-stop's* horizontal stabilizer with its propeller, a move sure to send the F-5 plummeting to earth.

OK, I guess he's got no guns...time to get away from this clown before he rams me...

In the brief moment it takes John to analyze and select a course of action, before he can actually execute an escape maneuver, the suicide plane's overtaxed engine seizes. The resulting gyroscopic force jerks the Zero into a violent roll, causing the pilot's head to strike the canopy frame with a force that breaks his neck. Had he ever learned the wisdom of securely snugging his seat belt and shoulder harness, his injury might not have proved fatal. The Zero, without engine and pilot, begins a fluttery, tumbling plunge to the ground.

John gets a quick glimpse of the Kamikaze plane, its propeller motionless and engine cowling mangled, as it drops back and down, away from his own aircraft. Now it made sense how the Zero was able catch up; its pilot had succeeded in destroying his plane and committing suicide, but he had failed to take John with him.

Too bad there's not a camera facing aft... I might have got a "kill"...

Suddenly, f-stop is alone in the sky again. The radio chatter fades. The photo mission continues.

As he approaches the southern end of Kyushu, just north of the head of Kagoshima Bay, the left oblique camera records a railroad track construction detail at work, with a small locomotive and several work cars, on the inland side of the heights overlooking Ariake Bay.

A short time later, John and his airplane leave Kyushu behind and head home to Kadena. The only aircraft he has to dodge now are friendly ones, heading north to unleash yet more destruction on the Japanese home islands.

For once, John gets back on the ground before Marge is awake.

"Take a look at this, gentlemen," Colonel Watkins says as he bends over one of the photographs from John Worth's last mission. "It looks like we've finally got some evidence that the Japs are building up fortifications in the Ariake Bay area."

He was referring to the railroad track-laying detail. The photo revealed they were constructing a spur into a cave network. "No doubt," Watkins says, "they'll be moving all kinds of heavy weapons and ammunition into those caves as soon as that track is finished. There is no road network there to transport heavy equipment. They're trying to do it by rail."

This information is immediately forwarded to MacArthur's G-2 at Manila. Intelligence sections throughout the theater have been scratching their heads for weeks looking for fresh, promising targets; they had already hit everything at least once. They finally have something new to bomb. The target is offered to the 20th Air Force, who gladly accepts it.

A flight of eight B-29's arrives the following afternoon. From their high altitude, the visibility for visual bombing is poor due to thick cloud cover. The big four-engined bombers are unopposed by Japanese fighters or anti-aircraft fire. The aiming point is to be the intersection of the main rail line and the new spur under construction, but it cannot be identified visually with the Norden bombsight. The radar bombsight of the lead aircraft provides an indistinct image, as there are few topographical features to distinguish the target. The lead bombardier takes his best shot and releases his bomb load, commanding the other aircraft to do the same.

His best shot is not good enough, however. The bombs miss their mark and over 80,000 pounds of high explosives devastate the forested hills to the west of the aiming point. No one on the ground is killed or injured. In fact, the area is deserted at the time of the raid. The tracks, the primary target of the bombers, are only slightly damaged.

On the return flight to Tinian, in the Marianas, one of the B-29's experiences electrical system problems and attempts to divert to Iwo Jima. That island--halfway between Japan and the Marianas--was seized by US Marines from the Japanese at great cost to serve as an emergency landing field for stricken bombers like this one. The resulting loss of radio and navigation equipment, however, coupled with an anxious, incorrect computation by the navigator that goes unchecked, causes an inability to find that island. The bomber ditches into the sea after running out of fuel and sinks soon after. Not knowing exactly where the off-course bomber has gone down, it takes the rescue seaplanes four days to stumble upon the crew floating in their rafts. Several of the crew have been injured in the ditching, but there are no fatalities.

A second B-29 is not so lucky. Its number 2 engine, inboard on the left wing, loses oil pressure on the return leg between Iwo Jima and Tinian and has to be shut down. On approach to Tinian, the number 1-- the other engine on that same wing--catches fire. It, too, is shut down and the fire extinguished, but handling this lumbering, asymmetrically powered beast in the strong, gusty winds, both engines on the left wing now dead, quickly proves more than the pilots can handle. It stalls and spins into the sea a mile short of the runway, its fuselage breaking open on impact and sinking quickly. There are no survivors.

The photo recon squadron tries but cannot record the results of the raid for two days, when the skies have finally cleared. By then, the minor damage to the tracks, which would not have been visible in the photos anyway, has been repaired.

The bombing mission is classified as "ineffective." They would have to try again. In the weeks that follow, the rail junction and the surrounding area are struck regularly by fighters and bombers of the 5th Air Force, rarely causing much damage and nothing that cannot be quickly repaired.

Chapter Thirty-One

"Gentlemen, today we work in conjunction with General LeMay's 20th Air Force," Colonel Harris says, beginning the briefing. "We will get the bomb assessment pictures of their raid on the Nakajima aircraft factory at Kokura. Captain Worth, your section will do the first photo run immediately after the raid."

This didn't come as much of a surprise; the squadron had been discussing the collaboration with the B-29 heavy bombers of the 20th Air Force all week. The only B-29's the recon pilots had seen so far were those that had diverted to Okinawa, limping in with mechanical problems or too low on fuel to get home to the Marianas. John could not wait to see one in action, up close. He had devoured all the technical data he could find on the new bomber and was in awe of its technical complexities and capabilities.

One hell of a machine, he thought.

John's section for this mission would boil down to him and Second Lieutenant Buddy Knox, a likeable rookie from North Carolina. The third pilot in the section was sick with dysentery. The fourth pilot slot in the section was unfilled, awaiting a replacement. John tried to get a fill-in from one of the other sections, but they were all short, too. Illnesses and mechanical problems were cited as well as reluctance to fly someone else's airplane; you just didn't know its quirks like your own machine, and that could cost your life. Buddy was a quick learner who seemed to accept his newcomer status with easy grace. John envied him that; he remembered the intense pressure he felt as a rookie not to screw up, always feeling he was seen as something of a liability. Sometimes he still felt it, to Marge's infuriation.

She had once yelled at him, *"Baby, don't you see that you're a goddamn legend around here? They think you're Superman with all the flying you do...a little nuts for still being here, perhaps, but still Superman!"*

He wanted to believe, but he just didn't.

John and Buddy Knox are approaching the rendezvous point with the B-29's over the Bungo Strait, just south of Shikoku, at 30,000 feet. The jetstream that often pushed aircraft all over the sky at this altitude is mild today, hence the plan for a daytime, high-altitude mission using precision bombing with high explosives. LeMay's aircrews welcomed the change from the nighttime, low-altitude "area" incendiary missions they were assigned all too often, where the stench of burned human flesh rising in the torrid air permeated their aircraft and made them nauseous. The darkness provided no hiding place as their planes were silhouetted against the raging fires below, easy pickings for Jap fighters lurking above and anti-aircraft gunners below.

The big bombers of the 20th Air Force are not in sight yet. As the photo planes orbit, waiting, Buddy suddenly cries into his radio: "Cap'n, my number one prop is acting up...erratic...I think it's gonna run away!" His plane is yawing violently as the troubled engine's power fluctuates wildly. Calmly, John talks him through the emergency procedure for the runaway propeller, something F-5 pilots faced all too often. Buddy responds evenly, his drawled replies belying the terror gripping him. It is no use; the prop rpm control is not responding. Buddy will have to pull the engine back, descend, and head for home.

As Buddy drops below 12,000 feet, he picks up an escort of two Navy F6F Hellcat fighters, but they are not able to stay with him long, called away to more urgent duties just south of Miyakonojo. Buddy plods ahead on his slow mount, the left engine at idle, toward Okinawa.

John, now alone, picks up the B-29's approaching from the east and establishes radio contact with the flight leader. The bombers pass, 16 strong, heading west to Kokura, their P-51 escorts weaving above. John follows them to the target.

The sky soon fills with enemy planes. The Japanese have really pulled out all the stops against this B-29 raid, throwing everything into the air that might get to the bombers' lofty altitude. The "Tony" interceptors have arrived first, trying to shoot the Americans down with their cannons and machine guns. They are immediately engaged by the P-51's. Some Kamikaze planes try to struggle up to altitude in front of the bomber formation, seeking head-on collisions. The P-51's are being spread thin in their efforts to protect the bombers.

John stays several miles behind the B-29 flight, weaving and orbiting to trade space for time, awaiting the completion of their bomb run. Seeing the massive B-29's at work for the first time, the most advanced and deadly bomber in the world, he is awestruck. The first combat aircraft with a pressurized cabin, Boeing's proud, four-engined creation is comfortable in the thin air and deadly cold of these high altitudes. The crew does not need to wear oxygen masks: compressed air maintains cabin pressurization and allows normal breathing. This same compressed air also provides heat for the crew compartments, so bulky flight clothing is not needed, either.

Inside *f-stop* at 30,000 feet, though, John is freezing. He has put his canteen inside his heavy flight jacket to keep the water inside from turning to ice. So far, no Japanese planes have paid him any attention.

The aerial battle in the sky ahead is a beautiful but deadly ballet, a snarl of white contrails and occasional streams of black smoke. The radio chatter is the usual cacophony of frightened, high-pitched voices screaming instructions and encouragement, crescendos of excitement about American victories quickly followed by somber recognition of American losses. The escorts' efforts have shifted to driving off the Kamikaze while the bombers' gunners work on the interceptors, but the gunners are having little success. Two B-29's have been damaged. One has been hit by cannon fire in both engines on the right wing; those engines are ablaze, threatening to engulf the fuel tanks within the wing. The second has taken numerous cannon rounds to the rear crew compartment, opening gaping holes which have caused the aircraft to depressurize. The three gunners in that compartment are badly wounded in their extremities from metal fragments; flak vests and steel helmets have protected their torsos and heads, but they need oxygen to breathe. None flows from their emergency masks, however; the supply lines have been severed. They struggle to reach portable oxygen bottles through the clouds of dust and frozen mist that accompany the depressurization. They do not make it. Slipping into unconsciousness, death from blood loss and hypoxia follows quickly. Those in the cockpit cannot help; they are separated from the gunners' compartment by the long tunnel through the bomb bays. The tail gunner is busy holding off Japanese planes. The other four machine gun turrets, now lacking the sophisticated fire control computer operated by the mortally wounded gunners, are of little use. Unable to maintain speed and altitude, both planes drop away from the formation, to be mauled by the interceptors. Their surviving crew members become prisoners of war after parachuting to Japanese soil.

The Kamikaze score only once. Most of their decrepit aircraft are attempting to fly beyond their performance capabilities and cannot attain the altitude of the bombers or keep up with their speed. One pilot, however, manages to get his plane, almost out of fuel and very light, above the bombers and dives into the top of a B-29's fuselage, where the main wing spar passes through the fuselage. The bomber's pilots had seen him coming from 12 o'clock high but too late for their attempts at evasion to take effect; while large aircraft possess many desirable flying traits, maneuverability is not one of them. Even the streams of .50 caliber bullets from the two top turrets did not stop the suicide plane.

The stricken bomber actually limps along for a few miles, mated with its unwelcome guest, until an explosion on board causes the spar to fail and the wings to fold, sending the shiny cylinder that is the fuselage plummeting to earth. It takes 10 Americans to their deaths, accompanied by one already dead Japanese pilot.

The remaining B-29's make it to Kokura, drop their bombs, and head back to their bases in the Marianas without further challenge from the enemy. John watches the bombs fall away, calculates their time to impact, and orbits three more times before beginning his camera run. The sky has few clouds, and the surface wind will carry the smoke from the bombs' explosions and resulting fires to the northeast. He decides to remain at 30,000 feet to take the pictures. He will make three passes, photographing the same objective each time: one straight and level, one banking to the left, and the final one banking to the right. This will replicate the images on all the cameras in case any decide to malfunction. The Japanese planes have vanished, low on fuel, oxygen, ammunition--or perhaps all three.

Since he is alone and unthreatened in the sky, John throttles back, decreasing his airspeed so the turns at the end of each camera run can be tighter. This will reduce both the distance flown and total time over the objective, saving some fuel. It is a good plan until turning to the third and final pass when he sees the two flecks in the sky over his right shoulder. The flecks get bigger quickly; they are heading right for him. In a moment, they grow wings--they are "Tony" fighters.

Cursing his decision to slow down, John shuts off the cameras, opens the throttles, releases the empty drop tanks, and pushes the nose over. He needs speed now and he needs it badly. The Tonys overshoot on their first pass, a deflection shot with a low chance of success, firing their guns but hitting nothing. As *f-stop* accelerates in its dive, her pursuers are behind and to the left, maneuvering for another shot. John, sweating in his heavy flying clothes despite the intense cold, taps his airspeed indicator with a gloved finger at the mark on the scale indicating maximum allowable speed; he is not quite there yet. He speaks the word "*compressibility*"--the phenomenon of excessive speed that will make it impossible to pull out of a dive-- several times in rapid succession. His throat feels like sandpaper. The Japanese fighters are still keeping pace; John wonders if they know they are chasing an unarmed airplane.

At this rate, they will be down to ground level in about two minutes. The *ground* in question here is the mountains of north central Kyushu; the highest, Kuju-san, rising almost 5000 feet. John must avoid getting caught in the twisting, turning valleys. He needs straight runs to capitalize on the F-5's speed; maneuverability is not her strong suit.

f-stop is finally putting some distance between herself and her Japanese pursuers. John begins to guide her out of the dive, putting gentle back pressure on the control column, relieved to feel the input take effect as her nose begins to rise. At this speed, the Tonys will never catch up. He wishes he was higher than 2000 feet as he speeds toward the mountains, but to climb means losing some of this lifesaving airspeed. To maintain this altitude means a dash down the valleys ahead. He chooses the valleys.

John removes his oxygen mask, wipes his sweaty face and takes a much needed drink of water. His bladder is sending the first signals of the need to urinate. He tries to ignore them. Okinawa is still two hours away. *f-stop* races into a valley.

Fortunately, this is a fairly straight valley, so the need for hair-raising high-speed maneuvering, with treed slopes rushing past on both sides, is held to a minimum.

Suddenly, the streams of little red balls, the telltale sign someone is shooting at you, are on either side of *f-stop*. At first, John thinks this is ground fire coming up at him, but no--they are coming from above and behind. Looking over his left shoulder, he is horrified to see two Japanese fighters diving down on him.

Are they the same two? Can't be!

John is right. They are not the same two he had just eluded. Fortunately, their marksmanship is no better, but *f-stop* is still a sitting duck, albeit a fast-moving one. The Japanese planes are getting really close.

SHIT!

The only trick that will work now is a rapid deceleration, one that puts your pursuers suddenly in front of you. To do that, John deploys his flaps and holds the control column forward to fight the tendency of the F-5 to balloon upward after flap extension at high speeds. He is too low to try anything else.

It works better than John could imagine. The two Japanese fighters suddenly end up in front of *f-stop*. In a panic, the pilots get their signals crossed and collide, their attempts at evasive maneuvering failing spectacularly. The two aircraft fall to the valley floor as one mass and disintegrate on impact.

Looking over his shoulder as he speeds away from the wreckage below, John thinks to himself, without emotion:

If the cameras were on, I could have claimed two kills.

When it is over, John feels no exhilaration, no cold-blooded thrill of victory, no heady feeling of invincibility--just the familiar relief to have survived once again. There is no satisfaction or validation in causing the death of a foe.

Maybe his flight school instructors had been right, that he did *lack aggressiveness*, but he no longer cared. He flew photo recon, he was damned good at it and he was proud of that fact. And Marge was right: he has done his share, maybe more.

Marge can tell right away: something has changed

in John. He seems suddenly unburdened--lighter--like he is 10 feet tall. His smile comes easily for a change.

"What's up with you?" she asks, curious and delighted.

"Nothing," he replies, beaming back at her. "Hey, you're off tonight! Let's go to the movies!"

Buddy Knox had returned, too. John breathed a sigh of relief after seeing his plane on the ramp while taxiing in, the mechanics already working on the propeller governor. Knox had encountered quite a bit of ground fire between the time the Navy escorts departed and leaving the shores of Kyushu, but he and his plane were none the worse for wear.

A week later, Buddy departs on a mission and never returns. No one knows what happened to him.

Chapter Thirty-Two

The Kadena Airfield outdoor theater is just a screen made of tarps hung between poles amidst a cluster of utility tents. Tonight's film is an old Charlie Chan mystery. You bring your own stool or just sit on the ground. Marge and John spread a blanket and share coffee from a thermos that is part of John's flying kit. He rarely used it on missions, though; coffee makes you urinate. There are several hundred male officers and enlisted men in attendance along with a far smaller number of nurses, those without male escort clustered together in mutual defense. Consumption of smuggled alcoholic beverages is inevitable; MPs hover to discourage trouble and promptly haul off anyone who misbehaves. So far, the MPs have little to do but enjoy the movie.

As soon as the film is over, Marge and John suddenly find themselves confronted by an inebriated Harmon Mann, who is loudly urging Marge to accompany him to a "fighterboys" party. When John tells him to "get lost," Mann throws down the gauntlet and says: "C'mon, asshole…let's you and me go man on man!"

This seems to Mann a safe show of bravado; somebody will break it up, probably before a punch is ever thrown. As for the MPs, he is quite sure there is no trouble with the law his birthright can't escape.

Marge, seeing John's face contort into a mask of hate and his fists already balled up, jumps in front of

John and tries to hold him back. Taking this in, Mann continues his taunt: "Let him go, Margie! C'mon, you Kodak douche bag… you and me got some business to settle!"

Other pilots from John's squadron begin to move in and keep them separated before it escalates to fisticuffs and the MPs get involved. Nobody from Mann's squadron bothers, though; they would love to see this strapping football player beat the soft, useless rich boy to a pulp.

It is Nancy Bergstrom who defuses the stand-off, though, sweeping in and grabbing Mann by the arm, pulling him forcefully away while saying, "C'mere, Harmon, I've got something to show you."

Once she has him isolated from the others, Nancy tells Mann, "Leave them alone, you drunken jerk! She's smart enough to have nothing to do with you and he looks about ready to kill you… probably could, too."

Mann tries to ignore her and rush back to taunt John some more, but Nancy, blocking his path, has more to say: "And if you keep making a scene, I'll tell everybody what a limp-dick, rotten lay you are right here, right now!"

Still ignoring her, Mann yells: "Hey, camera boy…take a picture of this!" while holding up the middle finger of his right hand. Then he tries to wrap his arms around Nancy's waist and slurs, "I guess it's you and me again, lover." But she bats his arms away and snarls, "Go fuck yourself, Captain!" before storming off.

By this time, Marge and John are well on their way to his tent. As John keeps looking back over his shoulder, eager for a fight, Marge pushes him along, saying, "C'mon, sweetie, nobody's going to the stockade tonight."

Later, as they lay together, their passion spent, Marge breaks the contented silence: "Lacks aggressiveness...HA!"

Chapter Thirty-Three

The first reports came from ships sailing near the Caroline Islands. Then more reports from ships and aircraft east of the Philippines indicated a major storm was growing in the western Pacific; it was to become Typhoon Louise.

Naval weather recon aircraft began a daily watch on this growing storm as it made its way to the northwest toward the Philippines, Formosa, and possibly Okinawa. Navy meteorologists on board the weather aircraft recorded the storm's track and made a prediction on its future path. They said it would pass north of the Philippines into the South China Sea.

They said it would miss Okinawa completely.

Several days passed with the storm behaving as predicted. Admiral Nimitz and his staff intently watched and studied as the meteorological data streamed in. He weighed the odds: should he accept the weathermen's report and assume this storm was not a threat or should he begin emergency preparations? A typhoon's strike squarely on Okinawa would be devastating to the invasion planning, as hundreds of ships, over 2000 aircraft, and 70,000 soldiers, marines and airmen, living in sprawling tent cities would be exposed and vulnerable.

Forty-eight hours prior to the predicted passing of the typhoon to the south of Okinawa, Nimitz made his decision. He ordered all naval vessels to evacuate the island's harbors. They were to sail east within 24 hours, away from the storm's predicted path--as well as the turn he feared it might make toward Okinawa-- and wait out its passing. Naval aircraft were to temporarily evacuate to the Philippines. He strongly suggested to MacArthur and his air force commander, General George Kenney, that they do the same with the planes of the 5th Air Force.

MacArthur, of course, initially rejected Nimitz's advice as alarmist, but Kenney did the math. It just made sense to be overly cautious. There were no missions planned that couldn't wait a few days. If they didn't evacuate and the typhoon struck, the inevitable damage could delay the invasion for months. MacArthur relented.

Emergency preparations on Okinawa went into high gear. Every aircraft that could fly would briefly relocate to the Philippines. Airfields there would be bursting to the seams with parked aircraft; special plans were made to stack them deep. Logisticians worked around the clock to ensure aviation gasoline, lubricants, and maintenance facilities would be available for all the visitors as well as those normally based there, although during a sudden change of plans on a scale like this shortages would be inevitable. Emergency priorities were established to deal with these shortages.

Naval vessels prepared to weigh anchor. Damaged and disabled vessels would be towed, if necessary; only a few were not capable of putting to sea. Admirals Spruance and Halsey prepared to provide defensive cover for the evacuee flotilla in the event of Japanese air and submarine attacks, although the weather made the risk of air attacks minimal.

The biggest problems would be the airfields, encampments, and depots on Okinawa; they could not be moved, only secured against the weather as much as possible. Virtually all of the shelters were tents. They would be destroyed immediately by the typhoon's winds of over 100 miles per hour if left erected. Virtually all of the stores of gasoline, oil, lubricants, rations, ammunition, and general supplies were in the open; sealing of storage tanks and containers against water ingress and securing against wind damage were absolutely essential.

The tentage was ordered struck and secured to the ground in place. Army engineers and Navy Seabees, using their heavy construction equipment, dug as many storm shelters and protective berms as possible in the short time available. The aircraft that could not be evacuated due to maintenance problems were faced into the expected wind and tied down to minimize damage, with lumber and sandbags tied to the tops of their wings to spoil lift and keep them from rising off the ground in winds strong enough to replicate flying airspeed. When the calm eye of the typhoon arrived, they would have to be turned 180 degrees and re-secured against the soon-to-be-reversed wind direction.

The typhoon posed a special problem for the field hospital. It currently had 48 patients, a few ill but most injured in accidents, some seriously. The ambulatory patients were temporarily sent to Navy hospital ships; some of the Army medical staff went along o care for them. Those who couldn't be easily evacuated were repositioned to the few Quonset huts available. Major McNeilly's remaining eight nurses, including Marge Braden and Nancy Bergstrom, would stay with them and provide care. The doctors and nurses did their best to weatherproof their stockpiles of medical supplies.

As the order to evacuate was implemented among the flying units, the photo recon squadron found itself with all but one of its aircraft ready to go. This F-5, Number 49, was having its right engine replaced. Its regular pilot, one of John Worth's section, was still in the hospital recovering from dysentery. He would have to remain on Okinawa. The mechanics worked like demons to complete the engine change so Number 49 could be evacuated. John Worth volunteered to return and ferry the aircraft after delivering *f-stop* to safety. Colonel Harris had no objections. Time was precious, though, and John had to depart with *f-stop* for the airfield on northern Luzon without seeing Marge, who was also racing the typhoon's arrival, relocating her patients to safety.

John's first flight went without a hitch; navigation across the open sea was easy as they flew in a group with a B-25 bomber as pathfinder. *f-stop* was turned over to Chuck Jaworski, who was in charge of the advance maintenance detachment dispatched to care for the evacuated photo recon aircraft. The typhoon began to veer northward toward Okinawa as John hitched a ride back on the last courier plane, another B-25, bringing crucial documents to 10th Army Headquarters. The storm would strike Okinawa in less than six hours.

Flying north, the B-25 passes high over the great pinwheel of nature's fury with the pilots, navigator, gunners, and John on oxygen. Some of the crew furiously snap pictures of the awesome 100-mile-wide storm. John muses that shortly he will return over the same route, hopefully in formation with the B-25. He makes notes on heading and wind drift for the return trip as he watches the navigator, who is busy with sun plots and low- frequency radio beacon tracking. John recalls the many times he has traversed large expanses of sea all alone, without benefit of a navigator or pathfinder aircraft, using only dead reckoning and prayer, never failing to find his destination; flights from Australia to New Guinea, New Guinea to Rabaul, New Guinea to the Philippines. He hopes Number 49 has film in the cameras so he can get some pictures of the typhoon for himself. He wonders if the engine change is even complete; if it is, he will evacuate the aircraft. If it is not, he will try to find Marge and ride out the storm with her.

The B-25 arrives at Kadena as the sky to the south turns dark and ominous and the winds grow strong, gusting to 50 miles per hour. The landing is very rough as the pilot grapples with the strong crosswind component. John drops through the hatch of the bomber before she even stops rolling and runs to Number 49, sitting on the ramp with anxious mechanics surrounding her; if John had been any later, they would have had to begin tying her down. John's preflight inspection is rapid but thorough and the engines, still warm from the run-up after the engine change, are fired up. All systems function normally, and John is pleased to see the mechanics have placed several chocolate bars and a fresh canteen of water in the cockpit. He will need them; he has not eaten all day. He begins the taxi to the far end of the runway for takeoff as the mechanics scramble to secure their equipment before seeking shelter for themselves. The storm will reach the southern tip of Okinawa in less than an hour.

Number 49 is lined up on the runway and John advances the throttles for takeoff. The crosswind component now actually exceeds the maximum allowed in the Aircraft Performance Manual. He does not know the exact wind values, but he can feel the dangerous conditions in the aircraft's behavior: the left wing wants to fly before the right wing and the nose is pulling hard to the right. John hopes he will not destroy the nose tire as he fights with the rudder pedals to keep the aircraft rolling straight. That could bring this takeoff or the next landing to a disastrous end as the steel wheel rim, bereft of a tire, digs into the runway. The plane gains flying speed quickly, though, and upon lifting off, John fights her wanting to roll hard right immediately. He keeps the nose down and retracts the landing gear, building as much airspeed as possible, skimming the ground for the entire length of the runway and beyond before trying to climb, all the while praying a sudden upset will not cause a wingtip or propeller to contact the ground. Fortunately, there are no trees or hills at the end of the runway in this direction and he will be over the water quickly. As the airspeed passes 150 knots and John gently pulls back the column to begin climbing, he breathes a sigh of relief as the altimeter begins to wind upward. Flying outside the performance envelope is nothing new to him, but that does not make it any less terrifying.

His relief is short-lived, however. At 1000 feet, the plane suddenly yaws right and loses airspeed. He doesn't even need to look at the engine gauges--the throbbing of out-of- sync propellers can be strongly felt in the seat of his pants.

Shit! Something's wrong with the goddamn prop governor on that new engine! Ain't this just fuckin' peachy!

He levels off to arrest the loss of speed and begins a slow turn to the left.

Never turn into the dead engine!

Now headed back over the airfield, he has time to play with the prop controls and plan his next move. If he cannot get it to respond, he will not be able to climb over the typhoon, and he will have to return immediately to Kadena.

Betcha the wrenches have all fled to shelter... Who can blame them? If I bring her back and manage not to crack up, there'll probably be nobody to tie her down but me... might not be able to in this wind and she'll get destroyed anyway and I'll probably get blown away trying. Gotta get control of this prop and stay upstairs!

That is just what he does, but it takes some experimenting and a fair knowledge of the workings of the prop governor. By alternately manipulating the manual override switch and rpm lever, he gets the blade pitch into a position where he can resume climb power. Once at altitude and above the storm, he will have to play with them again to get and keep a good cruise rpm setting. Even if the prop setting refuses to cooperate at that point, he can still maintain enough altitude and limp to Luzon with careful fuel management. A lesser pilot might have panicked and aborted the flight but John turns back to the south, into the path of Typhoon Louise, and continues his climb.

When he reaches the leading edge of the great storm--this massive pinwheel of dense cloud glistening in the bright sunlight--he is high above it at 20,000 feet. The cameras have indeed been loaded and John lets them click away. The view is breathtakingly beautiful, provided you could ignore the deadly havoc the storm is wreaking on the Earth's surface. His thoughts turn to Marge. He wishes he could have seen her, even just for a second. Mostly, he longs for her safety.

Back on Okinawa, Marge is every bit as concerned for John. Currently she, Nancy Bergstrom, one doctor, and three medics are caring for 10 badly injured patients in a cramped Quonset hut the engineers have deemed secure enough to withstand the deadly winds. She hopes the engineers are right; their chances of survival are bleak if this hut blows away. The nurses are running on caffeine and adrenaline. They have not slept or been off duty in over 24 hours.

Even though she has not heard from John, it is no secret the planes are being evacuated to the Philippines.

That crazy farm boy of mine is relaxing on Luzon right now, damn him!

Far from relaxing, though, John is ministering to his sick propeller, which is becoming more obstinate by the minute. Every time he gets it to an acceptable rpm setting, it drifts off, sometimes causing power loss, sometimes threatening to run away. Its constant demands are occupying almost all of John's attention. Ordinarily, such a situation is best remedied by shutting the engine down and descending to a lower altitude. The swirling mass of nature's destructive energy below him makes that not an option today.

The errant propeller is not his only problem. The voice in his head grows more nervous and uncertain with every passing minute.

Where the hell am I? I'd better not be drifting off course...ain't got that kind of fuel to play with. Fucking headwinds! I need to hit Luzon on the first try...can't go hunting around for it. Well, at least if I run out of gas, I'll be able to see the water I'm ditching into. Where the hell is that B-25? Why don't they answer?

The B-25 cannot answer John's radio call--it has crashed on takeoff at Kadena. Unable to deal with the winds, it veered off the runway and flipped onto its back. It came to rest right next to the Quonset hut

Marge and Nancy are occupying. One of the gunners is dead, his neck broken. The other four crewmen survive but are injured. All the medical staff, plus the three supply sergeants who were the normal occupants of the hut, raced to the mangled, inverted aircraft and pulled the crew out just as the wind-driven deluge began, alternating drenching the rescuers, knocking them down into the mud, and battering them with flying debris. The rain did serve one useful purpose; it smothered any ignition of the gasoline gushing from the wrecked bomber. The crewmen stumble into the hut if they can; they are carried if they cannot.

Nancy, soaking wet from the rain and dodging debris, yells to Marge, "Next time I set foot outside I'm wearing my fucking helmet!"

Marge, battered and covered in mud and gasoline, yells back, "There ain't gonna be no next time, honey!"

The one thing the medical staff had not expected was more patients *before* the storm passed, but the doctor and his nurses adapted as they always had, suturing lacerations and setting broken bones in the terribly crowded hut. The dead gunner was laid in a corner and covered with a blanket. The pilot had suffered a concussion and a badly cut scalp. Nancy talked continuously to keep him conscious while she cleaned and dressed the wound, and he was giving fairly lucid answers.

"...and this guy you gave a ride to, his name was Worth, you say?" Nancy asked. "John Worth?"

"Yeah, I think so," the groggy pilot said. "Looked like he had some engine trouble on takeoff, but the last we saw of him he was headed straight for the storm."

"Hey, Margie," Nancy called out, "don't be cursing loverboy just yet for lounging in Luzon..."

John is far from lounging anywhere. As he looks directly down into the eye of Typhoon Louise, he guesses he has another 60 miles--or 20 minutes--of flying before the winds at lower altitudes would be less than cyclonic strength; he prays the winds at his current altitude are not pushing him off course. Other than the blue-green patch of sea visible through the typhoon's eye, he can see nothing on the earth's surface, just the swirling bands of storm clouds below.

The propeller governor on the number 2 engine continues to give him fits but he has developed a routine for dealing with it, his left hand cycling that governor's circuit breaker, then fine-tuning the rpm with its manual override switch. This enables him to give at least some attention to the myriad other aspects of safe flight and steal an occasional glance at the photo of Marge that he always flies with now, tucked in the corner of the instrument panel. She seems so happy in the picture, in her brand new dress uniform on some stateside post, like a schoolgirl, bubbly and full of youthful joy, not a woman whose life has now been darkened by a year of war. He realizes he is more worried about her safety than his own at the moment.

Those fuel gauges...God, they can't be right! He doesn't know this airplane like his own; it would be easy to be misled by mechanical quirks. Number 49 seems to be using fuel more quickly than John had calculated. He wishes there had been time to fuel the drop tanks before departing. Empty, they were nothing but drag, and he had released them a while back when he first became suspicious of her thirst for fuel. The left tank had initially refused to release; it finally fell away on the fifth actuation of the toggle switch. Each successive try on that switch had been more frustrated and forceful than the preceding one. *I'm lucky it dropped before I broke the damn toggle off!* He had eaten the chocolate bars before going on oxygen, but despite the quick energy boost, they only made him realize how hungry he really was.

It occurs to him he has not once scanned for enemy fighters, a habit he thought was indelibly stamped in his subconscious. He comforts himself by thinking: *I guess deep down I don't believe any Japs would be hanging around a typhoon, even the ones real close in Formosa.*

But the wishful thinking wears off quickly: *That's just dumb. I'm here…why can't they be here, too? Pay attention, you idiot!*

As John clears the massive storm, it is bringing its full fury down on Marge. The medical staff, now back inside the Quonset hut with their newest patients, tries to clean up as best they can. Marge especially needs to get out of her gasoline-soaked fatigues and rinse her body. This is not easy in a hut crowded with men, but the exhausted yet resourceful nurses quickly fabricate a curtain behind which they are free to disrobe and wash. In the camaraderie of life-threatening crisis, the men respect their privacy without question. The nurses now realize the wisdom in Major McNeilly's insistence that they pack a change of clothes and extra dry socks. The wind outside is blowing over 100 miles per hour, the rain arriving in horizontal sheets. The hut creaks and groans as it strains against the storm; the boarded-up windward windows rattle as if announcing their intention to shatter at any moment. The leeward windows are open to prevent a pressure differential that would suck the hut off its foundation. It has grown quite dark outside even though it is early afternoon. The lighting in the hut depends on a gasoline-powered generator in its own exterior shelter and whatever filters in from the leeward windows. If the generator fails, they will have only lanterns and flashlights. When the calm of the eye arrives, the boarding and opening of windows must be reversed. The rain pounding on the arched, corrugated metal of the hut produces a menacing racket inside.

John has cleared the typhoon's trailing edge and begins to descend, pulling back the throttles on both engines, which temporarily alleviates the need to fight the balky propeller. As he drops through thick layers of cloud, he begins to view glimpses of the sea below. If visibility remains as obstructed as it is now, he probably will not be able to see land for another hour--assuming he is still on course.

If only those damn fuel gauges were reading a little higher...

Louise is spreading her mayhem across the length and breadth of Okinawa. The six vessels unable to leave the anchorage at Buckner Bay have been tossed about and spun around until their anchors drag. They are all grounded at the shoreline now. After the storm's eye passes and the wind direction reverses, they are pushed back into the bay: two sink and the others drift, still dragging anchor. Onshore, windblown debris is flying everywhere, causing casualties and damage. The 30 aircraft that had to remain are frequently struck by the debris, causing shattered canopies, punctured fuselages, and torn fabric on flight controls. Once a canopy is shattered, the cockpit floods quickly, ruining instruments and electrical wiring. The ground crews have done an excellent job of tying down, though, and only half a dozen aircraft are actually moved by the devastating wind, with three of those smashed together in one pile.

Louise rages across Okinawa for almost five hours, then heads northeast, buffeting some of the northern Ryukyus on her way out to sea. Other than higher-than-normal surf, she never affects the Japanese home islands. Marge and her team have everything under control in the Quonset hut. They takes turns catching much-needed naps. When it's Marge's turn, she finds it impossible to sleep, as her thoughts turn to her pilot.

Where are you, John? You'd better be OK...

Another hour passes and John, urging Number 49 and its balky right propeller, does not make landfall. Visibility seems limited to about 20 miles and all John sees is that distance of sea in all directions. His radio calls--to *any* listening station--are answered only by the dense static of storm activity. Trying to remain calm, he weighs his options.

All right...what do I do? If I've been blown off course, it will be to the west. But if I'm still on course and making less groundspeed than planned because of the headwind, a turn to the east will end up in the ocean, out of gas, northeast of Luzon...

His gloved fingers lightly touch Marge's photo.

What do you think, Marjorie? Which is it?

Scanning the vacant horizon once more, John takes a deep breath and makes a decision that relies far more on intuition and hope than science. He gambles and splits the difference, turning southeast, dropping still lower to get under some clouds. The needles in the fuel gauges quiver before inching a bit lower, like the minute hands of clocks in desperate need of winding, ticking their last seconds. He begins to weigh the pros and cons of shutting down the troublesome engine.

Half the fuel consumption...lower speed...longer

time to landing...can't climb if I run into more weather...

He elects not to shut the engine down. He has dealt with it this long, he can go a while longer.

His anxiety plays tricks on him. Several times, he mistakes banks of thin, low clouds for land. As he scans the horizon, losing hope, he cannot shake the image of the last night he spent with Marge, dancing in his tent to a record of Glen Miller's "Moonlight Serenade," clinging tightly to each other. But now Marge was fading away, dissolving in his imaginary grasp. The song modulates from its relaxed, contented sway to a disquieting dirge, *like funeral music,* he fears.

With composure born of inevitability, John comes to grips with his apparent fate. *So this is how it ends? In the water... Alone.*

Out of options but not quite out of gas, he plods ahead.

Fifteen minutes later, at 8000 feet, the coastline of Leyte Gulf--unmistakably *not* clouds--begins to fill his windshield, just where he hoped it would be. After another 15 minutes, with her fuel gauge needles sitting on zero, Number 49 touches down at its assigned Philippine airfield.

Chuck Jaworski pulls back the upper canopy and helps John out of the cockpit. He asks, "Where the hell were you, skipper? Sightseeing? What happened to my drop tanks? And you tore up the nose tire! We can almost see the air in it!"

John's eyes shoot daggers as he replies, "Sightseeing, my ass! Do something about the governor on that new engine, will you? It's all over the place... and stick the tanks, please. I'd like to know exactly how much gas is left...and don't lose the film!

Great pictures of the typhoon!"

Now standing on the ground, John looks up at Chuck, who is on the wing examining a fuel dipstick.

"How much?" John asks.

"You really want to know?"

"Of course I want to know!"

"You got less than five gallons, Captain. The gauges ain't kidding. The engines might have run for another minute or two."

The cold tremble of calamity averted once again passes through John Worth's body until a colonel walks up and asks: "Excuse me, Captain, but you didn't happen to come across my B-25 in your travels, did you?"

The worst devastation on Okinawa is to the food and medical supply depots. Most of their contents were ruined as water quickly saturated the cardboard boxes. Only canned goods survived. Some of the aviation gasoline became contaminated with water leakage, but the damage was isolated to just a few storage tanks. Numerous light vehicles were blown end over end and wound up in ditches and ravines. The Quonset huts that were not perpendicular to the wind direction were mostly blown out and destroyed, their flat ends taking the wind full force and collapsing. Those huts oriented in a perpendicular fashion, like the one Marge was in, survived unscathed as the wind deflected over their arched structures. The soil all over the island had turned into a soft, sticky mud that made movement by foot or vehicle difficult, often impossible. The large amount of Marsden matting--sheets of perforated steel planks comprising the runways, taxiways, and ramp areas of the airfields--was mostly unscathed. Among military personnel, there were 18 deaths and 56 injuries. Of the civilian inhabitants, several hundred perished, more than a thousand were injured, and 80 percent of their lightly-constructed dwellings were destroyed.

Within 24 hours of Louise's departing Okinawa, the airfields have been cleaned up by Army Engineers and Navy Seabees and are ready to take back their aircraft. The muddy ground begins to harden again. The ships of the Navy stream back to Buckner Bay. Seventy-two hours later, all evacuated aircraft and ships are back at Okinawa. Invasion preparations have continued simultaneously with the clean-up operation.

Logistics depots of the Pacific supply chain at Eniwetok, Kwajalein, and Ulithi atolls begin emergency resupply of fuel, food, medical supplies, additional tentage, and building supplies immediately. One week after the typhoon struck, all US military operations at Okinawa are back on track. The invasion date for Operation Olympic is affected slightly: originally planned for 1 November, it is moved to 7 November to accommodate the logistical catch-up required.

John Worth brings *f-stop* back to Kadena in the first wave of aircraft to return. His tent has already been restored and cleaned. The sign is up and he finds Marge sleeping peacefully in the hammock, wearing fatigue pants and his football jersey. She looks wonderful to him, though bruised and a bit disheveled, with bandages on her right wrist and forehead. He can hardly contain his joy that she is OK, but he does not wake her. The exhausted nurse will sleep soundly for another five hours, when she is expected back on duty.

Number 49 remained at Leyte a few more days, until the errant prop governor was repaired. John went back to give her a test flight and ferry her to Kadena as soon as she was ready.

And then life returns to normal, or as normal as things could get in war.

General Marshall and Admiral King commend Nimitz for his decision to evacuate Okinawa. He replies that it had been "no big deal, just prudent seamanship."

Chapter Thirty-Four

The young lovers lay quiet and still in the hammock, their afterglow-induced nap over. Marge is on top, her hands folded on John's chest, her chin resting on her hands. He props up his head with one arm to look straight at her. Smiling back at him, she opens her eyes, which shine a radiant green even in the pale light.

"I have something to confess," he says. "I really want to get this off my chest."

"Uh-oh," she replies, still smiling, not appearing in the least bit concerned.

"No, really, it's not that bad." He pauses, as if gathering courage. "But I don't know why I'm telling you this. Maybe I'm just an idiot..."

"That's probably true," Marge interrupts, with an impish grin.

He takes a deep breath before continuing. "But that first time we did it...I was upset for a minute that I wasn't your first."

"And how exactly did you know that, Farm Boy? Are you a doctor or something?" She is still smiling.

What's wrong with me? Why the hell did I ever bring this up? Thank God she's not pissed off... yet.

But he plows ahead anyway. "I don't have to be a doctor. It was just...so easy..."

"So easy to do what, John? Drive the train into the tunnel?"

John tenses for the assault he feels certain he has

unleashed. Being on the bottom like this, he is vulnerable to a knee in the groin, a punch in the nose-- *but dammit! She's taking this like it's some kind of joke!*

"Well, yeah," he says.

She is grinning even wider than before. "So you've plundered a lot of virgins in your time, eh, stud? Gee, I am absolutely crushed! And what part of the 19th century were you born in, again, Saint John?"

"Wait a minute, let me finish..."

"I don't know, Farm Boy, this has to be the strangest case of Catholic guilt I've ever heard of. But OK, go ahead," she says, assuming a quizzical look. "You do remember I'm a nurse and I could deceive you with any number of medical explanations?"

Still tense, he speaks slowly, choosing his words carefully. His gaze wanders to the tent's roof. "It's just that I love you so much...you know that...and I never dreamed I'd meet anybody like you, especially not here, in the middle of this damn war. I just don't want to think that someone was as close to you as I am now." His eyes lock on hers as he pleads: "Is that so silly?"

Her voice grows stern. "And you're not looking for an apology or anything, are you, John?"

"No."

"Good," she says. "Because I won't, no matter how much I love you."

For a few searing moments, he is sure he has shattered their bond beyond any hope of repair. Then Marge begins to giggle and snuggles her face to his chest. The giggling stops with a long sigh. Looking into his eyes, she says, "Don't try to be my first, baby, just be my last."

They are both smiling again as they fall back to

sleep.

When they wake again, Marge gently touches John's face and asks, "Baby, I'm not *your* first, am I? You certainly seemed to know what you were doing."

John, grinning sheepishly, replies: "No, honey, but you're real close. I've only had one real serious girlfriend... in college..."

Marge rolls her eyes. "My God, Farm Boy... you really are Catholic, aren't you?"

"But she was just with me because I played football. That's what she wanted to be, I think... a football player's girlfriend... just a reflection of him. I got so sick of hearing her talk with her friends, everything *Johnny this* and *Johnny that.* Some guys might like that but I couldn't put up with it."

She scolds him with mock indignation. "You rotten heartbreaker! And '*Some* guys might like that,' my foot! How about *most* guys!"

"Wait! I'm not finished," he says. "I like a woman with some backbone, who can stand up for herself." He plants a kiss on her forehead. "Like you."

Quietly, she basks in the compliment she has just received.

"Don't feel sorry for her," John says. "She moved on to someone else really quick."

"That's it? Just her? What about prostitutes? You've been in the Army quite a while. Surely..."

John cuts her off. "Nope, just her. I've never had a prostitute. Saved my money."

With a shy smile, he adds: "It's amazing I didn't go blind with all the jerking off..."

Coming from any other guy, Marge would have never believed it in a million years. From John, she accepted it as gospel. But she can't resist providing the punch line: "And you don't even need glasses yet!"

It takes a minute for them to stop giggling.

John asks, "Are you going to tell me your story now, sweetheart?"

"Somehow, I knew you were going to ask that. Well, OK...fair's fair." After a reluctant pause, she continues. "I've been with one other boy, John. I knew him most of my life. He was a bit older... his daddy was some big banker and good friends with my daddy. His family had lots of money."

"How long did you date him?"

"On and off through high school... never anything serious. When the war started, his daddy got him a *war-essential* job as a supervisor in a defense plant, building bombers, no less, although he didn't know anything about it. He just had to show up. I guess student nurses tend to get a little sexually adventurous sometimes...a little knowledge is a dangerous thing. Anyway, we started doing the deed my last year in nursing school. After a while, he really started to get on my nerves...always telling me what to do, what to think...When I graduated and told him I was thinking about joining up, he looked at me with such disdain and said: 'Don't be a jerk...let some other slob do it!' I signed up the next day and never saw him again. I picked the Army because the recruiting office was a block closer than the Navy's."

"He sounds like a real asshole, Marge."

"Yeah, he was." She begins to rant. "All those rich boys who think they're so damned entitled really piss me off now. They have those inflated views of themselves, which are completely unwarranted... think they own everybody..."

Her rant over, she kisses him and says, "I guess that's why I love you so much, John. You're just the opposite."

John begins to roll back on top of her.

"Hey! Hey!" Marge says in half-hearted protest. "No more foolin' around. I want you well rested for today's mission!"

John replies, "Baby, I can think of no better way to get back to sleep."

Chapter Thirty-Five

Major Kathleen McNeilly was quite pleased with what her nurses had managed to accomplish. Not only had they weathered the typhoon successfully, with patients new and old surviving without further trauma, but their invasion preparations were all current, actually a little ahead of schedule. She decided the nurses could work half shifts for a few days, as the present patient load was quite light. They could certainly use the rest.

Marge and Nancy elected to work their half shifts from 2200 to 0400. As they prepare to leave the hospital and enjoy their extended off-duty time, Major McNeilly announces casually that she is going over to the Navy hospital to see if she can barter some "swaps" of medical supplies.

As McNeilly leaves the tent, Nancy, with a mischievous smile, stage-whispers, "The only stuff the old dyke will be swapping over there are body fluids with her lady friend."

It is now 1700 as Marge sets out to look for John. Not finding him at mess or in his tent, she heads to the flight line; *f*-stop is parked with no one around her.

Marge's next stop is Base Operations. Upon entering the large tent, she runs straight into Captain Harmon Mann, still in his flying clothes and wrestling with some paperwork after another lifeguard mission.

"Well, hi there, Margie!" is Mann's delighted

response. "Looking for Ol' Harm, are you?"

They are alone in the tent. Marge wonders: *Where is everyone? Could the entire Operations Staff all be at mess?*

"No, Captain, I am not looking for *you,*" Marge says, her voice laden with annoyance and distaste. Have you seen Captain Worth, by any chance?"

"Camera Boy? No, haven't seen him. He must be out with his friends taking pictures of clouds or something...you know, very important war stuff."

Exasperated, Marge says, "Oh, knock it off, Captain! His airplane is parked right outside. Now if you'll excuse me." She heads out of the tent.

Mann rushes up behind her and grabs her by the arm, saying, "Wait a minute, sweetie...where you goin'? Stay and chat a while."

Tired of this game, Marge says, "Captain, let go of me!"

"I think you 'n me need to spend a li'l time together, Margie... How about we..."

Suddenly, a male voice booms from the other side of the tent. "The lady said 'let go,' Mann!"

With a smirk on his face, Mann turns to the voice, but the smirk quickly disappears, replaced by a look of uneasy surprise.

The object of Harmon Mann's uneasiness is Lieutenant Bob Kelly, US Navy, who had landed his Corsair at Kadena after a rain squall prevented his squadron from returning to their carrier. The carrier's planes were scattered across several airfields on Okinawa, where they would spend the night.

Kelly and Mann have history.

"Still menacing young ladies, I see. Are you all right, m'am?" Kelly asks.

"Yes, sir, I'm fine. I was just leaving," Marge

replies before scurrying out of the tent.

"Have a nice evening, then," Kelly says in her wake, then turns his attention back to Harmon Mann. "So tell me, dickhead, why am I so lucky to cross paths with a piece of shit like you halfway around the world? I should have killed you back at Yale. That pretty nurse might not have been looking for you, but I sure as hell am!"

"Big talk! You can't touch me and you know it!" Mann says, nervously trying to figure out his best path of escape.

"Now it seems I've got another reason to want you dead. Not only do I have that sexual assault on my sister that your Daddy got hushed up but now, you almost get one of my guys killed by fucking up a simple lifeguard mission... poor bastard was hurt and in the water for hours because you couldn't even mark a position and drop a raft correctly. It's a miracle the sharks didn't get him before the Dumbo found him."

Mann's eyes are wide with terror now as he says, "I don't know what the hell you're talking about! Why don't you kiss my ass..."

"Knock it off, shithead," Kelly says, stepping closer. "Since I had to land here anyway, I did a little checking. Imagine how thrilled I was to find the lifeguard was *you*. Your squadron mates don't have much of an opinion of you, by the way. Sounds like this isn't the first time you fucked up, either. Your mommy and daddy must be real proud of you, war hero."

"You and them can all go fuck yourselves," Mann replies, trying--and failing--to sound tough. "This lifeguard shit is hard work! Like findin' a fuckin' needle in a haystack!"

Kelly responds with a withering look of disdain--

and a wad of spit that he hurls at Mann.

"Anyway," Mann says, pretending there is no glob of spit clinging to his life vest, "you swabbies go down in the water, you're on your own. Don't expect the Army to come save you... And one more thing, Kelly, like me and Daddy said before... it ain't rape when they ask for it."

Before Mann can speak another word, Kelly's fist strikes him squarely in the jaw. He blacks out briefly as he crashes to the floor, landing flat on his back.

Towering over the prone Mann, Kelly says, "I've wanted to do that for a long time. I'd be more careful if I were you, Harmon... this ain't the Ivy League. You don't have any friends here. Do you think it's just chance this tent is deserted except for you and me? They were all thrilled to death when I asked for their cooperation and they don't even know me from Adam. Better tell your daddy to get you out of here before there's another *accident* that nobody manages to witness."

That said, Kelly kicks Mann's groggy, supine figure squarely in the groin, a powerful blow that locks Mann in the fetal position. "Until we meet again," Kelly says as he leaves the tent.

As he lies on the ground, alone and in great pain, Mann whispers, "I'll show all you sons of bitches..."

Marge finds John a few minutes after leaving the Operations tent. He had been at the machine shop with Chuck Jaworski, building another of his continuous improvements to *f-stop*, this time a field modification to the camera switches that would allow him to never take his hands off the control wheel and throttles during a camera run. He is surprised and delighted to see her.

"How come you ain't at work, honey?" he asks.

"McNeilly gave us half shifts. I'm not due back on duty until 2200."

"Great! You hungry?"

"I sure am! How about I help you with whatever you're doing and then we get some chow?"

John replies: "Swell! Shouldn't take but a few minutes." Marge's tenuous relationship with his airplane seemed to be improving lately, to his great delight.

The sun begins to set as the young pilot and nurse walk across the ramp to his aircraft, chatting happily. When they get there, Marge hops up on the tall plane's wing just like an old pro.

"I ran into our old friend Harmon Mann in the Operations tent, baby," Marge says.

John bristles. "He didn't try to bother you, did he?"

"No, not really. He was just being his usual stupid self, but some real tall Navy pilot was there who seemed to know him. Looked like he was going to kill him, too!"

"The Navy better get in line!" John says, as Marge laughs and nods in agreement.

Chapter Thirty-Six

The lone steel tower still rose above the desert emptiness on yet another early morning, three months since the first atomic bomb test failed. General Groves and Dr. Oppenheimer were ready to try again. This time, no tense words, no ultimatums were uttered as the firing sequence commenced. And this time, a split second after the button was pushed in the Control Bunker, there was the blinding flash as bright as the sun, followed by the shock wave and searing wind that incinerated the few living things in its path and would have flattened any structure for miles around. Moments later, after the ear-shattering boom, the mushroom cloud began its climb to the heavens, its top finally flattening at a height of 30,000 feet.

With blank faces, the scientist and the military man silently shook hands. Neither felt the joy nor the relief they had hoped would come from what they had just witnessed: the culmination of the Manhattan Project.

Chapter Thirty-Seven

Harmon Mann's testicles are still rather tender from Bob Kelly's kick. Walking slowly, Mann enters his squadron's *ready room* tent and orders the duty NCO to get his plane ready. Then he proceeds to don his flying gear, but getting the parachute harness straps between his legs and against his crotch makes him see stars once again.

As he heads to his aircraft--Number 43--his crew chief intercepts him and asks, "Where's the fire, Captain? There's no mission scheduled. We're still doing post-flight on the aircraft from your last run."

"Who asked you to do that? This plane should be ready to fly at all times," Mann replies, with dismissive arrogance.

"Excuse me, sir, but post-flight maintenance is *required*," the perplexed sergeant says.

"Get your ass in gear and get this aircraft ready... Now! Is that understood, Sergeant?"

With a reluctant sigh, the crew chief says, "Yes, sir. How much gas do you want?"

"How much is on board?" Mann asks.

"About 70 gallons, sir."

"Good...that's enough," Mann says.

"Ah, come on, Captain, let us give you a little more than that! That's hardly enough to go around the block a couple of times!"

"Sergeant, don't you understand English?"

With another heavy sigh, the crew chief says,

"Yes, sir. Will do." There is no point arguing with this fool. Another crew chief and pilot standing nearby overhear the entire exchange and roll their eyes; they figure they will be good witnesses at the board of inquiry for this brewing disaster.

The crew chief hurries his mechanics to complete what they are doing and stand by for departure. He then gives the P-47 a final once-over, signs the maintenance forms and presents them to Captain Mann, who is gingerly strapping himself into the cockpit, the sore groin still making its presence felt.

Stuffing the maintenance forms next to his seat without even looking at them, Mann says, "There...that wasn't so hard, was it, Sergeant?"

"No, sir. Have a good flight, wherever you're going. Stand by for clearance to start and..."

Mann interrupts him. "I don't need anybody's goddamn permission to start this aircraft, Sergeant! Now get yourself and your people the fuck out of my way! I'm going flying."

The crew chief does not bother to acknowledge as he scrambles off the wing. He directs his mechanics *not* to pull the chocks at the main wheels until *he* signals to do so--ignore the asshole in the cockpit. He doesn't want any of his crew, the battery cart used to turn the engine over, or the wheeled fire extinguisher to get run over by this impatient idiot. And, of course, he doesn't want the airplane damaged, either, but that will be out of his hands shortly.

Mann engages the starter and the big radial engine roars to life. After it warms up a moment, Mann signals for the chocks to be pulled. The mechanics stand still, looking to their crew chief. Mann, with great irritation, gives the signal to pull the chocks again.

But the mechanics on the chocks still do not move; their crew chief, standing to the left front of the aircraft, has given no signal; he is waiting until the ground equipment and those tending it are well clear. Mann, growing even more impatient, decides he will simply drive the big fighter out of the chocks and shoves the throttle forward. Hearing the engine accelerating and blasted by propwash, the men on the chocks flee to safety, leaving those chocks still in place. The crew chief frantically signals Mann to cut the throttle. Mann responds by making a gesture with his left hand, the middle finger extended.

As powerful as a P-47's engine is, it still cannot overcome properly installed wheel chocks. To try to do so is foolish and dangerous to the pilot, his aircraft, and those in the vicinity. As Mann continues to advance the throttle, the plane's tail starts to lift off the ground. Sensing the restrained plane is about to tip forward and her prop strike the ground, he chops the throttle and the tailwheel settles back down to the ground. As it does so, the front chocks, suddenly relieved of the pressure the main wheels had exerted against them, shoot forward a few inches.

By this time, Captain Mann's antics have drawn a crowd. Bets are being placed as to whether he will kill himself right there in the chocks or while actually attempting flight.

Mann advances the throttle a second time. The plane jumps forward slightly until it contacts the chocks again; then the tail again rises off the ground until Mann chops the throttle. As the tailwheel settles to the ground, the chocks slide forward a little more.

This cycle is repeated twice more, with Mann's plane still restrained by the chocks. On the fifth attempt, the chocks have been displaced sufficiently forward and to the side so when the throttle is advanced, the plane's forward motion strikes the chocks, then pushes them out of the way. Mann is free to do his worst. Those who bet he would die in the chocks fork over their stakes.

As Mann taxies to the runway, the control tower calls him on the radio to ask what his intentions are; they have no scheduled takeoff of a single P-47 listed at this time. The call is in vain, as Mann has never bothered to turn on his radio.

He holds short of the runway behind two B-24's preparing to take off. Once they are airborne, Mann takes the runway and begins his takeoff roll without bothering to get clearance. This comes as a tremendous shock to the pilot of a B-25 cleared for immediate landing on that same runway, with one of her two engines shut down, a victim of flak over Kagoshima. Only a quarter mile from touchdown, the B-25 pilot has little chance of executing the go-around the frantic controller in the tower is demanding. His aircraft has enough trouble maintaining altitude, let alone climbing, on one engine. The flight back to Kadena has been a long, gradual descent--a "drift-down"--and once on final approach he has no choice but to land. This intruder on the runway before him poses a good chance of causing a fiery ground collision or, at a minimum, the B-25 having to swerve off the runway, causing more damage than she already possesses.

Mann is oblivious to the twin-engined bomber bearing down on his tail. As he pushes his throttle forward for takeoff, his aircraft, much lighter than usual due to the minimal amount of fuel on board, begins to sprint eagerly down the runway and actually leaves a little room in its wake for the B-25 to land; when the bomber's main wheels touch down, its nose is perhaps 200 feet behind Mann's plane but traveling faster by about 50 mph. As Mann accelerates and the B-25 brakes firmly, the distance between the two aircraft shrinks to less than 10 feet. The bettors begin to quibble on how a ground collision would pay out under the terms of their wagers.

But there is to be no ground collision. The intersection of the acceleration and deceleration curves of the two planes is never achieved. Mann's aircraft breaks ground and the B-25 comes to a full stop. Her pilot takes a moment to regain his composure before taxiing to the ramp.

Now Mann can reveal the real purpose for this unauthorized flight. He is going to show everyone who denied him his due--all those sons of bitches who didn't recognize his superior status and entitlement by birthright, every woman who had refused his advances--why he is better than them. He will prove it with an aerobatic display.

After retracting the landing gear and flaps, he begins with a low-level high-speed pass down the flight line about 20 feet off the ground. Then, he pulls up sharply into an Immelmann turn, a half loop that reverses his direction of travel and leaves him upside down, setting up an inverted pass over the flight line in the opposite direction. This gets a little tricky and quickly overwhelms Mann's meager piloting skills. Not used to flying upside down, he panics as his plane sinks, bottom side up, toward a row of parked aircraft. He rams the stick forward to push the nose away from the approaching ground. The aircraft snaps straight up, shoots to 2000 feet and, as her airspeed bleeds off to nothing, comes to a standstill in a brief vertical hover. Hanging on the straining propeller, she swaps ends suddenly and plummets, nose down, straight back to earth.

Mann practically pulls the control stick out of its floor gimbal as he wrenches it back into his abdomen, asking--praying--for all the *up* elevator in his floundering ship's capability.

As the aircraft--going almost straight down–begins to accelerate, the elevator input begins to take effect and the nose begins to rise, slowly at first, then rapidly as the speed builds. She has achieved roughly level flight as her propeller, then her belly, strike the ground directly in front of the line of parked aircraft. The plane then slides along the ground, her engine seized and propeller tips bent over double, for several hundred feet, shedding parts all the way, finally coming to rest against a 2-1/2 ton truck that she impales broadside. The two occupants of the truck's cab, seeing the massive fighter sliding toward them, are able to escape out the far side door just before the impact. There is a brief fire, but Mann's plane has little fuel left to sustain it.

The crash crew is on site quickly. They douse the flames, jettison the canopy, and pull Mann from the cockpit by his parachute harness straps. He lets out a howl as the sudden pressure on the straps makes itself felt in his still-tender groin. Fearing internal injuries, the crash crew places him on a stretcher and prepares to load him into an ambulance.

Mann's commanding officer puts a stop to it. He stands over Mann and asks, "Are you injured, Captain?"

"No, Colonel, I do not believe I am," Mann replies, trying to summon some respect in his quivering voice.

"Just what the hell was that stunt all about, Captain?"

"I was just giving my plane a post-maintenance check flight, sir."

Growing furious, the colonel asks, "Was it damaged in combat or an accident?"

"No, sir."

"Then what the fuck did it need a check flight for, Captain?"

"Well, I deemed it necessary, sir."

The Colonel silences him with a wave of his hand. "Bullshit," he says. "You were hot-dogging during unauthorized flight and you managed to destroy an aircraft and a deuce and a half truck. You are grounded pending investigation of charges for court martial. Report to my office immediately."

"Yes, sir!" Mann replies, trying to sound like he gives a shit.

As the Colonel turns and walks away, a smirking Mann mutters to himself, "Court martial, my ass! We'll just see what Daddy has to say about that."

Chapter Thirty-Eight

Darkness fell as Colonel Ozawa and his small team prepared to move the nuclear device again, this time to Ariake Bay. The small locomotive had arrived and was being connected to a boxcar for personnel and support equipment. The flatcar carrying the device was attached behind. The journey had to be completed in darkness; the risk of air attack was too great in daylight. Ozawa's luck had held this time; the warehouse at Fukuoka, where the device had been hidden all these weeks, had never been bombed.

Major Watanabe, Ozawa's second-in-command, had selected and prepared the new hiding place at Ariake, a cave on the backside of the hills overlooking the bay, just large enough to accommodate the device on its flatcar. A spur several hundred yards long had been constructed from a main rail line right into the cave, allowing the flatcar to be backed in, then the track and cave mouth camouflaged with netting and vegetation. When the time came to deploy and detonate the device, the flatcar simply needed to be rolled out of the cave to the main line, then down the tracks to the coastal plain on the seaward side of the hills. No locomotive would be required; it was all downhill. Watanabe had also stockpiled spare track sections, ties, spikes, and tooling in case of bomb or shell damage.

General Takarabe, the 57th Army commander responsible for defending southeastern Kyushu, was advised to expect the "special" unit to arrive in the early morning darkness. He was still troubled that he knew nothing of this unit's mission or capabilities, but his mind was full of more urgent problems. His army had been trying to build defensive positions on the beaches and the plains immediately beyond but were making little progress. They could only work at night; any troops caught out in daylight were easy targets for the countless American fighters and bombers patrolling the skies above. He had few heavy anti-aircraft weapons; the light machine guns and rifles his units possessed were largely ineffective against aircraft. The Japanese planes that rose to counter the Americans might shoot a few down but never drove them off; there were just too many. When each night's work was completed, it had to be concealed with camouflage by day from the eyes of the Americans in the sky.

The defensive positions being constructed amounted to little more than trenches and fighting holes. Most lacked any sort of overhead cover as the lumber, concrete, and stone required had not been provided in any large amount. Furthermore, the work in the darkness had proven impossible to effectively supervise. Despite their best efforts, many of the positions dug would prove to be misplaced, with ineffective fields of fire, and have to be redone on subsequent nights. This cycle of planning, digging, correcting, and digging again went on for many weeks, wasting precious manpower.

During daylight hours, his troops hid amongst the civilians in the cities and villages and conducted pointless "civil defense" drills, arming the populace with bamboo sticks and farming tools to bolster the people's morale--and perhaps their own. But Takarabe had no intention of allowing civilian combatants on his battlefield; they would be nothing but a nuisance and a burden. Most Japanese generals felt the same way.

Both generals grappled with the concept of *beach* defense, a doctrine the Japanese forces had not utilized in all their previous island campaigns, preferring to offer only token opposition on the beaches and then fight a fierce battle of attrition from the hills, caves, and mountains beyond. Of course, the Americans had ultimately defeated them in all those campaigns; maybe it was not such a bad idea giving this new concept a try.

The small locomotive is making slow progress. Colonel Ozawa estimates the journey will take almost five hours, as much of the trip is uphill. Even at this slow pace, they should arrive at the new hiding place by 0300, with plenty of time before the sun rises again.

The slow pace becomes even slower, however, as the locomotive's boiler pressure drops and clouds of steam begin to envelop the small train; the drive piston for the right wheels is leaking badly. This locomotive, like everything else in Japan, is breaking down. The engineer shuts off the steam valve to the failed piston and attempts to move forward with just the left drive, but trying to pull all the weight with just one set of drive wheels on an uphill grade makes those wheels spin and slip on the track. The train progresses no farther.

After a discussion with Colonel Ozawa, the engineer backs the train several miles to a level section of the track, then tries to proceed forward again, hopefully building up some speed to negotiate the incline. The train is able to move forward this time and even develop some speed, but it bleeds away immediately at the incline. The train once again comes to a stop, the left drive wheels still slipping.

Their attempts to coax the faulty engine have consumed precious darkness. Ozawa is faced with two choices: return to the Fukuoka warehouse, running in reverse the entire way, or remain in his present position, 20 miles short of his destination, and wait for another locomotive. Either option will take hours and leave them exposed to the American planes at daylight. Ozawa chooses to remain at his current location and gamble on another engine arriving. The stricken locomotive, now without its load, slowly limps off, hoping to reach Ariake or Kagoshima, where the engineer might find a replacement. Ozawa and his few men remain with their device, immobile on the tracks.

Sunrise brings another locomotive and new hope. As soon as they are coupled and underway once again, however, US Navy planes appear overhead. They swoop down for a closer look and then, to Ozawa's astonishment, fly away.

Lieutenant Bob Kelly, in the lead plane, calls his boys off. "Forget it, guys, we're still not touching trains. Let's not kill our own POWs."

What providence is smiling on me this day? Ozawa wonders, as Kelly's flight disappears in the distance.

Soon, another American plane, this time one of those fork-tailed P-38 types, streaks by but does not circle back.

John Worth, the pilot of this aircraft, looks down from *f-stop's* cockpit as she flies north on this low-level photo run. "Holy Shit!" he says, "That looks like that damn beer barrel!" He rolls hard right for a view unobstructed by wing, engine, or tail boom. *f-stop's* right oblique camera captures the beer barrel clearly.

At the post-mission debrief, Colonel Watson and his staff note the *beer barrel* with intense interest. The markings on the railroad flatcar are identical to the first photo. When translated, they reveal nothing of the beer barrel's true nature.

The following morning, John is ordered to report to his C.O., Colonel Harris. When told of this order, Marge becomes thrilled. She asks: "You think you're going to get a medal?"

"Doubt it. Wait! Maybe I'm getting promoted!"

Marge likes the sound of that. "You're certainly due...And I wouldn't mind sleeping with a Major!"

With a big smile, he says, "Don't say that too loud. People might think you're easy."

"Oh, shut up, Farm Boy," she replies, moving in for her goodbye kiss. "Now hurry up. Don't keep the colonel waiting."

"You, me, and Colonel Watkins are going to Manila, John," Colonel Harris says. "That certain something in those photos of yours *really* interests them up at MacArthur's HQ. You seem to have the knack for finding that thing, whatever it is, so they want you with us. Pack a bag...our C-47 leaves at 1300."

John is shocked for two reasons: first, that he is actually going to MacArthur's HQ; second, that is the most Harris has ever said to him in the Colonel's brief, lackluster tenure as C.O.

When John tells Marge of the impending trip, she gushes with joy. "Now I know something great is going to happen! Even better, I'll bet they've decided you're too valuable and they're going to ground you!" She ignores, for this exhilarating moment, that such an event would probably entail his being shipped back to the States.

"I don't think so, Marge. Don't get your hopes up."

"OK, OK. So how long are you going to be gone, Farm Boy?"

"Sounds like two days, give or take the time to hitch a ride back here."

"Now don't go meeting any pretty girls in Manila," Marge says. She is upbeat, which almost makes it sound like she is kidding.

"No problem...and you keep those other ardent suitors away," John replies. He is dead serious, not kidding at all.

Chapter Thirty-Nine

Corporal Leonard Petrillo is hard at work but not happy. He is putting the finishing touches on a brake change, just about ready to drop the plane off the jack, but it is some other F-5, not *f-stop*. He is in a mood to grumble.

"Hey, Sarge," Petrillo says, "how come we spend so much time doing other guys' jobs? I swear, we work more on these other pieces of shit than we do on *f-stop*."

"It's simple," Chuck Jaworski replies. "Captain Worth is a mechanic who happens to be a pilot. These other guys are pilots pretending they understand mechanical stuff. When the Captain has a problem, he pretty much tells us exactly what's wrong down to the last nut and bolt. It's like having a pilot *and* a mechanic on board, so we nail *f-stop's* problems on the first try. Those other pilots are just describing symptoms that they get wrong half the time. With their airplanes, there're lots of do-overs, lots of extra work and wasted time, so we do our bit and help them out. Plus, Captain Worth never blames the airplane when he messes up...not like them other pilots. That's how come the other crews keep getting gripes they can't duplicate. There was never anything wrong with the plane in the first place...the pilot just made a mistake. More wasted time..."

Corporal Travis Lucas stops working on the engine and turns to Jaworski. "Captain Worth made a mistake?" Lucas says, looking genuinely surprised. "When'd that happen?"

"John Worth's damn good," Jaworski replies. "Best pilot I've ever seen. Better than all these hot shit fighter jocks...but nobody's perfect."

"Not even you, Sarge?" Lucas asks, with a sly grin.

"Not even me, redneck. And speaking of mistakes, did you get all the fuel cleaned up after that leak? I don't want to turn this engine over and get us another fireball."

"Keep your britches on, Sarge. I'm working on it."

As they work, the topic of conversation switches to the progress of the war against Japan. With great enthusiasm, Petrillo says, "These fuckin' Nips are gonna throw in the towel any minute! Everybody's sayin' it! They ain't got nothin' left! Our planes come and go as they fuckin' please. This squadron ain't lost one since Lieutenant Knox went missin'." Petrillo makes a rapid sign of the cross. "God knows what happened to him."

Lucas, still wiping spilled fuel out of the nacelle panels, replies, "Lenny, you dumb Yankee, don't believe them rumors. We ain't talkin' Brooklyn sissies here. We're talking Japs, and Japs don't surrender, they just die. Them Germans didn't surrender until we marched into Berlin and shot Hitler."

"Who you calling dumb, you ignorant cracker? We didn't march into Berlin, the Russians did. And Hitler committed suicide. Don't they teach you how to fuckin' read down south?"

The Confederate rebel in Travis Lucas boils to the surface. He stands defiant, arms crossed. "Who gives a goddamn shit how the son of a bitch died? And ain't the Russians on our side?"

"Supposed to be," Jaworski says, "but I see it this way. The Emperor won't quit until he gets a deal where Truman and MacArthur don't hang him. I think there's still going to be a lot of dying before that happens and it won't be him doing it."

"So you still think we're gonna invade, Sarge?" Petrillo asked.

"No doubt. Take a look around you, Leonard. Does anything here look permanent to you? This is an assembly point for an invasion. One way or another, you, me and all these machines are going to Kyushu soon." Dropping the big brother tone, Chuck Jaworski becomes the taskmaster again. "But there ain't going to be no goddamn invasion if you two goldbricks don't get this plane back into the sky! So knock off your jawing... the Civil War ended a long time ago. Now get back to work!"

Chapter Forty

General Marshall had just announced some very important news to the occupants of the Oval Office. Secretary of State James Byrnes was overtly delighted; the others took the news with some reserve.

"So the damned thing works, does it? Fantastic!" Byrnes says.

"That's correct, Mister Secretary," George Marshall replies. "The test was completely satisfactory. We now have a working atomic weapon."

President Truman is pensive. "So, General, when can a bomb be in theater, ready for use?"

"By the second week in November, Mister President."

"That's a bit longer than your original estimate. What happened?"

"There were delays in fabrication and construction. From what I am told, a major redesign was undertaken, but we have success at last, Mister President."

"OK, that's just great," Truman says as he contemplates the effect of Marshall's news on the invasion.

Admiral Leahy is more than a little concerned. "Mister President, we must give serious and immediate consideration to the question of using this terrible weapon at all."

Byrnes jumps up, ready as always to do verbal battle. "What are you talking about, Admiral? We now have the greatest power in the universe at our fingertips. Of course we're going to use it!"

"James," Leahy says, "you forget that apparently we are not the only ones with this power."

Byrnes shrugs off Leahy's admonition. "Yeah, maybe the Japs have it, too, but we can stop them and they can't stop us. They can't stop a B-29."

Admiral King, sitting next to Leahy, remains silent but privately amused. He supposes Jimmy Byrnes doesn't realize just how many B-29's have been lost over Japan.

General Arnold's body language is unmistakable: he cannot wait to drop this thing on a Japanese city teeming with civilians. His excitement is palpable, almost childlike. The others cannot help but remember that not so long ago Arnold had expressed no such enthusiasm about bombing German civilians. Instead, he chose to perpetuate the myth that his air forces in Europe had been practicing *precision* bombing, sparing civilians while striking purely military and industrial targets--despite all the evidence to the contrary.

Leahy plays devil's advocate. "Despite the fact many of our generals, including Eisenhower, are not in favor of it, there seems no doubt the Army is prepared to drop the atom bomb right now for no other reason except *we can*. But if we are to do so, we have several questions we must answer. First, what would we drop it on? Do we use it against a Japanese city? A military base? Or do we announce and perform a demonstration of this bomb's terrible power off the coast of Japan in the hope of bringing the Emperor and his war leaders to their senses? Most importantly, how does all this affect the invasion plans?"

Byrnes has no patience for this moralizing. "All Japanese military bases, even the ones on the Pacific islands we bypassed, are in or adjacent to centers of civilian populations, so your first two choices are really only one. And as to a demonstration at sea, do we really think we'll sway the Japanese, who seem determined to die to the last person, by killing fish?"

There is dead silence in the room for a few moments until Leahy says, "Professor Einstein and a host of our prominent scientists have urged a demonstration. They seem to be the only ones who begin to understand the universal chaos atomic weaponry will unleash. It is the only humane approach, except, of course, the option not to use the bomb at all."

"Your scientists are not responsible for bringing this war to a timely close," Byrnes says.

"No, Jimmy's right. I am the one responsible." Truman says, still preoccupied but obviously following the debate. The irony of Leahy's *humane* argument weighs heavily on his already burdened soul since they had been incinerating Japanese civilians by the hundreds of thousands in LeMay's firebombing raids for months.

The voices in Truman's head have many questions:

Should we unleash a method of massive devastation never before envisioned on an already-beaten foe?

Are the scientists right? Does this usher in a new era, bringing us a step closer to Armageddon?

Is Jimmy Byrnes right? Will it serve more than anything as a demonstration to "Uncle Joe" Stalin and keep him in line, now that he has finally stopped cooperating with Japan and will demand spoils in Asia?

Will it end this damn war?

Why the hell won't they just surrender right now and make it easy for me?

As his mind reels, Truman asks Arnold a question already made irrelevant by the discussion at hand. "What did General Groves say about your idea to use our bomb against a Japanese bomb?"

Somewhat puzzled, Arnold replies: "He was not in favor of the idea, Mister President."

"And I'll tell you why," Byrnes says. "Because unless their bomb is in the middle of a Japanese city, it's a goddamn waste of our bomb! The latest information puts it near an invasion beach, away from any big city, is that not correct?"

"That's correct, Mister Secretary," Marshall replies.

The room falls quiet again as they wait for a decision from their distraught president.

After a few moments, Truman recovers his focus. Thumbing through Groves' report on the successful test, he asks, "I understand *blast effects*, but what's this talk about *radiation?* What are the ramifications of it for our invasion troops?"

Admiral King finally speaks up. "Groves tells us that radioactive nuclear particles will remain in the area of an atomic blast and some will be carried away with the wind, affecting other areas. These particles remain active, emitting radiation for weeks, perhaps months, and have the potential to cause harmful effects to the human body, even death."

Byrnes waves his hand dismissively. "That doesn't sound very exact, Admiral."

"That's because it's uncharted territory, Mister Secretary," King says, with no hint of respect when speaking the man's title.

Truman turns to Marshall. "Do we have a list of

target cities prepared?"

"Yes, Mister President, we have such a list. All the cities are ones we have not extensively firebombed, so the level of devastation from the atomic blast will be readily apparent."

Leahy sinks into despair. Not only is it obvious to him Truman has decided to use the atom bomb against a Japanese city, he appears ready to continue the invasion, as well. The die is cast. Ethical considerations are not going to be a factor.

"How hard was it to come up with that list?" Leahy asks. "I thought LeMay burned almost everything to the ground already."

Unflustered, Marshall continues. "Of course, all the target cities are at least 50 miles from the invasion sites...and all are upwind...so effects from our bomb would be nonexistent for our troops."

"I see," the President says. "And LeMay's boys will deliver the bomb?"

"Yes, Mister President," Arnold replies, then pauses before nervously introducing a new issue. "There is one more thing about the bomb delivery, sir. As you know, General Spaatz is LeMay's theater commander, and he has insisted on *written* orders before dropping any atomic bomb."

Marshall, blindsided by Arnold's statement, is visibly upset, but before he can say a word Byrnes jumps up angrily and shouts, "Damn it! He'll do what he's told, written or not!"

King lets out a loud guffaw. "Tell Spaatz that won't help him at the war crimes trial. The Japs will behead him, anyway, along with the rest of us!"

Incensed, Truman holds up his hands, signaling for silence. "There will be no more talk like that in this chamber, Admiral King. Is that clear?"

"Yes, Mister President," King replies, trying to sound humble but not quite hitting the mark. "I was joking. I apologize."

Then the President turns his glare to the red-faced Marshall. "What's it going to be, General?"

Despite his annoyance with Arnold, Marshall replies calmly, without hesitation. "Orders for the atomic mission will be published by the end of the day, Mister President."

"Fine. Make that happen."

The President then turns toward the window and is stunned by the apparition that greets him. Despite the fact it is a bright, sunny fall afternoon, all he can see is a gray void. The trees, rather than turning vibrant colors, resemble charred skeletons. All of Washington, D.C. seems to have been consumed by fire. Nothing is alive.

Truman feels like his stomach is tied in knots. He fights the urge to vomit. There is an enormous weight on his chest, making it difficult to breathe. He had fought in a war and knew the vicious realities of politics, but nothing had prepared him for this.

The President realized he would carry the enormity of this decision to his grave. He really did not believe he had a choice, though. He had to use every weapon at his disposal to end this war as soon as possible while retaining his country's dominant position in world affairs. Nothing else mattered; damn the consequences. This steamroller had been set in motion long before he was forced into the presidency; he had little incentive to try and stop it.

He quickly turns back to the conference table. The motion makes him dizzy, like the room is spinning. His eyes fall on Leahy, his Chief of Staff, who is furiously writing.

Probably his resignation, Truman surmises.

The President steadies himself against the conference table and manages to ask one more question. "So, General Marshall...the invasion will begin 7 November?"

Marshall, puzzled by this inquiry of something that is common knowledge for those present, replies, "Yes...of course, Mister President."

Chapter Forty-One

John Worth sits uncomfortably in MacArthur's Manila conference room, feeling like a very small fish in a very big pond. Lieutenant General Sutherland, MacArthur's Chief of Staff, and Major General Willoughby, the G-2, are there, as are General George Kenney, Commander, Far Eastern Air Forces, and General Krueger, the 6th Army commander, who will lead the ground forces on Kyushu. MacArthur is not present.

Like any warrior seeing the conflict from his own isolated corner, where life and death revolve around just a few friends and foes, John had often wondered if the old men sitting in this room were real and not just abstractions--uncaring and unfeeling--whose grandiose plans sent younger men to their deaths so easily. Now he can see they, too, are flesh and blood, although he is still suspicious of the absent MacArthur. This newfound wisdom has not made him feel any more comfortable.

General Sutherland chairs the meeting in his commander's absence and begins it with a bang. "What dumb son of a bitch gave the directive to stop shooting up trains?"

General Willoughby sinks into his chair before speaking up. "I did. It seemed like a prudent idea at the time, knowing as little as we did about atom bombs."

Sutherland scowls. "Fine. Just get it rescinded immediately."

With a nod from Willoughby, a staff colonel scurries out of the room to do the General's bidding on the double.

Sutherland gets down to business. "Colonel Harris, your boys have been doing a fine job giving us the picture on Kyushu and, quite frankly, this picture is causing great hope of a successful invasion...note I didn't say 'easy,' but successful. The Navy's recon efforts have been largely wasted looking for Japanese naval assets that no longer exist, so we've depended on you and your boys entirely."

The Naval staff liaisons in the room squirm but remain silent.

Sutherland continues. "One thing gives us great concern, though, and it involves the object that only you, Captain Worth, seem to be able to locate. Now we realize this is mostly luck on your part, but we need that kind of luck if this object is what some of the staff think it is. What I am about to tell you, gentlemen, is top secret and is to remain so. Is that absolutely clear?"

Watkins, Harris, and Worth nod and speak in unison. "Yes, sir."

"Good. Now we believe this object, this 'beer barrel,' as you have been calling it, might...*just might*...be an atomic weapon. General MacArthur doesn't put much stock in this theory, but he's determined to err on the side of safety. I don't know how familiar any of you are with nuclear physics, but all you need to know for now is that such a weapon could have the explosive power of many thousands of tons of dynamite. That's a lot of killing power and could wipe out a great deal of our forces on the beach. The Navy was afraid it might be placed on a vessel and used against the invasion fleet, but this second sighting at an inland location points to it being used on land, somewhere in southern Kyushu. We suspect the Japanese would attempt to place such a weapon in the Ariake Bay area, but we're not completely sure. We are confident they have no capability to deliver such a weapon by an aircraft. It's just too damn big."

Sutherland's gaze falls on Colonel Harris. "Colonel, we expect you to assign a team headed by Captain Worth to the sole mission of locating this object so we can destroy it by whatever means available, be it aerial bombing, naval gunfire, or both. Scientists tell us it could be rendered useless in this manner without fear of a nuclear explosion, so our forces would not be harmed. No doubt they'll try to hide it until they're ready to use it, so this might get a little tricky. Our scientists also tell us it can't be most effective if it's submerged, buried, or stashed in a cave. At some point, we would get to see it in the open, perhaps camouflaged. Your mission, Colonel Harris, will not end until that thing is neutralized, *even if the invasion is already in progress.* And, as I stated before, this info is top secret and not to be divulged. We don't want to start a panic among our own troops. Am I understood?"

Once again, they nod and say: "Yes, sir."

But Sutherland is not finished. "Gentlemen, I will also tell you, in the strictest confidence, that we have developed an atom bomb, and we'll deliver it by aircraft wherever and whenever the President sees fit. Now, I'd like to introduce Lieutenant Commander Mark Colton, US Navy. Commander Colton is a nuclear weapons expert who will be working with you until this mission is successfully completed."

John Worth sits stoically, viewing the vacant faces on the senior officers around him. All he can think is:

Bullshit. Just a handful of guys and planes, led by

a junior officer, to find something supposedly this important? They don't really believe this thing exists and they don't care about finding it... they just want to look like they tried on the off chance this whole thing blows up, disturbs their precious invasion, and gets us all killed...they'll need somebody way down the chain of command to blame. No wonder MacArthur isn't even here.

But now I've got to care about finding the goddamn thing.

As they file out of the conference room, General Kenney pulls Colonel Harris aside and says, "See to it that young Worth gets promoted immediately."

Chapter Forty-Two

Marge had just finished an unusually easy shift at the hospital. Since John was away in Manila, she had lingered behind to chat with patients as well as the nurses on the opposite 12-hour rotation. She did not feel tired yet. Very few soldiers and airmen had gotten injured or sick lately; even the number of air crewmen wounded over Japan was at low ebb. Most of the nurses' time was being spent preparing the hospital for its planned move to Kyushu as part of the invasion.

After several animated conversations filling half an hour, tiredness finally overcomes her and she makes her way alone down the darkened walkway to the nurses' tents. Halfway there, she is startled to come face to face with the shadowy figure of Harmon Mann.

Nervously, she greets him. "Hello, Harm. Nice night, isn't it?"

He doesn't answer.

Where the hell are the MPs? she wonders. *They're usually all over the place.*

Smelling the alcohol on his breath, she tries to push past him, but he grabs her arm and half-shoving, half-dragging, propels her into a darkened, empty hospital tent.

"Harmon, stop it right now!" Marge shouts, not quite sure where the courage in her voice is coming from.

"C'mon, li'l Margie...I know you got a thing for Ol' Harm. We're birds of a feather, you know."

"Captain Mann...I'm going to ask you once more to stop this! Let go of me!"

"So you'd rather spread your legs for that dirt-poor plow boy? C'mon, baby...you got more class than that! Ol' Harm needs some lovin', too."

"Save that crap for your Mother!" Marge says, then rams a knee as hard as she can into Mann's groin.

She has hurt him some but enraged him more. After staggering back, still gripping her arm tightly, he recovers and shoves Marge into a curtained-off section of the tent. As he pushes her against the edge of a desk, she tries to strike his face with her free hand. Mann blocks the blow, then lands a right cross squarely to Marge's jaw. She falls backwards onto the desk, semi-conscious.

"All right, you teasin' little slut...you've had this coming for a long time."

Still standing, he leans over her limp form and undoes her fatigue pants. When he has pulled them down to her ankles, he begins to undo his own pants, slurring "I guarantee you ain't never had it so good, you..."

But his words are cut off by a powerful blow to the back of his head from a pipe-wielding assailant. He collapses in a heap to the floor, below Marge's dangling feet, his pants around his knees.

The two MPs who have been summoned are puzzled by what they find. Aside from the two groggy, semi-dressed officers, one a female with a badly bruised jaw and one a male bleeding from a scalp wound, there is a length of stout pipe on the floor a few feet away.

The MPs stand like statues, gawking at the half-naked Lieutenant Braden, until Major McNeilly rushes in, throws a blanket across Marge and commands the MP sergeant: "Arrest that man! He tried to rape this nurse!"

"Rape, my ass!" Mann groans from the floor. "She wanted it...she always wanted it!"

"Get this disgrace to the uniform out of here!" McNeilly bellows. The two burly MPs scoop Mann off the floor, repositioning his pants all in the same motion, and hustle him out of the tent.

On the way to the stockade, Mann mumbles, "Do you know who the fuck I am? Do you know who my daddy is?"

The MPs could not care less.

Major McNeilly holds Marge's battered face gently in her hands and says quietly, "Don't worry, Marjorie, he never touched you, aside from that wicked punch, of course. Now let's get some ice on that chin."

As Marge pulls herself together, McNeilly closes the tent flap and whispers to a shadowy figure lurking outside in the darkness, "Thanks for your help, Sergeant Jaworski."

Chapter Forty-Three

For a moment, Colonel Ozawa thought he was dreaming. But no, the inscrutable face of the old man staring down at him was real. So were the sounds of Major Watanabe ranting as he beat the sentry who should have been guarding the cave mouth but had fallen asleep at his post. The sentry stood at rigid attention, tears flowing down his cheeks as his head and body absorbed the blows from Watanabe's fists. He knew he deserved this discipline; he had failed in his duty. The responsibility for this mysterious but seemingly harmless intruder entering their cave was his alone.

Ozawa thought all civilians had been removed from the area. He had seen the dimly-lit processions in the night: miles-long lines of refugees on foot, leaving the coastal areas where the invasion was predicted, heading north, prodded on by soldiers. But no--here was a civilian standing before him, unimpressed by the colonel's authority, as if he had every right in the world to be there. This was most infuriating. Worse, the visitor could compromise the secrecy of his all-important mission.

"What are you doing here, old man?"

The visitor regards Ozawa coolly. "I could ask you the same, soldier."

"It is none of your concern. Be on your way."

"I would prefer not," the visitor says. "I hear airplanes approaching. I fear it is not safe to be walking these hills now. You hide from the airplanes, too, do you not?"

"Yes, we hide for now, but we will soon avenge the American air pirates."

The old man's indifference turns to outright skepticism. "And how will you do that? Does this giant barrel possess some magic power?"

"You ask too many questions, old man!"

"I fear you will bring death upon us all, soldier, and the Emperor will still kneel before the Americans..."

Ozawa has heard enough of this treasonous talk. But before he can say another word, Major Watanabe's sword finds its mark in the old man's belly. As the visitor sinks to his knees, mortally wounded, Watanabe withdraws the sword, then raises it high and beheads the old man with one quick stroke.

Ozawa stares at the severed head--the lifeless eyes seem to lock his gaze and bore into his soul.

Ozawa feels sure its lips have uttered the words *You will fail* in perfect English.

Chapter Forty-Four

General Kenney had had enough of Captain Harmon Mann. He hadn't forgotten the questions surrounding the strange death of Mann's section leader late last year, a death for which Mann was, quite possibly, responsible. He had initially chafed against the pressure from Washington to bury that incident but ultimately complied. It would have been politically foolish not to.

Then there was the unauthorized flight, the hot-dogging that ended with Mann destroying a P-47 and a ground vehicle, immediately followed by MPs finding him drunk and apparently engaging in a sex act at a field hospital with a nurse, which he claimed was consensual. The nurse's superior has accused Mann of rape; the nurse herself has not yet pressed charges.

When first hauled in by the MPs, Mann claimed during the *consensual encounter* he was assaulted by one Captain John Worth, a recon pilot with the 8th Photo Recon Squadron with an outstanding record and an incredibly long time in combat. Kenney knew, however, that Worth was standing before him in Manila on the day of the alleged attack; so did Mann's commander on Okinawa. When Mann was advised of this fact, he changed his story in an instant, reeling off a list of people who "have it in for me."

When told that one Major Kathleen McNeilly, US Army Nurse Corps, claimed she witnessed--and thwarted--Mann's physical attack and attempted sexual assault on her nurse, Mann's response was, "She's a lyin' ol' bitch!"

Kenney decided it was high time to get this dangerous incompetent with high-level political connections to a safe place until they could dress him up with some bullshit medal and send him home.

Chuck Jaworski is waiting on the ramp as the C-47 brings John and the two colonels back from Manila on a typically rainy afternoon. After saluting the brass, Chuck asks John for a moment of his time.

"What's up, Chuck?" John asks, as they hurry to the Operations tent, out of the rain and out of the colonels' earshot.

"I don't know any easy way to say this, John, so here it is. Mann tried to rape Lieutenant Braden. She's OK, nothing happened. Me and Major McNeilly put a stop to it."

John's face contorts into an expression of pain mixed with hatred. "I'm gonna kill that bastard."

"Not so fast, John. He's gone. Fifth Air Force whisked him out of here already."

"Why? Can't he be court-martialed right here?"

"Don't know nothing about that, John."

Chuck tells John how--two days ago in the early morning hours--he had followed Mann after seeing him skulking around the recon ramp, drunk and looking for trouble. Not finding John, Mann headed for the hospital. Chuck figured he was looking for Marge. Mann found her, too, walking back to her quarters alone. Major McNeilly had also seen him, summoned the MPs, and came running to help.

Then he lets John in on the secret to which only he and Kathleen McNeilly could bear witness. "I clubbed him with a pipe I found laying around. That knocked him out until the MPs got there and arrested him. He had punched her, but he never touched her down there. I could be in deep shit if they find out I hit an officer. Major McNeilly's swearing that she's the one swung that pipe. But you know how the brass can turn these things around."

Putting his hand on Chuck's shoulder, John says, "You won't be getting in any trouble, believe me. We're in debt to you for what you did, Chuck. Thank you...thank you very much."

"Anytime, Captain."

John finds Marge already at work at the hospital. Confronted by the ever-present Major McNeilly, he requests a minute of her nurse's time. She fetches Marge, telling her in a stage whisper loud enough for John to hear, "I'll give you five minutes to calm lover boy down, then I need you back in here."

Marge comes out, sporting the bruised chin that is still quite sore. She starts to explain, but John takes her in his arms and says, "I heard all about it. Are you sure you're OK?"

"I'm fine, baby. Nothing an ice pack won't fix."

"That son of a bitch is going to jail...if I don't kill him first."

She pulls away from his embrace. "Oh, John, stop it! Nothing is ever going to happen to him!"

"What do you mean? He attacked you!"

"Honey, you forget...my daddy is a lawyer. I've spent my whole life watching rich people protect themselves. They don't accumulate all that wealth so that they can be held *more* accountable for their actions. Nothing will happen to him...no court martial, no jail...absolutely nothing...no matter what you or I do. He'll tell the whole world something like *our meeting was consensual*, and *everybody* knows what sluts we nurses are, right? Let it go. Just be glad he's gone."

John is stunned by her attitude. "But that's not right, Marge!"

"Oh, Farm Boy, you've still got a lot to learn. But please, just let it go. For my sake."

That quiets him. But she can tell his need for revenge will not be extinguished quite so easily. She changes the subject.

"What happened in Manila, John?"

"Ahh, nothing big. We'll talk about it at breakfast. But you *will* have to start calling me 'Major.' "

"Oh, baby! That's great! I knew it would be something like that!" she says, jumping back into his arms. "OK, gotta go. I love you, Major!" After another quick kiss, she runs back into the hospital tent, back to work.

Later, at breakfast, a cheerful Marge asks, "So what else went on in Manila? Surely they didn't bring you there just to tell you you're going to be promoted, right?"

She doesn't like the look that comes across John's face as he sits, not speaking, not answering her question. It takes a moment before the awful realization strikes her.

"OH MY GOD!!! OH NO!!! What did you volunteer for this time? I knew there had to be a catch! Oh shit, John, not again!"

"Baby, it's OK. I won't be doing anything I don't already do every day."

"That's supposed to make me feel better? What is it? What do you have to do now? Fly to Tokyo and present the surrender papers yourself, maybe?"

No, baby, don't be silly. But I can't tell you. Believe me, you don't need to know… and I don't *want* you to know!"

"Not comforting, John! Not at all! I must really love you, Farm Boy, because here I am, about to be nauseous, and I'm not even sure why!"

Seeing the panicky look that comes over his face, she quickly adds, "No, you idiot! I'm not pregnant!"

Chapter Forty-Five

Marge Braden and Nancy Bergstrom are creating quite a stir on Kadena as they walk to the Officers' Mess dressed in their khaki uniform skirts and blouses, overseas caps perched on their heads, on their way to the promotion ceremony for John Worth and a few others. Officers and enlisted men in all directions stop dead in their tracks and watch the two nurses go by; they do not get to see actual female legs very often.

"We should have worn trousers," Marge says, looking worried.

"Nah, this is much more fun," Nancy replies, exaggerating the sway in her slender hips as she walks.

"Nancy! You are such a tramp!"

"Careful with the name-calling, sweetie. I'm not the only one who enjoys constant male company around here."

"True, but you've probably set an all-time record for the sheer number of males."

"Jealous, Margie?"

"Oh, shut up!" Marge says, playfully poking Nancy in the shoulder.

Nancy turns pensive. "You know, honey, if John was flying something with a trigger instead of a shutter, he would have been a full colonel a long time ago."

Marge ponders that for a moment, until her mind finishes Nancy's sentence...*or maybe dead a long time ago.* Then she becomes self-conscious once again from all the attention they are receiving. "I just hope we get there with our virtue still intact."

"Hell no, honey! Let's hope we don't," Nancy says as she blows a kiss to a group of admiring airmen.

The proceedings are quick and perfunctory. Colonel Harris says a few words about each of the officers being promoted: two second lieutenants to first, one first lieutenant to captain, and John, from captain to major. Details include their length of service, where they learned to fly, where they had been posted in their brief military careers. John has the longest combat career by far, and Harris appears overwhelmed by the details. The colonel gets so many of them wrong, his brief treatise on John's history becomes almost a parody, even referring to his aircraft's name as "*f for farmer.*" Maybe he means that to be a joke--but nobody laughs. The monologue has been painful enough to hear, as almost all assembled know far more of John's exploits than his commanding officer.

But everyone in attendance agrees with one of the colonel's points: John's record of time in combat is exceptional, surpassed by few mortal men, and deserving of high decoration.

Although such decoration will not be forthcoming, Marge thinks.

Before the speeches had started, Colonel Harris pulled John aside and, referring to the special mission to which he had been tasked, said quietly, "I hope this shows you how much faith the big brass have in you."

John nodded stoically, but in his mind nothing at all had changed: *Big deal...they're still just looking to cover their asses.*

Harris hands John his new insignia of rank, the

gold leaf. Marge, at John's request, steps forward to pin it to his collar. She cannot help but beam while doing it.

When done, she says, "Congratulations, Major Worth," and kisses him on the cheek.

A minute later, after a toast to all the promoted, John whispers in Marge's ear, "Damn, you look great!"

"OK, happy now? I wore a skirt. It's amazing we didn't get mauled just walking over here."

"Thank you, baby. I really mean that."

"Thank me better," Marge replies, leading him by the hand out of the mess tent.

Watching them leave, the knowing smile returns to Nancy's face once again. She turns to the flight surgeon standing next to her and asks, "Hey, Doc, buy a girl a drink?"

Chapter Forty-Six

November 1945

Colonel Ozawa and Major Watanabe look with satisfaction at their handiwork. The cave sheltering Professor Inaba's nuclear device and the railroad tracks leading to it are well concealed. This had been no small feat, considering the attention the area had received lately from American aircraft. They relax inside the cave and listen to the field wireless set, tuned to Radio Tokyo, waiting for a message.

Eastward across the Pacific, 30 troop ships and their escorts set sail from Pearl Harbor, carrying two "green" divisions, one Army, one Marine, to their invasion rendezvous point off the Marianas. More troop ships idle at the Marianas to embark the two veteran Marine divisions waiting there. On northern Luzon, still more ships await General Krueger's 6th Army.

Further east across the Pacific, at a naval shipyard in San Francisco Bay, Doctor Oppenheimer's atomic bomb is being loaded onto a US Navy warship for delivery to Tinian, the Marianas.

Further eastward still, in Washington, D.C., General Marshall informs President Truman that the war plan known as Operation Olympic, the invasion of southern Japan, has commenced. In addition, Marshall informs the President that their atomic bomb is being transported to an air base in the Marianas.

In the Imperial Palace, Tokyo, Prime Minister Suzuki stands at a window and looks despondently across the burned-out heart of Tokyo. Today, the Imperial War Council learned their once vaunted Kwangtung Army has been pushed out of Manchuria by the Russians, who have advanced into northern Korea. While the Russians still do not possess the capacity to attack across the Sea of Japan, the Japanese troops in East Asia are now totally cut off from the home islands, spelling an end to the Japanese domination of mainland Asia. The Emperor and the military leaders still refuse to consider surrender.

And the Americans will come very soon.

Major John Worth and his three-plane section had flown high-altitude missions almost constantly for the past week, using every hour of daylight, each plane scouting a different area of southern Kyushu, but they had not sighted or photographed the suspected device again. The other two pilots in John's section had not been told they were on a special mission from theater headquarters, although the repetitious sorties they have flown for the past week, covering nothing but rail routes, made them suspect the brass were looking for something specific.

As the Intelligence boys poured over the latest photos, eyes glued to the magnifiers perched above, Colonel Watkins thought to himself:

Did they get the damn thing off Kyushu? Why would they do that? Where would it go?

Admiral Nimitz had been wondering the same thing. He still harbored a fear the Japanese would try to use their bomb against a naval target, probably mounted on a suicide submarine. He had reaffirmed his order that the Navy's air recon units concentrate their

247

efforts against any vessels, especially submarines, found in the ports and waters around Kyushu. There had been little new maritime activity to report, however.

At MacArthur's headquarters, speculation of all sorts was rampant. Rumors had abounded of Kamikaze attacks planned against airfields and ports on Okinawa, the Philippines, and the Marianas, just like the September attack on Buckner Bay. Moreover, Intelligence had deduced that three Betty bombers, shot down over the sea recently by a Navy combat air patrol, had in fact been carrying suicide sappers for a sneak attack on a B-29 base in the Marianas. Apparently, their plan was to crash-land on an airfield amongst the parked American bombers and have each sapper blow up an aircraft and himself in the process. It was only luck that the Navy patrol had stumbled onto them. News of this prospect made the normally lax ground crews in the Marianas suddenly interested in carrying their weapons at all times. Even the flight crews started wearing their side arms when not flying.

At breakfast one morning, Marge says, "The invasion must be getting real close, baby. The hospital received its ready orders for the move to Kyushu last night, and you've been flying more than ever. Whatever it is they've got you doing, it must be terribly important. I can see how it's weighing on you. I wish you'd let me in. You know you can trust me, don't you? Maybe I can help you deal with it?"

"Marge, I can't. I've got orders from the big brass, and you've got enough on your mind already."

Yeah…like how to keep from going off my rocker after you get yourself killed.

As they walk from the mess tent to the hospital, Marge asks, "You're really not going to tell me, are you?"

"Like I said, baby, I can't. We *are* in the Army, you know. You do understand how these things work?"

"Don't be stupid. Of course I understand!" Tears begin to flow down Marge's cheeks. "I don't want to go to Japan...you know we'll get split up...I don't want to be without you...and I don't want to go home with just a memory of this wonderful dead guy I was in love with."

"Do you think *I* want any of those things? Honey, the only person I worry about more than me is *you*! But I've got to do my job."

They walk, saying nothing, as she resigns herself once more. It is Marge who finally breaks the silence. "Why won't this fucking war just end?"

At the wire fence surrounding the nurses' quarters, they kiss goodbye, and John once again promises, "I'll be back."

And Marge once again answers, "You'd better, Farm Boy. I mean it."

Today's mission does not start well. During the pre-dawn takeoff, First Lieutenant Lawrence "Rowdy" Chambers, of Lubbock, Texas, flying Number 36, strikes something with his nose gear, probably a wandering dog desperate for something to eat. He gets airborne and the gear seems to retract normally, but the rushing air noise that develops indicates the nose gear door is not properly closed. As airspeed increases, a vibration begins as well. Rowdy is a good flyer but does not have much time in the F-5. He doesn't want to abort his mission, though; he doesn't know what he is supposed to be looking for, but he is determined to find it.

Over the radio, John asks Rowdy to watch his fuel consumption. John maneuvers *f-stop* below and to the right of Rowdy's plane, but it is too dark to determine the condition of the nose gear door. The extra drag of an unfaired door might cause increased burn and fuel exhaustion before the planned end of the mission. When the sun comes up in about an hour, he would be able to make a better assessment.

Fifteen minutes after takeoff, the other pilot in John's section, Captain Paul "Frenchy" Laroix, of Montpelier, Vermont, flying Number 42, announces he must abort due to electrical problems. He has to use his flashlight to read the instruments still functioning: altimeter, airspeed indicator, compass, and artificial horizon. They require electricity only for background lighting; he needs to conserve the remaining battery power for propeller control. He should have just enough juice to get back to Kadena, although he will be landing in the dark, without lights. The entire scope of this mission will now fall to John and Rowdy, assuming Rowdy's aircraft can continue.

When the sun rises, John instructs Rowdy to maintain altitude while he slides *f-stop* beneath Number 36 to observe the troublesome nose gear door.

"OK, Rowdy, the leading edge of the door's bent a little...sticking into the airstream. The bottom edge looks rumpled, too. Shouldn't be any trouble extending for landing, though. How's your fuel consumption look?"

Chambers replies in his booming Texas voice, "It looks OK, boss, but my legs are getting a little numb from the vibration. I'll be fine, though. Do you think the vibration will mess up the cameras?" Rowdy normally speaks so loudly you would not think he would need the radio to communicate in flight.

"Maybe," John replies, "but they are shock mounted. They can probably handle it. If you've got enough gas, you can always slow down and try extending the gear for critical shots...that may eliminate the vibes. Hold still...I'm coming up on your right now."

"Roger, boss!"

As the two planes pass between Yaku-shima and Tane-ga-shima, John splits up the area Frenchy would have covered, giving half to Rowdy and revising his own flight plan to include the remaining half. Rowdy's fuel consumption looks acceptable; they should both have enough gas for the extra flying with no problem. A few minutes later, they separate to begin their respective camera runs.

John would fly the southeastern section of Kyushu, Rowdy would take the southwest. Their coverage will overlap the central area, from the head of Kagoshima Bay to Miyakanojo. Rowdy will fly over it at the beginning of his run; John's run will end there. This is the most suspect area, the last area the device had been seen. It needed all the coverage they could manage; by now, the recon pilots knew that ground intimately.

US Army and Navy aircraft are busy all over Kyushu. Emphasis in these final days before the invasion has returned to neutralizing the Japanese airfields: over 30 on southern Kyushu alone have been identified and hit repeatedly by bombers and fighters of both services. The number of aircraft on these fields does not seem to diminish, however. It is presumed that aircraft continue to be flown from the northern home islands under cover of darkness as the Japanese prepare for a last ditch effort to defeat the invasion forces, sacrificing the defenses of the other home islands to protect Kyushu from the imminent threat. Admiral Spruance's battleships and cruisers sit off the eastern coast at night, doing their part to pummel the airfields within range of their heavy guns, but yet the Japanese air arms still persist in great numbers.

Rowdy has gotten used to the vibration from the damaged nose gear door, regularly stamping his feet to alleviate the numbness it causes in his feet, ankles, and knees. The ground fire he receives seems heavier than usual, but he figures the Japs know the invasion is imminent and have heightened their defenses. His plane receives no hits, though. He prays the vibrations are not ruining his photos.

Near Sendai, as Rowdy approaches the western edge of his search area, the sky is full of broken cloud layers. He descends to get below the clouds and suddenly finds himself in a swarm of fighters, some Japanese, some US Navy.

"Wrong place, wrong time!" Rowdy's West Texas twang booms to no one in particular.

The other aircraft seem so close that his biggest worry is not bullets but collisions. Most of those planes are going in the opposite direction, appearing as little more than blue, green, or brown blurs as they whiz past. He figures the blue blurs are US Navy; the others must be Japanese. There is so much chatter on the radio it is impossible to make sense of it.

Suddenly, Rowdy seems alone again in the sky. It has all happened so fast; he has not had time to get nervous or frightened. He flies on for another moment, trying to salvage his photo run while scanning the empty sky around him.

He is alone for only a brief moment. There is a plane on his tail: a big, round engine with straight wings. Just like a Jap Oscar fighter.

Shit! That son of a bitch is right up my ass! Where the hell did he come from?

To escape, Rowdy needs speed; the only way to get that is to point the nose down and dive. He does so while releasing his empty drop tanks. As his speed picks up, the vibration becomes intense, then violent.

Hang on, girl! Don't shake yourself apart!

His next glance behind reveals there are now two aircraft chasing him, both with the same forward silhouette.

Damn! When it rains, it pours!

It is a small comfort that he is putting distance between himself and the two aircraft on his tail. Then, with a brief groan of rending metal, the vibration stops, replaced by a howling noise so loud he can hardly hear the drone of his engines.

Well, I might go deaf but at least I won't get shot down or bust apart right now!

The camera run all but abandoned in his fight for survival, Rowdy continues the high- speed descent, heading to the southwest. He is now beyond the coastline and can see the small islands of Koshikijima-Retto in the distance. As he scans behind him for probably the thousandth time in the past minute, he sees his pursuers--now far behind--give up the chase and roll into chandelles, rapidly reversing direction and climbing. Rowdy watches in amazement as the square-tipped blue wings--sporting white star and bars insignia--of US Navy Hellcat fighters are silhouetted against the sky.

Dammit! I'm running away from my own guys! Fucking Hellcats look just like Japs from the front! I like Corsairs better!

A Corsair's inverted gull wings made it very easy to distinguish, even at a quick glance.

The perplexed lead Hellcat pilot was just trying to be helpful. He had clearly identified Rowdy's plane as an unarmed F-5, not a gun-toting P-38, and was going to offer his services and those of his wingman as armed escorts. The Navy pilot had tried calling through the dense traffic on the common frequency but got no reply.

All the Hellcat pilot can think is *that stupid Army flyboy must have shit his pants in a panic.*

Rowdy regains his composure and flies back onshore; he will try to finish his camera run on the western side of Kagoshima Bay. As he slows the aircraft, the howling noise diminishes but never stops. He is sure the high-speed dive has caused the protruding nose gear door to rip right off. Now, instead of the door vibrating, he has to listen to the roar of air rushing through the open hole that is the nose wheel well.

The incessant radio chatter has finally died down. The skies that had been crowded with aircraft swirling in dogfights are now completely empty. Only a few wispy smoke trails mark the death plunges of the losers; even those oily black plumes are rapidly diminishing, blown to bits by the winds aloft. Rowdy transmits a call to John Worth, who replies immediately and reports his position about 10 miles behind at the northeast corner of Kagoshima Bay, heading south. His mission has gone somewhat less eventfully than Rowdy's, with only sporadic, ineffective ground fire; no aerial encounters with friend or foe and no aircraft malfunctions. The loss of the nose gear door has forced Rowdy to maintain the reduced speed, keeping the noise down. John is able to catch up 15 minutes later over the sea south of Kyushu. John slows *f-stop* to keep pace with Rowdy as both planes head home to Kadena.

Cruising at 10,000 feet, they get to view plenty of action above and below. Every aircraft they see is American, with the exception of a small flight of Japanese fighters below being mauled by P-38's over the island of Naka-no-shima. The P-38's are using their speed, diving from above, firing a burst, and then rapidly climbing away untouched. Nimitz's warships, too numerous to count, prowl the sea to the east of the Ryukyu's. A steady stream of 5th Air Force bombers lumber above the photo planes, heading north to continue the pre-invasion pummeling of Kyushu's airfields and harbors.

Over Okinawa, as they enter the downwind leg for landing at an altitude of 1000 feet, Rowdy tries to lower his landing gear. The nose gear will not extend.

"Hey, boss! My nose gear says it ain't down!" Rowdy bellows into his radio.

"OK, keep her level. I'll slide underneath and have a look."

Once below Rowdy's aircraft, John says, "Yeah, the gear's still stuck in the hole. Looks like a piece of the door got pushed up inside and got it jammed. The rest of the door is gone, though. Let me get out from under you…then you try a little dive with a quick pull out…see if the centrifugal force can break it loose."

With the two F-5's still stacked like pancakes, Rowdy screams into his radio:

"BIRDS! I'LL GO UP YOU GO DOWN!"

Rowdy's sudden climb does nothing to dislodge his nose gear, but it gets him clear of the oncoming flock of large seabirds. John is not so lucky. As he dives, it sounds and feels like a hundred birds impact *f-stop* in a very brief moment…and then it is over. John levels off at 650 feet and looks over his airplane. On the leading edge of the left wing, just outboard of the propeller arc, a jagged, V-shaped notch--oozing bird guts and feathers--has been carved several feet deep. John fears it has penetrated all the way to the wing's main spar. There is a loud buzz and some vibration from the left engine. The usual smooth, blurred disk of the spinning propeller now has an irregular appearance at the outer edge. Looking aft, the leading edge of the right vertical stabilizer sports a gouge and bird remains. The radio antenna, a "V" of wire stretching outward from the rear of the cockpit canopy to the tops of both vertical stabilizers, has snapped at the attach point to the right stabilizer and is now flapping straight back, slapping the horizontal stabilizer and elevator.

John throttles up the good right engine, leaving the left engine with the damaged propeller at idle, adjusts the rudder trim to compensate for the asymmetrical thrust, and continues preparations for landing. The damaged wing spar could be a deadly game- ender; the worst case scenario is the wing folds up and the plane goes spinning down.

Got to get you on the ground nice and gentle, ol' girl.

Rowdy is still struggling with his nose gear. He tries the dive trick to dislodge it but to no avail. The stuck gear continues to defy hydraulics, gravity, and prayer.

"Boss, I don't have a whole lot of gas to play around with."

"OK, Rowdy, do you want to land without the nose gear or bail out?

"What would you do, boss?"

"I'd bring her in."

"OK, that's what I'll do. Got any tips?"

"Yeah, Rowdy, try this...as soon as you get the

main gears on the ground, hold the nose off just like you always would, but kill the engines right away. The nose will settle pretty quickly after that. You'll still ruin the props, but the engines themselves stand a better chance of not being damaged when the props hit. You won't need the brakes to stop with the nose dragging the ground, so lay off them...there's less chance of ground-looping that way. Just get out fast after she stops just in case something on an engine does break loose and causes a fire."

After they both circle one more time to allow traffic to clear, Rowdy nervously begins final approach. *This will be a great story to tell the grandkids,* he tell himself, *if I live long enough to have kids in the first place.*

Rowdy knows why Major Worth had posed the bailout option. A lot could go wrong landing without the nose gear. Done indelicately, the nose could strike the ground hard enough to cause structural degradation and crush the pilot's legs. There is also the possibility of the nose digging in and the plane flipping end over end, coming to rest upside down with the pilot's head crushed. Landing with all the gear retracted is a direct ticket to the scrap heap and a chance for the pilot to die in a fire. Even if the plane is not that badly damaged, the bulldozer that would clear her expeditiously from the busy runway will finish her off.

He pushed those dire possibilities from his mind. *Dammit, these birds ain't exactly throw-aways. I'm supposed to be able to bring me and her back even when we're banged up and that's just what I'm fixing to do.*

His legs, no longer numb but now shaking badly, are having a rough time working the rudder pedals, but he manages to get the plane aligned with the runway.

The airspeed over the runway threshold is a bit high. As Rowdy flares her for touchdown, she begins a float that seems to go on forever as the speed slowly bleeds off. Fearing he is going to use up the entire length of the runway without actually touching the ground, Rowdy jumps ahead in the instructions John had given him and shuts the engines down while the plane is still a few feet off the ground.

A rapid deceleration results and the aircraft loses lift instantly. The impact of the main gear wheels with the runway is exceedingly firm. The left gear tire blows out immediately and before Rowdy can even think about holding the nose off, it strikes the ground violently. Clouds of sparks and dust fly from the Marsden Mat runway surface as the airplane slews off the runway and quickly comes to rest in the scrub. Rowdy, shaken but uninjured, has some trouble getting out of the cockpit but is assisted by the crash crew, who arrive moments after the plane comes to rest. There is no fire.

The control tower asks John to land on the same runway Rowdy has just barely managed to clear. They again have a backlog of traffic and need to use both runways simultaneously. John replies, "Affirmative," and sets his wounded machine down smoothly.

During the landing rollout, John notices something strange--he cannot move the control column forward. Glancing back at the tail, he sees the reason why. The antenna wire that had separated from the right vertical stabilizer is now wrapped around the upper counterbalance of the elevator. The counterbalances are small, football-shaped devices that protrude from the upper and lower elevator surfaces, between the vertical tails, at mid-span. Right now, snagged by the antenna wire, the counterbalance acts as an effective lock on the downward deflection of the elevator.

John blows a whistle of relief. He had never noticed any control problems because all this happened during low-speed flight. There is rarely any call during a normal approach and landing to use "down" elevator as the nose tends to drop at low speeds and low power settings. Most elevator input during landing is always in the "up" direction and the snagged antenna did not prevent this motion. Had this happened at high speed--perhaps while being pursued--this would have been a deadly problem.

As Corporal Petrillo guides *f-stop* into her parking spot, John can already see the agitation in Chuck Jaworski's facial expression and body language.

"JUST WHAT THE HELL DID YOU DO TO MY AIRPLANE NOW?" Jaworski says in mock reproach as he opens the cockpit canopy.

"Fucking birds, Sarge...fucking birds!" is John's exasperated reply.

At the debrief, the photos from this mission show no evidence of the nuclear device.

Rowdy's cameras are amazingly undamaged from the landing, but some of the photos are blurred and useless, no doubt the result of the inflight vibration.

The overall mission results are considered "satisfactory" by the Intelligence staff.

Chapter Forty-Seven

Colonel Ozawa anxiously thumbed the piece of paper in his hand for what must have been the hundredth time. Written on it were the words the Imperial High Command would broadcast over Radio Tokyo to authorize the deployment of the nuclear device. It would be delivered as a simple code, very much like the one used almost four years ago to signal the Pearl Harbor task force to execute its attack on the United States. Like that code, Ozawa's was made to sound like a weather report. The Pearl Harbor message had been the words *east wind rain*.

Colonel Ozawa listened to the wireless, awaiting the message printed on the paper in his hand, a voice that would say *east wind returns*.

The first Japanese sighting of the invasion fleet was on the morning of 4 November by the crew of a naval reconnaissance aircraft out of Formosa. They spotted the large fleet of warships and troop transports carrying the 6th Army's eight divisions between the Philippines and Okinawa, heading north to Kyushu. The Japanese aircraft was quickly shot down by US Navy fighters, but not before transmitting its message of warning.

Later that same day a Japanese submarine 450 miles southwest of Kyushu encountered the fleet of warships and transports carrying the three Marine divisions from the Marianas. It, too, got off its message before submerging and fleeing the depth charges sent its way. It lurked alone for another day, trying to penetrate the fleet's destroyer screen, finally succumbing to bombs from carrier-based aircraft when caught on the surface in daylight.

Combined, the two American fleets totaled over 3000 vessels. This included warships of all types, troop transports, and landing ships for tanks and vehicles. It did not count the myriad small landing craft the troop transports carried.

As Admiral Nimitz had supposed, the Japanese had their two to three day warning.

For the next two days, the sky above Kyushu was filled day and night with bombers of the 5th and 20th Air Forces, striking airfields and ports all over the large island. Population centers near the invasion sites were struck, as well, since large troop concentrations were suspected to be concealed there. During the day missions, Army fighters provided escort coverage for the bombers and strafed ground targets. The American bombers and fighters met heavy anti-aircraft fire but few opposing aircraft. Their losses were light. Over 1000 Japanese ground troops died in the bombings. Several thousand more were wounded and unable to fight. American estimates of Japanese aircraft destroyed on the ground were very high, if not purely speculative.

During the nights of 4 and 5 November, several hundred Kamikaze, each carrying a large high-explosive bomb, would fly off in search of the invasion fleets without fear of challenge from US Navy fighters, hoping to locate the blacked-out ships in the moonlight and destroy them. Many planes never found the ships, their woefully inexperienced pilots flying about blindly in the dark until they ran out of fuel and fell into the sea. Those that did find the ships had great difficulty executing their attacks against the moving targets in the darkness. It was not uncommon for a suicide plane to sight the luminous wake of a ship and dive on it, only to impact the sea adjacent to the target vessel. The Americans blindly put up volumes of anti-aircraft fire in fixed, predetermined patterns; the ships' losses were very light, almost negligible. Over 800 suicide aircraft and their pilots were expended before the invasion fleet was within sight of Kyushu, with no impact to the fleet's relentless progress. None of these aircraft had carried enough fuel for a round trip.

The morning of 6 November, over 1000 Kamikaze aircraft rose--for the first time in daylight--to fly against the invasion fleet, now less than 120 miles from Kyushu. US Army and Navy fighters were there to meet them before they even left the ground. The suicide planes, often decrepit, barely flyable, and with novice pilots at the controls, were easy pickings. They fell by the hundreds, both over their home island and en route to the American ships, but they had risen in such numbers that almost 400 managed to appear over the invasion fleet, to be further challenged by intense shipboard anti-aircraft fire. As in earlier Kamikaze attacks at the Philippines and Okinawa, the outer defensive ring of the fleet took the brunt of the attack. Of the 28 vessels actually struck by suicide aircraft that morning, 17 were destroyers on the outer ring. A total of eight vessels were sunk, with 34 sailors dead and 115 injured. Army and Marine casualties on the transports totaled 18 dead, 67 injured.

In the pre-dawn darkness of 7 November--"X" day plus zero, or simply X+0--Admiral Spruance's warships began the largest naval bombardment in history on the southern shores of Kyushu. Two thousand guns rained tens of thousands of shells on Miyazaki, Ariake Bay, and Kushikino, hammering the beaches and heights beyond. Landing ships modified to carry multiple rocket launchers instead of cargo lobbed thousands of 5-inch rockets into the landing zones.

When the naval bombardment ended two hours later, the landing ships and smaller landing craft full of invasion troops were already making their way to the beaches. Navy carrier aircraft swooped down to provide air support on demand. They were the first to see Japanese soldiers scurrying from caves and bunkers to their crude defensive positions after the naval bombardment had ended. Lacking overhead cover, these inexperienced troops fell to the guns and bombs of the Navy planes in large numbers. Several thousand were out of action before the first landing craft hit the beach.

The Kamikaze onslaught to the invasion fleet continued the morning of 7 November. There were approximately 1000 suicide aircraft and pilots left. While reports flowed to headquarters that "hundreds" of troop transports had been sunk and most of the invaders drowned, the commanders of the Kamikaze units knew better. As they had seen in past campaigns, their inexperienced pilots, under the extreme stress of combat and imminent death, tried to attack the first ship they saw, which was usually a small warship on the outer edge of the fleet. Few were able to discern the difference between a transport, destroyer, or light cruiser from high altitude. Heavy cruisers and battleships were almost impossible to differentiate. Only aircraft carriers were obvious, and they were the most well-protected vessels of all, sitting in the middle of multiple defensive rings. Hundreds of suicide planes had tried to attack carriers at Leyte and Okinawa; only a handful succeeded. The battle for Kyushu was to be no different. By nightfall on 7 November, less than 200 suicide aircraft and pilots had not yet flown; some of them would never fly due to lack of fuel. The almost 3000 who had gone before them in the last three days had managed to knock out of action only 5 percent of the invasion fleet, less than half of that number being troop transports. The American planes hovering over their airfields in great numbers had made all the difference; this was one advantage the Americans had lacked in the earlier Kamikaze campaigns at the Philippines and Okinawa.

The Japanese generals had been proven correct in their assessment that the American invasion forces would successfully storm the beaches. The Army divisions poured ashore at Miyazaki and Ariake Bay, the Marines at Kushikino. The fighting was intense and close-in. The Japanese generals were also correct when they said a beach defense would mitigate the broad American advantage in air and sea firepower. Nearly every yard gained by the invaders was the result of successful tactics at the company, platoon, and squad level. Wherever the invaders failed to make progress, it was due to the collapse of leadership and discipline at the same small unit levels.

The greatest progress was made by the Army at Miyazaki and the Marines at Kushikino. They met their objectives and by mid-afternoon had secured beachheads over a kilometer deep, despite intense opposition. Landing ships were then able to put ashore large numbers of tanks and artillery, further solidifying and expanding their gains. They did well for units comprised to a large degree of green troops. They maintained proper combat formations, used fire and maneuver effectively, and managed to prevail against the desperate efforts of the equally green Japanese defenders.

The Army forces at Ariake Bay, however, bogged down almost immediately. Navigation errors by several landing craft elements resulted in the jumbled and confused arrival of the 1st Cavalry and 43rd Infantry Divisions. Command and control quickly broke down while units tried to figure out where they were and how to get to where they were supposed to be while under murderous fire. Numerous companies just hunkered down on the beach, to be devastated by Japanese mortars and artillery. Only the ad hoc adjustments of the corps commander, stalking the beach in his jeep like a man convinced of his immunity to enemy fire, restored some sort of order to the debacle. By mid- afternoon, they had suffered heavy casualties, secured just a few hundred yards, and had landed little in the way of tanks and artillery. Only fire support from Navy aircraft kept them from being driven back into the sea. The Navy pilots had been effective and not confused as to the whereabouts of the *friendlies*, as they held only a thin ribbon at the shoreline. General Krueger was not able to bring his headquarters ashore that first day, further complicating communications between the three beachheads. The link-up between these beachhead elements, planned for 9 November, or X+2, was already in jeopardy.

Colonel Ozawa, waiting with the nuclear device in the cave, received no deployment order from Radio Tokyo. After hearing General Takarabe's report of the American failure at Ariake Bay, the Imperial War Council decided it was not yet time to use the nuclear device.

General MacArthur was not pleased with General Krueger once again. The poor performance at Ariake Bay was all too reminiscent of his sluggish start in the Philippine campaign. In a strongly worded communiqué, he urged Krueger to immediately deploy his reserves at Ariake and save that operation from collapsing. Krueger had kept his two reserve divisions on board ships southeast of Kyushu. He had expected to deploy at least part of his reserve to support the peripheral operations by elements of the 40th Infantry Division on the islands of Yaku-shima, Tane-ga-shima, and Koshiki Retto, but this had proved not to be necessary; those small garrisons fell easily. Furious planning began to facilitate the reserve divisions' landing at Ariake Bay on 8 November, at midday.

American aircraft were now the only ones in the sky above Kyushu. Their only opposition was the usual ground fire.

John Worth and his three-plane section flew as they had done every day for the past two weeks. Flying at medium to high levels to stay clear of the fray below, they had yet to sight or photograph the beer barrel shape of the suspected Japanese nuclear device.

One thought dominated John's mind: *Marge will land on Kyushu in two days...I've got to find this goddamn thing!*

Chapter Forty-Eight

MacArthur's headquarters had just transmitted its glowing report of Operation Olympic's initial "success" to Washington. The report made no specific mention of the dire situation at Ariake Bay, only that the reserves were to be employed there on X+1 to exploit certain *opportunities.*

Nimitz's report to Washington was unremarkable, saying only that the amphibious phase of Olympic had gone according to plan.

On Kyushu, the Japanese generals were not at all upset by the events of 7 November. Takarabe was, in fact, surprised and delighted with his force's success at Ariake Bay. The Americans there seemed so disorganized, so ineffective; he had hopes the Ketsu-Go plan might, in fact, succeed by dominating at Ariake, thereby splitting the invasion forces and laying the groundwork for their piecemeal destruction. He was sure, however, that MacArthur would not give up easily; more forces must be on the way to shore up the failing effort at Ariake.

Takarabe got his answer the mid-morning of 8 November--X+1--when the ships bringing Krueger's reserves appeared off Ariake Bay. The landings began as scheduled at midday, after a naval gun barrage that concentrated its firepower well beyond the small beachhead. The barrage was surprisingly effective, catching thousands of Japanese soldiers without overhead cover. These landings were made with far less confusion that those of X+0 and were far more effective. The depth of the beachhead doubled in just two hours, and by nightfall, it was almost a kilometer. American casualties were far lighter this day. While the Japanese continued to fight savagely, they employed generally poor tactics, usually remaining frozen in fixed positions as the invaders maneuvered, enveloped, and destroyed the inexperienced defenders in droves.

That evening, General Takarabe estimated in his report to the Imperial High Command that four to five divisions were now ashore at Ariake and gaining ground. He was doubtful his troops could prevail without immediate reinforcement. Reading Takarabe's report, the War Council could not believe their good fortune: the nuclear device could now wipe out almost twice the number of invaders than originally planned. The Council decided that 9 November--X+2--would be the day to employ the device.

In the early morning darkness of 9 November, Tokyo Radio broadcasts a weather report containing the words *east wind returns*.

Major Watanabe, who is monitoring the radio receiver in the cave, immediately wakes Colonel Ozawa with the news. Rousing the sleeping men of their section, they begin the preparations to deploy the nuclear device.

Their plan is simple: release the flatcar's brakes and let it roll down the gentle incline from the cave to the coastal plain, a distance of just over 2 kilometers. Ideally, they will stop the flatcar on a section of track 1.5 kilometers from the beach, within the device's optimum blast radius. At this location they will be flanked by thick woods on both sides. If they cannot complete their movement and preparations for detonation in the dark of night, by day the woods will make the device's detection from the air very difficult and impossible from the ground at the American beachhead.

In actuality, the plan proves anything but simple. Clearing the camouflage from the rail spur takes almost twice as long as planned and previously undetected track damage is found at the junction with the mainline track. Watanabe is prepared for such problems; the damaged section of track is quickly replaced and the brakes on the flatcar released once again. They progress only 200 meters before coming upon a section of track damaged by the latest naval barrage. This, too, is repaired, but it consumes precious time. The sun is rising. The device is still over 2.5 kilometers from the beachhead. It must be moved closer.

The sunrise coincides once again with the arrival of the American planes. *f-stop* is among them, and her pilot has never been a man more possessed. John's quest to find the elusive device will now be conducted at low altitude. He feels he has no other option, whatever the added hazards. No other recon technique has succeeded so far, and he desperately needs success. Even though his superiors have repeatedly expressed the hope that the beer barrel has already been destroyed by bombing or shelling, John has his doubts: *Who can count on that?*

The decision to fly at low level made it necessary to describe the object of their search to the other two pilots in the section. But John still could not tell them its suspected nature. Their orders state that if they spot it, they are to call for Tac Air immediately to destroy it, whether they have photographed it or not. At the briefing, Frenchy Laroix seemed unimpressed, silently puffing his pipe as he shuffled through John's old photos of the beer barrel. Rowdy Chambers took it all in with his usual humor, plus a healthy dose of skepticism. "Must be some real special kind of beer," he said. "Can't wait to taste it."

John covers the Ariake beachhead area. At 300 feet, *f-stop* is drawing some belated ground fire but none of it has hit the F-5 due to her high speed: the Japs on the ground just don't hear her coming.

John is banking left and right to get a better view of the ground immediately below for himself and the oblique cameras. On his second pass he sees it, unmistakable, rolling on its own on an open stretch of track leading to the beachhead. He pulls up sharply and turns hard left for another look while he calls for Tac Air. A Navy fighter section, Corsairs led by Lieutenant Bob Kelly, respond and are over the target in moments, attacking with bombs, rockets, and .50 caliber machine guns.

When the Corsairs are finished, the beer barrel is still there, seemingly undamaged. On his next pass, John can see a few people scurrying about the barrel and its flatcar, which is now stationary and still in the open. It does not appear to be neutralized.

John's mind is crystal clear. He embraces the cataclysmic importance of this moment.

I'm going to take this thing out...or die trying.

He calls for another air attack against his target, trying not to sound frantic as he begins his transmission with his call sign, "Focus 4-7."

He is horrified at the next response: a Navy fighter unit, different from the one John had just directed, is reporting the target destroyed!

"Focus 4-7, this is Blue Papa 6-1...we took it out already...we're done."

John sees what Blue Papa 6-1 is describing a short distance to the south. They had, in fact, attacked and destroyed a few rail cars--the wrong rail cars.

"Papa 6-1, this is Focus 4-7...that's the wrong target! Wrong coordinates! I need another strike now to the north of your position."

"Sorry, Focus...we're taking some fire here...we did our bit, we're heading home. Your target's destroyed."

Bob Kelly tries to intercede. "Papa 6-1, this is King 6-6...that's the wrong train. We've got another one about a mile or two north of your position."

"King 6-6...this is Papa 6-1. No can do, sir. It's just a damn train...we're done...OUT."

Despite John Worth's entreaties, no other Tac Air unit--Army or Navy--will respond for another strike at the beer barrel. They had all heard the radio conversations; they had just written it off as another case of the "fog of war."

No point getting yourself killed for somebody else's confusion...and they're only talking about a damn train, not some crucial target!

In desperation, John considers broadcasting what the device is and why it needs to be destroyed immediately, but who would believe him? They would have no idea what he was talking about and he simply could not disobey the order to keep it secret, no matter how little he thought of the wisdom and motivations of the high command at this moment.

But he cannot give up and run away.

Colonel Ozawa has only two men left, both wounded but not incapacitated. Watanabe and the others have been killed in Kelly's air attack. The nuclear device appears indestructible, if dented, from bullets and bomb fragments. They have trouble, however, finding the detonator equipment amidst the debris of the attack. When they finally locate all of it, the generator's plunger is damaged, but Ozawa is sure he can get it to work anyway. The wheels of the flatcar are miraculously still on the tracks, which have received some damage but look able to fulfill their purpose at least one more time. The Colonel turns the hand wheel that releases the brakes and the flatcar slowly resumes its downhill journey to the wooded hide.

John continues to orbit above, following Ozawa's progress. With their last few rounds, Bob Kelly and his section try one more strafing run to no apparent effect when viewed from John's perspective.

Ozawa has a decidedly different view of this last strafing. While it is true the Corsair's bullets did not harm the device, only denting the thick iron casing still more, they manage to kill his last two men, and fragments wound him in the left arm and leg. He is in great pain but not incapacitated. So close to his destiny, these wounds will not stop him.

All this action draws the aircraft closer to the American front line. To the frightened, green US troops manning an anti-aircraft section, it appears a twin-engined plane, possibly a Japanese Nakajima "Irving," having been pursued by some gull-winged US Navy Corsairs, is now heading their way at low altitude. John Worth's F-5, presenting only a thin forward silhouette as she approaches them, proves not as recognizable as the Corsairs. Even when she turns and flies north across their field of vision, showing a side view, the morning sun reflects brightly off the unpainted aluminum, obscuring the twin boom configuration and US markings. The terror of first combat overrides any doubt they may have of the aircraft's identity. They open up on her with their .50 caliber guns.

John feels the thump of a round's impact, then many more thumps a split second later, like the sound of dumping a basket of apples on a table. *f-stop's* right engine immediately gives signs of being mortally wounded; it vibrates badly as it trails oily smoke and glycol vapor. He tries to check the engine instruments but the cockpit has become a shambles. It is filling with electrical smoke. Instruments and switches on the right side of the forward panel are a tangle of severed wires and torn, jagged metal. His right arm hurts and bleeds. His face is cut, too. He suspects the rounds that hit him have come from the American lines. More little red balls--tracer rounds--come streaming past *f-stop's* nose, right to left--*friendly fire*. A few more thumps: the left engine starts to lose power, too. John knows he cannot keep her in the air much longer. He is too low to bail out.

The American gunners realize their collective mistake as the target turns left again, away from them, and completes a half-circle, trailing smoke. They still can't make out the national markings, but the P-38 shape is now unmistakable. The gunners look at each other, dumbfounded. A new, sickening despair replaces their whoops of triumph. They have killed one of their own. After a few moments, though, the denial mechanism of self-defense kicks in: *they* had fired at an *enemy* airplane; the *Japs* brought down the P-38.

John might have been dealt a bad hand, but he is far from dead. He knows an airstrip just to the south of Ariake Bay is in American hands; he had seen a few spotter planes already there, slow and vulnerable

Stinson L-5's that had island-hopped up the Ryukyu's from Okinawa. It is a little over 5 miles away; he points *f-stop* toward it. He hopes he can keep her in the air long enough to make an emergency landing at the airstrip--or at least crash-land within the American beachhead.

He keeps the dying right engine running, hoping it might deliver just enough thrust to get to the airstrip. But it seizes about halfway there. The left engine is still struggling on, though laboring and smoking badly. The engine gauges are among those shot away; he adjusts the engine power by the seat of his pants.

About a half mile out, he extends the landing gear and is relieved to get all three *down and locked* indications. John feels certain that *f-stop* is in the final moments of her flying life. She is too badly damaged to repair, *uneconomical* in logistics terminology. He would try to make this last, crippled landing as kind to her as possible.

She touches down gently on the airstrip's crude dirt runway, but John can feel immediately the right main gear tire is gone, destroyed by the friendly fire. Riding on just the steel wheel rim, the rollout is violently rough, the deceleration rapid as she slews to the right. In a great cloud of dust, *f-stop* comes to rest clear of the runway; her first landing on Japanese home island soil, her last landing ever.

Rapidly gathering his maps and charts, John propels himself from her cockpit as American soldiers approach to help. She is still smoking; he needs to get some distance in case she bursts into flame. But after he slides off the wing to the ground, he stops for a brief moment and hugs *f-stop's* tall nose gear. Softly, he says, "Thanks, old girl."

Gingerly, he peels off his bloody flight jacket to

get a better look at his wounds. *Great...a third Purple Heart...Marge will be so thrilled.* He pats his breast pocket, which now holds her miraculously undamaged photo, salvaged from the instrument panel.

An American captain appears before him and asks, "Are you Major John Worth, sir?"

"Yes, I am."

"General Krueger needs to see you immediately, sir."

While hurrying to Krueger's command post across the open ground pockmarked by pre-invasion bombing and shelling, John notices several steam locomotives and numerous freight cars on nearby tracks. *There're trains all over this damn island,* he thinks.

At the command post tent, a medic inspects John's wounds and finds them superficial. He applies antibiotics and bandages, then quickly departs. His services are in greater demand elsewhere.

Mark Colton enters the tent with General Krueger's Intelligence and Operations Officers. John is surprised to see the Navy physicist again, so far from the comforts of MacArthur's Manila headquarters.

"Didn't recognize you in working man's clothes, Mark."

"Swell to see you, too, John. Sounds like you found the damned thing. We heard the radio chatter, figured it was you. Don't worry, they know all about the beer barrel," Colton says, nodding to the other officers present.

"Yeah, I found it again...about 5 miles from here, just a little beyond our lines," John says, unfurling his map.

"We need to get Tac Air back on it and..." the Operations Officer begins, but John cuts him off.

"We probably don't have any time, sir. It's pretty well hidden from the air now, in a thick grove near here," John says, pointing to a spot on the map. "Navy Tac Air hit it twice, but it still looks alive. I saw some personnel with it, too."

"And what makes you so sure it's not already neutralized?" This question comes from General Krueger as he strides into the tent.

"At ease, gentlemen," the General commands as all present brace to attention.

John figures the General's question has been put to him, so he replies, "It was all water off a duck's back, sir. Doesn't look like we hurt it a bit. Probably needs a direct hit with a 500 pounder or better."

The General seems unimpressed. "I wasn't expecting to see you again in person, Major Worth. Are you hurt badly?"

"No, sir, I'm OK, but with all due respect, there's no time to organize another air strike. There are no eyes on the target now. Some Navy pilots tried to help, but they're gone, too. It'll be hit and miss just trying to find it again...there are rail cars scattered all over this goddamn place. Even artillery or shipboard guns would have only a small chance without someone in the air directing the fire."

"Tell me something I *don't* know, Major. Do you have a better plan?"

Pointing to the spot on his map, John asks, "Can't our ground troops just push up to there quickly, sir? It's not far from our lines. Isn't that what they're supposed to be doing, anyway?"

"No," Krueger says. "I don't need the Air Force's advice on tactics. The units on that part of the line are already worn out...finished...ineffective. I'm moving in replacements in the morning."

"By morning, we'll probably all be just hot dust, sir," Mark Colton says, his voice shaky, trying but failing to keep his fear down.

"Of course, Commander! I forgot your reason for being here for a moment. You still expect me to believe the Japs have such an unbelievable weapon?" the General asks.

"Yes, sir, I do. They're deploying it right now, right under our noses. We've got to do something!"

Krueger looks prepared to cut Mark Colton off at the knees. John Worth intercedes. "General, if I may?"

"Go ahead, Major."

"At first, I thought you might loan me one of the observation planes you have sitting here so I could adjust some artillery fire on it, but slow as they are, I'd probably just get knocked down again."

"True," Krueger says. "We've lost two to ground fire not far from here already. Why didn't you call for artillery fire yourself after the Navy flew away?"

"I would have loved to, sir, except I got shot down...by *your* guys, I believe. So how about this? The track the bomb is on runs right to our location. It's about a 5-mile distance. We have trains right here. Let's use one to mount a raid. Instead of fighting our way in on foot, we'll just drive in an iron locomotive. I don't think they'll be expecting that. Better than a tank!"

"And who the hell can drive a train?" the General asks.

"I can, sir," John replies. "Let's put a platoon into a couple of freight cars, stick an American flag on the roof so maybe our own pilots won't attack, and I'll drive them straight to the damn thing. Real quick, the platoon secures it, Commander Colton deactivates it, then we get the hell out of there. We need to get the word to our forward troops not to shoot us, though. I think it's our best shot."

John's words startle and horrify Mark Colton who, until this moment, had not seen himself as a hands-on participant in this war.

Krueger considers John's plan for a few moments, then asks, "When did you learn to drive a locomotive, Major?"

"I've known ever since I was a kid, sir...used to ride with my uncle. He was an engineer. He taught me."

After another moment deep in thought, Krueger says, "Tell you what, Major, I suppose I can spare a platoon. How long until you're ready to roll?"

"One of the locomotives looks like it was abandoned with its boiler still hot and its tender has plenty of coal. We should have steam up in about 20 minutes."

Krueger points to a colonel and says, "Get a fresh platoon from the 81st on the double...one that hasn't been on the line yet. Give them a couple of extra machine guns as well." Then turning to Worth and Colton, the General says, "I think this is a fool's game, gentlemen, but what the hell. I'll designate this operation 'Task Force Worth.' Good luck to you."

General Krueger had one further thought he did not dare to speak aloud: *and MacArthur has no intention of setting foot on Kyushu until this is put to bed.*

John Worth and Mark Colton climb into the locomotive's cab. Mark assumes the job of fireman, shoveling coal into the smoldering firebox as John studies the valves and gauges. Mark is decidedly grim-faced.

"Good job, Mark. Keep that coal coming. Get a good blaze going in there."

After a few moments of evaluation, John says, "This looks pretty simple. Ignore the markings in Japanese. Just follow the pipes."

Mark cannot answer. His nerves are getting the better of him. He has just vomited into the coal tender. *I hope to hell I don't piss my pants, too.* John manages a slight laugh, then helps Mark to his feet and says, "Buck up there, sailor...a lot of guys are counting on you right now." There are no words from Mark in response, just a sickly groan and a terrified stare into the distance.

John watches the boiler pressure build for about 15 minutes. Gingerly, he opens what he figures is the directional control valve fully in one direction, then opens what is obviously the throttle just a bit. With a chug, the locomotive moves slowly forward. John grabs and pulls another lever and the wheels stop with a screech. "OK," John says. "Now we know how to go forward, backward, and stop. All we have to do now is figure out how to keep the boiler from exploding. One of these must be the manual pressure relief valve." Slowly, he operates some valve handles until a big cloud of steam escapes a vent atop the boiler with a loud hiss. "That's the one!" John says, confident he now has the foreign machine mastered. Mark tries to force a smile of acknowledgement, but it will not come. He goes back to shoveling coal as John gives him a supportive pat on the back. "Stay with it, sailor. You're doing just fine."

Nearly an hour later, about 40 men--an infantry platoon--approach the train at a double-time march. Trailing a bit behind are two four-man teams, each team lugging a .30 caliber machine gun each plus many belts of ammunition.

A strapping lieutenant steps up to John, salutes. He introduces himself as First Lieutenant Malcolm "Bud" Davies, leader of Third Platoon, A Company, 127th Infantry, 81st Division.

"Bud Davies, the Michigan State fullback?"

"Yes, sir!"

"I'll be a son of a bitch," John says, extending his hand. "You were about the toughest ball carrier I ever tried to tackle. I'm John Worth. I played a little at Iowa State."

Bud's grin is wide and sincere. "Small world, sir! Glad to see you again... too bad the circumstances couldn't be better. What do you need me and my boys to do?"

Bud's breezy air of confidence comes as a great comfort to John Worth. Thankfully, they have not sent him some rookie second lieutenant fresh out of the box.

As John's mind wrestles with exactly how much he can tell Davies about their mission, General Krueger pulls up in his jeep and yells, "Did he tell you about his bomb yet, son?"

Holy shit! And here I am worried about contradicting orders, John thinks.

Mark just rolls his eyes in disbelief at the General's careless manner, afraid to open his mouth lest he upchuck again. Bud's platoon, standing at ease some distance away, has not heard what the General said.

John gives Bud the straight story. He takes it well, but the sight of the queasy Mark Colton does not inspire much confidence in their mission's *expert*.

Bud mulls over his role in the mission. "OK, when

we get to this thing, my platoon will neutralize any Japs and secure a perimeter while the Commander here deactivates it. And after he's done?"

"I plan on backing the hell out, straight back to here."

"And I plan on being with you, sir" Davies says. Gazing down the tracks toward the Japanese lines, he adds, "Look, Major, all my guys are green except me and my platoon sergeant. I don't think it's a good idea to tell them *everything* you just told me. It'll scare them shitless, worse than you just scared me. I should probably just tell them it's a *recon in force* and leave it at that."

"Whatever you think is best, Bud. I guess it doesn't matter one way or the other now. Just keep the Japs off us long enough to get this done."

"Roger, sir!"

John backs up the locomotive until, with a thud, its coupler engages two freight cars parked behind it. Lieutenant Davies briefs his platoon and divides them so two squads ride in the first car with one of the machine guns pointed out the open door to the right. His remaining two squads occupy the second car with the other machine gun pointed left. Bud Davies joins John and Mark in the locomotive's cab. Several of Bud's men have already spread and fastened an American flag on the first car's roof.

John opens the throttle and the train begins to chug forward, toward the Japanese device's hiding place.

Colonel Ozawa is not doing well. Slowed by his wounds, he is the last surviving member of his special suicide unit, one that has yet to fulfill its mission. Preparations for detonation, which should only have taken 10 minutes, have consumed over an hour so far, and completion is nowhere in sight.

He has managed to remove the access panel to the detonator and hook up the wires. Now, he has to connect the wires to the hand generator and push the plunger, just like the villains in American western movies used to do when blowing up something with dynamite. He remembers those silent movies as a teenager growing up in Hawaii before his father moved the family back to Tokyo. He isn't the villain of this story, he tells himself; he is the hero. Once he pushes that plunger, his mission and his life will be finished, and the Americans he hates so much will be dead, too. Japan will be victorious.

Although Japanese troops are all around, Ozawa has seen none. The terrified, inexperienced soldiers will not leave the defensive holes in which they cower, waiting for the invaders to advance. This strange railcar, with its huge barrel that is pockmarked but not penetrated by American bullets, holds no interest for them.

There is plenty of wire on a reel to connect the generator in case he must detonate the device from a remote, sheltered position while under fire. Ozawa has not bothered to play out the wire, though. He can just as easily detonate from right here on the flatcar. He has lost a lot of blood and is growing weaker.

When he grabs the generator to connect the wires, the plunger comes off in his hands and the generator topples off the flatcar, clattering to the ground. Ozawa lets out a curse as he begins the arduous task of climbing down off the flatcar, dragging the wire reel with him. It is too much to ask of his battered body and he tumbles to the ground, too, blacking out from the searing pain for a few moments. When he comes to, he pulls himself to his knees and slides the plunger back into the generator. He pushes down with all the might he can muster, but the handle just falls out again, sending the colonel sprawling. The generator is useless. He must find something--anything--to create an electric current.

As he lies on the ground, his mind searches for a solution through alternating waves of intense pain and enticing lapses of consciousness. He is jarred to awareness as a small aged truck cautiously approaches, carrying a jittery Japanese Army captain and his driver. They are couriers, looking for a specific commander to impart a message. They had seen the Corsairs attack and were curious about the flatcar and its strange cargo that seemed impervious to damage.

Seeing the colonel lying on the ground, they stop the truck next to the tracks, get out, and approach him. He is obviously in bad shape; they offer him a ride to an aid station, although they aren't sure where one can be found. The colonel declines the offer.

Ozawa had first wondered, in a brief moment of lucidity, if the truck's electrical system would set off the detonator until he realized the ancient truck had a hand crank starter and lacked a battery, whose terminals would have provided simple points of connection. He is no mechanical wizard, and in his present state he could probably never figure out how to make this idea work, and his shaky visitors were unlikely to be of much help.

Ozawa asks if they have a field radio. When the captain responds that they do, but it doesn't work, the colonel announces through his labored breathing that he is commandeering the radio's hand crank generator. The captain is reluctant, but orders are orders.

As the driver removes the generator from the back

of the truck, they all stop and turn as a strange sound fills the air. It is a train, rounding a gentle curve from the direction of the American lines, heading straight for them. As it comes into view through the trees, the captain and his driver see there are soldiers on board. As it gets still closer, these soldiers begin firing at them from the doors of the freight cars. They cannot hear shots over the noise of the train, but bullets are splashing up dirt and splintering trees all around them. The generator is dropped at Ozawa's feet; the captain and his driver jump back into the truck and speed away.

Ozawa, growing groggier by the moment, is having trouble grasping the situation. When the locomotive slams into the flatcar, finally comes to a stop, and soldiers begin to jump out in all directions, it becomes crystal clear. They are shouting in English! With all the strength he has left, Ozawa tries to run, crawling when he falls, seeking shelter in the thick stand of trees, dragging the generator and wire reel with him. The Americans have not seen him do this, perhaps thinking he, too, has escaped in the truck. Left behind on the flatcar are the two wrenches that made up the Ozawa's tool kit as well as his sidearm.

John, Mark, and Bud are amazed how easy this brief journey has been--until now.

The locomotive's brakes, which had seemed to work when John first tested them, have proved useless at higher speeds. He had only been able to decelerate by the last-minute action of throwing the drive wheels into reverse, their backward spinning against the rails diminishing the forward momentum some, but not enough, while throwing showers of sparks and unleashing a horrific squeal. The collision with the flatcar had been the ultimate brake, pushing it 50 yards down the track before the machinery slid to a halt. All the train's occupants were thrown forward on impact, but aside from assorted bumps and bruises, the collision caused no injuries.

"Brakes need a little work, sir," Bud Davies said as he leapt from the locomotive's cab.

They had traveled 5 miles total, the last three through enemy territory, and the first Japs they had seen had just fled in a truck. If anybody had fired at the train, its passengers were unaware. Now they are at their objective, and it is time to make history quickly. Japs had to be all around. The Americans' presence is no longer a secret. John wished Bud's platoon had not opened fire like that; it would have been easier and preferable to take the Japanese out at close range rather than firing wildly from a few hundred yards away and giving them a chance to escape. Bud had tried to stop the spontaneous, panicky fusillade, waving his arms in vain in a *cease fire* signal, but the fire discipline of his novice soldiers was poor.

Bud's platoon quickly tries to form a perimeter of 40 yards diameter around the train, but that proves no easy task in the limited visibility of the dense woods, where men 10 feet away are often not visible. The resulting protective circle is ragged. Bud and his platoon sergeant immediately set about tightening it up and filling the gaps. Mark Colton, much too busy to be nauseous now, races to the beer barrel and clambers onto its flatcar. John is right behind him.

Mark scans the beer barrel's structure, letting out a surprised whistle as he lays his hands on it. "What a piece of crap! Looks like they made this crude bastard in a junkyard out of scrap metal!" Then he sees the wire Ozawa has connected.

"John! This thing is wired to go!"

They cannot see how the wires are connected inside. They run beneath a hatch secured with many bolts that cannot be removed by hand. John tries to saw through the thick wires, first with his survival knife, then a bayonet, but it proves very difficult and will take much too long. He considers trying to shoot them apart with his pistol, but figures he would probably just blow his hand off and never damage the wires. If only they had some heavy wire cutters!

Jumping from the flatcar, John and Mark begin to follow the wires on a dead run into the thick woods flanking the track. But their dash ends quickly. John and Mark stand stock still, pistols drawn, pointed at an unarmed Japanese Army officer who looks to be at death's door. He is about 30 feet away, his back to a tree, kneeling before a small box with opposing crank handles protruding from either side. He is yelling in perfect English at the two Americans.

"YOU WILL NOT STOP ME, YOU BASTARDS. THIS IS MY DESTINY, JAPAN'S DESTINY, AND I WILL HAVE MY REVENGE!"

One hand on each handle, he slowly begins to turn the cranks. It is a difficult task as he is obviously weak and in great pain from his wounds.

Mark's eyes go wide with terror as he screams, "NO! STOP! YOU DON'T KNOW WHAT YOU'RE DOING!"

Ozawa knows full well what he is doing. He turns the cranks faster.

John breaks into a dead run again. He is going to tackle the Japanese officer, knocking him away from the generator. He does not hear the single shot that rings out just as he is about to make contact.

It is a vicious upper body tackle, shoulder to

shoulder. Their combined bodies bounce against the tree, then tumble to the ground, away from the generator. Roughly, John manhandles the much smaller Ozawa into a choke hold, but something feels very strange to John: *This guy ain't fighting back! It's like he's...*

Dead. John pulls his arm off Ozawa's neck. The sleeve of his flight suit is covered in blood--fresh blood.

The generator's crank handles coast to a stop.

Shit...I'm not hit, am I?

John rolls his adversary over to his back. The front of the man's shirt is covered in blood. There is still more flowing from a bullet wound dead center on his chest.

No, it ain't me bleeding, that's for sure.

John turns to see Mark Colton, his face ashen, his .45 caliber pistol still smoking in his outstretched hand.

"Gee! Nice shot, deadeye. Most people can't hit shit with a .45 from that distance," John says with a calmness that masks his astonishment--and his relief. He never felt the bullet that passed a fraction of an inch from him.

"I had to...couldn't wait anymore...didn't know how much juice that thing needed to blow," Mark says in a slow monotone, eyes glued to the body of the man whose life he has just taken.

But there is still much to be done. John pulls the wires from the generator and says, "I'm taking this thing with us." He starts to trot back to the flatcar, generator in one arm, pulling the shaken Mark with the other.

"You do much shooting?" John asks as he runs, still amazed at the marksmanship.

Mark mumbles his answer. "Never shot a gun in

my life."

"I guess I should count my blessings, then."

When they climb back on the flatcar, Mark Colton is still transfixed. John grabs him roughly by the collar. "C'mon, pal! We've gotta wrap this up fast! What do we do next?"

Mark begins to speak, slowly at first, snapping from his trance as the words begin to flow. "All we have to do is kill the detonator...it's probably just some high explosive. Pull it all out and break it up so it's useless. It's got to be under this hatch."

"Maybe it's nitro?" John asks.

"No, it can't be, John. Nitro's much too unstable for something like this."

Using the wrenches Ozawa left behind, they quickly remove the large nuts and bolts securing the hatch to the detonation chamber. It is very heavy; it takes both of them to lift the hatch off and lay it on the flatcar's deck. After peering inside for a few seconds, John says, "We don't need to pull this dynamite or whatever it is. It'll take too long, anyway! Let's just take this hatch with us. It's meant to keep the high-explosive blast inside, right? Like you said, a small explosion starts a big explosion. C'mon, let's grab it and go! We've gotta get the hell outta here!"

"Sounds like a plan, John."

They wrestle the hatch off the flatcar and run back to the locomotive. John signals Bud Davies to get his men on board on the double. On the run, Mark asks, "Hey, John...any chance of towing this piece of junk back with us? I'd love to keep it for a souvenir!"

"No, dammit, we can't. There's no coupler on the front of this locomotive. No chain to pull her with, either."

As soon as John says that, the first bullets from a

Japanese machine gun rake through Bud's collapsing perimeter. The couriers that had escaped the train's arrival had found the company commander they were looking for, who notified higher headquarters of the American "breakthrough." The commander was ordered to immediately counterattack; his troops are now converging on Task Force Worth from the north, south, and west. Only the east, the way back to the American lines, is still clear of ambushing Japanese for the moment.

"HOLY SHIT! THEY'RE EVERYWHERE!" are the words on the lips of every American as they try to catch sight of their attackers through the dense woods. Only a few of them begin shooting back.

The woods afford very poor fields of fire for everyone, and only a few of the combatants are hit despite the torrent of shots. Two of Bud's men are down and immobile, screaming their heads off. The sergeant and corporal who run to retrieve them are also hit and go down as they blunder into one of the few places the Japanese have a good lane of fire. Now there are four wounded Americans screaming their heads off. Bud repositions one of his machine guns and it answers the Japanese gun, silencing it for a few seconds while it, too, invisibly repositions. There is still plenty of lead flying the Americans' way, however, striking trees, freight cars, and the locomotive. There is as much splintered wood flying as steel, and they still must retrieve their wounded men before making good their escape.

In the locomotive's cab, John throws levers and valves to make the train go backwards; with loud *clanks*, the train slowly starts to move.

Bud Davies is still trying to retrieve his four wounded men. The rest of the platoon huddles in the bullet-scarred freight cars, some firing their weapons wildly while the rest simply cower and scream to whoever is driving this damn thing: "GET US OUT OF HERE! FUCK THE WOUNDED!"

Bud drags two of the wounded men to the door of the first car and hands them up. The train continues its slow acceleration, now at the speed of a casual walk. At this rate, he will never get the last two, much less himself, back on the train before it is out of reach. He needs help--now!

Bud grabs the arm of a young buck sergeant--a squad leader--hunkered down at the first freight car's door. "Sergeant, follow me."

The sergeant, whose expression and mannerisms are trying to convey that he is somehow not a part of all this, does not move.

"That's an order, sergeant!"

"I don't care if you court martial me, I ain't doin' it," the buck sergeant replies.

Bud now needs to walk briskly to keep up with the train. No one else in the car appears to be paying attention to him, each locked in his own terror. Giving up on the insubordinate sergeant, he starts running to retrieve the third man while turning to John Worth in the locomotive's cab, gesturing with outstretched arms: *I need help!*

John grabs Mark Colton, who is shoveling coal frantically, and says, "YOU DRIVE!"

Then he jumps from the cab and runs toward Bud, with Mark screaming after him, "WHAT? ARE YOU CRAZY? I DON'T KNOW HOW!"

As the train moves steadily backward, the cab comes squarely into the Jap's best field of fire. Bullets ping off the iron structure of the locomotive, sending hot metal fragments whizzing in all directions. Some bullets streak directly through the cab, in one window and out the other. Mark drops to the floor and lies prone, out of the line of fire, but is burned by several hot fragments that land on his back and legs once their velocity is spent bouncing around the cab.

The locomotive is driverless as its train continues to gradually accelerate rearward.

John and Bud are dragging the last two wounded to the train, which is now moving at a brisk jogging pace. The freight cars are beyond their reach; their only hope is to intersect the path of the locomotive's cab. Running as fast as possible, they aim for a point down the track to meet the cab's ladder. Despite their considerable athletic abilities and the adrenaline coursing through their veins, they really need Mark to back off the steam and stop the train's acceleration for a moment, but they cannot see him. He is still rolling around the floor of the cab, trying to shake off the searing metal fragments that are burning through his fatigues. But they can see Japs--plenty of them--some distance down the track chasing the locomotive, firing wildly on the run.

John and Bud hit their mark. As the cab's ladder sweeps by, they are both able to grab it with one hand while holding their wounded man by his web belt with the other. Bud gets one foot on the ladder, then the other, and climbs the four rungs into the cab, pulling his man up with him. John follows up the ladder with his man.

The train is now passing at a man's full-out running speed. The pursuing Japs give up the chase, dropping to one knee to try well-aimed but ineffective shots that bounce off the retreating locomotive.

As they catch their breath on the cab's floor, Bud looks to John, holds both hands over his head and says,

"Touchdown, sir!"

Less than 10 minutes later, with the train making excellent speed in reverse, they pass back through the American lines. The Japs had tried to spread the alarm down their forward positions, but the train traveled faster. Once they figure they are out of enemy territory, some soldiers from Bud's platoon climb on top of the freight cars and wave their arms frantically, hoping to persuade their fellow G.I.'s not to fire on them. Surprisingly, none do.

A few more minutes and the train coasts to a stop, without benefit of brakes, at its point of origin. The captured hatch is pushed from the locomotive to the ground. Mark Colton begins a manic, triumphant dance on their prize. Only a privileged few know why; the rest think he has flipped out, another case of combat fatigue crazily relishing a piece of junk as a war souvenir. Bud yells for medics to care for his wounded. He also tells his platoon sergeant to arrest and confine the young sergeant who had refused his order, pending court martial. The assembled platoon then marches off, with all except their lieutenant still ignorant of the true nature of their mission and their place in history.

John vents the remaining pressure from the locomotive's boiler, then vents himself with a big sigh of relief. Certainly, this mission has been beyond anything his imagination could conjure, but he has prevailed and survived once again. He is filled, just for a few seconds, with the heady satisfaction of having done something truly monumental.

Mark continues to strut around like he has just conquered the world. John puts his arm around Mark's shoulder. "Nice job, sailor. By the way, in the Air Force when you puke in somebody's machine, you have to clean it up!"

"Nice try, flyboy, but forget it! You ain't shitting in my mess kit right now! We're going to be telling our grandkids how we saved the world!"

"Don't get too carried away, Mark. We just got lucky. It could have turned into a SNAFU real easy."

Mark steps back, dumbfounded. "Are you kidding me? You do realize we just did something absolutely amazing? Totally unprecedented in all of science?

"Yeah, I realize it," John replies. "Believe me, I realize it. But this damn war still isn't over, so we'd better get a move on. I'm sure the general wants his after action-report on the double."

John starts to walk off, leaving Mark slack-jawed.

"Are you coming or what, sailor?"

Chapter Forty-Nine

On 9 November--X+2--MacArthur reported to Washington that excellent progress was being made on Kyushu: *Resistance, while stiff, is being overcome with increasing ease as the full weight of artillery assets are ashore and being brought to bear. Air assets continue to dominate: there is no longer any effective Japanese air resistance over Kyushu. Army Air Force units on Okinawa and the Philippines have begun relocating to the newly captured airfields. Large scale aerial bombardment of Honshu will commence in the next few days.*

As a miscellaneous comment, MacArthur added: *No credible evidence of Japanese nuclear capability has been found.*

After receiving General Krueger's message on the success of Task Force Worth, MacArthur arrived on Kyushu midday, X+3. His disembarkment from the B-17 that transported him to Japanese home soil was repeated numerous times for the cameras.

The after-action report verbally presented by John Worth, Mark Colton, and Bud Davies described the execution of Task Force Worth in great detail, right down to the steps taken to deactivate the nuclear device. At the end of this presentation, its transcript was immediately classified *Top Secret* and they were ordered never to divulge the nature of the mission they had just completed to anyone.

The official version of that report actually entered

into the 6th Army annals purged any mention of a nuclear device, merely stating: *A joint Army, Air Force, and Navy task force of approximately 50 men sought to exploit certain tactical opportunities behind enemy lines and was successful. The mission incurred four casualties, no fatalities, and employed indigenous rail assets to achieve mobility and surprise.*

The Japanese atomic bomb was never spoken of again.

Sitting at his desk in the Oval Office, Harry Truman put MacArthur's report down and relaxed in his chair. Half of his nuclear predicament had been solved.

At Hungnan Island, Japanese troops destroyed what was left of Professor Inaba's laboratory, lest it fall into Russian hands.

At the Imperial Palace, the Emperor's emissaries puzzled over a communiqué from the Swedish envoy, who appeared to be brokering an American peace proposal.

John had bunked in Mark Colton's tent the night of X+2. The following morning, he gathered his things hurriedly to hitch a ride on a C-47 back to his unit on Okinawa. With any luck at all, he'd get to see Marge one more time before the hospital shipped out to Kyushu. As he was saying his goodbyes to Mark, Bud Davies appeared at the entrance to the tent.

"What's cookin', Lieutenant?" John asks, obviously in a rush.

"I don't mean to hold you up, sir, but I was curious about something," Bud begins. "I need your opinion. Doesn't what we did deserve some kind of decoration? I mean, what does a guy have to do around here to get a medal? Nobody's said anything about it... just Purple Hearts for the wounded guys. I know we've all been ordered to keep our mouths shut, but still..."

Mark Colton is stunned by Bud's question. The voice in his scientist's mind cries out: *Who cares about some medal? The triumph of science is its own reward!*

John Worth is more pragmatic. "Bud, the brass aren't going to want to draw any attention to this atom bomb thing. They ran this whole invasion betting it wasn't real and can't have themselves proved wrong now. They're not likely to put on a big spectacle by making heroes out of any of us. Just be glad I didn't get us all killed."

Crestfallen, Bud says, "That doesn't sound right, sir."

"It's *not* right," John says, "but what's right and wrong out here depends on who you happen to be. And that buck sergeant you want to send to Leavenworth? Don't be surprised if that gets back-burnered, too. At most, he'll get a quick summary court martial, lose a stripe and get his ass shipped far away. The guys in your platoon still don't have a clue what that thing was, do they?"

"No, sir."

"One way or the other, Bud, I'm afraid that's the way it's going to stay."

Bud looks like he has been kicked in the gut. "OK, I get it," he mumbles. Then, in a stronger voice, he adds, "Well, it was a great honor working with both of you gentlemen. I really mean that."

Bud salutes. There are handshakes all around.

As Bud leaves the tent, Mark says, "Damn, John, I didn't realize just how big a cynic you are."

John replies, "A real smart young lady's been

teaching me."

Later that same day, X+3, American ground forces advance through the wooded area concealing the beer barrel. A Navy team headed by Mark Colton photographs, diagrams, and dismantles the device, leaving the empty iron shell where they found it. Soon after they are done, Mark is on a plane home with the documents, photos, and enriched uranium they had removed, sealed in a special lead box.

And on Tinian, in the Marianas, one B-29 is being loaded with one very big bomb.

Chapter Fifty

Tinian: one of several small islands in the Northern Marianas stocked to bursting with Boeing B-29's of the 20th US Army Air Force. The Americans who captured this 40 square mile limestone shelf thought its shape resembled Manhattan Island. It did, if you visualize Manhattan with its north-south axis squashed a bit. So they called it Manhattan, even naming the roads they built after its thoroughfares, like Broadway, 42nd Street, and 5th Avenue.

On this typically warm afternoon, the rain has stopped as if on cue, pushed on its way by a Pacific tradewind. One B-29 slowly moves backward along the puddled ramp, propelled by the tractor attached to her nose landing gear, guided by signalmen on foot at the wingtips and tail. When the silver, four-engined behemoth comes to rest, her two main landing gear straddle a deep pit, with the two gaping bomb bays in her belly directly above it.

The rear bomb bay is receiving an auxiliary fuel tank, which will help the plane balance the rotund, finned object being placed in the forward bomb bay: Dr. Oppenheimer's atomic bomb. Work progresses slowly and under a curtain of secrecy; MPs who do not know themselves exactly what is going on keep the unauthorized away. It will take many more hours to complete the loading and safety checks of the 5-ton bomb.

At Bomber Command headquarters on Tinian,

General Carl Spaatz, Commander, US Strategic Air Forces - Pacific, lights a cigarette and paces the floor. By special orders from Washington, "Tooey" Spaatz reports directly to the Joint Chiefs rather than MacArthur or Nimitz. The air forces he commands exist strictly to fulfill Washington's specific desires in this war unfiltered by the agenda or ego of any field commander. That meant the strategic bombing of cities and industry, including civilians. The need to keep the bombers out of the clutches of the field commanders keeps them based in the Marianas; Japan is just barely within the B-29's radius of operation from these islands. Now, in late 1945, there are places closer, like northern Luzon and Okinawa, but they are the turf of MacArthur and Nimitz, respectively.

Although the American atom bomb is being mated to an aircraft at this moment, Spaatz still has not received the written authorization he had demanded to drop the bomb on a Japanese city. "Tooey" is old school air corps, a military aviator since WWI, and, like most American generals, skeptical of the proposed uses and capabilities of atomic weapons. He is also mindful of the moral questions involved in unleashing such new, hypothetically terrible weapons against civilians. But Tooey Spaatz would not hesitate to use them if and when properly ordered. Wise in the ways of high command politics, however, he has no intention of being left holding the bag should the deployment of this bomb be a disastrous failure--or a disastrous success. In demanding the authorization in writing, he is fully prepared to be relieved of command for his stance.

He suspects the delay in receiving the authorization might be the result of some ethical debate in Washington on whether to drop it at all, now that the invasion is underway and seems to be going according to plan. But he also understands the current military and political mindset: *if you have a bigger weapon, you use it.* General LeMay, Spaatz's subordinate and the man leading the bomber command that would carry out this mission, thought his boss was nuts. While chomping on his ever-present cigar, LeMay had fumed in private: "Who the hell cares if the order is in writing or not? Let's drop the goddamn thing!"

Pending the expected arrival of the authorization, Spaatz had allowed preparations for the mission to begin. Advised these preparations had been completed at 2200 hours, he checks his chronometer and realizes it is 0700 of this same day in Washington. If he is going to receive his authorization this day, Washington time, it will likely arrive in the middle of the night, Marianas time. He directs the designated flight crews to plan a wake-up at 0300.

No such ethical debate like the one General Spaatz envisioned was taking place in Washington. It was just a question of waiting a little longer, hoping a message of surrender would be received now that American boots were firmly on Japanese home soil. There had been rumblings in European diplomatic channels of overtures from the Emperor's envoys, rumblings that contained a hint of "cessation of hostilities." Not "unconditional surrender," just "cessation."

By 0830, Truman decides he can wait no longer. Prodded by Secretary of State Byrnes, who had wanted to send the authorization days ago, before the bomb had even arrived on Tinian, the President orders Generals Marshall and Arnold to transmit the order to Spaatz immediately. Marshall and Admiral Leahy urge the President to wait just one more day, hoping the

European rumors might still possess some merit and solid information had merely been delayed while dispatches sat on some functionary's desk, awaiting coding or decoding. And, as always, the time differences between Tokyo, Europe, and Washington are driving Truman and his staff to distraction; they feel like their actions are always a day late.

But it is Byrnes who gains the upper hand. The waiting will cease. The authorization is teletyped to San Francisco, then to Hawaii, and finally to the Marianas, arriving there at 0230 local time. Spaatz, awoken by an aide, receives the news silently, expressing neither elation nor disappointment.

The three flight crews that comprise the first atomic bomb mission are hand picked; the cream of the crop. Having been roused and fed as planned at 0300, they assemble for briefing just before 0400. They are a bit surprised to see both LeMay and the big boss, Spaatz, in attendance; they know they are being tasked with something truly monumental; this just underlines it. Usually, no one higher than a colonel presides over a briefing.

Two of the planes will depart first and perform weather reconnaissance of the primary and three alternate target cities. Their crews would determine which cities had the best conditions for visual bombing, the preferred method of delivery over the less-accurate radar. A miss would be a colossal waste of expensive nuclear resources and might not properly demonstrate the effects of the new bomb. The third aircraft, which actually carries the bomb, will depart an hour later and rendezvous with the first two after their recon is complete; its aircraft commander will evaluate the recon information and decide which city they could best strike taking all operational factors into account, including fuel remaining, winds aloft, and any technical problems the aircraft might have developed. After the bomb is dropped, the recon planes will loiter at a safe distance, taking photos and scientific measurements of the detonation and its aftermath.

The two recon planes take off just before 0500 and head northwest, toward the southern half of the largest Japanese home island, Honshu. Stripped of weaponry but carrying a full fuel load, they are still below maximum takeoff weight, and in the relative coolness of early morning are airborne well before the far threshold of the runway. That runway, despite its 8500 foot length, never seems quite long enough to the B-29 pilots. It ends with an abrupt 10 foot drop to the sea. Overloaded B-29's often rolled off the end of the runway and dropped down towards the sea before gaining enough airspeed to climb. Sometimes they did not attain the requisite airspeed and splashed into the water.

The B-29 carrying the atomic bomb, Number 82, is definitely overloaded. Carrying the 5-ton bomb plus full fuel tanks and 600 gallons of ballast fuel puts her several thousand pounds beyond maximum takeoff weight. The pilots are used to this condition, however. Almost all of the nearly 3000 mile round-trip bombing missions to Japan start out this way. With a little luck and a lot of skill, they can get the overloaded monsters into the air. But if you crash on takeoff or have to immediately return for a mechanical problem and botch the overweight landing, the full load of aviation gasoline promises a spectacular inferno, with secondary explosions of the bomb load. There would be little chance of survival.

This poses an additional problem of cataclysmic proportions for a plane carrying an atomic bomb. A fiery crash of a bomber with its load of conventional high explosives cooking off was disastrous enough; a crash involving an atomic bomb could wipe the airfield and the island it sat on off the map. For this reason, the atomic bomb would only be made capable of detonating once airborne. A nuclear weapons specialist would be part of the flight crew and arm the bomb in flight, crawling into the bomb bay right after takeoff, before the plane was pressurized, to remove its safety devices installed at its manufacture and activate its triggering circuits. The specialist aboard Number 82 is a US Naval officer and physicist from Dr. Oppenheimer's staff who has accompanied the bomb all the way from the States.

The pilot of Number 82, a colonel and the group commander, is highly experienced at aerial bombardment. He began this war as a senior B-17 pilot bombing Germany with the 8th Air Force, moving steadily up the chain of command. Transferred to the Pacific theater, he was given command of a B-29 squadron last year in the aircraft's early operational days, when she was a temperamental lady prone to killing her crews. The 18 cylinder radial engines, each producing 2200 horsepower in its circular maze of cylinders, ducts, and wiring harnesses jammed into a tight cowling, had been prone to overheating and catching fire. The prototype had crashed during initial flight testing with such a problem, killing Boeing's chief test pilot. Modifications to the cowling's baffling and cooling flaps have made the B-29 friendlier to her operators and less of a firetrap. She was now free to fulfill her considerable promise.

Clearance for takeoff is received. The pilot aligns Number 82 to the runway's centerline in the pre-dawn darkness, manipulating the big red levers that protrude from the center console to steer by differential braking. The engines are run up to takeoff power while the pilot holds her in place with the brakes. With a confirmation from the flight engineer that all systems are in order, he releases the brakes and begins the headlong rush down the runway.

She gathers speed sluggishly, this overloaded beast, and reaches what would normally be flying speed about three quarters of the way down the runway. The pilot pulls back on the control column and the nose wheels lift off the ground, but after the brief moment that normally passes between the nose rising and the main wheels lifting off, she is not airborne. He puts the nose wheel gently back down on the runway until she can gain more speed. The crew cannot see the edge of land that marks the runway's end, but they are becoming more apprehensive by the moment of the dark, watery void beyond. Then, suddenly, without seeming to climb at all, the ground is no longer beneath them. The tail gunner, alone in his aft-most compartment, instinctively strains upward against his seat harness as if to keep his backside from skidding on the edge of the island as he feels the sickening drop toward the sea begin.

The pilot lets her descend, trading altitude for speed, gambling he will not use up that narrow margin of air and touch the water. The crewmen in the mid compartment, looking out the large, blister-shaped windows just aft of the wings, swear they can see wakes on the moonlit surface of the sea trailing her four huge propellers. The pilot offers a silent prayer that all the blacked-out naval vessels in the area are observing the safety zone beyond the runway's end, for he would not see them and cannot clear them if they lay in his path.

After gaining a few more knots of speed, the pilot eases back on the control column. The nose rises, but the airspeed quickly bleeds off and she does not climb. The nose is gently put back down. More speed is garnered: 160 knots. This time the nose rises, the airspeed holds, and she begins a slow climb. The crew discharges a collective sigh of relief.

After flying uneventfully for over four hours, the pilot of Number 82 is advised by his navigator they have arrived at the rendezvous point just southwest of Osaka. The big home island of Honshu sprawls below them, mostly shrouded in low clouds, its distant inland peaks jutting up as if floating on cotton. They orbit at 31,000 feet, awaiting the two recon ships, which arrive 25 and 30 minutes later, respectively--well past schedule--having taken extra time to reevaluate the four cities. Radio silence is broken briefly to convey the coded consensus: the best chance for visual bombing is at the primary target city, Hiroshima. All the alternates are currently obscured by cloud cover which is not likely to clear before Number 82 has burned so much fuel she cannot make it to Okinawa or Iwo Jima, the closest airfields that could accommodate a B-29. There is one further consideration: the B-29 crews have been informed that the airfields now occupied by the Americans on southern Kyushu are not suitable for their aircraft. You might land successfully, but you will never take off again. The runways are not long enough, assuming you could beg, barter, or steal some fuel. The choice makes itself: Number 82's pilot heads for Hiroshima, about 200 miles to the west.

They fly down the jagged coast delineating Honshu from the Iyo Sea. Approaching Hiroshima, it becomes apparent the favorable weather report might have been overly optimistic--the surface is obscured at least 50 percent by cloud cover. Aiming the drop visually might prove impossible; the bombardier cannot find the aiming point--a rail bridge in the center of the city--on their first pass.

It is time once again to weigh options. To follow orders to the letter, the bomb had to be aimed visually, not by radar. If they could not visually acquire the aiming point, the mission should be aborted. To land, the bomb would have to be deactivated. The pilot tells the nuclear weapons specialist to be prepared for the possibility of deactivation once the aircraft descends and depressurizes before landing. Only then could the hatch to the unpressurized bomb bay be opened. The flight engineer nervously taps the fuel quantity gauges, but wishing is not making them read any higher. The pilot turns the aircraft, orbiting for another pass over the city.

As the nuclear weapons specialist glumly opens his tool kit, he is dismayed by what he finds. There are supposed to be six deactivation plugs in the kit. He counts only five. If any of the plugs are not installed, the atomic bomb is not completely safe and would likely detonate as the high-explosive trigger cooked off in a post-crash fire.

In a panic, he dumps his kit on the floor at the rear of the cockpit between the navigator's table and the radio operator's station. Still only five plugs.

How the fuck could I have lost a plug! Did it fall out of the kit while I was still in the bomb bay? If it did, it will probably fall from the plane if the bomb bay doors are opened, that is if it didn't drop inside the door structure. Either way, I'll never see it again!

Frantically, he presses his face and his flashlight

to the small circular window in the pressure hatch leading to the darkened bomb bay, trying desperately to see if the green plug is there somewhere. He sees nothing but the big bomb hanging in its shackles. He repacks his tool kit in a frenzy, his mind reeling as he grapples for a quick salvation from this blunder of historic proportions. The other crewmembers, absorbed in their duties, are unaware of their collective plight.

The bomber lines up for her second pass over the city. The bombardier, hunched over the bombsight in the plexiglass-paneled nose, spins knobs and dials, trying to get a view of the aiming point through the thickening mass of cloud. He announces again, "I ain't got it."

As the aircraft is placed in yet another orbit, the pilot, flight engineer, and navigator discuss the deteriorating fuel situation. Every minute of extra flying they undertake diminishes their chances of getting to a safe landing field, and they have undertaken quite a few extra minutes so far. Now there is a new wrinkle: the flight engineer has only been able to transfer a small portion of the auxiliary fuel from the ballast tank in the aft bomb bay. For some unknown reason, the transfer to the main tanks has stopped, leaving almost 500 gallons of unusable fuel--3000 pounds of extra weight. Returning to the Marianas or even Iwo Jima is now out of the question. Okinawa is the only barely viable option remaining.

Turning to the nuclear weapons specialist, the pilot asks his opinion. He recognizes the specialist's agitated state right away but is not troubled: this man, who is a physicist by profession but a military officer only by circumstance, is obviously feeling the entire weight of the Manhattan Project on his shoulders at the moment.

Most understandable...

The pilot is not taken aback by the specialist's shakily expressed answer, either, because he is thinking exactly the same thing: "Let's go ahead and drop by radar. We'll get it close enough."

On the third pass, the navigator intently peers into his radar display, observing the glowing outline of the terrain features below. He feeds target and wind information to the bombardier, who uses it to set the cloud-blind Norden bombsight. This method will be much more difficult: picking your aiming point among a field of indistinct, glowing blotches rather than looking directly at it through a telescopic sight did not promote accuracy. The whole process would become an approximation. Precision bombing, their stock in trade, would not happen this mission.

Of course, with a bomb as powerful as the one their plane carried, how accurate did you really have to be? The aiming point had been selected due to its central location, so the blast effect would be greatest as it radiated out through the city in all directions. Would dropping a mile or so from the optimum aiming point make much difference?

Probably not, the pilot tells himself.

As Number 82 nears the center of Hiroshima for the third time, the navigator jerks his head back from the hooded radar scope, howling, "The fucking thing just quit! It's spoking!"

The radar technician sitting across the compartment does not need to be told. He can see the failure on his own scope and the radar unit's gauges. The navigator is correct: the system is "spoking." The magnetron--the electro-magnetic device producing the bursts of radio frequency energy that makes airborne radar feasible--is misfiring. This causes the bright symmetrical wedges resembling the spokes of a wheel that now clutter the screen, signaling the system's failure. The radar technician can probably fix it. He is a resourceful type; that is why he was picked for this crew. He has a spare magnetron on board but to replace it in flight is tricky, and it would take 15 minutes, maybe more. The fuel gauges are screaming their rebuttal to this option.

With all this going on--the flying in circles, the cloud cover gradually obscuring more of the surface, the agonizing over the fuel situation--neither the pilot nor the navigator are sure of their exact location anymore. They just know they are over the Iyo Sea somewhere south of Hiroshima. The co-pilot, who is actually flying the airplane while the pilot confers, is even less sure. His attempt to keep the same orbit track is approximate at best. That might be fine for dead reckoning navigation but it is not good enough for precision bombing.

The pilot is used to success. His entire military career has been one long success story. He is desperate not to fail at this mission. He can see the single star of a brigadier general perched on his shoulders very soon.

He tells the radar technician to proceed with the repair.

All they need right now is for some Jap fighters to show up and take a few shots at them. Number 82 has been stripped of all her defensive armament except the two tail guns to save weight. Luckily, no fighters are anywhere in sight. There are few left that could climb to this lofty altitude, anyway, and those that could tended not to pursue solitary B-29's. It was not worth the gas. Attacking formations of bombers was much more efficient.

Fifteen minutes pass, then 20, as the big bomber

continues to fly her lazy, broad circles, consuming precious fuel and time. The two recon ships, orbiting several miles away, keep radio silence while wondering *what the hell is going on?* The radar technician has worked feverishly and is in the final stages of the repair. He signals the navigator, at his station across the rear of the cockpit, that he will be done in another minute or two. The pilot, looking back from his seat, nods in acknowledgement.

The earth and water directly below are now almost completely obscured as clouds continue to roll in. The crew's rough points of reference for visual navigation are only the inland peaks of Honshu to the north, those of Shikoku to the south, and the sun. They will not know how far they might have strayed from Hiroshima city center until the radar is up and running again.

The repetitive orbiting is playing havoc on the navigator's wind corrections. His last precise calculation was now over one-half hour old. Using that as a baseline, the bomber should have drifted east-northeast as it circled. They would now need to correct back to the south-southwest as it prepared for their fourth--and hopefully final--run at the target. The bomb, when dropped from this altitude, would drift in the same manner. The navigator comes up with a course adjustment. The pilot applies it.

With a mechanical whirring noise, almost undistinguishable over the drone of the bomber's engines, the radar scope comes back to life. The radar technician, pleased with himself, gives a *thumbs up*. The navigator presses his face against the scope's hood once again.

He is confused by what he sees. The distinctive shape of the Hiroshima waterfront--the bay, the channels, the docks--is somehow different. Almost the same, but not quite.

"I'm not sure what I've got here, Colonel!" the navigator calls to the pilot without lifting his face from the hood.

With a hand motion to the co-pilot that says *your airplane*, the pilot leaves his seat and walks the few steps aft to the navigator's station. "Let's have a look," he says.

"What makes you think that's not the Hiroshima waterfront?" the pilot asks as he peers into the scope.

"The water, the channels…they're almost the right shape, sir…but not quite."

"I don't know about that…it looks pretty good to me. We're probably just getting a different echo because we're approaching from a different direction this time. Once we turn north again, you'll see," the pilot says as he returns to his seat. He takes back control of the aircraft from the co-pilot.

The navigator wishes he could believe that without reservation as he begins his plot once again. He wonders how many times the pilot has actually interpreted a radar display. *Not many*, he would bet. *And is this thing even working right after the repair?*

The overwrought nuclear weapons specialist sits on the cockpit floor with his back to the aft bulkhead, praying that they would just drop the damn thing. He does not want to abort. He does not want to be known in the Navy or at Caltech as *the guy who lost the plug*. He does not want to die in a post-crash nuclear holocaust.

After calling out the new course for the bomb run, the navigator keeps his face glued to the hood as the bomber turns north, now three miles from the release point according to his last calculation. The bombardier dials in the final bombsight data corrections.

The pilot might be right. After the turn north, the radar echoes do look somewhat different, but the navigator still is not totally convinced he is seeing the designated target on the screen. *But I'm pretty sure.*

Thirty seconds to bomb release. The pilot reminds the crew to put on the welder's goggles each has been issued to protect their eyes from the flash of nuclear detonation. The bomb bay doors open.

Twenty seconds…the navigator is still trying to reconcile what he is seeing against what he had expected to see.

Ten seconds…the bombardier flips open the safety guard on the manual drop button.

Five seconds…the bombardier raises his right hand, the ready signal…

Bomb away.

The pilot immediately puts Number 82 into a steep left bank to get as far as possible from the bomb's blast in the roughly 40 seconds until detonation. Unable to see the horizon or his instruments clearly while wearing the welder's goggles, however, he almost rolls her onto her back. Both pilot and co-pilot fling off their goggles in frustration.

As the plane banks sharply, the missing deactivation plug rolls out from under the box-like base of the radio operator's seat, where it had hidden all these hours, and comes to rest against the foot of the dumbstruck nuclear weapons specialist.

The shock wave feels like heavy flak as it buffets Number 82, now almost six miles distant. Her crew would have taken the bump in stride but they are still sightless from the brilliant flash seconds earlier. Even those who have kept the welder's goggles on cannot see for what seems an anxious eternity. The blindness only amplifies the stomach-wrenching gyrations of an airplane flown by blind men. As their collective eyesight returns a few moments later, they see the towering mushroom cloud--that column of hot air, dust, and debris that climbs into the sky until its peak cools and flattens--standing as a supernatural monument to what they have just done. They are silent, calm--not a peaceful calm, but the kind that accompanies a sober reflection of personal responsibility that cannot be escaped or undone.

Much too low on fuel, they head for Okinawa. They might not even make it there.

The dazed citizens of Hiroshima wonder what has just taken place. After the strange and massive explosion to the southwest of the city, there came a shower of rain, then a shower of dust. A few waterfront buildings have been destroyed, some small craft swamped, and possibly a few hundred people have been swept away, drowned in the sea swell that engulfed the waterfront after the explosion. Some who had been outdoors stagger through the streets, still blinded by the flash brighter than the sun. Aside from those things, there appears to be no other damage.

The mysterious flash and thunderous boom caused many rumors. The most prominent was an entire fleet of American fire-bombers had been destroyed in their entirety by the Kamikaze in one massive counterattack and had simultaneously exploded. In the past, Hiroshima had not received much attention from the Americans. Compared to what other cities had endured, whatever had just happened here seemed minor in comparison.

Chapter Fifty-One

The human reaction to failure is variable. Sometimes we are ashamed, remorseful, and filled with the desire to retry and succeed. Sometimes we refuse to acknowledge failure as such, seeing only new opportunities. Sometimes we seek scapegoats. Sometimes we simply fill with rage.

Harry Truman is currently in that last category. He stands behind his desk in the Oval Office like a coiled spring, leaning forward, palms on the blotter, in a room full of apprehensive men. General Marshall, the other joint chiefs, and cabinet members in attendance can sense he is about to blow. He has been standing like that, red-faced, since Marshal broke the news; it seems an hour ago, although it has only been a few seconds. Just one word--the wrong word--will send him into a full tirade.

Secretary of State James Byrnes paces the other side of the room, deep in thought.

Truman finally responds with all the civility he can muster. "General, describe exactly what the fuck you mean when you say the atom bomb drop *was not as effective as we hoped.*"

"The effect on the city of Hiroshima was minimal, Mister President. While the detonation occurred as expected, it appears the drop was off target by approximately four miles."

"Four fucking miles!" Truman says, turning to his Air Force chief. "General Arnold, is this what you consider 'precision' bombing? Two billion dollars in atomic bomb development gets dropped four miles off target?"

Before Arnold can say anything, Admiral King jumps in. He cannot wait to get his shot in at the Air Force. "Once again, gentlemen, the myth of *strategic bombing* is exposed for the colossal waste of war-fighting resources it always has been, from Billy Mitchell to…"

"THAT'S ENOUGH, ADMIRAL KING!" Truman says, having just heard that wrong word. The tirade is on. "I don't have the time for your interservice rivalry bullshit! Now, General Arnold, what is it you were trying to say, goddammit?"

Hap Arnold knows he is doomed. Whatever he says now, he is already in the trap. No excuse, no mitigating circumstance will redeem him. He decides to just tell it straight.

"They couldn't get a good visual of the target, Mister President. Too much cloud cover. They used radar. They thought they had good target confirmation, but the image was misleading or misinterpreted. They were actually still offshore, over the Iyo Sea, southwest of Hiroshima. The radar image of the offshore islands must have resembled the Hiroshima waterfront to them. The drop was about four miles off target, beyond the high ground west of the city. That high ground shielded the city from the blast. Damage assessment photos show the city virtually intact. The Japs are claiming no significant casualties. They're even saying they thwarted a major raid and destroyed all our bombers."

"Well, isn't that just dandy," Truman says, fuming. "Do they even know it was an atom bomb?'

"If they know, they're not saying, sir," Marshall

replies.

Admiral King pipes up again. "You know, Marshall, you might as well give Arnold his wish and make the Air Force a separate service. Get these expensive embarrassments out of the Army's hair."

Truman spins toward King, red-faced, but James Byrnes calmly strolls between them and says, "Gentlemen, I have a better idea."

"Oh, do tell, Jimmy," the seething president says.

Marshall and Arnold each take a deep breath, backing down for the moment from the internecine challenge King has posed.

"My good sirs," Secretary Byrnes says, "what we and the rest of the world have just witnessed was our *humane demonstration* of the awesome power of the atomic bomb."

"What the hell are you talking about, Jimmy?" Truman asks, quite impatient and more than a little confused.

Byrnes continues, "Look at it this way...we're finally sure the goddamn thing works now, even if the Air Force can't hit shit unless it's a blue sky day. We know what it *can* do, and with a little imagination, we can make the stinking Japs and the rest of the world see it, too. There's got to be some evidence of the bomb's power in the vicinity of Hiroshima, right?"

"Yes, Mister Secretary," Arnold replies with great eagerness. "We can see in the aerial photos that the terrain on the blast side of the high ground shielding the city is totally incinerated...same for the offshore islands. There is also some damage to the waterfront area. We suspect it was from sea surge caused by the bomb's shock wave."

"OK," Byrnes says. "Let's amplify that a bit...use words like *devastated, consumed, rendered uninhabitable, eradicated, wiped from the face of the earth.* A word like *destroyed* has *soooo* little meaning these days. We tell the world what benevolent, *humane* folks we are here in the good old US of A because we're giving them a chance to see what we're going to unleash if they don't surrender right quick...just like all our exalted scientists begged us to do. It's a win-win, gentlemen. How can we go wrong?"

"So you're saying we should claim success even though we failed at our mission?" Marshall asks.

With a sly smile, Byrnes replies, "General, you catch on fast. You're going to have a great future in politics."

"All right, Jimmy," Truman says, somewhat calmer. "I guess that's about the best we're going to make out of this mess. Who knows, it might just work, too. But General Arnold, I have one more question for you. Why didn't they just abort?"

"Mister President, these are very dedicated, determined warriors."

"Let's hope so, in case we have to do this shit all over again. And one more thing...Make sure that flight crew gets decorated generously. Make it look like they did a fucking fantastic job."

Chapter Fifty-Two

Looking down at the sea from the C-47 carrying him back to Kadena from Kyushu, it seems to John Worth there are so many vessels headed to Japan, you could just walk there--like stepping stones--from ship to ship. So many aircraft, too; the plane he rides seems to be the only one not heading north. The sheer size of the American military is almost incomprehensible to any one soldier, sailor, or airman, each in his own little pocket of the war.

It would be swell if every G.I. could get a load of what I'm seeing right now.

The wheels touch down uneventfully and the trusty transport taxies to its parking space. Gathering his flight bags, John spills from the plane onto the ramp, into the swirl of activity he had expected. Looking right, he sees a number of transport planes being loaded from trucks emblazoned with red crosses on their sides: the hospital units are preparing to depart for Kyushu. Hustling in this direction as fast as his aching body will take him, he sees Major McNeilly, hands on hips, supervising the loading. Behind her, he sees Marge among a group of nurses lugging baggage. Yelling her name is pointless. Nobody can hear anything above the noise of countless aircraft engines warming up.

He catches up with Marge at the boarding ladder. The starboard engine of her C-47 has just come to life with the usual belch of flame and smoke. The gasoline-tinged prop wash buffets them as they rush into each other's arms.

"Oh, John! What happened to you? I've been so worried! They told me you were OK." Marge yells into his ear, the need to be loud making her seem all the more frantic. "Oh my God...are you hurt, baby?"

Stroking her hair, he yells, "I'm OK, don't worry. I'm fine." Trying to sound reassuring is not easy at the top of your lungs; neither is saying goodbye to the woman you love. "And I found that damn thing I was looking for, but *f-stop* is out of action for good, though."

"Oh, good! No, no! Not good about your plane! Good that you found it, whatever it was! But, baby, when am I gonna see you again? We don't know exactly where we'll be."

"Don't worry, Marge. I'll be there before you know it, too."

Another aircraft engine roars to life. He must yell even louder. "I promise, I'll find you. I'll find you."

As her tears stream down, she buries her face in his shoulder, hugging him one more time. Looking up, she kisses his lips. Then she speaks into his ear with a tenderness totally at odds with the necessary volume, "Oh, honey, you already have!"

Then Marge runs up the ladder into the plane, past McNeilly's impatient glare. At the plane's door, Marge turns and yells, "See you in Japan, Farm Boy! I love you!"

John cannot hear her. He watches her plane taxi away, feeling something wonderful lost and found at the same time.

Chapter Fifty-Three

The exodus is in full swing. Air units are leaving Okinawa and heading to their new bases in Kyushu, the countless planes lined up for takeoff barely visible through the clouds of choking dust kicked up by the propwash. Those stuck on the ground are praying for the usual rain to hold down the dust, but it has yet to come today.

Colonel Harris sits at his desk, two pieces of paper before him. Both concern Major John Worth. The first is a secret communiqué from MacArthur's chief of staff directing Major Worth be reassigned to a stateside post immediately upon his return to Okinawa. A similar message was sent to Bud Davies' division commander on Kyushu. Soon after its receipt, Bud found himself on a plane to Hawaii, via Guam, with a brand new set of captain's bars on his collar. As he looked out the window to the glistening sea below, he reflected on how correct Major Worth had been: *don't expect any trumpets--now excuse us while we stick you in some out-of-the-way closet. Take your promotion and be quiet.*

And of course, Mark Colton was long gone, halfway to California. The Navy had seen to that.

The other piece of paper was from the International Red Cross and had been forwarded through military channels. A week had already passed since its origination date. It contained the message that John Worth's mother was terminally ill, dying of cancer. She had been given a month, maybe less. John's sister had sent him a letter weeks ago explaining the sad situation in detail, but it was still far from delivery, slowly making its way across the Pacific by ship, one logistical depot to the next. He would never receive it.

Military personnel overseas had experienced in time-delay the births, dire illnesses, and deaths of loved ones since this war began. They did not get to go running home; those were the rules. The military could not afford to lose manpower over something as trivial as life events.

Harris had not seen John Worth for two days, when he departed for what would turn out to be his last mission. The colonel did not know how many missions John had flown in his combat career; he had never bothered to find out. But he was sure there were more than enough to justify sending him home. Harris was also sure Worth would put up a fuss. There was that nurse he was cozy with--surely when a man gets that lucky he will be in no hurry to leave. Even if he and his lover ended up being posted far apart in Japan, Worth was a clever boy with access to airplanes.

John's reaction does not disappoint the colonel.

"Negative, sir! With all due respect, I request permission to remain with the unit!" are the first words out of John's mouth.

"At ease, Worth. You look a mess. You're wounded, tired. You've been here too long, son. You're not thinking clearly. You've done your job admirably, honorably. I'm sending you home. They need you there. Your mother needs you."

"Colonel, my wounds are superficial. I've had worse. Why am I suddenly so lucky? Nobody gets to go home for an impending death in the family." His voice was taking on a pleading tone.

"Major, you're getting on that plane if I have to put you on bodily. Do you understand me?"

John understands all too well: *Shit. I guess I already forgot that little speech I gave Bud Davies. Better that those of us who know of the Japanese bomb get scattered and nudged out of the picture. Easier to hush it up that way. I wonder if Mom is really sick at all. I wouldn't put it passed them to make that up as an excuse.*

"I asked you a question, Major Worth. Do you understand me?"

"Yes, sir," John replies with dispirited voice as he salutes.

"Good. Your plane leaves tomorrow morning, 0600. Get packed, Worth. Good luck to you."

As he walks to his tent, John has never felt more alone in his life. Being on Okinawa without her is bad enough. The thought of being half a world away is unbearable. *It's a good thing I don't have to fly today, because if I did--for the first time in my flying career-- I would fake it at sick call and sit the mission out.*

When he gets to his tent, he begins the long letter to Marge, a letter he never expected to write. He explains he is being ordered home. They had discussed the possibility of that before, considering how long he has been here and how much he had flown. His mother's illness is a side note, for they are both well aware that is no reason to be sent home. He says nothing of the Japanese atomic bomb. Pledging he will be waiting for her back in the States, he instructs her to write him at his Iowa address, one she knows by heart, until he can advise her of his new posting. A dozen times he reiterates how much he loves her, but somehow it does not seem enough.

John writes the letter twice. He gives one copy to Rowdy Chambers, the other to Chuck Jaworski. Both men would move with the squadron to Kyushu in two days. Better to have some insurance. This was still a dangerous business; some people would still die. At least one of them would find her.

Then he starts to pack. Writing the letter had eased the pain some, each word reinforcing the bond he felt between them. Packing rips him apart again. Almost every one of his few possessions brings back a memory of Marge. The old football jersey cuts the deepest. As he stuffs it into the duffel, he remembers the last time he had seen her wearing it, asleep in his hammock after the typhoon. He was so grateful to find her alive. Now he is grateful there is nobody around to see him like this.

In the cool, early morning darkness, John makes his way across the ramp to the silver four-engined transport that will fly him away. It is a Navy plane, an R5D, military equivalent of the new Douglas DC-4 airliner. The Army calls her a C-54. He drags himself, his duffel, and his flight bag up to the boarding ladder. A young naval airman, the plane's radio operator, helps him with the baggage.

The plane looks brand new, her aluminum skin gleaming in the moonlight and the headlights of ramp vehicles. None of the typical wear and tear around the loading doors, floor, and cabin sidewalls you usually see on transports. Even the tires look fresh, unworn, like they have only kissed the ground a handful of times since leaving the factory. The rubber deicing boots on the leading edges of the wings and stabilizers are still smooth, clean, not eroded. The big, round nacelles, each housing a 14 cylinder, 1700 horsepower radial engine, show no leaks, either.

An old airman's joke: *A radial engine not leaking? It must be out of oil!*

The co-pilot, a naval ensign, his gold wings still shiny, right out of the box, greets John in the cabin and says with all the enthusiasm of a rookie, "She looks good, doesn't she, sir? You'll be going home in style!"

John gives only a weak smile in reply, for going home is the last thing he wants right now. He settles into one of the dozen or so airline-style passenger seats in the aft end of the cabin; spartan affairs, but better than the usual bench seats along the cabin sidewall, for the long, multi-legged flight. The cabin forward of the seats is without furnishings; it is full of cargo that has been loaded through the oversized door in the aft left fuselage side, which is now closed. Only the passenger door, a smaller, integral part of that oversized cargo door, is still open, accepting passengers and crew.

This is basically a courier flight, with some passengers along for the ride. Boxes full of documents, records, routine requisitions--the usual paper trail of a mammoth military operation--comprise the cargo load. Three of the passengers--two Army officers and an NCO--are the designated couriers accompanying the boxes, guardians of the bureaucracy. The other passengers, six in number, are five Marine Corps infantry officers and John Worth. As they settle in, the aircraft commander, a Navy full lieutenant, climbs aboard, greets his passengers, and casually gives them the standard pre-flight safety briefing for an overwater flight. The pilot covers the location of life vests, rafts, and survival kits. Seeing the wings on John's flight jacket, he apologizes in advance if he bores him with such details. He offers that once airborne, they are free to wander the cabin and visit the cockpit. In addition to himself and his co-pilot, the crew will consist of a flight engineer, radio operator, flight mechanic, and navigator, all petty officers. The navigator, a chief petty officer, looks old enough to be the father of everybody else on board. They will be at their first stop, Guam, in six hours.

The big transport takes off on schedule and turns east, toward the gray horizon trimmed with pink, announcing the dawn. The crew settles in for the long, monotonous overwater flight, made easier by the autopilot which is now flying the plane and will continue to do so until descent for landing, when the humans take back control. The flight engineer surveys the cockpit gauges and periodically strolls the cabin, looking out the windows with satisfaction at the four humming radials spinning their propellers at cruise rpm. He does not have much to do on this spanking new ship, where everything seems to be working as advertised. The old navigator, jokingly referred to as "The Ancient Mariner" by the other, younger crewmen, peers regularly into the scope of his LORAN receiver, does some calculations and passes the resulting information to the pilots. John can sense the slight changes in heading, the gentle, shallow banks the airplane makes after each correction of just a few degrees as the pilot dials the navigator's information into the autopilot. The radio operator taps out regular position reports, presumably received at their destination, Guam. The flight mechanic, untroubled, sleeps like a log.

The bored, weary passengers sometimes nap, sometimes chat, talking vague generalities of the war, unable to comprehend and disinterested in each others' specific realms. The Marine officers--a major, two captains and two lieutenants--are headquarters staff, returning to Guam with reports on Okinawa's logistical situation. All are combat infantry veterans of the island-hopping campaigns across the South Pacific. The Army couriers are all veterans on rotation home, savvy enough to latch onto this temporary duty as a reliable way to ensure quick transportation.

John is lost in his thoughts, unable to sleep. He chats intermittently, feeling no camaraderie with his fellow travelers. The news of his mother's terminal illness has not caused him much distress; he had never been close to her, always feeling she had coldly kept all her children at a distance, as if they were some kind of imposition that existed merely as potential sources of embarrassment. He remembers something his father had told him when he was a young boy, "Your Mother...she's not a *warm* woman." Young John had no idea what he was talking about; that lesson would take some years. Now that he has known Marge, he cannot imagine being with a woman who was anything but warm.

Marge--every time he thinks of her it is like there is not enough air to breathe, like he is flying too high and should be on oxygen. The disappointment of leaving has turned into the constant dull ache of missing her, a clamp-like pressure on his chest that makes him gasp. They were well aware separation might be forced on them; they had vowed it would not matter. Now they would put that vow to the test.

John is surprised to realize he has no qualms leaving his unit and not flying. He really has changed, and it is Marge that has changed him. He definitely feels he has done his share--*more* than his share. It is not of his doing that he is on his way home. His conscience is clear, his duty done. For three long years he had flown combat missions with all the dedication and naiveté of a child. In three short months, this woman has made him see the light. The only reason for wanting to remain is Marge. She has gotten her wish, though, doled out with a cruel dose of irony: he is out of combat; they are thousands of miles apart.

He allows himself a few moments of nostalgia for *f-stop*. Of all the machines he has known in his life, she had been the finest--his favorite--no doubt due to the expert ministrations of Chuck Jaworski. Machines are like pets: you love them; they die; you get another one to love. She had never failed him, but she was finished now, used up, beyond repair; the eventual fate of all machines of war. There are not enough Jaworskis around to keep them all running forever. She had not burned after her last landing; the electrical fire had extinguished after John shut her down for the last time. Now she was a ball of scrap metal, bulldozed out of the way at the field where she made her final landing. He will never forget her.

When they touch down on Guam, it is late morning of a typically warm sunny day. They do not stay long. Most of the cargo boxes are removed, a few more added. The Marine Corps passengers say goodbye and march away, seemingly in formation by rank. A new, larger relief crew arrives, with an extra pilot, flight engineer, and navigator beyond the normal complement for the next leg to Midway, twice the distance they had just covered, almost 12 hours in the air. The original flight crew, after briefing the newcomers, immediately racks out, the officers in the bunks at the rear of the cockpit, the NCOs on hammocks and mattresses scattered throughout the cabin. There will be 17 souls on board. The last detail to be completed is refueling. The tanks are refilled to the brim with 100 octane gasoline after some brief confusion over paperwork is resolved. The engines are restarted. After a lengthy dash down the long runway, the R5D is airborne once again, heavy with fuel but unburdened by much cargo or passenger weight. *So far,* John thinks, *these naval aviators have done OK.*

John is determined to get some sleep this leg. He finds that if he imagines Marge is next to him, it helps. He talks softly to his imaginary bunkmate. No one else can hear him over the steady drone of the engines and the even, wind-like noise of the plane slipping through the air as she levels off at cruise altitude. He can hear Marge's voice in the steady, comforting background noises of the machine in flight.

John senses the change in the noises immediately, at the same time as the flight crew. Looking forward to the cockpit, he can see the pilots leaning closer to the engine instruments on the forward panel, their hands working the forest of levers that sprout from the pedestal between them. Frantic words, unheard from John's far aft position, are being exchanged. The sleeping crew members are suddenly all awake. They sense it, too: the engines are losing power. All four of them. John makes his way to the cockpit as the plane begins a steep turn back toward Guam. Maybe he can help.

He stands at the entrance to the cockpit, his further progress forward prevented by the crowd of Navy airmen already choking its confined space. There are urgent shouts of "Get the nose down! Fuel Pressure! Try a richer mixture! Descend to warmer air!" Of one thing they are all certain: *this big machine will fast turn into the world's worst glider if they don't get those engines making power again.*

The Navy pilots have not yet reconciled

themselves that they are headed for a ditching. They are too preoccupied with troubleshooting the problem and devising corrective actions. Reconciliation begins rapidly, however, when the number 4 engine quits. Preparations for ditching are smoothly begun, as every man on board--save the couriers--is an airman. Life vests are donned, rafts readied for inflation once outside the aircraft, and survival kits secured to the rafts. Raft assignments are delegated like choosing sides for a sandlot pickup game. Nobody is particularly concerned. If they have to go *in the drink,* they will be picked up in no time. They are not that far from Guam. The flight engineers may still overcome the problem, and they could return to Guam under their own steam.

In the cockpit, it is looking less and less likely this problem is going to be overcome anytime soon. Number 1 engine now sputters, coughs, and dies. The only engines still running, numbers 2 and 3, are doing so in a most sickly manner, producing little power, but lots of drag from the anemically windmilling props. Any attempt to advance their throttles much above idle causes them to start coughing and dying, as well. The plane is sinking steadily, trading altitude for airspeed. The way things are going, this tradeoff will end in the water about 100 miles northeast of Guam.

Spirits lift momentarily when, after much coaxing, number 3 roars back to life, but this elation is quickly dampened as the engine starts an oscillating cycle of backfiring, running normally, then backfiring again. This cycling soon ends as number 3 backfires once more, coughs a few times, then quits, its feathered propeller motionless like that of numbers 1 and 4. Number 2, still barely running, never gives any inkling of returning to life. Final position reports are prepared and passed to the radio operator for his MAYDAY transmission. He begins tapping furiously on the key, his Morse code the only link to their would-be rescuers. The pilots comfort each other that the sea looks fairly calm; the ditching should not be too difficult. Hell, she might still be afloat when the *Dumbo* seaplanes arrive, making her really easy to find! They are less than 2000 feet from the ocean's surface now. The Navy radio station on Guam acknowledges receipt of the MAYDAY. The crew makes a final attempt to restart the dead engines. It fails.

After a few more minutes, they hit the water.

Chapter Fifty-Four

On a squalid Manila back street, where the desperate, violent cycle of life has only been amplified by four years of Japanese occupation and the recent recapture by MacArthur's forces, a solitary American officer lies in the gutter bleeding to death, his throat slit by a prostitute's knife. It is just past midnight.

The two patrolling MPs who stumble across him see no reason for a sense of urgency, as his condition is obviously hopeless. He has lost too much blood already. The dying officer has been trying to tell them something, but his wound prevents any sound other than a gurgling rasp to escape. The MPs begin to open the victim's collar to check his dog tags. They also plan to rifle his pockets, in case his assailant has left any loose cash behind. The blood spilling down the front of his uniform shirt makes the dog tag check a most distasteful prospect, however, and they put that first task on hold as they proceed with the latter.

This officer had made the mistake, in his drunken haze, of attempting to avail himself of the prostitute's services without providing the appropriate fee in advance. When she continued to insist, in broken English *You pay first! You pay first!* he just laughed and continued to force himself on her, as if it was his right, his privilege. She did not give a damn about his privilege and his belief that in his world he was entitled to whatever he wanted. She only knew he was a cheat and a thief who was not playing by the inviolable rules. In her world, this smirking drunk deserved to die.

It was an unfortunate coincidence death would come to this officer at this place and time. He had been scheduled to return to the United States later this same day, his overseas tour declared finished by the 5th Air Force brass. Although he had once been a pilot, he was recently assigned to a ground staff job at Air Force headquarters in Manila, just marking time until rotation home. He did not give a damn about being permanently grounded; he cared not a whit about flying. All he ever wanted to do was strut around wearing the wings. To actually fulfill the duties that the wearing of those wings entailed had always seemed beneath someone of his birthright.

And here, on this night before rotation home, it was customary to have a big *going away* party thrown in your honor. No such party had occurred. Few at his post knew who he was or had ever seen him, as his attendance at his job was somewhat spotty. He could usually be found at the bar, though, a drunken, obnoxious presence who nobody cared to get to know. He decided *Fuck 'em...I'll have my own party* and went looking for some female companionship. He found it in the woman destined to be his killer.

When the report of his murder arrives at headquarters, the adjutant has to rummage through the personnel records to confirm this officer is actually assigned there. He finally finds it, a thin file with little to distinguish his wartime service one way or the other. The name on the file is *Mann, Harmon--Captain, US Army Air Force.*

The adjutant has one final encounter with the file of the deceased Captain Mann. He is instructed by Commanding General, 5th US Army Air Force, to process Captain Mann for a posthumous Silver Star *for extraordinary heroism and valiant service to his country in time of war.*

The words Mann had been trying to say to the MPs, words he could no longer voice, were simply these: *Do you know who my daddy is?*

Chapter Fifty-Five

The teletype printers at the War Department in Washington had not paused, even for an instant, all morning. It was the same at the State Department. They poured out endless inquires from allied countries and military commands all over the world about conditions, timetables, and protocols for the *cessation of hostilities* the Emperor of Japan had announced the evening of this same day, Tokyo time.

The Washington establishment had been busily reading between the lines of the Emperor's announcement. At no time did he use the word *surrender*, let alone *unconditional*. A spirited debate raged around what *cessation* implied for the political future of Japan and the status of the Asian lands it occupied.

What caused the most debate, however, was the Emperor's statement that he was "accepting the terms of the Supreme Commander, United States Forces." Who, exactly, was that? Did he mean the President, who had never offered anything less than *unconditional surrender*? Not likely. If not the President, what authority did this person have to make offers to foreign governments?

The smart money was on MacArthur. So smart, in fact, that nobody would take the bet.

As the day progressed, the story slowly came together. Through the offices of the Swedish ambassador to Japan, a secret, backchannel negotiation had been going on for some weeks with MacArthur, first in Manila, then Kyushu, whose aims were, for the most part, little different from Washington's: Japanese forces at home and throughout Asia were to lay down their arms. Captured territories were to be relinquished. Allied forces were to occupy Japan.

Then came the kicker, crossing a line in the sand the President and his Secretary of State had drawn which nobody had dared cross until now: the Emperor would be allowed to keep his throne. He would be a figurehead, subject to the will of the American military governor. He would be immune from prosecution for war crimes. But these were *conditions*, and they were forbidden.

General Marshall and the chiefs of staff were used to President Truman's fits of rage, but this one was on a whole new order: objects thrown, swear words fit only for the barracks, lunatic pacing while ranting. They were sure he would wear a path in the Oval Office carpeting before long.

"Just who the fuck does that son of a bitch think he is that he can usurp the President of the United States? Well, General Marshall?"

Marshall, composed and dignified as always, has an answer to that question but elects to remain silent and endure the president's invective. Words like "messianic," "mercurial," and "seditious" would lace such an answer, but there is no point in speaking right now.

"I'm firing that arrogant bastard. General Marshall, draw up the orders relieving him."

Calmly, Marshall asks, "Who would you suggest succeed him, Mister President?"

"I suggest you, General Marshall."

That response catches George Marshall

completely off guard. Though he had often been considered for and greatly desired a major field command, his insight and extraordinary managerial and diplomatic talents had always been recognized as unique to the Washington realm and best put to use there. This sudden suggestion that he run off to Japan must be indicative of the President's short-term distress; things would surely return to normal in a moment. In the meantime, Marshall is speechless. The opportunity excites him, but how could he possibly leave all he is responsible for in Washington?

Secretary of State Byrnes picks this moment to refocus the discussion. "Does this mean you're not going to accept the Emperor's offer to stop fighting, Mister President? The war is to continue?"

"Who said anything about that?" Truman replies. "Of course not!"

Byrnes is relieved. "Oh, OK. I just needed to clarify that. But as far as MacArthur…"

Truman cuts him off. "I will not have that man strutting around like he won the goddamn war single-handedly."

"We can easily make sure that doesn't happen, Mister President," Byrnes says in a soothing tone.

"And how do you propose we do that, Jimmy?"

"Simple. He wants nothing more than to be military governor of Japan. Tell him he's on thin ice. If he doesn't keep his mouth shut you'll give the job to Nimitz."

Admiral King really likes that idea. General Marshall breathes an irresolute sigh of relief. Admiral Leahy is happy, period; whatever the semantics, the war is finally at an end.

"But the unmitigated gall!" Truman says. "And how could any ambassador, envoy, or what-have-you possibly think MacArthur speaks for this country's elected government?"

"Mister President," Byrnes begins, "perhaps they're not as current on American civics as we'd like them to be. I'm sure any foreign envoy is not going to question the credentials of an American theater commander to seek terms of peace. In MacArthur's mind, he probably thinks he's done you a favor, and just maybe he did, even though he's just a self-serving bastard who'll take any shortcut to dominate his nemesis, Japan. But firing him will send the wrong message to the country and the world. Doing anything other than accepting with a smile will make us look *not benevolent.* We can't have those Russian monsters calling us *savages,* now, can we? And our beleaguered allies are certainly ready to end this thing. This is a golden opportunity. Let's not throw it away."

"And what happened to all your talk about not backing down from unconditional surrender, Jimmy? And how could such a thing be going on without our... no, make that *your* knowledge?"

"Apparently, Mister President, MacArthur employed diplomatic channels that proved very effective and very secret, channels to which we had turned a deaf ear. State had no idea what he was up to, neither did War," Byrnes says, casting an intimidating glance at Secretary of War Patterson, a glance meant to silence. "Things change, Mister President. Make the most of it."

Truman mulls that for a few moments, then calmly says, "Fine...but I'll get that insubordinate son of a bitch someday if it's the last thing I do."

"Of course you will, Mister President. Just don't do it right now," Byrnes replies, smiling like a salesman closing the deal.

In a commandeered palace on southern Kyushu, the country home of a Japanese aristocrat, General Douglas MacArthur sits in his office alone, thoroughly pleased with himself. He has won the gamble. That little haberdasher from Missouri, the accidental president, would no longer be standing in his way with his bumbling, amateur statesmanship:

Did he really think that he, a bumpkin, a mere National Guard captain of artillery at the same time I was already a highly decorated colonel in World War I, might understand military matters and diplomacy better than I? I, who had retired from the US Army to command the Philippine military only to have the Army beg me to come out of retirement when Japan rattled its saber? If we had done it his way, we'd be fighting our way through the home islands for another year or two, atomic bombs or not. Such a waste! I was born to lead...born to rule...and I'm not getting any younger. This was so much easier, so much better. He should be thanking me for saving his bacon. Sure, he might have tried to fire me, call me disloyal, but that would have seemed disingenuous. Surely that clerk Marshall or that devious scoundrel Byrnes would dissuade him.

I deserve Japan.

In Tokyo, Prime Minister Suzuki heard of the American acquiescence to the Emperor's announcement with overwhelming relief. This long and costly war that had started with such heady promise for the Empire, then turned into a horrifying process of attrition that almost left it destroyed in its entirety, was finally over. The Americans were already here, and there would be many more of them very soon, but occupation on these terms had to be a better result than what the nihilism of the military would have achieved. He felt an exhaustion of mind and body from which there would be no recovery, just an accommodation to the inexorable descent to one's own mortality.

Not far away, General Umezu was breathing his own sigh of relief. He had offered his life in atonement to the Emperor should the plan to use Professor Inaba's atomic device fail. After arriving at the Imperial Palace, baring his abdomen and kneeling in the anteroom of the Imperial Council Chamber to perform the act of hara-kiri, he was told by an emissary to rise and depart: the Emperor had absolved him of his obligation. His death would not be required. No other explanation was given. Confused but obedient, Umezu took his leave.

As for the Emperor, he had not been surprised when he received MacArthur's overtures:

This naïve and foolish American president had painted himself into an unyielding corner with his Potsdam Declaration and needed a way to save face and end this war by simply coming to terms. Surely, Mister Truman, you were not looking forward to a continued slog up the home islands and through mainland Asia, a campaign that might drag on for years, promising only an occupation of a hostile nation without end. The new miracle weapons, the atomic bombs you threaten us with, neither your words nor your bombs scare us. You had done far worse and we did not capitulate. Despite your military and industrial might, you cannot dominate a people who will not be dominated. What better way to affect an honorable end than to use a clandestine intermediary? MacArthur had been perfect: a man of sufficient stature on the world stage to be credible but still a military man who could be controlled by his government. How brilliant! You must have some very cunning advisors, Mister Truman. You need them.

But even the Emperor knew that, eventually, death gets too close. It was one thing for his subjects to die for him; it was quite another matter to sacrifice himself and the living deity myth, the cornerstone of Japanese culture, the basis of his privilege. If the American bombs did not kill him, their noose would.

Envoys of the Emperor would sign a document of surrender on the deck of a US Navy battleship, beneath the massive guns, but it was not the unconditional surrender Truman had demanded. And while the leaders of nations sought refuge in their illusions, delusions, and rationalizations, the conflict that was World War II came to a halt, leaving in its path the unresolved animosities, beaten down for a brief moment, that would sow the seeds of discord and conflict for the rest of the Twentieth Century and beyond.

Chapter Fifty-Six

November 1955
Miami International Airport (Wilcox Field)

The Lockheed Constellation stands proud and shining on the humid airport ramp, mid-morning of a typical South Florida day. The low, billowy white clouds with their flat bottoms are in stunning contrast to the brilliant blue sky above. Soon, this four-engined airliner with its distinctive triple tail, wearing the logo of Eastern Airlines, will be winging its way north through that sky, carrying its load of winter-vacationing *snowbirds* home to their frozen nests in the Northeast.

It is still almost two hours to departure time, but the captain is already on board, well ahead of his crew. While not typical of flight crew hierarchy and protocol, it is common for this particular man. He has begun the pre-flight inspections on the big machine, one he has piloted many times before, first as a co-pilot and now as captain. Soon after, the flight engineer arrives. He and the captain are old friends, their bond extending back to World War II in the Pacific. They fly together often. Their passengers, despite the general admiration for aviators that is part of American folklore, will never be able to fully appreciate just how capable are the hands flying them to their destination this day.

Chuck Jaworski, flight engineer, stows his flight bags and turns to John Worth, asking, "You get the outside yet, Skipper?"

"Just a general look-see, Sarge. I saved the dirty stuff for you. I'll get the interior while you do that."

"Always a pleasure serving with you and Mister Lockheed, Captain," Chuck jokes, as the two have spent so much of their careers in military and civil aviation with Lockheed machines. Then he exits to the ramp to pay serious attention to the engines, hydraulics, and landing gear, the *dirty stuff.*

John Worth finishes his inspection of the flight deck and moves back into the cabin. The stewardesses arrive and begin their own cabin checks. *Pretty young girls,* John thinks, amazed that they all look little more than teenagers from his lofty perch of 33 years of age. Most would find husbands and be gone in little more than a year, no longer meeting the *unmarried* requirement of their jobs. He remembered how tempted he had been by the *stews* when he first began as an airline pilot right after the war, especially the outrageously flirtatious southern girls. Yet he had not succumbed to their charms. He was waiting for someone else.

He had been very lucky to land an airline job so quickly. He had returned to Iowa, a return delayed by five days floating in a life raft near Guam, to find his mother already dead and buried a week. Assigned to an Army Air Force training unit in Tampa, he was to be quickly discharged in the exodus from the service that followed the Japanese capitulation. He had seen an advertisement in a local newspaper that Captain Eddie Rickenbacker, head of Eastern Airlines, was hiring pilots at the airline's base in Miami. Captain Eddie, the World War I flying ace, ran his airline with an iron fist and selected all his pilots personally.

John hopped a bus to Miami and got an interview.

Captain Eddie was immediately taken with John; they shared a very unique experience. Both had spent time in a life raft in the Pacific during the war. Captain Eddie, during a fact-finding mission for the government, had been on board a plane that had gotten lost over the vastness of the ocean and ditched, its occupants spending 24 days in a raft before being rescued. Several of the others had died during the ordeal, but Captain Eddie was a tough old bird.

John's experience seemed almost benign by comparison. The ditching had been fairly routine. The first contact of the plane's belly with the sea was light, skipping like a stone across the surface. The next contact was firm, the resulting deceleration rapid. The plane did not break apart; all her occupants exited safely onto the wings and into the two rafts. They were confident they would be rescued shortly, before the sunset three hours away. Captain Eddie had chuckled at that part.

No rescuers came; not that day, not that night. Not the next day, either. It had taken the spanking new R5D a day and a half to finally slip beneath the surface, her very brief life ending in this watery grave. Her crew and passengers drifted in their rafts for four days and four nights, never seeing a ship or plane. Finally, on the morning of the fifth day, a US Navy seaplane tender--a floating repair and support ship for the PBY Catalinas and PBM Mariners of the Pacific fleet--stumbled across them, totally by chance. They were hungry, badly sunburned and dehydrated, but all 17 survived. There had been little fresh water left. The survival kit supplies had been depleted, and it had only rained once, allowing the rainfall collectors in the kits to be put to good use. They had been careless about rationing water and food, though. They could not believe rescue would take so long. Much longer and they would have started to die off, one by one, the weakest first. Captain Eddie nodded in somber assent.

"What went wrong with the airplane, son? Bad fuel?" Captain Eddie asked.

"Yes, sir, that was the assumption. As I said, the plane was brand new. Turns out the fuel filters had only been replaced once since leaving the factory and were due to be changed again immediately upon her return flight to the States. The Navy figured the residual factory debris from the wing tanks, plus the water in the contaminated fuel set up an icy clog in the filter elements at high altitude that just took too long to clear once we descended. We had gone up to almost 12,000 feet to catch some tailwinds. There had been some discussion over the fuel paperwork before departure, too. Something didn't add up, like that batch might never have been accepted and approved for use. The fuel we got was actually slated to be condemned, but they were real slow red-tagging the storage tank."

"I see...And how did you end up off course?" Captain Eddie asked.

"Actually, sir, we weren't. The plane's radio log shows the accurate location of our ditching, right on our flight plan routing. The station radio log at Guam had one digit different. They started looking for us a hundred miles away. Then we started drifting. There's no telling which radio operator made the error."

"Well, son, you survived, that's the important thing." Captain Eddie said as he turned to the window overlooking the airport. He liked this young pilot before him immensely. He was a survivor, full of character. And he could sense they shared a deep, innate understanding of all things mechanical. Captain Eddie offered him a job on the spot.

As John reaches overhead at the open cabin door to check the escape rope stowed there, the Florida sun reflects brightly off his wedding band and fills his mind with warm thoughts of his wife of nine years, Marjorie Braden Worth. It had taken nearly a year for Marge to follow John home as she served with the occupation forces in a US Army hospital in Japan, collecting "points" for rotation home and discharge. That year had not been easy for either of them. It began for Marge as Chuck Jaworski and that funny Texan Rowdy Chambers showed up at her hospital soon after her arrival in Japan and presented her with two identical letters from John. She read one, then the other, hoping the second would contain some correction, some revision in orders that would keep John close or maybe just expose the whole thing as a joke as John suddenly appeared, as if he had been hiding behind a curtain. He would not do that, though. He was not one to play those kinds of jokes, not about something as devastating as this. He really was gone. She thanked Chuck and Rowdy, excused herself and sought a private place to cry her eyes out, the first of many good cries she would allow herself over the next year. Kathleen McNeilly found Marge alone and sobbing and immediately thought the worst. When McNeilly found out John was not, in fact, dead--only rotated home--she let out a great sigh of relief. Throwing her arm around Marge, she said, "Honey, look at it this way…half your problems are over! He's going to be alive when you get home!"

Then there were the confusing reports two weeks later that first announced John was OK, he had been rescued from a raft in the Pacific and was safely back in the States. The following day came one that said he was missing in the Pacific after the plane bringing him home had ditched. Marge chalked that humorous anticlimax up to the usual, disjointed path of the unofficial communications pipeline the war had spawned. But it was over two months before she actually received a letter from him, talking about his impending discharge at Tampa and the possibility of an airline pilot job, events that might have already occurred. She thought it odd he would seek work with an airline. She had always assumed he would return to college to finish his engineering degree. They had never really discussed the future in much detail, only that they wanted to spend it together. And the damned mail took so long; at least he had received some of the constant stream of letters she had written.

On one point they totally agreed: they ached for each other physically and emotionally.

Marge found herself in a larger group of nurses at the occupation hospital in Japan. The old gang was still there. McNeilly was still in charge and Nancy Bergstrom was at her promiscuous best. Among some of the other nurses, though, Marge found soulmates: "The Old Maids Club" they called themselves, married women and those planning to be wed immediately on discharge, bound into a protective social circle, warding off the ever-present male advances. Only one of their number, married, ever sought male comfort outside the circle.

It was Major Kathleen McNeilly, however, who gave Marge the greatest diversion from her own troubles. McNeilly had been delighted to find her lover, Lieutenant Commander Martha Simpson, posted in Japan at a Navy hospital not far from her own. Her world collapsed one day when Martha informed Kathleen she need not come around any more. She had taken up with another Navy nurse, younger and proximal. Thanks and goodbye.

All McNeilly's considerable strengths betrayed her and she suffered a nervous breakdown. The Army did not know what to do. It had no plan to care for psychologically damaged women in its ranks; it could barely deal with men damaged from combat fatigue. Mental illness was misunderstood, ignored, shunted away. So they did what came naturally to government organizations when faced with an unknown; they confined her to the stockade. Marge, suddenly the acting head nurse, became enraged and demanded the major be released to her care. Kathleen McNeilly was not a criminal. She was ill, and she should be cared for at the hospital. Nancy used some heavy-handed persuasion on one of the doctors, a married man with whom she was frequently intimate, to sign the medical order for McNeilly's care. The mention of a tattletale letter to the doctor's wife was all it took.

Marge and her nurses, using the very limited psychiatric training they had received in nursing school to the best of their abilities, established a peaceful, quiet setting in the hospital for Kathleen McNeilly to recuperate. Marge was fiercely protective of her charge and guided her recovery until she was well enough to be sent home, back to her husband, a quiet San Francisco pathologist, who continued nursing her back to health after her honorable discharge. Marge and Nancy had seen to the proper medical documentation for that, as well. Kathleen McNeilly fully recovered and corresponds with Marge to this day.

What had seemed like eternity finally ended in August 1946. First Lieutenant Marjorie Braden was finally coming home. John had finagled some time off, not an easy feat for a junior co-pilot, and hitched a ride on a company DC-3 from Miami to Chicago, stopping in Atlanta and Nashville. The typical summer storms had delayed their arrival and John barely made it to Union Station to meet her train. John was not even sure how much money he threw at the cabbie before sprinting inside. When he saw her across the lobby it was like that first time he laid eyes on her in that dispensary tent on Okinawa; despite the throngs of people milling about, there was no one there but her. He ran straight to Marge, who was running as fast as she could toward him, their paths intersecting in the middle of the lobby. They dissolved into a wordless embrace, sobbing unashamedly. Passersby paid them no heed. Scenes like this had become commonplace since the war ended, although it was usually the man wearing the uniform. Still, they were hardly worth a look.

For the second time in his life, John realized he was speechless. The first time had been when he found Marge safe after Maria Carbone's shooting death at the field hospital in Okinawa. He could not know it now, but this would occur twice more in his life, both times after the birth of their sons. When their first, Eli, was born in 1947, an exhausted but radiant Marge clung to the infant and repeated over and over again, "Isn't he beautiful?" to John's involuntary silence, as tears of joy streamed down his face. On the birth of Charlie two years later, Marge beamed as she said to John, "You still can't talk, can you, baby? He's beautiful, too!"

Married life in Miami has become pleasant, familiar. The warmth, the ocean sky, and sea breezes remind John and Marge of Okinawa, the only other place in the world they had ever spent any time together. They bought a cozy, pastel house in Miami Springs, right near the airport. John flew as co-pilot, first on DC-3's, moving up to DC-4's, and finally, Constellations. He was promoted to captain last year. Chuck and Suzy Jaworski, their two kids now teenagers, live a few blocks away. Marge waded back into nursing part-time at first, eventually becoming a head nurse at the new Hialeah Hospital, her experience and abilities too obvious to ignore.

Of course, the Worth home features a hammock in a secluded corner of the back yard. Marge refuses to make love in it, though. When John coaxed her once, trying to rekindle the spirit of their Okinawan passion, she dismissed his efforts with, "Oh, John, we would have done it in the dirt back then!" He had to remind her that, on occasion, they had, indeed, after their youthful enthusiasm had tumbled them from the hammock.

Among the family pictures that adorn the walls are many of *f-stop,* some on the ramp in Okinawa, usually with John, Marge, or both waving from their perch on her wing. Others show her in flight with John at the controls, photographed from one of the other recon ships. Even Marge speaks of *f-stop* with great fondness now. Chuck Jaworski just smiles when he sees those pictures; he has plenty of his own.

It is almost boarding time. John Worth returns to the cockpit from Operations with the current weather information and flight plan in hand, dragging their new co-pilot in tow. As John excuses himself for a moment, the young co-pilot, fresh from the US Air Force where he had flown transports during the Korean Conflict, turns to Chuck Jaworski and asks, "Hey, I hear the skipper is some kind of war hero. He flew fighters?"

Chuck pauses a moment, never comfortable with these questions. While his belief in John's heroism is unshakable and always has been, it was only in strictest confidence that he knew the little he did about John's last mission. It was not his place to go telling the world. He responds without looking away from his panel. "Yeah, he's a great hero. And yeah, he flew a fighter."

"How many kills did he have?" the co-pilot asks, wide-eyed.

After a long pause, Chuck turns, looks the co-pilot dead in the eye and replies:

"No kills...just one *real big* save."

About the Author:

William P. Grasso writes on historical and aviation topics. He is retired from the aircraft maintenance industry and served in the US Army. He also participated in Desert Storm as a flight crew member with the Civil Reserve Air Fleet (CRAF). He resides with his wife in Tulsa, Oklahoma.

Contact Me Online:

eastwindreturns@cox.net